"This book blew my mind! Utterly original and unique."
—SOPHIE HANNAH

THE 7½ DEATHS OF — EVELYN HARDCASTLE

a novel

STUART TURTON

PRAISE FOR *THE 7½ DEATHS* OF *EVELYN HARDCASTLE*

"Dazzling. A revolving door of suspects (and narrators); a sumptuous country-house setting; a pure-silk Möbius strip of a story. This bracingly original, fiendishly clever murder mystery—Agatha Christie meets *Groundhog Day*—is quite unlike anything I've ever read, and altogether triumphant. I wish I'd written it."

—A. J. Finn, #1 *New York Times* bestselling author of
The Woman in the Window

"I hereby declare Stuart Turton the Mad Hatter of Crime. *The 7½ Deaths of Evelyn Hardcastle* is unique, energizing, and clever. So original, a brilliant read."

—Ali Land, *Sunday Times* bestselling author of
Good Me Bad Me

"Pop your favorite Agatha Christie whodunit into a blender with a scoop of *Downton Abbey*, a dash of *Quantum Leap*, and a liberal sprinkling of *Groundhog Day*, and you'll get this unique murder mystery."

—*Harper's Bazaar*

"Turton's debut is a brainy, action-filled sendup of the classic mystery."

—*Kirkus Reviews*

"If Agatha Christie and Terry Pratchett had ever had LSD-fueled sex, then *The 7½ Deaths of Evelyn Hardcastle* would be their acid trip book baby. Darkly comic, mind-blowingly twisty, and with a cast of fantastically odd characters, this is a locked room mystery like no other."

—Sarah Pinborough, *New York Times* bestselling author

"This novel is so ingenious and original that it's difficult to believe it's Turton's debut. The writing is completely immersive... Readers may be scratching their heads in delicious befuddlement as they work their way through this novel, but one thing will be absolutely clear: Stuart Turton is an author to remember."

—*Booklist*, Starred Review

"Atmospheric and unique, this is a mystery that adds 'Who am I?' to the question of whodunit, with existentially suspenseful results."

—*Foreword Reviews*

"This book blew my mind! Utterly original and unique."

—Sophie Hannah, international bestselling author

"Agatha Christie meets *Downton Abbey* with a splash of red wine and *Twin Peaks*. Dark and twisty, lush and riddled with gorgeous prose, part of me will always be trapped in Blackheath."

—Delilah S. Dawson, *New York Times* bestselling author

"A kaleidoscopic mystery that brilliantly bends the limits of the genre and the mind of the reader. *The 7½ Deaths of Evelyn Hardcastle* is urgent, inventive, creepy, and, above all, a blast to read!"

—Matthew Sullivan, author of
Midnight at the Bright Ideas Bookstore

"Absolute envy-making bloody murderous brilliance."

—Natasha Pulley, author of
The Watchmaker of Filigree Street

"I'm green with envy; I wish I'd written this book."

—Jenny Blackhurst, author of *How I Lost You*

"Gloriously inventive, playful, and clever, this is a must for mystery fans. I wish I'd written it myself…"

—Robin Stevens, author of
the Wells and Wong Mystery series

"Stuart Turton's debut novel is dazzling in its complexity, astonishing in its fiendishness, and shocking in its sheer audacity. Every page, every character, and every deliciously dark secret is an absolute treat. Turton is going places."

—Anna Stephens, author of the Godblind trilogy

"Audaciously inventive, gripping, and original."

—Louise O'Neill, author of
Only Ever Yours and *Asking for It*

"This book had me mesmerized from the very first page to the last. A totally unique premise and a beautifully plotted tale told with breathtaking skill. One of the best books I've read in a long time. Every page either sparkles or fizzes with beauty or danger. This is a real mind-melter of a novel from a writer who has complete mastery over his work. If more people could write like this, who'd need cinema?"

—Imran Mahmood, author of *You Don't Know Me*

"Bonkers but brilliant. It's an Agatha Christie manor-house mystery—with a *Black Mirror* twist. Kept me engrossed and guessing throughout, and I still didn't figure it out."

—Kirsty Logan, author of *The Gracekeepers*

"Brilliant, brilliant, brilliant! It's a work of sheer genius. An amazing, unique book that blew my mind."

—Sarah J. Harris, author of *The Color of Bee Larkham's Murder*

THE 7½ DEATHS — OF — EVELYN HARDCASTLE

STUART TURTON

Published by Sourcebooks Landmark, an imprint of Sourcebooks
P.O. Box 4410, Naperville, Illinois 60567-4410
(630) 961-3900
sourcebooks.com

Originally published as *The Seven Deaths of Evelyn Hardcastle* in 2018 in
the UK by Bloomsbury Raven, an imprint of Bloomsbury Publishing.

The Library of Congress has cataloged the hardcover edition as follows:

Names: Turton, Stuart, author.
Title: The 7 1/2 deaths of Evelyn Hardcastle / Stuart Turton.
Other titles: Seven and one half deaths of Evelyn Hardcastle
Description: Naperville, Illinois : Sourcebooks Landmark, [2018]
Identifiers: LCCN 2017032577 | (hardcover : acid-free paper)
Subjects: LCSH: Murder--Investigation--Fiction. | GSAFD: Mystery fiction.
Classification: LCC PR6120.U79 A615 2018 | DDC 823/.92--
dc23 LC record available at https://lccn.loc.gov/2017032577

Printed and bound in the United States of America.
WOZ 20 19 18 17

To my parents, who gave me everything and asked for nothing. My sister, first and fiercest of my readers from the bumblebees onward. And my wife, whose love, encouragement, and reminders to look up from my keyboard once in a while made this book so much more than I thought it could be.

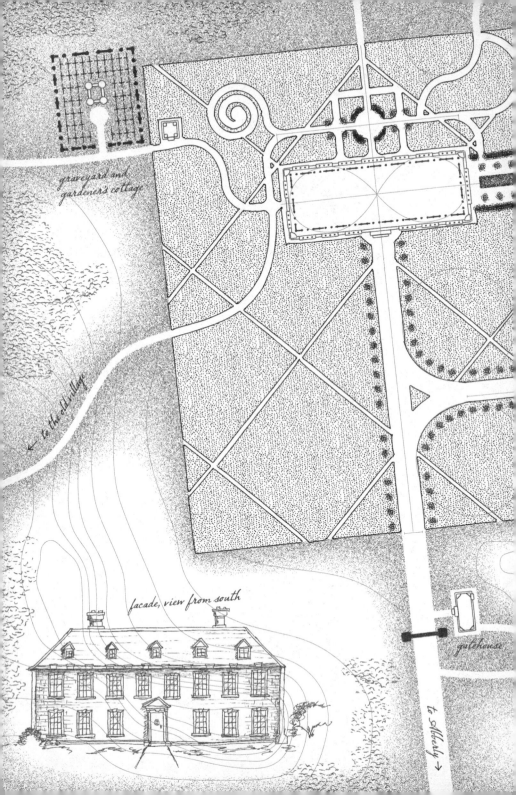

graveyard and
gardener's cottage

← to the old village

facade, view from south

gatehouse

to Solsbury →

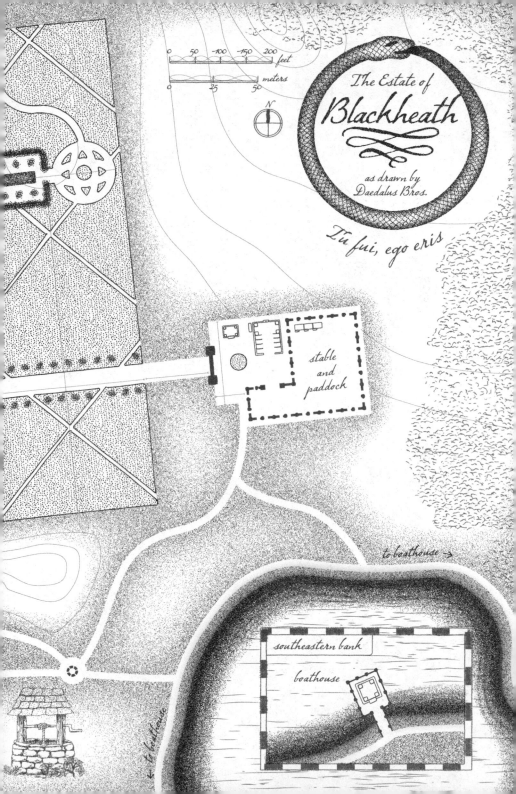

YOU ARE CORDIALLY INVITED to

BLACKHEATH HOUSE for

The Masquerade

INTRODUCING YOUR HOSTS,

the HARDCASTLE FAMILY

LORD PETER HARDCASTLE AND LADY HELENA HARDCASTLE

- & -

THEIR SON, **MICHAEL HARDCASTLE**

THEIR DAUGHTER, **EVELYN HARDCASTLE**

NOTABLE GUESTS

→ EDWARD DANCE, CHRISTOPHER PETTIGREW & PHILIP SUTCLIFFE, FAMILY SOLICITORS

→ GRACE DAVIES & HER BROTHER, DONALD DAVIES, SOCIALITES

→ COMMANDER CLIFFORD HERRINGTON, NAVAL OFFICER (RETIRED)

→ MILLICENT DERBY & HER SON, JONATHAN DERBY, SOCIALITES

→ DANIEL COLERIDGE, PROFESSIONAL GAMBLER

→ LORD CECIL RAVENCOURT, BANKER

→ JIM RASHTON, POLICE OFFICER

→ DR. RICHARD (DICKIE) ACKER

→ DR. SEBASTIAN BELL

→ TED STANWIN

PRINCIPAL HOUSEHOLD STAFF

→ THE BUTLER, ROGER COLLINS

→ THE COOK, MRS. DRUDGE

→ FIRST MAID, LUCY HARPER

→ STABLE MASTER, ALF MILLER

→ ARTIST IN RESIDENCE, GREGORY GOLD

→ LORD RAVENCOURT'S VALET, CHARLES CUNNINGHAM

→ EVELYN HARDCASTLE'S LADY'S MAID, MADELINE AUBERT

WE ASK ALL GUESTS TO KINDLY REFRAIN FROM DISCUSSING

THOMAS HARDCASTLE and **CHARLIE CARVER**,

AS THE TRAGIC EVENTS SURROUNDING THEM STILL GRIEVE THE FAMILY GREATLY.

⌒ 1 ⌒

DAY ONE

I forget everything between footsteps.

"Anna!" I finish shouting, snapping my mouth shut in surprise.

My mind has gone blank. I don't know who Anna is or why I'm calling her name. I don't even know how I got here. I'm standing in a forest, shielding my eyes from the spitting rain. My heart's thumping, I reek of sweat, and my legs are shaking. I must have been running, but I can't remember why.

"How did—" I'm cut short by the sight of my own hands. They're bony, ugly. A stranger's hands. I don't recognize them at all.

Feeling the first touch of panic, I try to recall something else about myself: a family member, my address, age…anything, but nothing's coming. I don't even have a name. Every memory I had a few seconds ago is gone.

My throat tightens, breaths coming loud and fast. The forest is spinning, black spots inking my sight.

Be calm.

"I can't breathe," I gasp, blood roaring in my ears as I sink to the ground, my fingers digging into the dirt.

You can breathe; you just need to calm down.

There's comfort in this inner voice, cold authority.

Close your eyes. Listen to the forest. Collect yourself.

Obeying the voice, I squeeze my eyes shut, but all I can hear is my own panicked wheezing. For the longest time it crushes every other sound, but slowly, ever so slowly, I work a hole in my fear, allowing other noises to break through. Raindrops are tapping the leaves, branches rustling overhead. There's a stream away to my right and crows in the trees, their wings cracking the air as they take flight. Something's scurrying in the undergrowth, the thump of rabbit feet passing near enough to touch. One by one, I knit these new memories together until I've got five minutes of past to wrap myself in. It's enough to stanch the panic, at least for now.

I get to my feet clumsily, surprised by how tall I am, how far from the ground I seem to be. Swaying a little, I wipe the wet leaves from my trousers, noticing for the first time that I'm wearing a dinner jacket, the shirt splattered with mud and red wine. I must have been at a party. My pockets are empty and I don't have a coat, so I can't have strayed too far. That's reassuring.

Judging by the light, it's morning, so I've probably been out here all night. No one gets dressed up to spend an evening alone, which means somebody must know I'm missing by now. Surely, beyond these trees, a house is coming awake in alarm, search parties striking out to find me? My eyes roam the trees, half-expecting to see my friends emerging through the foliage, pats on the back and gentle jokes escorting me back home, but daydreams won't deliver me from this forest, and I can't linger here hoping for rescue. I'm shivering, my teeth chattering. I need to start walking, if only to keep warm, but I can't see anything except trees. There's no way to know whether I'm moving toward help or blundering away from it.

At a loss, I return to the last concern of the man I was.

"Anna!"

Whoever this woman is, she's clearly the reason I'm out here, but I can't picture her. Perhaps she's my wife, or my daughter? Neither feels right, and yet there's a pull in the name. I can feel it trying to lead my mind somewhere.

"Anna!" I shout, more out of desperation than hope.

"Help me!" a woman screams back.

I spin, seeking the voice, dizzying myself, glimpsing her between distant trees, a woman in a black dress running for her life. Seconds later, I spot her pursuer crashing through the foliage after her.

"You there, stop!" I yell, but my voice is weak and weary; they trample it underfoot.

Shock pins me in place, and the two of them are almost out of sight by the time I give chase, flying after them with a haste I'd never have thought possible from my aching body. Even so, no matter how hard I run, they're always a little ahead.

Sweat pours off my brow, my already weak legs growing heavier until they give out, sending me sprawling into the dirt. Scrambling through the leaves, I heave myself up in time to meet her scream. It floods the forest, sharp with fear, and is cut silent by a gunshot.

"Anna!" I call out desperately. "Anna!"

There's no response, just the fading echo of the pistol's report.

"Thirty seconds," I mutter. That's how long I hesitated when I first spotted her, and that's how far away I was when she was murdered. Thirty seconds of indecision…thirty seconds to abandon somebody completely.

There's a thick branch by my feet, and picking it up, I swing it experimentally, comforted by the weight and rough texture of the bark. It won't do me very much good against a pistol, but it's better than investigating these woods with my hands in the air. I'm still panting, still trembling after the run, but guilt nudges me in the direction of Anna's scream. Wary of making too much noise, I brush aside the low-hanging branches, searching for something I don't really want to see.

Twigs crack to my left.

I stop breathing, listening fiercely.

The sound comes again, footsteps crunching over leaves and branches, circling around behind me.

My blood runs cold, freezing me in place. I don't dare look over my shoulder.

The cracking of twigs moves closer, shallow breaths only a little behind me. My legs falter, the branch dropping from my hands.

I would pray, but I don't remember the words.

Warm breath touches my neck. I smell alcohol and cigarettes, the odor of an unwashed body.

"East," a man rasps, dropping something heavy into my pocket.

The presence recedes, his steps retreating into the woods as I sag, pressing my forehead to the dirt, inhaling the smell of wet leaves and rot, tears running down my cheeks.

My relief is pitiable, my cowardice lamentable. I couldn't even look my tormentor in the eye. What kind of man *am* I?

It's some minutes before my fear thaws sufficiently for me to move, and even then, I'm forced to lean against a nearby tree to rest. The murderer's gift jiggles in my pocket, and dreading what I might find, I plunge my hand inside, withdrawing a silver compass.

"Oh!" I say, surprised.

The glass is cracked and the metal scuffed, the initials *SB* engraved on the underside. I don't understand what they mean, but the killer's instructions were clear. I'm to use the compass to head east.

I glance at the forest guiltily. Anna's body must be near, but I'm terrified of the killer's reaction should I arrive upon it. Perhaps that's why I'm alive, because I didn't come any closer. Do I really want to test the limits of his mercy?

Assuming that's what this is.

For the longest time, I stare at the compass's quivering needle. There's not much I'm certain of anymore, but I know murderers don't show mercy. Whatever game he's playing, I can't trust his advice and I shouldn't follow it, but if I don't... I search the forest again. Every direction looks the same: trees without end beneath a sky filled with spite.

How lost do you have to be to let the devil lead you home?

This lost, I decide. Precisely this lost.

Easing myself off the tree, I lay the compass flat in my palm. It yearns for north, so I point myself east, against the wind and cold, against the world itself.

Hope has deserted me.

I'm a man in purgatory, blind to the sins that chased me here.

2

The wind howls, the rain has picked up and is hammering through the trees to bounce ankle high off the ground as I follow the compass.

Spotting a flash of color among the gloom, I wade toward it, coming upon a red handkerchief nailed to a tree—the relic of some long-forgotten child's game, I'd guess. I search for another, finding it a few feet away, then another and another. Stumbling between them, I make my way through the murk until I reach the edge of the forest, the trees giving way to the grounds of a sprawling Georgian manor house, its redbrick facade entombed in ivy. As far as I can tell, it's abandoned. The long gravel driveway leading to the front door is covered in weeds, and the rectangular lawns either side of it are marshland, their flowers left to wither in the verge.

I look for some sign of life, my gaze roaming the dark windows until I spot a faint light on the second floor. It should be a relief, yet still I hesitate. I have the sense of having stumbled upon something sleeping, that uncertain light the heartbeat of a creature vast and dangerous and still. Why else would a murderer gift me this compass, if not to lead me into the jaws of some greater evil?

It's the thought of Anna that drives me to take the first step. She lost her life because of those thirty seconds of indecision, and now I'm faltering again. Swallowing my nerves, I wipe the rain from my eyes and cross the lawn, climbing the crumbling steps to the front door. I hammer it with a child's fury, dashing the last of my strength on the wood. Something terrible happened in that forest, something that can still be punished if I can only rouse the occupants of the house.

Unfortunately, I cannot.

Despite beating myself limp against the door, nobody comes to answer it.

Cupping my hands, I press my nose to the tall windows either side, but the stained glass is thick with dirt, reducing everything inside to a yellowy smudge. I bang on them with my palm, stepping back to search the front of the house for another way in. That's when I notice the bellpull, the rusty chain tangled in ivy. Wrenching it free, I give it a good yank and keep going until something shifts behind the windows.

The door is opened by a sleepy-looking fellow so extraordinary in his appearance that for a moment we simply stand there, gaping at each other. He's short and crooked, shriveled by the fire that's scarred half his face. Overlarge pajamas hang off a coat-hanger frame, a ratty brown dressing gown clinging to his lopsided shoulders. He looks barely human, a remnant of some prior species lost in the folds of our evolution.

"Oh, thank heavens. I need your help," I say, recovering myself.

He looks at me, mouth agape.

"Do you have a telephone?" I try again. "We need to send for the authorities."

Nothing.

"Don't just stand there, you devil!" I cry, shaking him by the shoulders, before pushing past him into the entrance hall, my jaw dropping as my gaze sweeps the room. Every surface is glittering, the checked marble floor reflecting a crystal chandelier adorned with dozens of candles. Framed mirrors line the walls, a wide staircase with an ornate railing sweeping up toward a gallery, a narrow red carpet flowing down the steps like the blood of some slaughtered animal.

A door bangs at the rear of the room, half a dozen servants appearing from deeper in the house, their arms laden with pink and purple flowers, the scent just about covering the smell of hot wax. All conversation stops when they notice the nightmare panting by the door. One by one, they turn toward me, the hall holding its breath. Before long, the only sound is the dripping of my clothes on their nice, clean floor.

Plink.

Plink.

Plink.

"Sebastian?"

A handsome blond fellow in a cricket sweater and linen trousers is trotting down the staircase two steps at a time. He looks to be in his early fifties, though age has left him decadently rumpled rather than weary and worn. Keeping his hands in his pockets, he crosses the floor toward me, cutting a straight line through the silent servants who part before him. I doubt he even notices them, so intent are his eyes upon me.

"My dear man, what on earth happened to you?" he asks, concern crumpling his brow. "Last I saw—"

"We must fetch the police," I say, clutching his forearm. "Anna's been murdered."

Shocked whispers spring up around us.

He frowns at me, casting a quick glance at the servants, who've all taken a step closer.

"Anna?" he asks in a hushed voice.

"Yes. Anna. She was being chased."

"By whom?"

"Some figure in black. We must involve the police!"

"Shortly, shortly. Let's go up to your room first," he soothes, ushering me toward the staircase.

I don't know if it's the heat of the house, or the relief of finding a friendly face, but I'm beginning to feel faint, and I have to use the banister to keep from stumbling as we climb the steps.

A grandfather clock greets us at the top, its mechanism rusting, seconds turned to dust on its pendulum. It's later than I thought, almost 10:30 a.m.

Passages either side of us lead off into opposite wings of the house, although the one into the east wing is blocked by a velvet curtain that's been hastily nailed to the ceiling, a small sign pinned to the material proclaiming the area under decoration.

Impatient to unburden myself of the morning's trauma, I try again to raise the issue of Anna, but my Samaritan silences me with a conspiratorial shake of the head.

"These damnable servants will smear your words up and down the house in half a minute," he says, his voice low enough to scoop off the floor. "Best we talk in private."

He's away from me in two strides, but I can barely walk in a straight line, let alone keep pace.

"My dear man, you look dreadful," he says, noticing that I've fallen behind.

Supporting my arm, he guides me along the passage, his hand at my back, fingers pressed against my spine. Though a simple gesture, I can feel his urgency as he leads me along a gloomy corridor with bedrooms either side, maids dusting inside. The walls must have been recently repainted for the fumes are making my eyes water, further evidence of a hurried restoration gathering as we progress along the passage. Mismatched stain is splashed across the floorboards, rugs laid down to try and muffle creaking joints. Wingback chairs have been arranged to hide the cracks in the walls, while paintings and porcelain vases attempt to lure the eye from crumbling cornices. Given the extent of the decay, such concealment seems a futile gesture. They've carpeted a ruin.

"Ah, this is your bedroom, isn't it?" says my companion, opening a door near the end of the corridor.

Cold air slaps me in the face, reviving me a little, but he walks ahead to close the raised window it's pouring through. Following behind, I enter a pleasant room with a four-poster bed set in the middle of the floor, its regal bearing only slightly let down by the sagging canopy and threadbare curtains, their embroidered birds flying apart at the seams. A folding screen has been pulled across the left side of the room, an iron bathtub visible through the gaps between the panels. Other than that, the furniture's sparse—just a nightstand and a large wardrobe near the window, both of them splintered and faded. About the only personal item I can see is a King James Bible on the nightstand, its cover worn through and pages dog-eared.

As my Samaritan wrestles with the stiff window, I come to stand beside him, the view momentarily driving all else from my mind. Dense forest surrounds us, its green canopy unbroken by either a village or road. Without that compass, without a murderer's kindness, I'd never have found this place, and yet I cannot shake the feeling that I've been lured into a trap. After all, why kill Anna and spare me, if there wasn't some grander plan behind it? What does this devil want from me that he couldn't take in the forest?

Slamming the window shut, my companion gestures to an armchair next to a subdued fire, and passing me a crisp white towel from the cupboard, he sits down on the edge of the bed, tossing one leg across the other.

"Start at the beginning, old love," he says.

"There isn't time," I say, gripping the arm of the chair. "I'll answer all your questions in due course, but we must first call for the police and search those woods! There's a madman loose."

His eyes flicker across me, as though the truth of the matter is to be found in the folds of my soiled clothing.

"I'm afraid we can't call anybody. There's no line up here," he says, rubbing his neck. "But we can search the woods and send a servant to the village, should we find anything. How long will it take you to change? You'll need to show us where it happened."

"Well." I'm wringing the towel in my hands. "It's difficult. I was disoriented."

"Descriptions, then," he says, hitching up a trouser leg, exposing the gray sock at his ankle. "What did the murderer look like?"

"I never saw his face. He was wearing a heavy black coat."

"And this Anna?"

"She was also wearing black," I say, heat rising into my cheeks as I realize this is the extent of my information. "I... Well, I only know her name."

"Forgive me, Sebastian. I assumed she was a friend of yours."

"No..." I stammer. "I mean, perhaps. I can't be certain."

Hands dangling between his knees, my Samaritan leans forward with a confused smile. "I'm missing something, I think. How can you know her name, but not be certain—"

"My memory is lost, damn it," I interrupt, the confession thudding on the floor between us. "I can't remember my own name, let alone those of my friends."

Skepticism billows up behind his eyes. I can't blame him; even to my ears, this all sounds absurd.

"My memory has no bearing on what I witnessed," I insist, clutching at the tatters of my credibility. "I saw a woman being chased. She screamed and was silenced by a gunshot. We have to search those woods!"

"I see." He pauses, brushing some lint from a trouser leg. His next words are offerings, carefully chosen and even more carefully placed before me.

"Is there a chance the two people you saw were lovers? Playing a game in the woods, perhaps? The sound might have been a branch cracking, even a starting pistol."

"No, no. She called for help; she was afraid," I say, my agitation sending me leaping from the chair, the dirty towel thrown on the floor.

"Of course, of course," he says reassuringly, watching me pace. "I do believe you, my dear fellow, but the police are so precise about these things and they do delight in making their betters look foolish."

I stare at him helplessly, drowning in a sea of platitudes.

"Her killer gave me this," I say, suddenly remembering the compass, which I tug from my pocket. It's smeared with mud, forcing me to wipe it clean with my sleeve. "There are letters on the back," I say, pointing a trembling finger toward them.

He views the compass through narrowed eyes, turning it over in a methodical fashion.

"SB," he says slowly, looking up at me.

"Yes!"

"Sebastian Bell." He pauses, weighing my confusion. "That's your name, Sebastian. These are your initials. This is *your* compass."

My mouth opens and closes, no sound coming out.

"I must have lost it," I say eventually. "Perhaps the killer picked it up."

"Perhaps." He nods.

It's his kindness that knocks the wind out of me. He thinks I'm half mad, a drunken fool who spent the night in the forest and came back raving. Yet instead of being angry, he pities me. That's the worst part. Anger's solid; it has weight. You can beat your fists against it. Pity's a fog to become lost within.

I drop into the chair, my head cradled in my hands. There's a killer on the loose, and I have no way of convincing him of the danger.

A killer who showed you the way home?

"I know what I saw," I say.

You don't even know who you are.

"I'm sure you do," says my companion, mistaking the nature of my protest.

I stare at nothing, thinking only of a woman called Anna lying dead in the forest.

"Look, you rest here," he says, standing up. "I'll ask around the house, see if anybody's missing. Maybe that will turn something up."

His tone is conciliatory but matter of fact. Kind as he's been to me, I cannot trust his doubt will get anything done. Once that door closes behind him, he'll scatter a few halfhearted questions among the staff, while Anna lays abandoned.

"I saw a woman murdered," I say, getting to my feet wearily. "A woman I should have helped, and if I have to search every inch of those woods to prove it, I'll do so."

He holds my gaze a second, his skepticism faltering in the face of my certainty.

"Where will you start?" he asks. "There are thousands of acres of forest out there, and for all your good intentions, you could barely make it up the stairs. Whoever this Anna is, she's already dead and her murderer's fled. Give me an hour to gather a search party and ask my questions. Somebody in this house must know who she is and where she went. We'll find her, I promise, but we have to do it the right way."

He squeezes my shoulder.

"Can you do as I ask? One hour, please."

Objections choke me, but he's right. I need to rest, to recover my strength, and as guilty as I feel about Anna's death, I do not want to stalk into that forest alone. I barely made it out of there the first time.

I submit with a meek nod of the head.

"Thank you, Sebastian," he says. "A bath's been run. Why don't you clean yourself up? I'll send for the doctor and ask my valet to lay out some clothes for you. Rest a little. We'll meet in the drawing room at lunchtime."

I should ask after this place before he leaves, my purpose here, but I'm impatient for him to start asking his questions so we can get on with our search. Only one question seems important now, and he's already opened the door by the time I find the words to ask it.

"Do I have any family in the house?" I ask. "Anybody who might be worried about me?"

He glances at me over his shoulder, wary with sympathy.

"You're a bachelor, old man. No family to speak of beyond a dotty aunt somewhere with a hand on your purse strings. You have friends, of course, myself among them, but whoever this Anna is, you've never mentioned her to me. Truth be told, until today, I've never even heard you say the name."

Embarrassed, he turns his back on my disappointment and disappears into the cold corridor, the fire flickering uncertainly as the door closes behind him.

3

I'm out of my chair before the draft fades, pulling open the drawers in my nightstand, searching for some mention of Anna among my possessions, anything to prove that she isn't the product of a lurching mind. Unfortunately, the bedroom is proving remarkably tight-lipped. Aside from a pocketbook containing a few pounds, the only other personal item I come across is a gold-embossed invitation, a guest list on the front and a message on the back, written in an elegant hand.

> *Lord and Lady Hardcastle request the pleasure of your company at a masquerade ball celebrating the return of their daughter, Evelyn, from Paris. Celebrations will take place at Blackheath House over the second weekend of September. Owing to Blackheath's isolation, transport to the house will be arranged for all of our guests from the nearby village of Abberly.*

The invitation is addressed to Doctor Sebastian Bell, a name it takes me a few moments to recognize as my own. My Samaritan mentioned it earlier, but seeing it written down, along with my profession, is an altogether more unsettling affair. I don't feel like a Sebastian, let alone a doctor.

A wry smile touches my lips.

I wonder how many of my patients will stay loyal when I approach them with my stethoscope on upside down.

Tossing the invitation back into the drawer, I turn my attention to the Bible on the nightstand, flipping through its well-thumbed pages. Paragraphs are underlined, random words circled in red ink, though for the life of me I can't make sense of their significance. I'd been hoping to find an inscription or a letter concealed inside, but the Bible's empty of wisdom. Clutching it in both hands, I make a clumsy attempt at prayer, hoping to rekindle whatever faith I once possessed, but the entire endeavor feels like foolishness. My religion has abandoned me along with everything else.

The cupboard is next, and though the pockets of my clothes turn up nothing, I discover a steamer trunk buried beneath a pile of blankets. It's a beautiful old thing, the battered leather wrapped in tarnished iron bands, a heavy clasp protecting the contents from prying eyes. A London address—my address presumably—is written in the slip, though it stirs no recollection.

Taking off my jacket, I heave the trunk onto the bare floorboards, the contents clinking with every jolt. A murmur of excitement escapes me as I press the button on the clasp, transforming into a groan when I discover the damned thing is locked. I tug at the lid, once, twice, but it's unyielding. I search the open drawers and sideboard again, even dropping to my stomach to look under the bed, but there's nothing under there but rat poison pellets and dust.

The key isn't anywhere to be found.

The only place I haven't searched is the area around the bathtub, and I round the folding screen like a man possessed, nearly leaping out of my skin when I discover a wild-eyed creature lurking on the other side.

It's a mirror.

The wild-eyed creature looks as abashed as I at this revelation.

Taking a tentative step forward, I examine myself for the first time, disappointment swelling within me. Only now, staring at this shivering, frightened fellow, do I realize that I had expectations of myself. Taller, shorter, thinner, fatter, I don't know, but not this bland figure in the glass. Brown hair, brown eyes, and no chin to speak of. I'm any face in a crowd; just the Lord's way of filling in the gaps.

Quickly tiring of my reflection, I continue searching for the key to my trunk, but aside from some toiletries and a jug of water, there's nothing back here. Whoever I used to be, it appears I tidied myself away before disappearing. I'm on the verge of howling in frustration when I'm interrupted by a knock on the door, an entire personality conveying itself in five hearty raps.

"Sebastian, are you there?" says a gruff voice. "My name's Richard Acker, I'm a doctor. I was asked to look in on you."

I open the door to find a huge gray mustache on the other side. It's a remarkable sight, the tips curling off the edge of the face they're theoretically attached to. The man behind it is in his sixties, perfectly bald, with a bulbous nose and bloodshot eyes. He smells of brandy, but cheerfully so, as though every drop went down smiling.

"Lord, you look dreadful," he says. "And that's my professional opinion."

Taking advantage of my confusion, he strolls past me, tossing his black medical case onto the bed and having a good look around the room, paying particular attention to my trunk.

"Used to have one of these myself," he says, running an affectionate hand across the lid. "Lavolaille, isn't it? Took me to the Orient and back when I was in the army. They say you shouldn't trust a Frenchman, but I couldn't do without their luggage."

He gives it an experimental kick, wincing as his foot bounces off the obstinate leather.

"You must have bricks in there," he says, cocking his head at me expectantly, as though there's some sensible response to such a statement.

"It's locked," I stammer.

"Can't find the key, hmmm?"

"I...no. Doctor Acker, I—"

"Call me Dickie, everybody else does," he says briskly, going to the window to peer outside. "I've never enjoyed the name truth be told, but I can't seem to shake it. Daniel says you've suffered a misfortune."

"Daniel?" I ask, just about holding onto the back of the conversation as it streaks away from me.

"Coleridge. Chap who found you this morning."

"Right, yes."

Doctor Dickie beams at my bafflement.

"Memory loss, is it? Well, not to worry, I saw a few of these cases in the war, and everything came back after a day or so, whether the patient wanted it to or not."

He shoos me toward the trunk, making me sit down on top of it. Tilting my head forward, he examines my skull with a butcher's tenderness, chuckling as I wince.

"Oh, yes, you've a nice bump back here." He pauses, considering it. "Probably banged your head at some point last night. I'd imagine that's when it all spilled out, so to speak. Any other symptoms? Headaches, nausea, that sort of thing?"

"There's a voice," I say, a little embarrassed by the admission.

"A voice?"

"In my head. I think it's my voice, only, well, it's very certain about things."

"I see," he says thoughtfully. "And this...voice. What does it say?"

"It gives me advice. Sometimes it comments on what I'm doing."

Dickie's pacing behind me, tugging his mustache.

"This advice, is it... How should I say? All aboveboard? Nothing violent, nothing perverse?"

"Absolutely not," I say, riled by the inference.

"And are you hearing it now?"

"No."

"Trauma," he says abruptly, raising a finger in the air. "That's what it'll be. Very common, in fact. Somebody bangs their head and all manner of strange things start going on. They see smells, taste sounds, hear voices. Always passes in a day or two, month at the outside."

"A month!" I say, spinning on the trunk to look at him. "How am I going to manage like this for a month? Perhaps I should visit a hospital?"

"God no, terrible things, hospitals," he says, aghast. "Sickness and death swept into corners, diseases curled up in the beds with the patients. Take my advice and go for a stroll, root through your belongings, talk to some friends. I saw you and Michael Hardcastle sharing a bottle at dinner last night, several bottles actually. Quite an evening by all accounts. He should be able to help, and mark my words, once your memories return, that voice will be no more."

He pauses, tutting. "I'm more concerned by that arm."

We're interrupted by a knock on the door, Dickie opening it before I can protest. It's Daniel's valet, delivering the pressed clothes he promised. Sensing my indecision, Dickie takes the clothes, dismisses the valet, and lays them out on the bed for me.

"Now, where were we?" he says. "Ah, yes, that arm."

I follow his gaze to find blood drawing patterns on my shirtsleeve. Without preamble, he tugs it up to reveal ugly slashes and tattered flesh beneath. They look to have scabbed over, but my recent exertions must have reopened the wounds.

Bending my stiff fingers one by one, he then fishes a small brown bottle and some bandages from his bag, cleaning my injuries before dabbing them with iodine.

"These are knife wounds, Sebastian," he says in a concerned voice, all his good cheer turned to ash. "Recent ones, too. It looks like you held your arm up to protect yourself, like so."

He demonstrates with a glass dropper from his medical bag, slashing violently at his forearm, which he's raised in front of his face. His reenactment is enough to bring me out in goose bumps.

"Do you recall anything of the evening?" he says, binding my arm so tightly that I hiss in pain. "Anything at all?"

I push my thoughts toward my missing hours. Upon waking, I'd assumed everything was lost, but now I perceive this isn't the case. I can sense my memories just out of reach. They have weight and shape, like shrouded furniture in a darkened room. I've simply misplaced the light to see them by.

With a sigh, I shake my head.

"Nothing's forthcoming," I say. "But this morning I saw a—"

"Woman murdered," interrupts the doctor. "Yes, Daniel told me."

Doubt stains every word, but he knots my bandage without voicing any objection.

"Either way, you need to inform the police immediately," he says. "Whoever did this was trying to cause you significant harm."

Lifting his case from the bed, he clumsily shakes my hand.

"Strategic retreat, my boy. That's what's required here," he says. "Talk to the stable master. He should be able to arrange transport back to the village, and from there, you can rouse the constabulary. In the meantime, it's probably best you keep a weather eye out. There are twenty people staying in Blackheath this weekend, and thirty more arriving for the ball tonight. Most of them aren't above this sort of thing, and if you've offended them…well…" He shakes his head. "Be careful. That's my advice."

He lets himself out, and I hurriedly take the key from the sideboard to lock the door after him, my shaking hands causing me to miss the hole more than once.

An hour ago, I'd thought myself a murderer's plaything, tormented, but beyond any physical threat. Surrounded by people, I felt safe enough to insist we try recovering Anna's body from the forest, thereby spurring the search for her killer. That's no longer the case. Somebody's already tried to take my life, and I have no intention of staying long enough for them to try again. The dead cannot expect a debt from the living, and whatever I owe Anna will have to be paid at a distance. Once I've met with my Samaritan in the drawing room, I'm going to follow Dickie's advice and arrange transport back to the village.

It's time I went home.

～ 4 ～

Water slops over the edges of the bathtub as I quickly slough off the second skin of mud and leaves coating me. I'm inspecting my scrubbed pink body for birthmarks or scars, anything that might trigger a memory. I'm due downstairs in twenty minutes, and I know nothing more of Anna than when I first stumbled up Blackheath's steps. Banging into the brick wall of my mind was frustrating enough when I thought I'd be helping with the search, but now my ignorance could scupper the entire endeavor.

By the time I'm finished washing, the bathwater is as black as my mood. Feeling despondent, I towel myself dry and inspect the pressed clothes the valet dropped off earlier. His selection of attire strikes me as rather prim, but peering at the alternatives in the wardrobe, I immediately understand his dilemma. Bell's clothing—for truly, I can't yet reconcile us—consists of several identical suits, two dinner jackets, hunting wear, a dozen shirts, and a few waistcoats. They come in shades of gray and black, the bland uniform of what appears thus far to be an extraordinarily anonymous life. The idea that this man could have inspired anybody to violence is quickly becoming the most outlandish part of this morning's events.

I dress quickly, but my nerves are so ragged, it takes a deep breath and a stern word to coax my body toward the door. Instinct prompts me to fill my pockets before I leave, my hand leaping toward the sideboard only to hover there uselessly.

I'm trying to collect possessions that aren't there and I can no longer remember. This must be Bell's old routine, a shadow of my former life haunting me still. The pull is so strong, I feel damn queer coming away empty-handed. Unfortunately, the only thing I managed to carry back from the forest was that damnable compass, but I can't see it anywhere. My Samaritan—the man Doctor Dickie called Daniel Coleridge—must have taken it.

Agitation pricks me as I step into the corridor.

I only have a morning's worth of memories, and I can't even keep hold of those.

A passing servant directs me to the drawing room, which turns out to be on the far side of the dining hall, a few doors down from the marble entrance hall I entered this morning. It's an unpleasant place, the dark wood and scarlet drapes bringing to mind an overlarge coffin, the coal fire breathing oily smoke into the air. A dozen people are gathered within, and though a table's been laid with cold cuts, most of the guests are flopped in leather armchairs or standing at the leaded windows, staring mournfully at the frightful weather, while a maid, with jam stains on her apron, slips unobtrusively among them, gathering dirty plates and empty glasses onto a huge silver tray she can barely hold. A rotund fellow in green hunting tweeds has set himself up on the pianoforte in the corner and is playing a bawdy tune that causes offense only for the ineptness of its delivery. Nobody is paying much attention to him, though he's doing his best to rectify that.

It's almost midday, but Daniel is nowhere to be seen, and so I busy myself inspecting the various decanters in the drinks cabinet without any clue as to what they are, or what I enjoy. In the end, I pour myself something brown and turn to stare at my fellow guests, hoping for a flash of recognition. If one of these people is responsible for the wounds on my arm, their irritation at seeing me hale and healthy should be obvious. And surely my mind wouldn't conspire to keep their identity secret should they reveal themselves? Assuming, of course, my mind can find some way of telling them apart. Nearly every man is a braying, beef-faced bully in hunting tweeds, while the women are dressed soberly in skirts, linen shirts, and cardigans. Unlike their boisterous husbands, they move in hushed tones, finding me from the corner of their eyes. I have the impression of being surreptitiously observed, like a rare bird. It's terribly unsettling, though understandable I suppose. Daniel couldn't have asked his questions without revealing my condition in the process. I'm now part of the entertainment, whether I like it or not.

Nursing my drink, I attempt to distract myself by eavesdropping on the surrounding conversations, a sensation akin to sticking my head into a rosebush. Half of them are complaining, the other half are being complained at. They don't like the accommodations, the food, the indolence of the help, the isolation, or the fact they couldn't drive up themselves (though heaven knows how they would have found the place). Mostly, though, their ire is reserved for the lack of a welcome from Lady Hardcastle, who has yet to surface, despite many of them having arrived in Blackheath last night—a fact they appear to have taken as a personal insult.

"'Scuse me, Ted," says the maid, trying to squeeze past a man in his fifties. He's broad chested and sunburned beneath a thinning crop of red hair. Hunting tweeds stretch around a thick body that's slipping toward fat, his face lit by bright-blue eyes.

"Ted?" he says angrily, grabbing her wrist and squeezing hard enough to make her wince. "Who the hell do you think you're talking to, Lucy? It's Mr. Stanwin to you. I'm not downstairs with the rats anymore."

She nods, shocked, searching our faces for help. Nobody moves, even the piano bites its tongue. They're all terrified of this man, I realize. To my shame, I'm little better. I'm frozen in place, watching this exchange from the corner of my lowered eyes, desperately hoping his vulgarity doesn't turn in my direction.

"Let her go, Ted," says Daniel Coleridge from the doorway.

His voice is firm, cold. It clatters with repercussions.

Stanwin breathes through his nose, staring at Daniel out of narrowed eyes. It shouldn't be a contest. Stanwin is squat and solid and spitting venom. Yet there's something in the way Daniel stands there, hands in his pockets, head tilted, that gives Stanwin pause. Perhaps he's wary of being hit by the train Daniel appears to be waiting for.

A clock drums up its courage and ticks.

With a grunt, Stanwin releases the maid, brushing past Daniel on his way out, muttering something I can't quite hear.

The room breathes, the piano resumes, the heroic clock carrying on as though nothing happened.

Daniel's eyes weigh us one by one.

Unable to face his scrutiny, I stare at my reflection in the window. There's disgust on my face, revulsion at the endless shortcomings of my character. First the murder in the woods, and now this. How many injustices will I allow to walk by before I pluck up the courage to intervene?

Daniel approaches, a ghost in the glass.

"Bell," he says softly, laying a hand on my shoulder. "Do you have a minute?"

Hunched beneath my shame, I follow him into the study next door, every pair of eyes at my back. It's even gloomier in here, untrimmed ivy shrouding the leaded windows, paintings in dark oils soaking up what little light manages to squirm through the glass. A writing desk has been arranged with a view onto the lawn, and looks recently vacated, a fountain pen leaking ink onto a torn piece of blotting paper, a letter opener beside it. One can only imagine the missives written in such an oppressive atmosphere.

In the opposite corner, near a second door out of the room, a puzzled young man in hunting tweeds is peering down the speaker of a gramophone, clearly wondering why the spinning record isn't flinging sound into the room.

"A single term at Cambridge and he thinks he's Isambard Kingdom Brunel," says Daniel, causing the young man to look up from his puzzle. He's no more than twenty-four, with dark hair and wide, flattened features that give the impression of his face being pressed up against a pane of glass. Seeing me, he grins broadly, the boy in the man appearing as if through a window.

"Belly, you bloody idiot, there you are," he says, squeezing my hand and clapping me on the back at the same time. It's like being caught in an affectionate vice.

He searches my face expectantly, his green eyes narrowing at my lack of recognition.

"It's true, then, you can't remember a thing," he says, tossing a quick glance at Daniel. "You lucky devil! Let's get to the bar so I can introduce you to a hangover."

"News travels fast in Blackheath," I say.

"Boredom's very flat ground," he says. "Name's Michael Hardcastle. We're old friends, though I suppose we're better described as recent acquaintants now."

There's no hint of disappointment in the statement. In fact, he seems amused by it. Even at first meeting, it's evident Michael Hardcastle will be amused by most things.

"Michael was sitting next to you at dinner last night," says Daniel, who's taken up Michael's inspection of the gramophone. "Come to think of it, that's probably why you went out and coshed yourself on the head."

"Play along, Belly. We're hoping one day he'll accidentally say something funny," says Michael.

There's an instinctive pause for my rejoinder, the rhythm of the moment collapsing under the weight of its absence. For the first time since I woke up this morning, I feel a yearning for my old life. I miss knowing these men. I miss the intimacy of this friendship. My sorrow is mirrored on the faces of my companions, an awkward silence digging a trench between us. Hoping to recover at least some of the trust we must once have shared, I roll up my sleeve to show them the bandages covering my arm, blood already beginning to seep through.

"I wish I had coshed myself on the head," I say. "Doctor Dickie believes somebody attacked me last night."

"My dear fellow," gasps Daniel.

"This is because of that damn note, isn't it?" says Michael, his eyes tracing my injuries.

"What note?" asks Daniel. "Are you saying you know something about this, Hardcastle? Why didn't you mention it earlier?"

"Because the way you described it, all of Belly's misfortunes came about this morning," he says. "The note came last night. I didn't put the two things together until now."

"I think an explanation is in order," says Daniel.

"There's not much more to it," says Michael sheepishly, digging at the thick carpet with the toe of his shoe. "A maid brought a note to the table during our fifth bottle of wine. Next thing I know Belly's making his excuses and trying to remember how doors work." He looks at me shamefaced. "I wanted to go with you, but you were adamant you had to go alone. I assumed you were meeting some woman or other, so I didn't press the issue, and that was the last I saw of you until now."

"What did the message say?" I ask.

"Haven't the foggiest, old bean. I didn't see it."

"Do you remember the maid who brought it, or if Bell mentioned anybody called Anna?" asks Daniel.

Michael shrugs, wrapping his entire face around the memory. "Anna? Doesn't ring any bells, I'm afraid. As for the maid, well…" He puffs up his cheeks, blowing out a long breath. "Black dress, white apron. Oh, dash it all, Coleridge. Be reasonable. There's dozens of them. How's a man meant to keep track of their faces."

He hands each of us a helpless look, Daniel meeting it with a disgusted shake of the head.

"Don't worry, old boy; we'll get to the bottom of all this," he says to me, squeezing my shoulder. "And I've an idea how."

He motions toward a framed map of the estate hanging on the wall. It's an architectural drawing, rain spotted and yellowing at the edges, but quite beautiful in its depiction of the house and grounds. As it turns out, Blackheath is a huge estate with a family graveyard to the west and a stable to the east, a trail winding down to a lake with a boathouse clinging to the bank. Aside from the driveway, which is actually a stubborn road cutting straight toward the village, everything else is forest. As the view from the upper windows suggests, we're quite alone among the trees.

A cold sweat prickles my skin.

I was meant to disappear in that expanse, as Anna did this morning. I'm searching for my own grave.

Sensing my disquiet, Daniel glances at me.

"Lonely sort of place, isn't it?" he murmurs, tapping a cigarette loose from a silver case. It dangles from his lower lip as he searches his pockets for a lighter.

"My father brought us out here when his political career keeled over," says Michael, lighting Daniel's cigarette and taking one for himself. "The old man fancied himself a country squire. Didn't work out quite the way he'd hoped, of course."

I raise a questioning eyebrow.

"My brother was murdered by a chap called Charlie Carver, one of our groundskeepers," says Michael calmly, as though he were declaring the racing results.

Aghast that I could forget something so horrific, I stammer out an apology.

"I'm…I'm sorry, that must have been—"

"A terribly long time ago," interrupts Michael, a hint of impatience in his voice. "Nineteen years, in fact. I was only five when it happened, and truthfully, I can barely recall it."

"Unlike most of the gutter press," adds Daniel. "Carver and another fellow drank themselves into a mania and grabbed Thomas near the lake. They half drowned him, then finished the job with a knife. He was seven or so. Ted Stanwin came running and drove them off with a shotgun, but Thomas was already dead."

"Stanwin?" I ask, struggling to keep the shock from my voice. "The lout from lunch?"

"Oh, I wouldn't go saying that too loudly," says Daniel.

"He's very well thought of by my parents, is old Stanwin," says Michael. "He was a lowly gamekeeper when he tried to save Thomas, but Father gave him one of our African plantations in thanks and the blighter made his pile."

"What happened to the murderers?" I ask.

"Carver swung," says Daniel, tapping ash onto the carpet. "The police found the knife he used under the floorboards in his cottage, along with a dozen pilfered bottles of brandy. His accomplice was never caught. Stanwin says he clipped him with the shotgun, but no one turned up at the local hospital with an injury and Carver refused to give him up. Lord and Lady Hardcastle were hosting a party that weekend, so it could have been one of the guests, but the family were adamant that none of them knew Carver."

"Rum business all round," says Michael tonelessly, his expression black as the clouds crowding the windows.

"So the accomplice is still out there?" I say, dread creeping up my spine. A murder nineteen years ago and a murder this morning. Surely that can't be a coincidence.

"Does make you wonder what the police are for, doesn't it?" says Daniel, falling silent.

My eyes find Michael, who's staring into the drawing room. It's emptying out as the guests drift toward the entrance hall, carrying their conversations with them. Even from here, I can hear the stinging, swirling swarm of insults touching on everything from the rundown state of the house to Lord Hardcastle's drunkenness and Evelyn Hardcastle's icy demeanor. Poor Michael. I can't imagine how it must feel to have one's family so openly ridiculed, in their own home no less.

"Look, we didn't come here to bore you with ancient history," says Daniel, fracturing the quiet. "I've been asking around after Anna. It's not good news, I'm afraid."

"Nobody knows her?"

"There isn't anybody by that name among the guests or the staff," says Michael. "More to the point, nobody's missing from Blackheath."

I open my mouth to protest, but Michael holds his hand up, silencing me. "You never let me finish, Belly. I can't gather a search party, but the chaps are going hunting in about ten minutes. If you give me a vague idea where you woke up this morning, I'll make sure we head in that direction and keep our eyes open. Fifteen of us are going out, so there's a good chance we'll spot something."

Gratitude swells in my chest.

"Thank you, Michael."

He smiles at me through a cloud of cigarette smoke. "I've never known you to over-egg the pudding, Belly, so I can't imagine you're doing it now."

I stare at the map, eager to do my part, but I have no clue where I spotted Anna. The murderer pointed me east, and the forest disgorged me toward the front of Blackheath, but I can only guess for how long I walked or where I may have started from. Taking a breath and trusting to providence, I prod the glass with my fingertip as Daniel and Michael hover over my shoulder.

Michael nods, rubbing his chin.

"I'll tell the chaps." He looks me up and down. "You'd better get changed. We'll be leaving soon."

"I'm not coming," I say, my voice strangled by shame. "I have to… I just can't…"

The young man shifts awkwardly. "Come now—"

"Use your head, Michael," interrupts Daniel, clapping a hand on my shoulder. "Look what was done to him. Poor Bell barely got out of that forest. Why would he want to go back?"

His tone softens.

"Don't you worry, Bell. We'll find your missing girl, and the man who murdered her. It's in our hands now. Get yourself as far away from this mess as you can."

5

I stand at the leaded window, half concealed by the velvet drapes. Out on the driveway, Michael is mingling with the other men. They're heaving beneath their thick coats, shotguns crooked over their elbows, laughing and chatting, cold breath escaping their lips. Freed from the house with a slaughter to enjoy, they seem almost human.

Daniel's words were comforting, but they can't absolve me. I should be out there with them, searching for the body of the woman I failed. Instead, I'm running away. The very least I can do is endure the shame of watching them set off without me.

Dogs pass by the window, straining at leads their masters are struggling to hold. The two commotions merge, striking off across the lawn toward the forest, in precisely the direction I indicated to Daniel, although I can't see my friend among them. He must be joining the group later.

I wait for the last of them to disappear among the trees before returning to the map on the wall. If it's correct, the stables aren't too far from the house. Surely that's where I'll find the stable master. He can arrange a carriage to the village, and from there, I'll catch a train home.

I turn for the drawing room, only to find the doorway blocked by a huge black crow.

My heart leaps, and so do I, straight into the sideboard, sending family photographs and trinkets clattering to the floor.

"You don't need to be afraid," says the creature, taking a half step out of the gloom.

It's not a bird at all. It's a man dressed as a medieval plague doctor, his feathers a black greatcoat, the beak belonging to a porcelain mask, glinting in the light of a nearby lamp. Presumably this is his costume for the ball tonight, though that doesn't explain why he's wearing such sinister garb in the middle of the day.

"You startled me," I say, clutching my chest and laughing in embarrassment as I try to shake off my fright. He cocks his head, examining me as if I'm a stray animal he's found sitting on the carpet.

"What did you bring with you?" he asks.

"I'm sorry?"

"You woke up with a word on your lips. What was it?"

"Do we know each other?" I ask, glancing through the door into the drawing room, hoping to see another guest. Unfortunately, we're alone, which was almost certainly his intention, I realize with growing alarm.

"I know you," he says. "That's enough for now. What was the word, please?"

"Why not take off the mask so we might speak face-to-face," I say.

"My mask is the least of your concerns, Doctor Bell," he says. "Answer the question."

Though he's said nothing threatening, the porcelain muffles his voice, adding a low animal rumble to every sentence.

"Anna," I say, clamping my hand on my thigh to stop my leg from jogging.

He sighs. "That's a pity."

"Do you know who she is?" I say hopefully. "Nobody else in the house has ever heard of her."

"I'd be surprised if they had," he says, waving away my question with a gloved hand. Reaching into his coat, he pulls out a golden pocket watch, tutting at the time. "We'll have work to do before long, but not today and not while you're in this state. We'll speak again soon, when everything's a little clearer. In the meantime, I'd advise you to acquaint yourself with Blackheath and your fellow guests. Enjoy yourself while you can, Doctor. The footman will find you soon."

"The footman?" I say, the name ringing an alarm bell somewhere deep within me. "Is he responsible for Anna's murder, or the wounds on my arm?"

"I very much doubt it," says the Plague Doctor. "The footman isn't going to stop with your arm."

There's a tremendous thump behind me, and I spin toward the noise. A small splash of blood smears the window, a dying bird thrashing the last of its life away among the weeds and withered flowers below. The poor thing must have flown into the glass. I'm startled by the pity I feel, a tear creeping into my eye at this wasted life. Resolving to bury the bird before I do anything else, I turn around, intending to make my excuses to my enigmatic companion, but he's already left.

I look at my hands. They're clutched so tightly my fingernails are digging into my palms.

"The footman," I repeat to myself.

The name means nothing, but the feeling it evokes is unmistakable. For some reason, I'm terrified of this person.

Fear carries me over to the writing desk and the letter opener I saw earlier. It's small, but sharp enough to draw blood from the tip of my thumb. Sucking the wound, I pocket the weapon. It's not much, but it's enough to stop me barricading myself in this room.

Feeling a touch more confident, I head for my bedroom. Without the guests to distract from the décor, Blackheath is a melancholy pile indeed. Aside from the magnificent entrance hall, the other rooms I pass through are musty, thick with mildew and decay. Pellets of rat poison have been piled up in the corners, dust covering any surface too high for a maid's short arm to reach. The rugs are threadbare, the furniture scratched, the smeared silver crockery arranged behind the dirty glass of display cabinets. As unpleasant as my fellow guests seem,

I miss the thrum of their conversations. They're the lifeblood of this place, filling up the spaces where otherwise this grim silence would fall. Blackheath's only alive so long as people are in it. Without them, it's a depressing ruin waiting on the mercy of a wrecking ball.

I collect my coat and umbrella from my bedroom and make my way outside where rain is bouncing off the ground, the air smothered by the stink of rotten leaves. Uncertain of which window the bird crashed against, I follow the verge until I locate its body, and using the letter opener as a makeshift shovel, I bury it in a shallow grave, soaking my gloves in the process.

Already shivering, I consider my route. The cobbled road to the stables skirts the bottom edge of the lawn. I could cut across the grass, but my shoes seem ill suited to the venture. Instead, I take the safer option, following the gravel driveway until the road appears on my left. Unsurprisingly, it's in a terrible state of disrepair. Tree roots have overturned the stones; untrimmed branches hang low like pilfering fingers. Still unsettled by my meeting with the strange man in the plague doctor costume, I clutch the letter opener and move slowly, wary of losing my footing, afraid of what might spring out at me from the woods if I do. I'm not sure what his game is, dressing up like that, but I can't seem to shrug off his warnings.

Somebody murdered Anna and gave me a compass. It's doubtful that same person attacked me last night only to save me this morning, and now I must contend with this footman. Who must I have been to assemble so many enemies?

At the end of the road is a tall, redbrick arch with a shattered glass clock at the center, and beyond that a courtyard, stables and outbuildings arranged around its edge. Troughs overflow with oats, and carriages stand wheel to wheel, draped in green canvas covers to keep the weather off.

The only things missing are the horses.

Every stable is empty.

"Hello?" I call out tentatively, my voice echoing around the yard but meeting no response.

A plume of black smoke is escaping the chimney of a little cottage, and finding the door unlocked, I chase my hollered greetings inside. No one's home, which is curious as a fire's burning in the hearth, porridge and toast laid out on the table. Removing my soggy gloves, I hang them on the kettle pole above the fire, hoping to spare myself a little discomfort on the walk back.

Touching the food with a fingertip, I discover it's lukewarm, so not long abandoned. A saddle lies discarded beside a leather patch, suggesting an interrupted repair. I can only assume whoever lives here has rushed out to deal with some emergency, and I consider waiting for them to return. It's not an unpleasant refuge, though the air's thick with burning coal and smells rather strongly of polish and horse-hair. Of greater concern is the cottage's isolation. Until I know who attacked me last night, everybody in Blackheath must be treated with caution, including the stable master. I will not meet him alone, if it can be helped.

A work roster hangs on a nail by the door, a pencil dangling from a piece of string beside it. Taking it down, I turn the sheet over intending to leave a message requesting a ride to the village, but there's a note already written there.

Don't leave Blackheath, more lives than your own are depending on you. Meet me by the mausoleum in the family graveyard at 10:20 p.m. and I'll explain everything. Oh, and don't forget your gloves. They're burning.

Love, Anna

Smoke fills my nostrils, and I swing around to see my gloves smoldering above the fire. Snatching them down, I stamp the ashes out, eyes wide and heart pounding, as I search the cottage for some indication as to how the trick might have come to pass.

Why don't you ask Anna when you meet her tonight?

"Because I saw her die," I snarl at the empty room, embarrassing myself.

Recovering my composure, I read the note once more, the truth of it no nearer at hand. If Anna's survived, she'd have to be a cruel creature to play such games with me. More likely, after word of this morning's misadventure spread around the house, somebody has decided to play a trick on me. Why else would they choose such a sinister location and hour for the meeting?

Is this somebody a fortune-teller?

"It's a foul day. Anybody could have predicted I'd dry my gloves once I arrived."

The cottage listens politely, but even to my ears that reasoning's desperate. Almost as desperate as my urge to discredit the message. So defective is my character, I'd happily abandon any hope of Anna being alive in order to flee this place with a clean conscience.

Feeling miserable, I pull on my singed gloves. I need to think, and walking seems to help.

Heading around the stables, I come upon an overgrown paddock, the grass grown waist high and the fences so badly rotted they've all but collapsed. On the far side, two figures huddle beneath an umbrella. They must be following a hidden path as they're moving easily, arm in arm. Heaven knows how they spot me, but one of them raises a hand in greeting. I return the gesture, sparking a brief moment of distant kinship, before they disappear into the gloom of the trees.

Lowering my hand, I make my decision.

I told myself that a dead woman could lay no claim to me, and that's why I was free to leave Blackheath. It was a coward's reason, but at least it had a ring of truth to it.

If Anna's alive, that's no longer the case.

I failed her this morning, and it's all I've thought about since. Now that I have a second chance, I cannot turn my back. She's in danger and I can help, so I must. If that's not enough to keep me at Blackheath, I don't deserve the life I'm so fearful of losing. Come what may, I must be in the graveyard at 10:20 p.m.

6

"*Somebody wants me dead.*"

It feels strange to say it out loud, as though I'm calling fate down upon myself, but if I'm to survive until this evening, I'll need to face down this fear. I refuse to spend any more time cowering in my bedroom. Not while there are so many questions to answer.

I'm walking back to the house, scouring the trees for any sign of danger, my mind running back and forth across the morning's events. Over and over again, I wonder about the slashes on my arm and the man in the plague doctor costume, the footman and this mysterious Anna, who now appears to be alive and well, and leaving enigmatic notes for me to find.

How did she survive in the forest?

I suppose she could have written the note earlier this morning, before she was attacked, but then how did she know I'd be in that cottage, drying my gloves over the fire? I didn't tell anybody about my plans. Did I speak out loud? Could she have been watching?

Shaking my head, I take a step away from that particular rabbit hole.

I'm looking too far forward, when I need to be looking back. Michael told me that a maid delivered a note to the dinner table last night, and that was the last he saw of me.

Everything started with that.

You need to find the servant who brought the note.

I'm barely through Blackheath's doors when voices pull me toward the drawing room, which is empty aside from a couple of young maids clearing the lunchtime detritus onto two huge trays. They work side by side, heads bowed in hushed gossip, oblivious to my presence at the door.

"...Henrietta said she'd gone mad," says one girl, brown curls tumbling free of her white cap.

"It's not right to say that about Lady Helena, Beth," scolds the older girl. "She's always been good to us, treated us fair, hasn't she?"

Beth weighs this fact against the wealth of her gossip.

"Henrietta told me she was raving," she continues. "Screaming at Lord Peter. Said it was probably on account of being back in Blackheath after what happened to Master Thomas. Does funny things to a person, she said."

"She says a lot of things, does Henrietta. I'd put them out of your mind. Not like we haven't heard them fighting before, is it? Besides, if it were serious, Lady Helena would tell Mrs. Drudge, wouldn't she? Always does."

"Mrs. Drudge can't find her," says Beth triumphantly, the case against Lady Helena well and truly proven. "Hasn't seen her all morning, but—"

My entrance slaps the words out of the air, the maids attempting startled curtsies that swiftly devolve into a tangle of arms, legs, and blushes. Waving away their confusion, I ask after the servants who served dinner last night, prompting only blank stares and mumbled apologies. I'm on the verge of giving up, when Beth ventures that Evelyn Hardcastle is entertaining the ladies in the sunroom toward the rear of the house and would certainly know more.

After a brief exchange, one of them leads me through a communicating door into the study where I met Daniel and Michael this morning. There's a library beyond it, which we cross briskly, exiting the room into a dim connecting passage. Darkness stirs to greet us, a black cat drifting out from beneath a small telephone table, its tail dusting the wooden floor. On silent feet, it pads up the corridor, slipping through a door left slightly ajar at the far end. A warm, orange light is seeping through the gap, voices and music on the other side.

"Miss Evelyn's in there, sir," says the maid.

Her tone succinctly describes both the room and Evelyn Hardcastle, neither of which she seems to hold in particularly high regard.

Brushing off her scorn, I open the door, the heat of the room hitting me full in the face. The air is heavy, sweet with perfume, stirred only by a scratchy music that soars and glides and stuns itself against the walls. Large leaded windows look out over the garden at the rear of the house, gray clouds piling up beyond a cupola. Chairs and chaise longues have been gathered around the fire, young women draped over them like wilted orchids, smoking cigarettes and clinging to their drinks. The mood in the room is one of restless agitation rather than celebration. About the only sign of life comes from an oil painting on the far wall, where an old woman with coals for eyes sits in judgment of the room, her expression conveying her distaste for this gathering.

"My grandmother, Heather Hardcastle," says a woman from behind me. "It's not a flattering picture, but then she wasn't a flattering woman by all accounts."

I turn to meet the voice, reddening as a dozen faces swim up through their boredom to inspect me. My name runs laps of the room, a sudden excited buzz chasing it like a swarm of bees.

Sitting either side of a chess table are a woman I must assume to be Evelyn Hardcastle and an elderly, extremely fat man wearing a suit that's a size too small for him. They're an odd couple. Evelyn's in her late twenties and rather resembles a shard of glass with her thin, angular body and high cheekbones, her blond hair tied up away from her face. She's wearing a green dress, fashionably tailored and belted at the waist, its sharp lines mirroring the severe expression on her face.

As for the fat man, he can't be less than sixty-five, and I can only imagine what contortions must have been necessary to persuade his enormous bulk behind the table. His chair's too small for him, too stiff. He's a martyr to it. Sweat is gleaming on his forehead, the soaking wet handkerchief clutched in his hand testifying to the duration of his suffering. He's looking at me queerly, an expression somewhere between curiosity and gratitude.

"My apologies," I say. "I was—"

Evelyn slides a pawn forward without looking up from the board. The fat man returns his attention to the game, engulfing his knight with a fleshy fingertip.

I surprise myself by groaning at his mistake.

"You know chess?" Evelyn asks me, her eyes still fixed on the board.

"It appears so," I say.

"Then perhaps you would play after Lord Ravencourt?"

Ignorant of my warning, Ravencourt's knight swaggers into Evelyn's trap, only to be cut down by a lurking rook. Panic takes hold of his play as Evelyn urges her pieces forward, hurrying him when he should be patient. The game's over in four moves.

"Thank you for the diversion, Lord Ravencourt," says Evelyn, as he topples his king. "Now, I believe you had somewhere else to be."

It's an eloquent dismissal, and with an awkward bow, Ravencourt disentangles himself from the table and limps out of the room, offering me the slightest of nods on the way.

Evelyn's distaste chases him through the door, but it evaporates as she gestures to the seat opposite.

"Please," she says.

"I'm afraid I can't," I say. "I'm looking for a maid who brought me a message at the dinner table last night, but I know nothing more of her. I was hoping you could help."

"Our butler could," she says, restoring the pieces of her bedraggled army to their line. Each is placed precisely at the center of a square, its face turned toward the enemy. Clearly, there's no place for cowards on this board.

"Mr. Collins knows every step every servant takes in this house, or so he leads them to believe," she says. "Unfortunately, he was assaulted this morning. Doctor Dickie had him moved to the gatehouse, so he could rest more comfortably. I've actually been meaning to look in on him myself. Perhaps I could escort you."

I momentarily hesitate, weighing the danger. One can only assume that if Evelyn Hardcastle intended me harm, she wouldn't announce our intention to go off together in front of an entire room of witnesses.

"That would be very kind," I respond, earning a flicker of a smile.

Evelyn stands, either not noticing or pretending not to notice the curious glances nudging us. There are french doors onto the gardens, but we forgo them, departing instead from the entrance hall, so we might collect our coats and hats from our bedrooms first. Evelyn's still tugging hers on as we step out of Blackheath into the blustery, cold afternoon.

"May I ask what happened to Mr. Collins?" I say, wondering if perhaps his assault might be linked to my own last night.

"Apparently he was set upon by one of our guests, an artist named Gregory Gold," she says, knotting her thick scarf. "It was an unprovoked attack by all accounts, and Gold managed to thrash him pretty soundly before somebody intervened. I should warn you, Doctor, Mr. Collins has been heavily sedated, so I'm not sure how helpful he'll be."

We're following the gravel driveway that leads to the village, and once again, I'm struck by the peculiarity of my condition. At some point in the last few days, I must have arrived along this very road, happy and excited, or perhaps annoyed at the distance and isolation. Did I understand the danger I was in, or did it come later during my stay? So much of me is lost, memories simply blown aside like the leaves on the ground, and yet here I stand, remade. I wonder if Sebastian Bell would approve of this man I've become. If we'd even get along?

Without a word, Evelyn links an arm through my own, a warm smile transforming her face. It's as though a fire has been kindled within, her eyes sparkling with life, banishing the shrouded woman of earlier.

"It's so good to be out of that house," she cries, tipping her face to meet the rain. "Thank goodness you came along when you did, Doctor. Honestly, a minute later and you'd have found me with my head in the grate."

"Lucky I stopped by, then," I say, somewhat startled by her change in mood. Sensing my confusion, Evelyn laughs lightly.

"Oh, don't mind me," she says. "I loathe getting to know people, so whenever I meet somebody I like, I just assume a friendship immediately. It saves a great deal of time in the long run."

"I can see the appeal," I say. "May I ask what I did to earn a favorable impression?"

"Only if you allow me to be frank in my answer."

"You're not being frank now?"

"I was trying to be polite, but you're right. I never seem to land on the right side of the fence," she says with mock regret. "Well, *to be frank*, I like your pensiveness, Doctor. You strike me as a man who'd much rather be somewhere else, a feeling I can wholeheartedly sympathize with."

"Am I to assume you're not enjoying your homecoming?"

"Oh, this hasn't been my home in a very long time," she says, skipping over a large puddle. "I've lived in Paris for the last nineteen years, ever since my brother was killed."

"What about the women I saw you with in the sunroom, are they not your friends?"

"They arrived this morning, and truth be told, I didn't recognize a single one of them. The children I knew have shed their skins and slithered into society. I'm as much a stranger here as yourself."

"At least you're not a stranger *to* yourself, Miss Hardcastle," I say. "Surely you can take some solace in that?"

"Quite the contrary," she says, looking at me. "I imagine it would be rather splendid to wander away from myself for a little while. I envy you."

"Envy?"

"Why not?" she says, wiping the rain from her face. "You're a soul stripped bare, Doctor. No regrets, no wounds, none of the lies we tell ourselves so we can look in the mirror each morning. You're..." She bites her lip, searching for the word. "Honest."

"Another word for that is 'exposed,'" I say.

"Am I to take it you're not enjoying *your* homecoming?"

There's a crook in her smile, a slight twist of the lips that could easily be damning, yet somehow comes across as conspiratorial.

"I'm not the man I'd hoped to be," I say quietly, surprised by my own candor. Something about this woman puts me at ease, though for the life of me I can't tell what it is.

"How so?" she asks.

"I'm a coward, Miss Hardcastle," I sigh. "Forty years of memories wiped away and that's what I find lurking beneath it all. That's what remains to me."

"Oh, do call me Evie. That way, I can call you Sebastian and tell you not to fret about your flaws. We all have them, and if I were newly born into this world, I might be cautious too," she says, squeezing my arm.

"You're very kind, but this is something deeper, instinctive."

"Well, so what if you are?" she asks. "There are worse things to be. At least you're not mean-spirited or cruel. And now you get to choose, don't

you? Instead of assembling yourself in the dark like the rest of us—so
that you wake up one day with no idea of how you became this person—
you can look at the world, at the people around you, and choose the parts
of your character you want. You can say, 'I'll have that man's honesty, that
woman's optimism, as if you're shopping for a suit on Savile Row.'"

"You've made my condition into a gift," I say, feeling my spirits lift.

"Well, what else would you call a second chance?" she asks. "You
don't like the man you were. Very well. Be somebody else. There's
nothing stopping you, not anymore. As I said, I envy you. The rest of
us are stuck with our mistakes."

I have no response to that, though one is not immediately required.
We've arrived upon two giant fence posts, fractured angels blaring
their noiseless horns on top. The gatehouse is set back among the trees
on our left, splashes of its red-tile roof showing through the dense
canopy. A path leads toward a peeling green door, which is swollen
with age and riddled with cracks. Ignoring it, Evelyn pulls me by the
fingers toward the back of the house, pushing through branches so
overgrown they're touching the crumbling brickwork.

The back door is held fast with a simple latch, and undoing it, she
lets us into a dank kitchen, a layer of dust coating the countertops, the
copper pans still on the stove top. Once inside, she pauses, listening
intently.

"Evelyn?" I say.

Motioning for quiet, she takes a step closer to the corridor.
Unsettled by this sudden caution, my body tenses, but she breaks the
spell with laughter.

"I'm sorry, Sebastian. I was listening out for my father."

"Your father?" I say, puzzled.

"He's staying here," she says. "He's supposed to be out hunting,
but I didn't want to risk bumping into him if he was running late. I'm
afraid we don't like each other terribly much."

Before I have the chance to ask any more questions, she beckons me into a tiled hallway and up a narrow staircase, the bare wooden steps shrieking beneath our feet. I keep to her heels, snatching backward glances every few steps. The gatehouse is narrow and crooked, doors set into the walls at odd angles like teeth grown wild in a mouth. Wind whistles through the windows carrying with it the smell of the rain, the entire place seeming to rattle on its foundations. Everything about this house seems designed to unseat the nerves.

"Why put the butler all the way out here?" I ask Evelyn, who's trying to choose between the doors either side of us. "There must have been somewhere more comfortable."

"All the rooms in the main house are full, and Doctor Dickie ordered peace and quiet, and a good fire. Believe it or not, this might be the best place for him. Come on, let's try this one," she says, rapping lightly on a door to our left, pushing it open when there's no response.

A tall fellow in a charcoal-stained shirt is bound by his wrists and dangling from a hook on the ceiling, his feet only barely touching the floor. He's unconscious, a head full of dark curly hair slumped against his chest, blood speckling his face.

"Nope, must be the other side," says Evelyn, her voice bland and unconcerned.

"What the devil?" I say, taking a step back in alarm. "Who is this man, Evelyn?"

"This is Gregory Gold, the fellow who assaulted our butler," says Evelyn, eyeing him as one would a butterfly pinned to a corkboard. "The butler was my father's batman during the war. Seems Father's taken the assault rather personally."

"Personally?" I say. "Evie, he's been strung up like a pig!"

"Father's never been a subtle man, or a particularly clever one," she shrugs. "I suspect the two things go hand in hand."

For the first time since I awoke, my blood is boiling. Whatever this man's crimes, justice can't be served by a length of rope in a locked room.

"We can't leave him like this," I protest. "It's inhuman."

"What he did was inhuman," says Evelyn, her chill touching me for the first time. "Mother commissioned Gold to tidy up a few of the family portraits, nothing more. He didn't even know the butler, and yet this morning, he took after him with a poker and beat him half to death. Believe me, Sebastian, he deserves worse than what's happening to him here."

"What's to become of him?" I ask.

"A constable is coming from the village," says Evelyn, ushering me out of the small room, and closing the door behind us, her mood brightening immediately. "Father wants to let Gold know of his displeasure in the meantime, that's all. Ah, this must be the one we wanted."

She opens another door on the opposite side of the hall, and we enter a small room with whitewashed walls and a single window blinded by dirt. Unlike the rest of the house, there's no draft in here and a good fire's burning in the grate, plenty of wood stacked nearby to feed it. There's an iron bed in the corner, the butler shapeless beneath a gray blanket. I recognize this chap. It's the burned man who let me in this morning.

Evelyn was right. He's been cruelly treated. His face is hideously bruised and livid with cuts, dried blood staining the pillowcase. I might have mistaken him for dead if it weren't for his constant murmuring, distress poisoning his sleep.

A maid sat beside him in a wooden chair, a large book open in her lap. She can't be more than twenty-three, small enough to tuck into a pocket, with blond hair spilling from beneath her cap. She looks up as we enter, slamming the book closed and leaping to her feet when she realizes who we are, hastily smoothing out her white apron.

"Miss Evelyn," she stammers, eyes on the floor. "I didn't know you'd be visiting."

"My friend here needed to see Mr. Collins," says Evelyn.

The maid's brown eyes flick toward me, before pinning themselves to the ground once more.

"I'm sorry, miss, he hasn't stirred all morning," says the maid. "The doctor gave him some tablets to help him sleep."

"And he can't be woken?"

"Haven't tried, miss, but you made an awful racket coming up them stairs and he didn't bat an eyelid. Don't know what else would do it, if that didn't. Dead to the world, he is."

The maid's eyes find me once again, lingering long enough to suggest some sort of familiarity, before resuming their former contemplation of the floor.

"I'm sorry, but do we know each other?" I ask.

"No, sir, not really, it's just...I served you at dinner last night."

"Did you bring me a note?" I ask, excitedly.

"Not me, sir. It was Madeline."

"Madeline?"

"My lady's maid," interrupts Evelyn. "The house was short-staffed so I sent her down to the kitchen to help out. Well, that's fortunate." She checks her wristwatch. "She's taking refreshments out to the hunters, but she'll be back around 3:00 p.m. We can question her together when she returns."

I turn my attention back to the maid.

"Do you know anything more about the note?" I ask. "Its contents, perhaps?"

The maid shakes her head, wringing her hands. The poor creature looks quite on the spot, and taking pity on her, I offer my thanks and leave.

～ 7 ～

We're following the road to the village, the trees drawing closer with every step. It's not quite what I'd anticipated. The map in the study conjured images of some grand labor, a boulevard hewn from the forest. The reality is little more than a wide dirt track, wretched with potholes and fallen branches. The forest hasn't been tamed so much as bartered with, the Hardcastles winning the barest of concessions from their neighbor.

I don't know our destination, but Evelyn believes we can intercept Madeline on her way back from the hunt. Secretly, I suspect she's simply looking for an excuse to prolong her absence from the house. Not that any subterfuge is necessary. This last hour in Evelyn's company is the first time since waking that I've felt myself a whole person, rather than the remnants of one. Out here, in the wind and rain, with a friend by my side, I'm happier than I have been all day.

"What do you believe Madeline can tell you?" asks Evelyn, picking a branch off the path and tossing it into the forest.

"The note that she brought me last night lured me out into the woods so somebody could attack me," I say.

"Attack!" interrupts Evelyn, shocked. "Here? Why?"

"I don't know, but I'm hoping Madeline can tell me who sent the note. She might even have peeked at the message."

"There's no 'might' about it," says Evelyn. "Madeline was in Paris with me. She's loyal and she makes me laugh, but she's an atrocious maid. She probably considers peeking at other people's mail a perk of the job."

"That's very lenient of you," I say.

"I have to be, I can't pay very well," she says. "And after she's revealed the contents of the message, what then?"

"I tell the police," I say. "And hopefully put this matter to bed."

Turning left at a crooked signpost, we follow a small trail into the woods, dirt tracks crisscrossing each other until the way back is impossible to discern.

"Do you know where you're going?" I ask nervously, swiping a low-hanging branch from my face. The last time I entered this forest, my mind never made it back.

"We're following these," she says, tugging at a fragment of yellow material nailed to a tree. It's similar to the red one I found when I stumbled upon Blackheath this morning, the memory only serving to unsettle me further.

"They're markers," she says. "The groundskeepers use them to navigate in the woods. Don't worry. I'll not lead you too far astray."

The words are barely out of her mouth when we enter a small clearing with a stone well at its center. The wooden shelter has collapsed, the iron wheel that once raised the bucket now left to rust in the mud, almost buried by fallen leaves. Evelyn claps in delight, laying an affectionate hand on the mossy stone. She's clearly hoping I haven't noticed the slip of paper tucked between the cracks, or the way her fingers are now covering it. Friendship compels me to play along, and I hastily avert my attention when she looks back toward me. She must have some suitor in the house, and I'm ashamed to say I'm jealous of this secret correspondence and the person on the other side of it.

"This is it," she says with a theatrical sweep of her arm. "Madeline will be passing through this clearing on her way back to the house.

Shouldn't be too long now. She's due back at the house by 3:00 to help finish setting up the ballroom."

"Where are we?" I ask, looking around.

"It's a wishing well," she says, leaning over the edge to peer into the blackness. "Michael and I used to come here when we were children. We'd make our wishes with pebbles."

"And what sorts of things did young Evelyn Hardcastle wish for?" I ask.

She wrinkles her brow, the question flummoxing her.

"You know, for the life of me, I can't remember," she says. "What does a child who has everything want?"

More, just like everybody else.

"I doubt I could have told you even when I did have my memories," I say, smiling.

Dusting the grime from her hands, Evelyn looks at me quizzically. I can see the curiosity burning inside her, the joy at encountering something unknown and unexpected in a place where everything is familiar. I'm out here because I fascinate her, I realize with a flash of disappointment.

"Have you thought about what you'll do if your memories don't return?" she says, softening the question with the gentleness of her tone.

Now it's my turn to be flummoxed.

Since my initial confusion passed, I've tried not to dwell upon my condition. If anything, the loss of my memories has proven a frustration rather than a tragedy, my inability to recall Anna being one of the few moments when it's seemed anything more than an inconvenience. Thus far, in the excavation of Sebastian Bell, I've unearthed two friends, an annotated Bible, and a locked trunk. Precious little return for forty years on this earth. I don't have a wife weeping for our lost time together, or a child worrying that the father she loved might not return. At this distance, Sebastian Bell's life seems an easy one to lose and a difficult one to mourn.

A branch snaps somewhere in the forest.

"Footman," says Evelyn, my blood immediately running cold as I recall the Plague Doctor's warning.

"What did you say?" I ask, frantically searching the forest.

"That noise, it's a footman," she says. "They're collecting wood. Shameful, isn't it? We don't have enough servants to stock all the fireplaces, so our guests are having to send their own footmen to do it."

"They? How many are there?"

"One for every family visiting, and there's more coming," she says. "I'd say there's already seven or eight in the house."

"Eight?" I say in a strangled voice.

"My dear Sebastian, are you quite all right?" says Evelyn, catching my alarm.

Under different circumstances I would welcome this concern, this affection, but here and now, her scrutiny only embarrasses me. How can I explain that a strange chap in a plague doctor costume warned me to keep an eye out for a footman—a name that means nothing to me, and yet fills me with a crippling fear every time I hear it?

"I'm sorry, Evie," I say, shaking my head ruefully. "There's more I need to tell you, but not here, and not quite yet."

Unable to hold her questioning stare, I look around the clearing for a distraction. Three trails intersect before striking off into the forest, one of them cutting a straight path through the trees toward water.

"Is that—"

"A lake," says Evelyn, looking past me. "The lake, I suppose you'd say. That's where my brother was murdered by Charlie Carver."

A shiver of silence divides us.

"I'm sorry, Evie," I say at last, embarrassed by the poverty of the sentiment.

"You'll think me awful, but it happened so long ago it barely seems real," she says. "I can't even remember Thomas's face."

"Michael shared a similar sentiment," I say.

"That's not surprising. He was five years younger than me when it happened." She's hugging herself, her tone distant. "I was supposed to be looking after Thomas that morning, but I wanted to go riding and he was always pestering me, so I arranged a treasure hunt for the children and left him behind. If I hadn't been so selfish, he'd never have been at the lake in the first place, and Carver wouldn't have got his filthy hands on him. You can't imagine what that thought does to a child. I didn't sleep, barely ate. I couldn't feel anything that wasn't anger or guilt. I was monstrous to anybody who tried to console me."

"What changed?"

"Michael." She smiles wistfully. "I was vile to him, positively horrid, but he stayed by my side, no matter what I said. He saw I was sad, and he wanted to make me feel better. I don't even think he knew what was happening, not really. He was just being nice, but he kept me from drifting away completely."

"Is that why you went to Paris, to get away from it all?"

"I didn't choose to leave. My parents sent me away a few months after it happened," she says, biting her lip. "They couldn't forgive me, and I wouldn't have been allowed to forgive myself if I'd stayed. I know it was supposed to be a punishment, but exile was a kindness, I think."

"And yet you came back?"

"You make it sound like a choice," she says bitterly, tightening her scarf as the wind carves through the trees. "My parents ordered my return. They even threatened to cut me out of the will should I refuse. When that didn't work, they threatened to cut Michael out of the will instead. So here I am."

"I don't understand. Why would they behave so despicably and then throw you a party?"

"A party?" she says, shaking her head. "Oh, my dear man, you really have no idea what's happening here, do you?"

"Perhaps if you—"

"My brother was murdered nineteen years ago tomorrow, Sebastian. I don't know why, but my parents have decided to mark the occasion by reopening the house where it happened and inviting back the very same guests who were here that day."

Anger is rising in her voice, a low throb of pain I'd do anything to make go away. She's turned her head to face the lake, her blue eyes glossy.

"They're disguising a memorial as a party, and they've made me the guest of honor, which I can only assume means something dreadful is coming for me," she continues. "This isn't a celebration, it's a punishment, and there'll be fifty people in their very finest clothes watching it happen."

"Are your parents really so spiteful?" I ask, shocked. I feel much as I did when that bird hit the window earlier this morning, a great swell of pity mingled with a sense of injustice at life's sudden cruelties.

"My mother sent me a message this morning, asking me to meet her by the lake," she says. "She never came, and I don't think she ever meant to. She just wanted me to stand out there, where it happened, remembering. Does that answer your question?"

"Evelyn... I...I don't know what to say."

"There's nothing to say, Sebastian. Wealth is poisonous to the soul, and my parents have been wealthy a very long time—as have most of the guests who will be at this party. Their manners are a mask; you'd do well to remember that."

She smiles at my pained expression, taking my hand. Her fingers are cold, her gaze warm. She has the brittle courage of a prisoner walking their final steps to the gallows.

"Oh, don't fret, dear heart," she says. "I've done all the tossing and turning it's possible to do. I see little benefit in your losing sleep over it also. If you want, you could make a wish in the well on my behalf, though I'd understand if you have more pressing concerns."

From her pocket, she pulls out a small coin.

"Here," she says, handing it to me. "I don't think our pebbles did much good."

The coin travels a long way, hitting rock rather than water at the bottom. Despite Evelyn's advice, I hitch no hopes for myself to its surface. Instead, I pray for her deliverance from this place, for a happy life and freedom from her parents' machinations. Like a child, I close my eyes in the hope that when I open them again, the natural order will be overturned, the impossible made plausible by desire alone.

"You've changed so much," mutters Evelyn, a ripple of emotion disturbing her face, the slightest indication of discomfort when she realizes what she's said.

"You knew me before?" I say, surprised. Somehow, it never occurred to me that Evelyn and I might have had a relationship prior to this one.

"I shouldn't have said anything," she says, walking away from me.

"Evie, I've been in your company for over an hour, which makes you my best friend in this world," I say. "Please, be honest with me. Who am I?"

Her eyes crisscross my face.

"I'm not the right person to say," she protests. "We met two days ago, and only briefly. Most of what I know is innuendo and rumor."

"I'm sitting at an empty table. I'll take whatever crumbs I'm fed."

Her lips are tight. She's tugging her sleeves down awkwardly. If she had a shovel, she'd dig herself an escape tunnel. The deeds of good men are not related so reluctantly, and I'm already beginning to dread what she has to tell me. Even so, I cannot let this go.

"Please," I plead. "You told me earlier I could choose who I wanted to be, but I cannot do that without knowing who I was."

Her obstinacy flickers, and she looks up at me from under her eyelashes.

"Are you certain you wish to know?" she asks. "The truth isn't always a kindness."

"Kind or not, I need to understand what's been lost."

"Not a great deal, in my opinion," she sighs, squeezing my hand in both of hers. "You were a dope dealer, Sebastian. You made your living alleviating the boredom of the idle rich, and quite a living it was too, if your practice on Harley Street is anything to go by."

"I'm a…"

"Dope dealer," she repeats. "Laudanum's the fashion, I believe, though from what I understand, your trunk of tricks has something to cater to every taste."

I slump within myself. I wouldn't have believed I could be so wounded by the past, but the revelation of my former profession tears a hole right through me. Though my failings were numerous, against them was always stacked the small pride of being a doctor. There was nobility in that course, honor even. But no, Sebastian Bell took the title and twisted it to his own selfish ends, making it perverse, denying what little good remained to him.

Evelyn was right, the truth isn't always a kindness, but no man should discover himself this way, like an abandoned house stumbled upon in the darkness.

"I shouldn't worry about it," says Evelyn, cocking her head to catch my averted eye. "I see little of that odious creature in the man before me."

"Is that why I'm at this party," I ask quietly. "To sell my wares?"

Her smile is sympathetic. "I suspect so."

I'm numb, two steps behind myself. Every strange glance over the course of the day, every whisper and commotion as I walked into a room, is explained. I thought people were concerned for my well-being, but they were wondering when my trunk would reopen for business.

I feel such a fool.

"I have to…"

I'm moving before I understand how that sentence ends, my body carrying me back through the forest at an ever-increasing pace. I'm almost running by the time I arrive on the road. Evelyn's at my heels, struggling to keep up. She's trying to anchor me with words, reminding me of my desire to meet Madeline, but I'm impervious to reason, consumed by my hatred for the man I was. His flaws I could accept, perhaps even overcome, but this is a betrayal. He made his mistakes and fled, leaving me holding the tatters of his scorched life.

Blackheath's door stands open, and I'm up the staircase and into my room so quickly the smell of damp earth still clings to me, as I stand panting over the trunk. Is this what drove me into the forest last night? Is this what I spilled blood for? Well, I'm going to smash it all, and with it any connection to the man I was.

Evelyn arrives to find me ransacking my bedroom for something heavy enough to break the lock. Intuiting my purpose, she ducks into the corridor, returning with the bust of some Roman emperor or other.

"You're a treasure," I say, using it to hammer the lock.

When I yanked the trunk out of the cupboard this morning, it was so heavy it took all my strength to lift, but now it's sliding backward with each blow. Once again, Evelyn comes to the rescue, sitting on the trunk to keep it in place, and after three enormous strikes, the lock clatters to the floor.

Tossing the bust on the bed, I lift the heavy lid.

The trunk's empty.

Or at least mostly empty.

In a dark corner is a solitary chess piece with Anna's name carved into the base.

"I think it's time you told me the rest of your story," says Evelyn.

8

Darkness presses up against my bedroom window, its cold breath leaving frost on the glass. The fire hisses in response, the swaying flames my only light. Steps hurry down the corridor beyond my closed door, a jumble of voices on their way to the ball. Somewhere in the distance, I hear the tremble of a violin coming awake.

Stretching my feet toward the fire, I wait for silence. Evelyn asked me to attend both dinner and the party, but I can't mingle with these people knowing who I am and what it is they really want from me. I'm tired of this house, their games. I'm going to meet Anna at 10:20 p.m. in the graveyard, and then I'll have a stable hand take us to the village, away from this madness.

My gaze returns to the chess piece I found in the trunk. I'm holding it up to the light in the hope of worrying loose some further memories. Thus far, it's kept quiet and there's little about the piece itself to illuminate my memory. It's a bishop, hand carved and freckled with white paint; a far cry from the expensive ivory sets I've seen around the house, and yet…it means something to me. Regardless of any memory, there's a feeling associated with it, a sense of comfort almost. Holding it brings me courage.

There's a knock on the door, my hand tightening around the chess piece as I start from the chair. The closer I come to the meeting in the graveyard the more highly strung I've become, practically leaping out the window every time the fire pops in the grate.

"Belly, you in there?" asks Michael Hardcastle.

He knocks again. It's insistent. A polite battering ram.

Placing the chess piece on the mantel above the fireplace, I open the door. The hall's awash with people in costume, Michael wearing a bright-orange suit and fiddling with the straps of a giant sun mask.

"There you are," he says, frowning at me. "Why aren't you dressed yet?"

"I'm not coming," I say. "It's been…"

A wave toward my head, but my sign language is too vague for him.

"Are you feeling faint?" he asks. "Should I call Dickie? I just saw him—"

I have to catch Michael's arm to prevent him from flying off down the corridor in search of the doctor.

"I simply don't feel up to it," I say.

"Are you sure? There are going to be fireworks, and I'm certain my parents have been cooking up a surprise all day. Seems a shame to—"

"Honestly, I'd rather not."

"If you're certain," he says reluctantly, his voice as crestfallen as his face. "I'm sorry you've had such a wretched day, Belly. Here's hoping tomorrow will be better, with fewer misunderstandings, at least."

"Misunderstandings?" I say.

"The murdered girl?" He smiles in confusion. "Daniel told me it was all a big mistake. I felt a right bloody fool calling off the search halfway through. No harm done, though."

Daniel? How could he possibly have known Anna was alive?

"It *was* a mistake, wasn't it?" he asks, noting my bafflement.

"Of course," I say brightly. "Yes…terrible mistake. I'm sorry to have bothered you with it."

"Not to worry," he says, slightly dubiously. "Think no more about it."

His words are stretched thin, like overburdened elastic. I can hear his doubt, not only in the story, but in the man standing before him.

After all, I'm not the person he knew, and I think he's coming to realize that I no longer wish to be. This morning I'd have done almost anything to repair the fracture between us, but Sebastian Bell was a drug peddler and a coward, the consort of vipers. Michael was a friend of that man, so how could he ever be a friend of mine?

"Well, I'd best be off," he says, clearing his throat. "Feel better, old man."

Rapping the doorframe with his knuckle, he turns away, following the rest of the guests on their way to the party.

I watch him go, digesting the news. I'd quite forgotten about Anna's flight through the woods this morning, our imminent meeting in the graveyard sapping much of the horror from my first memory. And yet, something momentous clearly happened, even if Daniel has been telling people it didn't. I'm certain of what I witnessed, the gunshot and the fear. Anna was chased by a figure in black, whom I must now assume to have been the footman. Somehow she survived, as did I after my assault last night. Is that what she wants to talk about? Our mutual enemy, and why he wants us dead? Perhaps he's after the drugs? They're clearly valuable. Maybe Anna's my partner and she removed them from the trunk to keep them out of his hands? That would, at least, explain the presence of the chess piece. Maybe it's some sort of calling card?

After taking my coat from the wardrobe, I wrap myself in a long scarf and slip my hands into a thick pair of gloves, pocketing the letter opener and chess piece on the way out. I'm rewarded by a crisp, cold night. As my eyes adjust to the gloom, I breathe in the fresh air, still damp with the storm, and follow the gravel path around the house toward the graveyard.

My shoulders are tense, my stomach unsettled.

I'm frightened of this forest, but I'm more frightened by this meeting. When I first awoke, I wanted nothing more than to rediscover myself, but last night's misadventure now seems a blessing. Injury has given me the chance to start again, but what if meeting Anna brings all my old memories flooding back? Can this higgledy-piggledy personality I've cobbled together over the course of the day survive such a deluge, or will it be washed away entirely?

Will I be washed away?

The thought is almost enough to turn me around by the shoulders, but I cannot confront the person I was by running from the life he built. Better to make a stand here, confident of whom I wish to become.

Gritting my teeth, I follow the path through the trees, coming upon a small gardener's cottage, the windows dark. Evelyn's leaning against the wall, smoking a cigarette, a lantern burning by her feet. She's wearing a long beige coat and Wellington boots, an outfit somewhat at odds with the blue evening dress beneath it and the diamond tiara sparkling in her hair. She's really quite beautiful, though she carries it awkwardly.

She notices me noticing.

"I didn't have time to change after dinner," she says defensively, tossing her cigarette away.

"What are you doing here, Evie?" I ask. "You're supposed to be at the ball."

"I slipped away. You didn't think I'd miss all the fun?" she says, grinding the cigarette beneath her heel.

"It's dangerous."

"Then it would be foolish for you to go alone. Besides, I brought some help."

From her clutch, she pulls out a black revolver.

"Where on earth did you find that?" I ask, feeling shocked and slightly guilty. The idea that my problem has put a weapon in Evelyn's hand seems like a betrayal somehow. She should be warm and safe in Blackheath, not out here in harm's way.

"It's my mother's, so the better question might be where she found it,"

"Evie, you can't—"

"Sebastian, you're my only friend in this dreadful place, and I'm not going to let you stroll into a graveyard alone, without knowing what's waiting for you. Somebody's already tried to kill you once. I have no intention of letting them try again."

A lump of gratitude lodges itself in my throat.

"Thank you."

"Don't be silly. It's either this or I stay in that house with everybody's eyes upon me," she says, lifting the lantern into the air. "I should be thanking you. Now, shall we go? There'll be hell to pay if I'm not back for the speeches."

Darkness weighs heavy on the graveyard, the iron fence buckled, trees bent low over crooked gravestones. Thick piles of rotting leaves smother the plots, the tombs cracked and crumbling, taking the names of the dead with them.

"I spoke with Madeline about the note you received last night," says Evelyn, pushing open the squeaking gate and leading us inside. "I hope you don't mind."

"Of course I don't," I say, looking around nervously. "It slipped my mind, truth be told. What did she say?"

"Only that the note was given to her by Mrs. Drudge, the cook. I spoke to her separately, and she told me it had been left in the kitchen, though she couldn't say by whom. There was too much coming and going."

"And did Madeline read it?" I ask.

"Of course," says Evelyn, wryly. "She didn't even blush when she admitted to it. The message was very brief; it asked you to come immediately to the usual spot."

"That was all? No signature?"

"I'm afraid not. I'm sorry, Sebastian. I'd hoped to have better news."

We've reached the mausoleum at the far end of the graveyard, a large marble box watched over by two broken angels. A lantern hangs from one of their beckoning hands, and though it flickers in the gloom, there's nothing of note to illuminate. The graveyard's empty.

"Perhaps Anna's running a little late," says Evelyn.

"Then who left the lantern burning?" I ask.

My heart is racing, damp seeping up my trousers as I wade through ankle-deep leaves. Evelyn's watch assures us of the time, but Anna's nowhere to be seen. There's just that damnable lantern, squeaking as it sways in the breeze, and for fifteen minutes or more, we stand stiff beneath it, the light draping our shoulders, our eyes searching for Anna and finding her everywhere: in the shifting shadows and stirring leaves, the low-hanging branches disturbed by the breeze. Time and again one of us taps the other on the shoulder, drawing their attention to a sudden sound or startled animal darting through the underbrush.

As the hour grows later, it's difficult to keep one's thoughts from venturing to more frightening places. Doctor Dickie believed the wounds on my arms were defensive in nature, as though I'd been fending off an assault with a knife. What if Anna isn't an ally, but an enemy? Perhaps that's why her name was fixed in my mind? For all I know, she penned the note I received at the dinner table and has now lured me out here to finish the job started yesterday evening.

These thoughts spread like cracks through my already brittle courage, fear pouring into the hollowness behind. Only Evelyn's presence keeps me upright, her own courage pinning me in place.

"I don't think she's coming," says Evelyn.

"No, I rather think not," I say, speaking quietly to mask my relief. "Perhaps we should head back."

"I think so," she says. "I'm so sorry, dear heart."

With an unsteady hand, I take the lantern down from the angel's arm and follow Evelyn toward the gate. We've only taken a couple of steps when Evelyn clutches my arm, lowering her flame toward the ground. Light splashes the leaves, revealing blood splattered across their surface. Kneeling down, I rub the sticky substance between my thumb and forefinger.

"Here," says Evelyn quietly.

She's followed the drips to a nearby tombstone, where something glitters beneath the leaves. Sweeping them aside, I find the compass that led me out of the forest this morning. It's bloodstained and shattered, yet still unwavering in its devotion to north.

"Is that the compass the killer gave you?" says Evelyn, her voice hushed.

"It is," I say, weighing it in my palm. "Daniel Coleridge took it from me this morning."

"And then it appears somebody took it from him."

Whatever danger Anna intended on warning me about, it seems to have found her first, and Daniel Coleridge was involved somehow.

Evelyn lays a hand on my shoulder as she squints warily into the darkness beyond the glow of the lantern.

"I think it's best we get you out of Blackheath," she says. "Go to your room and I'll send a carriage to fetch you."

"I have to find Daniel," I protest weakly. "And Anna."

"Something awful is happening here," she hisses. "The slashes on your arm, the drugs, Anna, and now this compass. These are pieces in a game neither of us knows how to play. You must leave, for me, Sebastian. Let the police deal with all of this."

I nod. I've not the will to fight. Anna was the only reason I stayed in the first place, the shreds of my courage convincing me there was some honor to be found in obeying a request delivered so cryptically. Without that obligation, the ties binding me to this place have been severed.

We return to Blackheath in silence, Evelyn leading the way, her revolver poking at the darkness. I trail behind quietly, little more than a dog at her heel, and before I know it, I'm saying goodbye to my friend and opening the door into my bedroom.

All is not how I left it.

There's a box sitting on my bed, wrapped in a red ribbon that comes loose with a single tug. Sliding away the lid, my stomach flips, bile rushing into my throat. Stuffed inside is a dead rabbit with a carving knife stabbed through its body. Blood has congealed at the bottom, staining its fur and almost obscuring the note pinned to its ear.

From your friend,
The footman.

Black swims up into my eyes.

A second later, I faint.

∽ 9 ∼

DAY TWO

A deafening clanging jolts me upright, my hands flying to my ears. Wincing, I look around for the source of the noise to find I've been moved in the night. Instead of the airy bedroom with the bathtub and welcoming fire, I'm in a narrow room with whitewashed walls and a single iron bed, dusty light poking through a small window. There's a chest of drawers on the opposite wall beside a ratty brown dressing gown hanging from a door peg.

Swinging my legs from the bed, my feet touch cold stone, a shiver dancing up my spine. After the dead rabbit, I immediately suspect the footman of perpetrating some new devilry, but this incessant noise is making it impossible to concentrate.

I pull on the dressing gown, nearly choking on the smell of cheap cologne, and poke my head into the corridor beyond. Cracked tiles cover the floor, whitewashed walls ballooning out with damp. There are no windows, only lamps staining everything with a dirty, yellow light that never seems to settle. The clanging is louder out here, and covering my ears, I follow the din until I reach the bottom of a splintered wooden staircase, leading up into the house. Dozens of large tin bells are attached to a board on the wall, each with a plaque beneath it naming a section of the house. The bell for the front door is shaking so hard I'm worried it's going to unsettle the foundations.

Hands pressed to my ears, I stare at the bell, but short of ripping it from the wall, there's no obvious way of quietening the clamor beyond answering the door. Belting the dressing gown tight, I rush up the stairs, emerging at the rear of the entrance hall. It's much quieter here, the servants moving through in a calm procession, their arms filled with bouquets of flowers and other decorations. I can only assume they're too busy clearing away the detritus of last night's party to have heard the noise.

With an annoyed shake of the head, I open the door to find myself confronted by Doctor Sebastian Bell.

He's wild-eyed and dripping wet, shivering with cold.

"I need your help," he says, spitting panic.

My world empties.

"Do you have a telephone?" he continues, the desperation terrible in his eyes. "We need to send for the authorities."

This is impossible.

"Don't just stand there, you devil!" he cries out, shaking me by the shoulders, the cold of his hands seeping through my pajamas.

Unwilling to wait for a response, he pushes past me into the entrance hall, searching for aid.

I try to make sense of what I'm seeing.

This is me.

This is me yesterday.

Somebody is speaking to me, tugging on my sleeve, but I can't focus on anything except the imposter dripping on the floor.

Daniel Coleridge has appeared at the top of the staircase.

"Sebastian?" he says, descending with one hand on the banister.

I watch him for the trick, some flicker of rehearsal, of jest, but he pads down the steps exactly as he did yesterday, just as light of foot, just as confident and admired.

There's another tug on my arm, a maid placing herself in my eyeline. She's looking at me with concern, her lips moving.

Blinking away my confusion, I focus on her, finally hearing what she's saying.

"…Mr. Collins? You all right, Mr. Collins?"

Her face is familiar, though I can't place it.

I look over her head to the stairs, where Daniel is already ushering Bell up to his room. Everything's happening precisely as it did yesterday.

Pulling free of the maid, I rush to a mirror on the wall. I can barely look at it. I'm badly burned, my skin mottled and rough to the touch like fruit left too long in the sweltering sun. I know this man. Somehow, I've awoken as the butler.

My heart hammering, I turn back to the maid.

"What's happening to me?" I stammer, clutching at my throat, surprised by the hoarse northern voice coming out of it.

"Sir?"

"How did…"

But I'm asking the wrong person. The answers are caked in dirt and trudging up the stairs to Daniel's room.

Picking up the edges of my dressing gown, I hurry after them, following a trail of leaves and muddy rainwater. The maid is calling my name. I'm halfway up when she bolts past me, planting herself in the way with both hands pressed against my chest.

"You can't go up there, Mr. Collins," she says. "There'll be merry hell to pay if Lady Helena catches you running around in your smalls."

I try to go around her, but she steps sideways, blocking me again.

"Let me pass, girl!" I demand, immediately regretting it. This isn't how I speak, blunt and demanding.

"You're having one of your turns, Mr. Collins, that's all," she says. "Come down to the kitchen. I'll make us a pot of tea."

Her eyes are blue, earnest. They flick over my shoulder self-consciously, and I look behind me to find other servants gathered at the bottom of the stairs. They're watching us, their arms still laden with flowers.

"One of my turns?" I ask, doubt opening its mouth and swallowing me.

"On account of your burns, Mr. Collins," she says quietly. "Sometimes you say things or see things that ain't right. A cup of tea's all it takes. A few minutes and you're right as rain."

Her kindness is crushing, warm and heavy. I'm reminded of Daniel's pleas yesterday, his delicate way of speaking, as though I might fracture if pressed too hard. He thought I was mad, as this maid does now. Given what's happening to me, what I *think* is happening to me, I can't be certain they're wrong.

I offer her a helpless look, and she takes my arm, guiding me back down the steps, the crowd parting to let us through.

"Cup of tea, Mr. Collins," she says reassuringly. "That's all you need."

She leads me like a lost child, the soft grip of her calloused hand as calming as her tone. Together we leave the entrance hall, heading back down the servants' staircase and along the gloomy corridor into the kitchen.

Sweat stands up on my brow, heat rushing out of ovens and stoves, pots bubbling over open flames. I smell gravy, roasted meats, and baking cakes, sugar and sweat. Too many guests and too few working ovens, that's the problem. They've had to start preparing dinner now to make sure everything goes out on time later.

The knowledge bewilders me.

It's true, I'm certain of it, but how could I know that unless I really am the butler?

Maids are rushing out carrying breakfast, scrambled eggs and kippers heaped on silver platters. A wide-hipped, ruddy-faced elderly woman is standing by the oven bellowing instructions, her pinafore covered in flour. No general ever wore a chestful of medals with such conviction. Somehow, she spots us through the commotion, her iron glare striking the maid first, then me.

Wiping her hands on her apron, she strides over to us.

"I'm sure you've somewhere to be, haven't you, Lucy," she says with a stern look.

The maid hesitates, considering the wisdom of objecting.

"Yes, Mrs. Drudge."

Her hand releases me, leaving a patch of emptiness on my arm. A sympathetic smile and she's gone, lost among the din.

"Sit yourself down, Roger," says Mrs. Drudge, her tone aspiring to gentleness. She has a split lip, bruising beginning to show around her mouth. Somebody must have struck her, and she winces when she speaks.

There's a wooden table at the center of the kitchen, its surface covered in platters of tongue, roasted chickens, and hams piled high. There are soups and stews, trays of glistening vegetables, with more being added all the time by the harassed kitchen staff, most of whom look to have spent an hour in the ovens themselves.

Pulling out a chair, I sit down.

Mrs. Drudge slides a tray of scones from the oven, putting one on a plate with a small curl of butter. She brings it over, placing the plate in front of me and touching my hand. Her skin's hard as old leather.

Her gaze lingers, kindness wrapped in thistle, before she turns away, bellowing her way back through the crowd.

The scone is delicious, the melting butter dripping off the sides. I'm only a bite into it when I see Lucy again, finally remembering why she's familiar. This is the maid who will be in the drawing room at lunchtime—the one who will be abused by Ted Stanwin and rescued by Daniel Coleridge. She's even prettier than I recall, with freckles and large, blue eyes, red hair straying from beneath her cap. She's trying to open a jam jar, her face screwed up with effort.

She had jam stains all over her apron.

It happens in slow motion, the jar slipping from her hands and hitting the floor, glass spraying across the kitchen, her apron splattered with dripping jam.

"Oh, bloody hell, Lucy Harper," somebody cries, dismayed.

My chair clatters to the floor as I dart from the kitchen, racing down the corridor and back upstairs. I'm in such a rush that as I turn the corner onto the guest corridor, I collide with a wiry chap, curly black hair spilling down his brow, charcoal staining his white shirt. Apologizing, I look up into the face of Gregory Gold. Fury wears him like a suit, his eyes empty of all reason. He's livid, trembling with rage, and only too late do I remember what comes next, how the butler looked after this monster did his work.

I attempt to back away, but he takes hold of my dressing gown with his long fingers.

"You don't need—"

My vision blurs, the world reduced to a smudge of color and a flash of pain as I crash into a wall, then drop to the floor, blood trickling from my head. He's looming over me, an iron poker in his hand.

"Please," I say, trying to slide backward, away from him. "I'm not—"

He kicks me in the side, emptying my lungs.

I reach out a hand, trying to speak, beg, but that only seems to infuriate him further. He's kicking me faster and faster until there's nothing I can do but curl up in a ball as he pours his wrath upon me.

I can barely breathe, barely see. I'm sobbing, buried by pain.

Mercifully, I pass out.

~ 10 ~

DAY THREE

It's dark, the net on the window fluttering in the breath of a moonless night. The sheets are soft, the bed comfortable and canopied.

Clutching the eiderdown, I smile.

It was a nightmare, that's all.

Slowly, beat by beat, my heart quiets down, the taste of blood fading with the dream. It takes me a few seconds to remember where I am, another to pick out the dim shape of a large man standing in the corner of the room.

My breath catches in my throat.

Sliding my hand through the covers toward the bedside table, I reach for the matches, but they seem to slither away from my searching fingers.

"Who are you?" I ask the darkness, unable to keep the tremor from my voice.

"A friend."

It's a man's voice, muffled and deep.

"Friends don't lurk in the gloom," I say.

"I didn't say I was your friend, Mr. Davies."

My blind fumbling almost knocks the oil lamp off the bedside table. Attempting to steady it, my fingers find the matches cowering at its base.

"Don't worry about the light," says the darkness. "It will little profit you."

I strike the match with a trembling hand, touching it to the lamp. Flame explodes behind the glass, driving the shadows deep into the corners and illuminating my visitor. It's the man in the plague doctor costume I met earlier, the light revealing details I'd missed in the gloom of the study. His greatcoat is scuffed and tattered at the edges, a top hat and porcelain beak mask covering all of his face except for the eyes. Gloved hands rest on a black cane, an inscription inlaid in sparkling silver down the side, though the writing's much too small to read at this distance.

"Observant, good," remarks the Plague Doctor. Footsteps sound from somewhere in the house, and I wonder if my imagination is sufficient to conjure the mundane details of such an extraordinary dream.

"What the hell are you doing in my room?" I demand, surprising myself with this outburst.

The beak mask ceases its exploration of the room, fixing on me once again.

"We have work to do," he says. "I have a puzzle that requires a solution."

"I think you've mistaken me for somebody else," I say angrily. "I'm a doctor."

"You were a doctor," he says. "Then a butler, today a playboy, tomorrow a banker. None of them is your real face, or your real personality. Those were stripped from you when you entered Blackheath, and they won't be returned until you leave."

Reaching into his pocket, he pulls out a small mirror and tosses it onto the bed.

"See for yourself."

The glass shakes in my hand, reflecting a young man with striking blue eyes and precious little wisdom behind them. The face in the glass isn't that of Sebastian Bell, or the burned butler.

"His name's Donald Davies," says the Plague Doctor. "He has a sister called Grace and a best friend called Jim, and he doesn't like peanuts. Davies will be your host for today, and when you wake up tomorrow, you'll have another. That's how this works."

It wasn't a dream after all, it really happened. I lived the same day twice in the bodies of two different people. I talked to myself, berated myself, and examined myself through somebody else's eyes.

"I'm going mad, aren't I?" I say, looking at him over the top of the mirror.

I can hear the cracks in my voice.

"Of course not," says the Plague Doctor. "Madness would be an escape, and there's only one way to escape Blackheath. That's why I'm here. I have a proposition for you."

"Why have you done this to me?" I demand.

"That's a flattering notion, but I'm not responsible for your predicament, or Blackheath's for that matter."

"Then who is?"

"Nobody you'd care to meet or need to," he says, dismissing the notion with a wave of his hand. "Which brings me back to my proposition—"

"I must speak with them," I say.

"Speak with whom?"

"The person who brought me here, whoever can free me," I say through gritted teeth, struggling to keep hold of my temper.

"Well, the former is long gone, and the latter is before you," he says, tapping his chest with both hands. Perhaps it's the costume, but the movement seems somehow theatrical, almost rehearsed. I suddenly have the sense of taking part in a play in which everybody knows their lines but me.

"Only I know how you can escape Blackheath," he says.

"Your proposition?" I say suspiciously.

"Precisely, though 'riddle' might be closer to the truth of it," he says, lifting out a pocket watch and checking the time. "Somebody's going to be murdered at the ball tonight. It won't appear to be a murder, and so the murderer won't be caught. Rectify that injustice and I'll show you the way out."

I stiffen, gripping the sheets.

"If freeing me is within your power, why not just do it, damn you!" I say. "Why play these games?"

"Because eternity is dull," he says. "Or maybe because playing is the important part. I'll leave you to speculate. Just don't procrastinate for too long, Mr. Davies. This day will be repeated eight times, and you'll see it through the eyes of eight different hosts. Bell was your first, the butler your second, and Mr. Davies the third. That means you only have five hosts left to discover. If I were you, I would move quickly. When you have an answer, bring it to the lake, along with proof, at 11:00 p.m. I'll be waiting for you."

"I will not play these games for your amusement," I snarl, leaning toward him.

"Then fail out of spite, but know this: if you don't solve this problem by midnight in your final host, we'll strip your memories and return you to the body of Doctor Bell and this will all begin again."

He checks his watch, dropping it into his pocket with an irritated *tut*. "Time runs away from us. Cooperate and I'll answer more of your questions next time we meet."

A breeze slips through the window, extinguishing the lamp and draping us in darkness. By the time I find the matches and relight it, the Plague Doctor is gone.

Confused and afraid, I jump out of bed as if stung, throwing open the bedroom door and stepping into the cold. The corridor's black. He could be standing five paces away and I'd never see him.

Closing the door, I fly toward the wardrobe, dressing myself in whatever comes to hand first. Whomever I'm wearing, he's skinny and short with a penchant for the garish, and when I'm finished, I'm splashed in purple trousers, an orange shirt, and a yellow waistcoat. There's a coat and scarf at the back of the cupboard, and I pull them on, before heading out. Murder in the morning and costumes at night, cryptic notes and burned butlers; whatever's happening here, I will *not* be yanked around like some puppet on a string.

I must escape this house.

The grandfather clock at the top of the stairs points its weary arms at 3:17 a.m., tutting at my haste. Though I'm loath to wake the stable master at such a frightful hour, I can see no other choice if I'm to escape this madness, so I take the staircase two steps at a time, nearly tripping over this peacock's ridiculously tiny feet.

It wasn't like this with Bell or the butler. I feel myself pressed up against the walls of this body, straining at its seams. I'm clumsy, almost drunk.

Leaves scatter inside as I open the front door. It's blowing a gale outside, rain swirling in the air, the forest cracking and swaying. It's a filthy night, the color of tossed soot. I'll need more light if I'm to find my way without falling and breaking my neck.

Retreating inside, I head down the servants' staircase at the rear of the entrance hall. The wood of the banister is rough to the touch, the steps rickety. Thankfully, the lamps are still leaking their rancid light, though the flames burn low and quiet, their flicker indignant. The corridor is longer than I remember, the whitewashed walls sweating with condensation, the smell of earth spilling through the plaster. Everything's damp, rotten. I've seen most of Blackheath's dirty edges, but none so purposefully neglected. I'm surprised the place has any staff at all, given how little regard they appear to be held in by their masters.

In the kitchen, I bounce between the stacked shelves until I find a hurricane lamp and matches. Two strikes to light it and I'm bounding back up the stairs and through the front door into the storm.

The lamp claws at the darkness, the rain stinging my eyes.

I follow the driveway to the cobbled road leading up to the stables, the forest heaving around me. Slipping over the uneven stones, I strain my eyes for the stable master's cottage, but the lamp's too bright, concealing much of what it should reveal. I'm beneath the arch before I see it, sliding on horse manure. As before, the yard is a crush of carriages, each covered in a rippling canvas sheet. Unlike earlier, the horses are in the stables, snorting in their sleep.

Shaking the manure from my feet, I throw myself on the mercy of the cottage, banging the knocker. The light comes on after a few minutes, the door opening a crack to reveal the sleepy face of an old man in his nightshirt.

"I need to leave," I say.

"At this hour, sir?" he asks dubiously, rubbing his eyes and glancing at the pitch-black sky. "You'll catch your death."

"It's urgent."

He sighs, taking in the scene, then gestures me inside, opening the door fully. Putting on a pair of trousers, he tugs the suspenders over his shoulders, moving in that sluggish daze that marks someone roused unaccountably from their sleep. Taking his jacket from the peg, he drags himself outside, motioning for me to stay where I am.

I must confess I do so happily. The cottage bulges with warmth and homeliness, the smell of leather and soap a solid, comforting presence. I'm tempted to check the roster by the door to see if Anna's message is already written there, but no sooner have I reached out my hand than I hear a god-awful commotion, lights blinding me through the window. Stepping into the rain, I find the old stable master sitting in a green automobile, the entire thing coughing and shuddering as if afflicted by some terrible disease.

"Here you go, sir," he says, getting out. "I got her started for you."

"But…"

I'm at a loss for words, aghast at the contraption before me.

"Are there no carriages?" I ask.

"There are, but the horses are skittish around thunder, sir," he says, reaching under his shirt to scratch an armpit. "With respect, you couldn't keep hold of them."

"I can't keep hold of this," I say, staring at the dreadful mechanical monster, horror strangling my voice. Rain is pinging off the metal and making a pond of the windshield.

"Easy as breathing it is," he says. "Grip the wheel and point it where you want to go, then press the pedal to the floor. You'll make sense of it in no time."

His confidence pushes me inside as firmly as any hand, the door closing with a soft click.

"Follow this cobbled road until the end, and then turn left onto the dirt track," he says, pointing into the darkness. "That will lead you to the village. It's long and straight, a bit uneven, mind. Takes anywhere between forty minutes and an hour, depending on how carefully you drive, but you can't miss it, sir. If you wouldn't mind, leave the automobile somewhere obvious and I'll have one of my boys collect it first thing in the morning."

With that, he's gone, disappearing back into his cottage, the door slamming shut behind him.

Gripping the wheel, I stare at the levers and dials, trying to find some semblance of logic in the controls. I tentatively press the pedal. The dreaded contraption lurches forward, and applying a little more pressure, I urge the automobile beneath the arch and along the bumpy cobbled road, until we reach the left turn the stable master mentioned.

Rain blankets the glass, forcing me to lean out the window to see where I'm going. The headlamps shine on a dirt track littered with leaves and fallen branches, water cascading across its surface. Despite the danger, I keep the accelerator pedal pinned to the floor, elation replacing my unease. After everything that's happened, I'm finally escaping Blackheath, each mile of this bumpy track taking me farther from its madness.

Morning arrives in a smudge, a gray half-light that taints rather than illuminates, though it at least brings an end to the rain. As promised, the road continues straight, the forest unending. Somewhere among those trees, a girl is being murdered and Bell is coming awake to see it. A killer will spare his life with a silver compass that points to a place that doesn't make sense, and, like a fool, he'll think himself saved. But how can I be in that forest and in this car—and a butler in between? My hands tighten around the wheel. If I was able to talk to the butler when I was Sebastian Bell, then presumably, whoever I'll be tomorrow is already walking around Blackheath. I might even have met him. And not just tomorrow, but the man I'll be the day after that and the day after that. If that's the case, what does that make me? Or them? Are we shards of the same soul, responsible for each other's sins, or entirely different people, pale copies of some long-forgotten original?

The fuel gauge nudges red as fog comes rolling out of the trees, thick upon the ground. My earlier sense of triumph has waned. I should have arrived at the village long ago, but there's no chimney smoke in the distance and no end to the forest.

Finally, the car shudders and stills, its dying breath a screech of grinding parts as it comes to a stop mere feet from the Plague Doctor, whose black greatcoat is in stark contrast to the white fog he's emerging from. My legs are stiff and my back sore, but anger propels me out of the car.

"Have you got this foolishness out of your system yet?" asks the Plague Doctor, both hands resting on his cane. "You could have done so much with this host; instead you waste him on this road, accomplishing nothing. Blackheath won't let you go, and while you're tugging on your lead, your rivals are pressing ahead with their investigations."

"And *now* I have rivals," I say contemptuously. "It's one trick after another with you, isn't it? First you tell me I'm trapped here, and now it's a competition to escape."

I'm marching toward him, fully intending to beat an exit out of him.

"Don't you understand yet?" I say. "I don't care about your rules, because I'm not going to play. Either you let me leave, or I'll make you sorry I stayed."

I'm two steps away when he points his cane at me. Though it hovers an inch from my chest, no cannon was ever so threatening. The silver lettering along the side is pulsing, a faint shimmer rising from the wood, burning away the fog. I can feel the heat of it through my clothes. If he desired, I'm certain this benign-looking stick could rip a hole straight through me.

"Donald Davies is always the most childish of your hosts," he tuts, watching me take a nervous step backward. "But you don't have time to indulge him. There are two other people trapped in this house, wearing the bodies of guests and servants, just like you. Only one of you can leave, and it will be whoever brings me the answer first. Now do you see? Escape isn't to be found at the end of this dirt road; it's through me. So run if you must. Run until you can't stand, and when you wake up in Blackheath again and again, do so in the knowledge that nothing here is arbitrary, nothing overlooked. You'll stay here until I decide otherwise."

Lowering the cane, he tugs loose his pocket watch.

"We'll speak again soon, when you've calmed down a little," he says, putting the watch away again. "Try to use your hosts more wisely from now on. Your rivals are more cunning than you can imagine, and I guarantee they won't be so frivolous with their time."

I want to charge him, fists flying, but now the red mist has passed, I can see it's a preposterous idea. Even taking away the bulk of his costume, he's a large man, more than capable of weathering my assault. Instead, I veer around him, the Plague Doctor heading back to Blackheath, as I press into the fog ahead. There may be no end to this road, no village to be found, but I can't give up until I know for sure.

I won't return willingly to a madman's game.

～ 11 ～

DAY FOUR

I awake wheezing, crushed beneath the tremendous monument of my new host's stomach. The last thing I remember is collapsing exhausted on the road after walking for hours, howling in desperation at a village I couldn't reach. The Plague Doctor was telling the truth. There's no escape from Blackheath.

A carriage clock by the bed tells me it's 10:30 a.m., and I'm about to rise when a tall man enters through a connecting room carrying a silver tray, which he lays on the sideboard. He's in his mid-thirties, I'd guess, dark-haired and clean-shaven, blandly attractive without being memorable in any way. A pair of glasses have slipped down his small nose, his eyes looking over them at the curtains he's walking toward. Without saying a word, he draws them and pushes open the windows, revealing views of the garden and forest.

I watch him in fascination.

There's something oddly precise about this man. His actions are small and quick, without any wasted effort. It's as though he's saving his energy for some great labor ahead.

For a minute or so, he stands at the window with his back to me, letting the room breathe cold air. I feel as though something is expected of me, that this pause has been manufactured for my benefit, but for the life of me, I can't guess what I should be doing. No doubt sensing my indecision, he abandons his vigil, slipping his hands under my armpits and tugging me into a sitting position.

I pay for his assistance in shame.

My silk pajamas are soaked through with sweat, and the odor rising from my body is so pungent it brings tears to my eyes. Oblivious to my embarrassment, my companion retrieves the silver tray from the sideboard and places it on my lap, lifting the dome cover. The platter beneath is piled high with eggs and bacon, a side helping of pork chops, a pot of tea, and a jug of milk. Such a meal should be daunting, but I'm ravenous and tear into it like an animal, while the tall man—who I can only assume is my valet—disappears behind a screen, the sound of pouring water issuing forth.

Pausing for breath, I take this opportunity to examine my surroundings. In contrast to the frugal comforts of Bell's bedroom, this place is awash in wealth. Red velvet drapes flow down the windows, piling up on a thick blue carpet. Art spots the walls, the lacquered mahogany furniture polished to a shine. Whoever I am, he's held in high esteem by the Hardcastle family.

The valet returns to find me mopping grease from my lips with a napkin, panting with the effort of eating. He must be disgusted. I am disgusted. I feel like a pig in a trough. Even so, no flicker of emotion shows on his face as he removes the tray and slides my arm across his shoulders to better help me out of bed. God only knows how many times he's been through this ritual, or what he's paid to do it, but once is enough for me. Like a wounded soldier, he half walks, half drags me behind the screen where a steaming hot bath has been prepared.

That's when he begins to undress me.

I have no doubt this is all part of the routine, but the shame's too much to bear. Though this isn't my body, I'm humiliated by it, appalled by the waves of flesh lapping against my hips, the way my legs rub together as I walk.

I shoo my companion away, but it's pointless.

"My lord, you can't..." He pauses, collecting his words together carefully. "You're not going to be able to get in and out of the bath alone."

I want to tell him to go hang, to leave me in peace, but he is, of course, correct.

Squeezing my eyes shut, I nod my submission.

In practiced motions, he unbuttons my pajama top and pulls down the bottoms, lifting my feet one at a time so I don't become tangled in them. In a few seconds I'm naked, my companion standing at a respectful distance.

Opening my eyes, I find myself reflected in a full-length mirror on the wall. I resemble some grotesque caricature of the human body, my skin jaundiced and swollen, a flaccid penis peeking out of an unkempt crop of pubic hair.

Overcome by disgust and humiliation, I let out a sob.

Surprise lights up the valet's face and then, just for a moment, delight. It's a patch of raw emotion, gone as quickly as it appeared.

Hurrying over, he helps me into the bathtub.

I remember the euphoria I felt climbing into the hot water as Bell, but there's none of that now. My immense weight means the joy of getting into a warm bath is eclipsed by the certain humiliation of getting out of it again.

"Will you require the reports this morning, Lord Ravencourt?" asks my companion.

Sitting stiff in the bath, I shake my head, hoping he'll leave the room.

"The house has prepared a few activities for the day: hunting, a forest walk, they asked—"

I shake my head again, staring at the water. How much more must I endure?

"Very well, then it's just the appointments."

"Cancel them," I say quietly. "Cancel them all."

"Even with Lady Hardcastle, my lord?"

I find his green eyes for the first time. The Plague Doctor claimed I must solve a murder to depart this house, and who better than the lady of the house to help me sift through its secrets.

"No, not that one," I say. "Remind me where we're meeting again?"

"One thirty in your parlor, my lord. Unless you wanted me to change it?"

"No, that will suffice."

"Very well, my lord."

The last of our business concluded, he departs with a nod, leaving me to wallow in peace, alone with my misery.

Closing my eyes, I rest my head on the edge of the bath, trying to make sense of my situation. Finding their soul cut loose from their body would suggest death to some, but deep down I know this isn't the afterlife. Hell would have fewer servants and better furnishings, and stripping a man of his sins seems a poor way to sit in judgment on him.

No, I'm alive, though not in any state I recognize. This is something next to death, something more devious, and I'm not alone. The Plague Doctor claimed there are three of us competing to escape Blackheath. Could the footman who left me the dead rabbit be trapped as I am? That would explain why he's trying to scare me. After all, a race is hard to win if you're afraid of reaching the finish line. Perhaps this is what the Plague Doctor considers entertainment, setting us against each other, like half-starved dogs in a pit.

Maybe you should trust him.

"So much for trauma," I mutter at the voice. "I thought I'd left you in Bell."

I know it's a lie even as I say it. I'm connected to this voice in the same way I'm connected to the Plague Doctor and the footman. I can feel the weight of our history, even if I can't remember it. They're part of everything that's happening to me, pieces of this puzzle I'm scrambling to solve. Whether they're friends or enemies I can't be certain, but whatever the voice's true nature, it hasn't led me astray so far.

Even so, trusting my captor strikes me as naive at best. The idea that all of this will end should I solve a murder seems preposterous. Whatever the Plague Doctor's intent, he came concealed by mask and midnight. He's wary of being seen, which means there's leverage to be found in ripping that mask free.

I glance at the clock, weighing my options.

I know he'll be in the study talking with Sebastian Bell—a previous *me*, I still can't quite wrap my head around it!—after the hunt departs, which would seem an ideal time to intercept him. If he wishes me to solve a murder, I'll do so, but it won't be my only task today. If I'm to ensure my freedom, I must know the identity of the man who has taken it from me, and for that I'm going to need some help.

By the Plague Doctor's count, I've already wasted three of my eight days in this house, those belonging to Sebastian Bell, the butler, and Donald Davies. Including myself, that means I have five remaining hosts, and if Bell's encounter with the butler is any guide, they're walking around Blackheath, as I am.

That's an army in waiting.

I just need to work out who they're wearing.

～ 12 ～

The water's long cold, leaving me blue and shivering.
Vainglorious though it may be, I can't bear the thought of Ravencourt's valet lifting me out of this bath like a sodden sack of potatoes.

A polite knock on the bedroom door relieves me of the decision.

"Lord Ravencourt, is all well?" he calls, entering the room.

"Quite well," I insist, my hands numb.

His head appears around the edge of the screen, his eyes taking hold of the scene. After a moment's scrutiny, he approaches without my beckoning, rolling up his sleeves to pull me out of the water with a strength that belies his thin frame.

This time I do not protest. I have too little pride left to salvage.

As he helps me out of the bathtub, I spot the edge of a tattoo poking from beneath his shirt. It's smeared green, the details lost. Noticing my attention, he hurriedly pulls his sleeve down.

"Folly of youth, my lord," he says.

For ten minutes I stand there, quietly humiliated, as he towels me dry, mothering me into my suit; one leg then the next, one arm then the other. The clothes are silk, beautifully tailored but tugging and pinching like a roomful of elderly aunts. They're a size too small, fitting Ravencourt's vanity rather than his body. When all is done, the valet combs my hair, rubbing coconut oil into my fleshy face before handing me a mirror that I might better inspect the results. The reflection is nearing sixty, with suspiciously black hair and brown eyes the color of weak tea. I search them for some sign of myself, the hidden man working Ravencourt's strings, but I'm obscured. For the first time, I wonder who I was before coming here, and the chain of events that led me into this trap.

Such speculation would be intriguing if it weren't so frustrating.

As with Bell, my skin prickles when I see Ravencourt in the mirror. Some part of me remembers my real face and is perplexed by this stranger staring back.

I hand the mirror to the valet.

"We need to go to the library," I say.

"I know where it is, my lord," he says. "Shall I fetch you a book?"

"I'm coming with you."

The valet pauses, frowning. He speaks hesitatingly, his words testing the ground they're tiptoeing across.

"It's a fair walk, my lord. I fear you may find it…tiring."

"I'll manage. Besides, I need the exercise."

Arguments queue behind his teeth, but he fetches my cane and an attaché case and leads me into a dark corridor, oil lamps spilling their warm light across the walls.

We walk slowly, the valet tossing news at my feet, but my mind is fixed on the ponderousness of this body I'm dragging forward. It's as though some fiend has remade the house overnight, stretching the rooms and thickening the air. Wading into the sudden brightness of the entrance hall, I'm surprised to discover how steep the staircase now appears. The steps I sprinted down as Donald Davies would require climbing equipment to surmount this morning. Little wonder Lord and Lady Hardcastle lodged Ravencourt on the first floor. It would take a pulley, two strong men, and a day's pay to hoist me into Bell's room.

Requiring frequent rests at least allows me to observe my fellow guests as they make their way around the house, and it's immediately evident that this is not a happy gathering. Whispered arguments spill out of nooks and crannies, raised voices moving hurriedly up the stairs only to be cut off by slamming doors. Husbands and wives goad each other, drinks gripped too tightly, faces flushed red with barely controlled rage. There's a needle in every exchange, the air prickly and dangerous. Perhaps it's nerves, or the hollow wisdom of foresight, but Blackheath seems fertile ground for tragedy.

My legs are trembling by the time we arrive at the library, my back aching with the effort of holding myself erect. Unfortunately, the room offers scant reward for such suffering. Dusty, overburdened bookshelves line the walls, a moldy red carpet smothering the floor. The bones of an old fire lie in the grate, opposite a small reading table with an uncomfortable wooden chair placed beside it.

My companion sums up his feelings in a single *tut*.

"One moment, my lord. I'll fetch you a more comfortable chair from the drawing room," he says.

I'll need it. My left palm is blistered where it's rubbed against the top of the cane, and my legs are wobbling beneath me. Sweat has soaked through my shirt, leaving my entire body itchy. Crossing the house has left me a wreck, and if I'm to reach the lake tonight before my rivals, I'm going to need a new host, preferably one capable of conquering a staircase.

Ravencourt's valet returns with a wingback chair, placing it on the floor in front of me. Taking my arm, he lowers me into the green cushions.

"May I ask our purpose here, my lord?"

"If we're very lucky, we're meeting friends," I reply, mopping my face with a handkerchief. "Do you have a piece of paper to hand?"

"Of course."

He retrieves some foolscap and a fountain pen from his attaché case, standing ready to take dictation. I open my mouth to dismiss him, but one look at my sweaty, blistered hand dissuades me. In this instance, pride is a poor cousin to legibility.

After taking a minute to arrange the words in my head, I begin speaking aloud.

"It's logical to believe that many of you have been here longer than I and possess knowledge of this house, our purpose here, and our captor, the Plague Doctor, that I do not."

I pause, listening to the scratching of the pen.

"You have not sought me out, and I must assume there's good reason for that, but I ask you now to meet me in the library at lunchtime and help me apprehend our captor. If you cannot, I ask you to share what you've learned by writing it on this paper. Whatever you know, no matter how trivial, may be of use in helping speed our escape. They say two heads are better than one, but I believe in this case our combined head may be sufficient."

I wait for the scribbling to end, then look up at my companion's face. It's mystified, though also a touch amused. He's a curious fellow, this one, not at all the straight edge he first appears.

"Should I post this, my lord?" he asks.

"No need," I say, pointing toward the bookshelf. "Slide it within the pages of the first volume of the *Encyclopedia Britannica*. They'll know where to find it."

He eyes me, then the note, before doing as I ask, the page slipping neatly inside. It seems a fitting home.

"And when should we expect a response, my lord?"

"Minutes, hours, I can't be certain. We'll have to keep checking back."

"And until then?" he asks, wiping the dust from his hands with a pocket square.

"Talk to the servants. I need to know if any of the guests has a medieval plague doctor costume in their wardrobe."

"My lord?"

"Porcelain mask, black greatcoat, that sort of thing," I say. "In the meantime I'm going to have a nap."

"Here, my lord?"

"Indeed."

He watches me with a frown, trying to stitch together the scraps of information scattered before him.

"Should I light a fire?" he asks.

"No need, I'll be quite comfortable," I say.

"Very well," he says, hovering.

I'm not sure what he's waiting for, but it never arrives, and with a final look, he leaves the room, his confusion creeping out quietly behind him.

Placing my hands on my stomach, I close my eyes. Every time I've slept I've woken up in a different body, and while it's risky sacrificing a host this way, I can't see what more I can accomplish in Ravencourt. With any luck, when I awaken, my other selves will have made contact through the encyclopedia and I'll be among them.

~ 13 ~

DAY TWO (CONTINUED)

Agony.

I scream, tasting blood.

"I know, I know. I'm sorry," says a woman's voice.

A pinch, a needle enters my neck. Warmth melts the pain.

It's hard to breathe, impossible to move. I can't open my eyes. I hear rolling wheels, hooves on cobbles, a presence by my side.

"I—" I start coughing.

"Shush, don't try to talk. You're back in the butler," says the woman in an urgent whisper, laying a hand on my arm. "It's been fifteen minutes since Gold attacked you, and you're being taken by carriage to the gatehouse to rest."

"Who are—?" I croak.

"A friend. It doesn't matter yet. Now, listen. I know you're confused, tired, but this is important. There are rules to all of this. There's no use trying to abandon your hosts the way you did. You get a full day in each of them, whether you want it or not. That's from whenever they wake up until midnight. Understand?"

I'm dozing, struggling to stay awake.

"That's why you're back here," she continues. "If one of your hosts falls asleep before midnight, you'll jump back into the butler and carry on living this day. When the butler falls asleep, you'll be returned. If the host slept past midnight, or if they died, you'll jump into somebody new."

I hear another voice. Rougher. From the front of the carriage.

"Gatehouse coming up."

Her hand touches my forehead.

"Good luck to you."

Too tired to hold on, I slip back into the dark.

~ 14 ~

DAY FOUR (CONTINUED)

A hand rocks my shoulder.

Blinking my eyes open, I find myself back in the library, back in Ravencourt. Relief washes over me. I'd thought nothing could be worse than this bulk, but I was wrong. The butler's body felt like a bag of broken glass, and I'd live a lifetime as Ravencourt before I'd go back to that torment, though it doesn't appear I have a choice. If the woman in the carriage is telling the truth, I'm destined to be pulled back there again.

Daniel Coleridge is looking down at me through a cloud of yellow smoke. A cigarette dangles from his lip, a drink in his hand. He's wearing the same scuffed hunting clothes as when he talked with Sebastian Bell in the study. My eyes flick to the clock; it's twenty before lunch. He must be on his way to that meeting now.

He hands me the drink and sits down on the edge of the table opposite, the encyclopedia now lying open beside him.

"I believe you were looking for me," says Daniel, blowing smoke from the corner of his mouth.

He sounds different through Ravencourt's ears, the softness shed like an old skin. Before I can answer him, he begins reading from the encyclopedia.

"It's logical to believe that many of you have been here longer than I and possess knowledge of this house, our purpose here and our captor, the Plague Doctor, that I do not." He closes the book. "You called and I answered."

I search the shrewd eyes fixed upon me.

"You're like me," I say.

"I am you, just four days ahead," he says, pausing to let my mind ram itself against the idea. "Daniel Coleridge is your final host. Our soul, his body, if you can make any sense of that. Unfortunately, it's his mind, too." He taps his forehead with his forefinger. "Which means you and I think differently."

He holds up the encyclopedia.

"Take this, for example," he says, letting it drop on the table. "Coleridge would never have thought to write to our other hosts asking for help. It was a clever idea, very logical, very Ravencourt."

His cigarette flares in the gloom, illuminating the hollow smile beneath. This is not the Daniel of yesterday. There's something colder, harder in his gaze, something trying to pry me open so it might peer inside. I don't know how I didn't see it when I was Bell. Ted Stanwin did, when he backed down in the drawing room. The thug's cleverer than I gave him credit for.

"So you've already been me…this me, Ravencourt, I mean?" I say.

"And those who follow him," he says. "They're a difficult bunch. You should enjoy Ravencourt while you can."

"Is that why you're here? To warn me about my other hosts?"

The notion seems to amuse him, a smile touching his lips before drifting away with the cigarette smoke.

"No, I've come because I remember sitting where you are and being told what I'm about to tell you."

"Which is?"

There's an ashtray on the far side of the table, and he reaches across, drawing it toward him.

"The Plague Doctor has asked you to solve a murder, but he didn't mention the victim. It's Evelyn Hardcastle—that's who's going to die at the ball tonight," he says, tapping ash into the ashtray.

"Evelyn?" I say, struggling to sit upright, splashing a little of my forgotten drink across my leg. Panic has hold of me, a terror of my friend being hurt, a woman who went out of her way to be kind to me even as her own parents filled the house with cruelty. "We must warn her!" I demand.

"To what end?" asks Daniel, dousing my alarm with his calm. "We cannot solve the murder of somebody who isn't dead, and without that answer, we cannot escape."

"You would let her die?" I say, shocked by his callousness.

"I've lived this day eight times over, and she's died every evening regardless of my actions," he says, running his finger along the edge of the table. "Whatever happened yesterday, it will happen tomorrow and the day after. I promise you, however you may consider interfering, you've already tried and it's already failed."

"She's my friend, Daniel," I say, surprised at the depth of my feeling.

"And mine," he says, leaning closer. "But every time I've tried to change today's events, I've ended up becoming the architect of whatever misery I was trying to prevent. Believe me, trying to save Evelyn is a waste of time. Circumstances beyond my control brought me here, and very soon, sooner than you can imagine, you'll find yourself sitting where I am, explaining it as I have, and wishing you still had the luxury of Ravencourt's hope. The future isn't a warning my friend—it's a promise—and it won't be broken by us. That's the nature of the trap we're caught in."

Rising from the table, he wrestles with a window's rusty handle and pushes it open. His eyes are fixed on some distant point, a task four days beyond my comprehension. He has no interest in me, my fears or hopes. I'm just part of some old story he's tired of telling.

"It makes no sense," I say, hoping to remind him of Evelyn's qualities, the reasons she's worth saving. "Evelyn's kind and gentle, and she's been away for nineteen years. Who'd want to harm her now?"

Even as I say it, a suspicion begins to dawn on me. In the forest yesterday, Evelyn mentioned that her parents had never forgiven her for letting Thomas wander off alone. She blamed herself for his murder at Carver's hands, and, worst of all, so did they. Their ire was so great, she believed they were plotting some terrible surprise at the ball. Could this be it? Could they really hate their own daughter enough to murder her? If so, my meeting with Helena Hardcastle could prove fortuitous indeed.

"I don't know," says Daniel, a note of irritation in his voice. "There are so many secrets in this house, it can be difficult to pick the right one from the pile. If you heed my advice, though, you'll start looking for Anna immediately. Eight hosts may sound a great deal, but this task needs double that number. You're going to need all the help you can get."

"Anna," I exclaim, remembering the woman in the carriage with the butler. "I thought she was an acquaintance of Bell's?"

He takes a long drag of his cigarette, considering me through narrowed eyes. I can see him sifting through the future, working out how much to tell me.

"She's trapped here like us," he says eventually. "She's a friend, as much as somebody can be in our situation. You should find her quickly, before the footman does. He's hunting us both."

"He left a dead rabbit in my room—Bell's room, I mean—last night."

"That's only the beginning," he says. "He means to kill us, though not before he's had his fun."

My blood runs cold, my stomach nauseated. I'd suspected as much, but to hear the fact laid out so baldly is something else entirely. Closing my eyes, I let a long breath out through my nose, releasing my fear with it. It's a habit of Ravencourt's, a way of clearing the mind, though I couldn't say how I know that.

When I open my eyes again, I'm calm.

"Who is he?" I ask, impressed by the strength in my voice.

"I've no idea," he says, blowing smoke into the wind. "I'd call him the devil if I thought this place anything so mundane as hell. He's picking us off one by one, making sure there's no competition when he delivers his answer to the Plague Doctor tonight."

"Does he have other bodies, other hosts, like us?"

"That's the curious thing," he says. "I don't believe he does, but he doesn't seem to need them. He knows the faces of every one of our hosts, and he strikes when we're at our weakest. Every mistake I've made, he's been waiting."

"How do we stop a man who knows our every step before we do?"

"If I knew that, there'd be no need of this conversation," he says irritably. "Be careful. He haunts this house like a bloody ghost, and if he catches you alone…well, don't let him catch you alone."

Daniel's tone is dark, his expression brooding. Whoever this footman is, he has taken hold of my future self in a way that's more unsettling than all the warnings I've heard. It's not hard to understand why. The Plague Doctor gave me eight days to solve Evelyn's murder and eight hosts to do it. Because Sebastian Bell slept past midnight, he's now lost to me.

There goes day one.

My second and third hosts were the butler and Donald Davies. The woman in the carriage didn't mention Davies, which seems a curious omission, but I'm assuming the same rules apply to him as the butler. They both have plenty of hours left until midnight, but one of them is severely injured and the other asleep on a road, miles from Blackheath. They're practically useless. So much for days two and three.

I'm already on my fourth day, and Ravencourt is proving a burden rather than a boon. I don't know what to expect from my remaining four hosts—though Daniel seems capable enough—but it feels as though the Plague Doctor is stacking the deck against me. If the footman truly knows my every weakness, then God help me, because there's plenty to exploit.

"Tell me everything you've already learned about Evelyn's death," I say. "If we work together, we can solve it before the footman has a chance to harm us."

"The only thing I can tell you is that she dies promptly at 11:00 p.m. every single night."

"Surely, you must know more than that."

"A great deal more, but I can't risk sharing the information," he says, glancing at me. "All my plans are built around things you're going to do. If I tell you something that stops you doing those things, I can't be certain they'll play out the same way. You might blunder into the middle of an event settled in my favor, or be elsewhere when you should have been distracting the fellow whose room I'm sneaking into. One wrong word could leave all my plans in ruins. This day must proceed as it always does, for your sake as much as mine." He rubs his forehead, all of his weariness seeming to pour out of the gesture. "I'm sorry, Ravencourt. The safest course is for you to go about your investigation without interference from me or any of the others."

"Very well," I say, hoping to keep my disappointment from him. It's a foolish notion, of course. He's me. He remembers this disappointment for himself. "But the fact you're counseling me to solve this murder suggests you trust the Plague Doctor," I say. "Have you uncovered his identity?"

"Not yet," he says. "And trust is too strong a word. He has his own purpose in this house, I'm certain of it, but for the moment, I can't see any other course beyond doing as he demands."

"And has he told you why this is happening to us?" I ask.

We're interrupted by a commotion at the door, our heads turning toward Ravencourt's valet, who's halfway out of his coat and trying to extricate himself from the clutches of a long purple scarf. He's wind tussled and slightly out of breath, his cheeks swollen with cold.

"I received a message that you required me urgently, my lord," he says, still tugging at the scarf.

"My doing, old love," says Daniel, deftly slipping back into character. "You've a busy day ahead, and I thought Cunningham here could be of use. Speaking of busy days, I must be going myself. I've got a midday appointment with Sebastian Bell."

"I won't leave Evelyn to her fate, Daniel," I say.

"Neither did I," he says, flicking his cigarette into the verge and shutting the window. "But fate found her anyway. You should prepare yourself for that."

He's gone in a few long strides, the library filling with the burble of voices and the loud clatter of cutlery as he tugs open the door on his way to the study and passes through into the drawing room. The guests are gathering for lunch, which means Stanwin will soon threaten the maid, Lucy Harper, while Sebastian Bell watches from the window, feeling himself a fraction of a man. A hunt will depart, Evelyn will collect a note from the well, and blood will be spilt in a graveyard while two friends wait for a woman who'll never arrive. If Daniel's right, there's little I can do to disrupt the day's course, though I'll be damned if I'm going to lie down before it. The Plague Doctor's puzzle may be my way out of this house, but I'll not step over Evelyn's body to escape. I mean to save her, no matter the cost.

"How can I be of service, my lord?"

"Pass me paper, a pen, and some ink, would you? I need to write something down."

"Of course," he says, retrieving the items from his attaché case.

My hands are too clumsy for flowing penmanship, but amidst the smeared ink and ugly blots, the message reads clearly enough.

I check the clock. It's 11:56 a.m. Almost time.

After airing the paper to dry the ink, I fold it neatly and press the creases down, handing it to Cunningham.

"Take this," I say, noticing the traces of greasy black dirt on his hands as he reaches for the letter. His skin's pink with scrubbing, but the dirt's etched into the whorls of his fingertips. Aware of my attention, he takes the letter and clasps his hands behind his back.

"I need you to go directly to the drawing room where they're serving lunch," I say. "Stay there and observe events as they unfold, then read this letter and return to me."

Confusion paints his face. "My lord?"

"We're about to have a very strange day, Cunningham, and I'm going to need your absolute trust."

I wave away his protests, gesturing for him to help me out of the seat.

"Do as I ask," I say, getting to my feet with a grunt. "Then return here and wait for me."

As Cunningham heads for the drawing room, I retrieve my cane and make my way to the sunroom in the hopes of finding Evelyn. Being early, it's only half full, ladies pouring themselves drinks from the bar, wilting over chairs and chaise longues. Everything seems to be a very great effort for them, as though the pale flush of youth were a burden, their energy exhausting. They're muttering about Evelyn, a ripple of ugly laughter directed toward the chess table in the corner, where a game is laid out before her. She has no opponent, her concentration fixed on outwitting herself. Whatever discomfort they're hoping to heap upon her, she seems oblivious to it.

"Evie, can we speak?" I say, hobbling over.

She lifts her head slowly, taking a moment to register me. As yesterday, her blond hair is tied up into a ponytail, tugging her features into a gaunt, rather severe expression. Unlike yesterday, it doesn't soften.

"No, I don't think so, Lord Ravencourt," she says, returning her attention to the board. "I've quite enough unpleasant things to do today, without adding to the list."

Hushed laughter turns my blood to dust. I crumble from the inside out.

"Please, Evie, it's—"

"It's Miss Hardcastle, Lord Ravencourt," she says pointedly. "Manners maketh man, not his bank account."

A pit of humiliation opens in my stomach. This is Ravencourt's worst nightmare. Standing in this room, a dozen pairs of eyes digging at me, I feel like a Christian waiting for the first rocks to be thrown.

Evelyn ponders me, sweating and shaking. Her eyes narrow, glittering.

"Tell you what: play me for it," she says, tapping the chessboard. "You win and we'll have a conversation; I win and you leave me be for the rest of the day. How would that suit?"

Knowing it's a trap, but in no position to argue, I wipe the sweat from my brow and wedge myself into the small chair opposite her, much to the delight of the assembled ladies. She could have forced me into a guillotine and I would have been more comfortable. I spill over the sides of the seat, the low back offering so little support that I tremble with the effort of keeping myself upright.

Unmoved by my suffering, Evelyn crosses her arms on the table and pushes a pawn across the board. I follow it with a rook, the pattern of the middle game weaving itself in my mind. Although we're evenly matched, discomfort is digging holes in my concentration, my tactics proving too ramshackle to overpower Evelyn. The best I can do is prolong the match, and after half an hour of counters and feints, my patience is exhausted.

"Your life is in danger," I blurt out.

Evelyn's fingers pause on her pawn, a little tremor of her hand sounding loud as a bell. Her eyes skirt my face, then those of the ladies behind us, searching for anybody who might have heard. They're frantic, working hard to scrub the moment from history.

She already knows.

"I thought we had a deal, Lord Ravencourt," she interrupts, her expression hardening once more.

"But—"

"Would you prefer I leave?" she says, her glare strangling any further attempts at conversation.

Move after move follows, but I'm so perplexed by her response, I pay little heed to strategy. Whatever's going to happen tonight, Evelyn seems to be aware of it, and yet her greater fear seems to be that somebody else will find out. For the life of me, I can't imagine why that would be, and it's clear she's not going to open her heart to Ravencourt. Her disdain for this man is absolute, which means if I'm to save her life, I must either put on a face she likes or press forward without her help. It's an infuriating turn of events, and I'm desperately trying to find a way of reframing my argument when Sebastian Bell arrives at the door, provoking the queerest of sensations within me. By any measure this man is me, but watching him creep into the room like a mouse along a skirting board, I struggle to believe it. His back is stooped, his head low, arms stiff by his sides. Furtive glances scout every step, his world seemingly filled with sharp edges.

"My grandmother, Heather Hardcastle," says Evelyn, watching him examine the portrait on the wall. "It's not a flattering picture, but then she wasn't a flattering woman by all accounts."

"My apologies," says Bell. "I was—"

Their conversation proceeds exactly as it did yesterday, her interest in this frail creature prompting a pang of jealousy, though that's not my principal concern. Bell's repeating my day exactly, and yet he believes himself to be making his choices freely, as I did. Likely then I'm blindly following a course plotted by Daniel, which makes me what...an echo, a memory or just a piece of driftwood caught in the current?

Flip over the chessboard. Change this moment. Prove yourself unique.

My hand reaches out, but the thought of Evelyn's reaction, her disdain, the laughter of the assembled ladies, is too much. Shame cripples me, and I jerk my hand back. There'll be further opportunities, I need to keep watch for them.

Thoroughly demoralized and with defeat unavoidable, I dash the last few moves, putting my king to the sword with unseemly haste before staggering from the room, Sebastian Bell's voice fading behind me.

～ 15 ～

As ordered, Cunningham's waiting for me in the library.
He's sitting on the edge of a chair, the letter I gave him unfolded
and trembling slightly in his hand. He stands as I enter, but in my
desire to put the sunroom behind me, I've moved too quickly. I can
hear myself breathing, wheezy desperate bursts from my overburdened lungs.

He doesn't venture to help.

"How did you know what was going to happen in the drawing
room?" he asks.

I try to answer, but there isn't room for both words and air in my
throat. I choose the latter, guzzling it with the same appetite as everything else in Ravencourt's life, while staring into the study. I'd hoped
to catch the Plague Doctor while he chatted with Bell, but my futile
attempt to warn Evelyn dragged on longer than I expected.

Perhaps I shouldn't be surprised.

As I saw on the road to the village, the Plague Doctor seems to
know where I'll be and when, no doubt timing his appearances so I
can't ambush him.

"It happened exactly as you described it," continues Cunningham,
staring at the paper in disbelief. "Ted Stanwin insulted the maid, and
Daniel Coleridge stepped in. They even spoke the words you wrote
down. They spoke them *exactly*."

I could explain, but he hasn't got to the section troubling him yet.

Instead, I hobble over to the chair, lowering myself onto the cushion with a great deal of effort. My legs throb in pitiful gratitude.

"Was it a trick?" he asks.

"No trick," I say.

"And this…the final line, where you say…"

"Yes."

"…that you're not Lord Ravencourt."

"I'm not Ravencourt," I say.

"You're not?"

"I'm not. Get a drink. You're looking a little pale."

He does as I say, obedience seemingly being the only part of him that hasn't thrown its hands up in defeat. He returns with a glass of something and sits down, sipping it, his eyes never leaving mine, legs pressed together, shoulders bowed.

I tell him everything, from the murder in the forest and my first day as Bell, right through to the never-ending road and my recent conversation with Daniel. Doubt flickers on his face, but every time it seems to have a foothold, he glances at the letter. I almost feel sorry for him.

"Do you need another drink?" I ask, nodding toward his half-empty glass.

"If you're not Lord Ravencourt, where is he?"

"I don't know."

"Is he alive?"

He can barely make eye contact.

"Would you rather he wasn't?" I ask.

"Lord Ravencourt's been good to me," he says, anger flashing across his face.

That doesn't answer the question.

I look at Cunningham again. Downcast eyes and dirty hands, a smeared tattoo from a troubled past. In a flash of intuition, I realize he's afraid, but not of what I've told him. He's afraid of what somebody who's already seen this day unfold might know. He's hiding something, I'm certain of it.

"I need your help, Cunningham," I say. "There's lots to do, and while I'm shackled to Ravencourt, I don't have the legs to do any of it."

Draining his glass, he gets to his feet. The drink's painted two spots of color on his cheeks, and when he speaks, his voice drips with the bottle's courage.

"I'm going to take my leave now and resume service tomorrow when Lord Ravencourt has"—he pauses, considering the right word—"returned."

He bows stiffly, before heading for the door.

"Do you think he'll take you back when he knows your secret?" I say abruptly, an idea dropping into my head like a stone into a pond. If I'm right and Cunningham is hiding something, it may be shameful enough to use as leverage.

He stops dead beside my chair, hands clenched tight.

"What do you mean?" he says, staring straight ahead.

"Look beneath the cushion of your seat," I say, trying to keep the tension from my voice. The logic of what I'm attempting is sound, but that doesn't mean it will actually work.

He glances at the chair, then back toward me. Without a word he does as I say, discovering a small white envelope. Triumph twists a smile from my lips as he tears it open, his shoulders sagging.

"How did you know?" he asks, his voice cracked.

"I don't know a thing, but when I wake up in my next host, I'm going to dedicate myself to the task of uncovering your secret. I'm then going to return to this room and place the information in that envelope for you to find. Should this conversation not go the way I want, I'll place the envelope where the other guests can find it."

He snorts at me, his contempt a slap in the face.

"You may not be Ravencourt, but you sound exactly like him."

The idea is so startling it momentarily silences me. Until now, I'd assumed my personality—whatever that might be—was carried into each new host, filling them as pennies fill a pocket, but what if I was wrong?

None of my previous hosts would have thought to blackmail Cunningham, let alone had the stomach to act on the threat. In fact, looking back at Sebastian Bell, Roger Collins, Donald Davies, and now Ravencourt, I can see little in their behavior to suggest a common hand at work. Could it be that I'm bending to their will, rather than the other way around? If so, I must be wary. It's one thing to be caged in these people, quite another to abandon oneself entirely to their desires.

My thoughts are interrupted by Cunningham, who's setting fire to a corner of the letter with a lighter from his pocket.

"What is it you want from me?" he says in a hard, flat voice, dropping the burning paper into the grate.

"Four things, initially," I say, counting them off on my thick fingers. "First, I need you to find an old well off the road into the village. There'll be a note tucked into a crack in the stone. Read it, put it back, and return to me with the message. Do it soon, the note will be gone within the hour. Second, you need to find that plague doctor costume I asked about earlier. Third, I want you scattering the name Anna around Blackheath like confetti. Let it be known Lord Ravencourt is looking for her. Finally, I need you to introduce yourself to Sebastian Bell."

"Sebastian Bell, the doctor?"

"That's the chap."

"Why?"

"Because I remember being Sebastian Bell, but I don't remember meeting you," I say. "If we change that, I prove to myself that something else can be changed today."

"Evelyn Hardcastle's death?"

"Precisely."

Letting out a long breath, Cunningham turns to face me. He seems diminished, as though our conversation were a desert he's spent a week crossing.

"If I do these things, can I expect the contents of this letter to stay between us?" he says, his expression conveying more hope than expectation.

"It will. You have my word."

I extend a sweaty hand.

"Then it seems I have no choice," he says, shaking it firmly, only the slightest flicker of disgust showing on his face.

He departs in a hurry, probably wary of being burdened with more tasks should he linger. In his absence, the damp air seems to settle upon me, sinking through my clothes and into my bones. Judging the library too cheerless to stay in any longer, I struggle out of my seat, using my cane to hoist myself onto my feet.

I pass through the study on my way to Ravencourt's parlor, where I'll settle myself ahead of my meeting with Helena Hardcastle. If she's plotting to murder Evelyn this evening, then, by Lord, I mean to have it out of her.

The house is still, the men out hunting and the women drinking in the sunroom. Even the servants have disappeared, scattering back belowstairs to prepare for the ball. In their wake a great hush has fallen, my only company the rain tapping at the windows, demanding to be let inside. Bell missed the noise, but as somebody finely tuned to the malice of others, Ravencourt finds this silence refreshing. It's like airing a musty room.

Heavy steps disturb my reverie, each one deliberate and slow, as if determined to draw my attention. I've reached as far as the dining hall, where a long oak table is overlooked by the mounted heads of long-slaughtered beasts, their fur faded and thick with dust. The room is empty, and yet the steps seem to be all around, mimicking my hobbling gait.

I stiffen, coming to a halt, sweat beading my brow.

The steps stop in turn.

Dabbing my forehead, I look around nervously, wishing Bell's letter opener were to hand. Buried in Ravencourt's sluggish flesh, I feel like a man dragging an anchor. I can neither run nor fight, and even if I could, I'd be swinging at air. I'm quite alone.

After a brief hesitation, I begin walking again, those ghostly steps trailing me. I stop suddenly, and they stop with me, a sinister giggle drifting out of the walls. My heart's pounding, hair standing up on my arms as fright sends me lurching toward the safety of the entrance hall visible through the drawing-room door. By now, the steps aren't bothering mimicking me, they're dancing, that giggle seeming to come from every direction.

I'm panting by the time I reach the doorway, blinded by sweat and moving so fast I'm in danger of tripping over my own cane. As I pass into the entrance hall, the laughter stops abruptly, a whisper chasing me out.

"We'll meet soon, little rabbit."

～ 16 ～

Ten minutes later, the whisper's long faded, but the terror it provoked echoes still. It wasn't the words themselves, so much as the glee they carried. That warning was a down payment on the blood and pain to come, and only a fool wouldn't see the footman behind it.

Holding my hand up, I check to see how badly it's trembling, and deciding that I'm at least moderately recovered, I continue onward to my room. I've only taken a step or two when sobbing draws my attention to a dark doorway at the back of the entrance hall. For a full minute I hover on the periphery, peering into the dimness, fearing a trap. Surely the footman wouldn't try something so soon, or be able to summon up these pitiable gulps of sadness I'm hearing now?

Sympathy compels me to take a tentative step forward, and I find myself in a narrow gallery adorned with Hardcastle family portraits. Generations wither on the walls, the current incumbents of Blackheath hanging nearest the door. Lady Helena Hardcastle is sitting regally beside her standing husband, both of them dark-haired and dark-eyed, beautifully supercilious. Next to them are the portraits of the children, Evelyn at a window, fingering the edge of the curtain as she watches for somebody's arrival, while Michael has one leg flung over the arm of the chair he's sitting in, a book discarded on the floor. He looks bored, shimmering with a restless energy. In the corner of each portrait is a splashed signature; that of Gregory Gold if I'm not very much mistaken. The memory of the butler's beating at the artist's hands is still fresh, and I find myself gripping my cane, tasting the blood in my mouth once again. Evelyn told me Gold had been brought to Blackheath to touch up the portraits and I can see why. The man may be insane, but he's talented.

Another sob issues from the corner of the room.

There are no windows in the gallery, only burning oil lamps, and it's so dim I have to squint to locate the maid slumped in the shadows, weeping into a soggy handkerchief. Tact would advise that I approach quietly, but Ravencourt's ill designed for stealth. My cane raps the floor, the sound of my breathing running on ahead, announcing my presence. Catching sight of me, the maid leaps to her feet, her cap coming loose, curly red hair springing free.

I recognize her immediately. This is Lucy Harper, the maid Ted Stanwin abused at lunch, and the woman who helped me down to the kitchen when I awoke as the butler. The memory of that kindness echoes within me, a warm rush of pity shaping the words in my mouth.

"I'm sorry, Lucy. I didn't mean to startle you," I say.

"No, sir, it's not… I shouldn't…" She casts around for some escape, miring herself further in etiquette.

"I heard you crying," I say, attempting to push a sympathetic smile onto my face. It's a difficult thing to achieve with somebody else's mouth, especially when there's so much flesh to move around.

"Oh, sir, you shouldn't… It was my fault. I made a mistake at lunch," she says, dabbing the last of her tears away.

"Ted Stanwin treated you atrociously," I say, surprised by the alarm rising on her face.

"No, sir, you mustn't say that," she says, her voice hurdling an entire octave. "Ted, Mr. Stanwin, I mean, he's been good to us servants. Always treated us right, he has. He's just… Now he's a gentleman, he can't be seen…"

She's on the verge of tears again.

"I understand," I say hastily. "He doesn't want the other guests treating him like a servant."

A smile swallows her face.

"That's it, sir. That's just it. They'd never have caught Charlie Carver if it weren't for Ted, but the other gentlemen still look at him like he's one of us. Not Lord Hardcastle, though. He calls him Mr. Stanwin and everything."

"Well, as long as you're quite all right," I say, taken aback by the pride in her voice.

"I am, sir. Really I am," she says earnestly, emboldened enough to scoop her cap from the floor. "I should be getting back. They'll be wondering where I've got to."

She takes a step toward the door, but is too slow to prevent me throwing a question in her path.

"Lucy, do you know anybody called Anna?" I ask. "I was thinking she could be a servant."

"Anna?" She pauses, tossing the full weight of her thought at the problem. "No, sir, can't say as I do."

"Any of the maids acting strangely?"

"Now, sir, would you believe, you're the third person to ask that question today," she says, twisting a lock of her curly hair around her finger.

"Third?"

"Yes, sir, Mrs. Derby was down in the kitchen only an hour ago wondering the same thing. Gave us a right fright she did. High-born lady like that wandering around downstairs, ain't ever heard of such a thing."

My hand grips my cane. Whoever this Mrs. Derby is, she's acting oddly and asking the same questions I am. Perhaps I've found another of my rivals.

Or another host.

The suggestion makes me blush, Ravencourt's familiarity with women extending only so far as acknowledging their existence in the world. The thought of becoming one is as unintelligible to him as a day spent breathing water.

"What can you tell me about Mrs. Derby?" I ask.

"Nothing much, sir," says Lucy. "Older lady, sharp tongue. I liked her. Not sure if it means anything, but there was a footman as well. Came in a few minutes after Mrs. Derby asking the same question: any of the servants acting funny?"

My hand squeezes the knob of my cane even tighter, and I have to bite my tongue to keep from cursing.

"A footman?" I say. "What did he look like?"

"Blond hair, tall, but..." She drifts off, looking troubled. "I don't know, pleased with himself. Probably works for a gentleman, sir, they get like that, pick up airs and graces they do. Had a broken nose, all black and purple, like it only recently happened. I reckon somebody took exception to him."

"What did you tell him?"

"Wasn't me, sir, was Mrs. Drudge, the cook. Said the same thing she said to Mrs. Derby, that the servants were fine, it was the guests gone..." She blushes. "Oh, begging your pardon, sir. I didn't mean—"

"Don't worry, Lucy. I find most of the people in this house as peculiar as you do. What have they been doing?"

She grins, her eyes darting toward the doors guiltily. When she speaks again, her voice is almost low enough to be drowned out by the creaking of the floorboards.

"Well, this morning Miss Hardcastle was out in the forest with her lady's maid, French she is, you should hear her, *quelle* this and *quelle* that. Somebody attacked them out by Charlie Carver's old cottage. One of the guests apparently, but they wouldn't say which one."

"Attacked, you're certain?" I say, recalling my morning as Bell, and the woman I saw fleeing through the forest. I assumed it was Anna, but what if I was wrong? It wouldn't be the first assumption to trip me up in Blackheath.

"That's what they said, sir," she says, falling shy in the face of my eagerness.

"I think I need to have a chat with this French maid. What's her name?"

"Madeline Aubert, sir, only I'd prefer it if you didn't let on who told you. They're keeping quiet about it."

Madeline Aubert. That's the maid who gave Bell the note at dinner last night. In the confusion of recent events, I'd quite forgotten about his slashed arm.

"My lips are sealed, Lucy. Thank you," I say, miming the action. "Even so, I must speak with her. Could you let her know I'm looking for her? You don't have to tell her why, but there's a reward in it for both of you if she comes to my parlor."

She looks doubtful, but agrees readily enough, bolting before I have time to slip any more promises around her neck.

If Ravencourt were able, I'd have a bounce in my step as I depart the gallery. Whatever apathy Evelyn may feel toward Ravencourt, she's still my friend and my will is still bent on saving her. If somebody threatened her in the forest this morning, it's not a stretch to assume the same person will play some part in her murder this evening. I must do everything in my power to intercept them, and hopefully this Madeline Aubert will be able to help. Who knows, by this point tomorrow I might have the murderer's name in hand. If the Plague Doctor honors his offer, I could escape this house with hosts to spare.

This jubilation persists only as far as the corridor, my whistling faltering with each step farther away from the brightness of the entrance hall. The footman's presence has transformed Blackheath, its leaping shadows and blind corners populating my imagination with a hundred horrible deaths at his hands. Every little noise is enough to set my already overburdened heart racing. By the time I reach my parlor, I'm soaked with sweat, a knot in my chest.

Closing the door behind me, I let out a long shuddering breath. At this rate, the footman won't need to kill me, my health will give out first.

The parlor's a beautiful room, a chaise longue and an armchair beneath a chandelier reflecting the flames of a roaring fire. A sideboard is laid with spirits and mixers, sliced fruit, bitters, and a bucket of half-melted ice. Beside that sits a teetering pile of roast beef sandwiches, mustard running down the severed edges. My stomach would drag me toward the food, but my body's collapsing beneath me.

I need to rest.

The armchair takes my weight with ill temper, the legs bowing under the strain. Rain's thumping the windows, the sky bruised black and purple. Are these the same drops that fell yesterday, the same clouds? Do rabbits dig the same warrens, disturbing the same insects? Do the same birds fly the same patterns, crashing into the same windows? If this is a trap, what kind of prey is worthy of it?

"I could do with a drink," I mutter, rubbing my throbbing temples.

"Here you go," says a woman from directly behind me, the drink arriving over my shoulder in a small hand, the fingers bony and calloused.

I attempt to turn, but there's too much of Ravencourt and too little of the seat.

The woman shakes the glass impatiently, rattling the ice inside.

"You should drink this before the ice melts," she says.

"You'll forgive me if I'm suspicious of taking a drink from a woman I don't know," I say.

She lowers her lips to my ear, her breath warm on my neck.

"But you do know me," she whispers. "I was in the carriage with the butler. My name's Anna."

"Anna!" I say, trying to raise myself from the seat.

Her hand is an anvil on my shoulder, pushing me back down onto the cushions.

"Don't bother. By the time you get up, I'll be gone," she says. "We'll meet soon, but I need you to stop looking for me."

"*Stop* looking, why?"

"Because you're not the only one searching," she says, withdrawing a little. "The footman's hunting me as well, and he knows we're working together. If you keep looking, you're going to lead him straight to me. We're both safe while I'm hidden, so call off the dogs."

I feel her presence recede, steps moving toward the far door.

"Wait," I cry. "Do you know who I am, or why we're here? Please, there must be something you can tell me."

She pauses, considering it.

"The only memory I woke up with was a name," she says. "I think it's yours."

My hands clutch the armrests.

"What was it?" I ask.

"Aiden Bishop," she says. "Now, I've done as you asked, so do as I ask. Stop looking for me."

"Aiden Bishop," I say, wrapping my tongue around the vowels.
"Aiden…Bishop. Aiden, Aiden, Aiden."

I've been trying different combinations, intonations, and deliveries of my name for the last half hour, hoping to lure some memories from my recalcitrant mind. Thus far, all I've managed to do is give myself a dry mouth. It's a frustrating way to pass the time, but I've few alternatives. One thirty has come and gone, with no word from Helena Hardcastle to explain her absence. I summoned a maid to fetch her, but was informed that nobody's seen the lady of the house since this morning. The damn woman has disappeared.

To make matters worse, neither Cunningham nor Madeline Aubert has visited me, and while I'd hardly expected Evelyn's maid to answer my summons, Cunningham's been gone for hours. I can't imagine what's keeping him, but I'm growing impatient. We've so much to do, and little time left to do it.

"'Allo, Cecil," says a rasping voice. "Is Helena still here? I heard you were meeting with her."

Standing at the door is an elderly lady buried beneath a huge red coat, hat, and mud-spattered Wellington boots that almost reach her knees. Her cheeks are raw with cold, a scowl frozen on her face.

"I haven't seen her, I'm afraid," I say. "I'm still waiting for her."

"You too, eh? Bloody woman was supposed to meet me in the garden this morning, left me shivering on a bench for an hour instead," she says, stomping over to the fire. She's wearing so many layers a spark will send her up like a Viking funeral.

"Wonder where she's got to?" she says, tugging off her gloves and tossing them on the seat next to mine. "It's not like there's a lot to do in Blackheath. Fancy a drink?"

"Still working on this one," I say, waving my glass in her direction.

"You've got the right idea. I got it into my head to go for a stroll, but when I came back, I couldn't get anybody to open the front door. I've been banging on windows for the last half hour, but there's not a servant to be seen. The whole thing's positively American."

Decanters scrape free of their fittings, glasses thumping down on the wood. Ice tinkles against glass, crackling as alcohol is poured on top. There's a fizz and a satisfying plop, followed by a gulp and a long sigh of pleasure from the old lady.

"That's the stuff," she says, a fresh round of clinking glass suggesting the first was a warm-up. "I told Helena this party was a terrible idea, but she wouldn't hear of it and now look: Peter's hiding in the gatehouse, Michael's holding the party together with his fingernails, and Evelyn's playing dress-up. The entire thing will be a disaster, mark my words."

Drink in hand, the elderly lady resumes her position in front of the fire. She's shrunken magnificently after discarding a few layers, revealing pink cheeks and small pink hands, a crop of gray hair running wild on her head.

"What's this then," she says, lifting a white card off the mantel. "Were you going to write to me, Cecil?"

"Sorry?"

She hands me the card, a simple message written on the front.

Meet Millicent Derby

A.

Anna's work, no doubt.

First burning socks and now introductions. As strange as it is having somebody scattering breadcrumbs throughout my day, it's nice to know I have a friend in this place, even if it does put paid to my theory about Mrs. Derby being one of my rivals, or even another host. This old lady's much too herself to be anybody else underneath.

Then why was she sniffing around the kitchen, asking questions about the maids?

"I asked Cunningham to invite you for drinks," I say smoothly, taking a sip of my whiskey. "He must have got distracted while writing the message down."

"That's what happens when you trust the lower classes with important tasks," sniffs Millicent, dropping into a nearby chair. "Mark my words, Cecil, one day you'll find he's emptied your accounts and done a bunk with one of your maids. Look at that damnable Ted Stanwin. Used to waft about this place like a soft breeze when he was a groundskeeper, now you'd think he owns the place. The nerve of it."

"Stanwin's an objectionable fellow, I agree, but I've a soft spot for the household staff," I say. "They've treated me with a great deal of kindness. Besides, word has it you were down in the kitchen earlier, so you can't find them all bad."

She waves her glass at me, splashing whiskey over my objection.

"Oh, that. Yes…" She trails off, sipping her drink to buy herself time. "I think one of the maids stole something from my room, that's all. It's like I say, you never know what's going on underneath. Remember my husband?"

"Vaguely," I say, admiring the elegance with which she's switched topic. Whatever she was doing in the kitchen, I doubt it had anything to do with theft.

"Same thing," she sniffs. "Dreadful lower-class upbringing, yet built himself forty-odd cotton mills without ever being anything less than an absolute ass. In fifty years of marriage, I didn't smile till the day I buried him and haven't stopped since."

She's interrupted by a creaking sound from the corridor, followed by the squeak of hinges.

"Maybe that's Helena," says Millicent, pushing herself out of the chair. "Her room is next door."

"I thought the Hardcastles were staying in the gatehouse?"

"Peter's staying in the gatehouse," she says, raising an eyebrow. "Helena's staying here, insisted on it, by all accounts. Was never much of a marriage, but it's disintegrating quickly. I tell you, Cecil, it was worth coming for the scandal alone."

The old lady heads into the corridor, calling out Helena's name, only to fall suddenly silent. "What on earth…" she mutters, before poking her head into my parlor again. "Get up, Cecil," she says nervously. "Something odd is going on."

Concern drags me to my feet and into the hall, where Helena's bedroom door creaks back and forth in a breeze. The lock has been shattered, splinters of wood crunching underfoot.

"Somebody broke in," hisses Millicent, staying behind me.

Using my cane, I slowly push the door open, allowing us to peer inside.

The room's empty, and has been for some time by the looks of things. The curtains are still drawn, light delivered secondhand from the lamps lining the corridor. A four-poster bed is neatly made, a vanity table overflowing with face creams, powders, and cosmetics of every sort.

Satisfied that it's safe, Millicent appears from behind me, offering me a level glance best described as a belligerent apology, before making her way around the bed to wrestle the heavy curtains open, banishing the gloom.

The only thing that's been disturbed is a chestnut bureau with a roll-down top, its drawers hanging open. Among the ink bottles, envelopes, and ribbons scattered on it, there's a large lacquered case with two revolver-shaped hollows in the cushion. The revolvers themselves are nowhere to be seen, though I suspect Evelyn brought one of them to the graveyard. She did say it was her mother's.

"Well, at least we know what they wanted," says Millicent, tapping the case. "Doesn't make any damn sense, though. If somebody wanted a gun, they could just as easily steal one from the stables. There's dozens of them. Nobody would bat an eyelid."

Pushing aside the case, Millicent unearths a moleskin day planner and begins leafing through the pages, running her finger across the meetings and events, reminders and notes crammed inside. The contents would suggest a busy, if rather dull life, if it weren't for the torn-out last page.

"That's curious. Today's appointments are missing," she says, her irritation giving way to suspicion. "Now, why would Helena rip those out?"

"You believe she did it herself?" I say.

"What use would anybody else have for them?" says Millicent. "Mark my words: Helena has something foolish in mind, and she doesn't want anybody finding out about it. Now, if you'll excuse me, Cecil, I'm going to have to find her and talk her out of it. As usual."

Tossing the planner on the bed, she stalks out of the bedroom and up the corridor. I barely notice her leave. I'm more concerned with the black smudged fingerprints on the pages.

My valet's been here, and it appears he's looking for Helena Hardcastle as well.

~ 18 ~

The world's shriveling beyond the windows, darkening at the edges and blackening at the center. The hunters are beginning to emerge from the forest, waddling across the lawn like overgrown birds. Having grown impatient in my parlor waiting for Cunningham's return, I'm heading to the library to inspect the encyclopedia.

It's already a decision I regret.

A day of walking has sapped all my strength, this ponderous body growing heavier by the second. To make matters worse, the house is alive with activity, maids plumping cushions and arranging flowers, darting this way and that like schools of startled fish. I'm embarrassed by their vigor, cowed by their grace.

By the time I enter the entrance hall, it's filled with hunters shaking the rain from their caps, puddles forming at their feet. They're soaking wet and gray with cold, the life washed right out of them. They've clearly endured a miserable afternoon.

I pass into the group nervously, my eyes downcast, wondering if any of these scowling faces belongs to the footman. Lucy Harper told me he had a broken nose when he visited the kitchen, which gives me some hope that my hosts are fighting back, not to mention an easy way of picking him out.

Seeing no disfigurement, I continue more confidently, the hunters standing aside, allowing me to shuffle through on my way to the library, where the heavy curtains have been drawn and a fire set in the grate, the air touched with a faint perfume. Fat candles sit on plates, plumes of warm light pockmarking the shadows, illuminating three women curled up on chairs, engrossed in the books open on their laps.

Heading to the bookshelf where the encyclopedia should be, I grope about in the darkness, finding only an empty space. Taking a candle from a nearby table, I pass the flame across the shelf hoping it has been moved, but it's definitely gone. I let out a long breath, deflating like the bellows of some awful contraption. Until now, I hadn't realized how much hope I'd invested in the encyclopedia, or in the idea of meeting my future hosts face-to-face. It wasn't only their knowledge I craved, but the chance to study them, as one might one's own twisted reflections in a hall of mirrors. Surely in such observation, I'd find some repeated quality, a fragment of my true self carried through into each man, unsullied by the personalities of their hosts? Without that opportunity, I'm not certain how to identify the edges of myself, the dividing lines between my personality and that of my host. For all I know, the only difference between myself and the footman is the mind I'm sharing.

The day's leaning on my shoulders, forcing me into a chair opposite the fire. Stacked logs pop and crackle, heat shimmering and sagging in the air.

My breath catches in my throat.

Among the flames lies the encyclopedia, burned to ash but holding its shape, a breath away from crumbling.

The footman's work no doubt.

I feel like I've been struck, which was no doubt the intention. Everywhere I go, he seems to be a step ahead of me. And yet, simply winning isn't enough. He needs me to know it. He needs me to be afraid. For some reason, he needs me to suffer.

Still reeling from this blatant act of contempt, I lose myself in the flames, piling all my misgivings onto the bonfire until Cunningham calls me from the doorway.

"Lord Ravencourt?"

"Where the devil have you been?" I snap, my temper slipping away from me completely.

He strolls around my chair, taking a spot near the fire to warm his hands. He looks to have been caught in the storm, and though he's changed his clothes, his damp hair is still wild from the towel.

"It's good to see Ravencourt's temper is still intact," he says placidly. "I'd feel positively adrift without my daily dressing down."

"Don't play the victim with me," I say, wagging my finger at him. "You've been gone hours."

"Good work takes time," he says, tossing an object onto my lap.

Holding it up to the light, I stare into the empty eyes of a porcelain beak mask, my anger evaporating immediately.

Cunningham lowers his voice, glancing at the women, who are watching us with open curiosity. "It belongs to a chap called Philip Sutcliffe," he says. "One of the servants spotted it in his wardrobe, so I crept into his room when he left for the hunt. Sure enough, the top hat and greatcoat were in there as well, along with a note promising to meet Lord Hardcastle at the ball. I thought we could intercept him."

Slapping my hand against my knee, I grin at him like a maniac. "Good work, Cunningham, good work indeed."

"I thought you'd be happy," he says. "Unfortunately, that's where my good news ends. The note waiting for Miss Hardcastle at the well, it was…odd, to say the least."

"Odd, how so?" I say, holding the beak mask over my face. The porcelain's cold, clammy against my skin, but aside from that it's a good fit.

"The rain had smeared it, but best I could tell, it said, 'Stay away from Millicent Derby,' with a simple little drawing of a castle beneath it. Nothing else."

"That's a peculiar sort of warning," I say. "I wonder who it's from?"

"Warning? I took it as a threat," says Cunningham.

"You think Millicent Derby's going to take after Evelyn with her knitting needles?" I say, raising an eyebrow.

"Don't dismiss her because she's old," he says, prodding some life into the dwindling fire with a poker. "At one time, half the people in this house were under Millicent Derby's thumb. There wasn't a dirty secret she couldn't ferret out, or a dirty trick she wouldn't use. Ted Stanwin was an amateur in comparison."

"You've had dealings with her?"

"Ravencourt has and he doesn't trust her," he says. "The man's a bastard, but he's no fool."

"That's good to know," I say. "Did you meet with Sebastian Bell?"

"Not yet. I'll catch him this evening. I wasn't able to turn over anything about the mysterious Anna either."

"Oh, no need. She found me earlier today," I say, picking at a loose piece of leather on the arm of the chair.

"Really, what did she want?"

"She didn't say."

"Well, how does she know you?"

"We didn't get around to it."

"Is she a friend?"

"Possibly."

"Profitable meeting then?" he says slyly, replacing the poker on its stand. "Speaking of which, we should get you into a bath. Dinner's at 8:00 p.m., and you're beginning to smell a bit ripe. Let's not give people any more reason to dislike you than they already do."

He moves to help me up, but I wave him back.

"No, I need you to shadow Evelyn for the rest of the evening," I say, struggling to raise myself from the chair. Gravity, it seems, is opposed to the idea.

"To what end?" he asks, frowning at me.

"Somebody's planning to murder her," I say.

"Yes, and that somebody could be me for all you know," he says blandly, as though suggesting nothing more important than a fondness for music halls.

The idea strikes me with such force, I drop back into the seat I've half escaped, the wood cracking beneath me. Ravencourt trusts Cunningham completely, a trait I've adopted without question despite knowing he has a terrible secret. He's as much a suspect as anybody.

Cunningham taps his nose.

"Now you're thinking," he says, sliding my arm over his shoulders. "I'll find Bell when I've got you into the bath, but to my mind, you're better off shadowing Evelyn yourself when you're next able. In the meantime, I'll stick by your side so you can rule me out as a suspect. My life's complicated enough without having eight of you chasing me around the house accusing me of murder."

"You seem well versed in this sort of thing," I say, trying to scrutinize his reaction from the corner of my eye.

"Well, I wasn't always a valet," he says.

"And what were you?"

"I don't believe that information was part of our little arrangement," he says, a grimace on his face as he tries to lift me.

"Then why don't you tell me what you were doing in Helena Hardcastle's bedroom?" I suggest. "You smeared the ink while you were rifling through her day planner. I noticed it on your hands this morning."

He lets out a whistle of astonishment.

"You *have* been busy." His voice hardens. "Strange you haven't heard about my scandalous relationship to the Hardcastles, then. Oh, I wouldn't want to spoil the surprise for you. Ask around. It's not exactly a secret, and I'm sure somebody will get a thrill from telling you."

"Did you break in, Cunningham?" I demand. "Two revolvers were taken, and a page torn from her day planner."

"I didn't have to break in. I was invited," he says. "Couldn't tell you about those revolvers, but the day planner was whole when I left. Saw it myself. I suppose I could explain what I was doing there, and why I'm not your man, but, if you've got any sense, you wouldn't believe a word of it, so you might as well find out for yourself. That way you can be certain it's the truth."

We rise in a damp cloud of sweat, Cunningham dabbing the perspiration from my forehead before handing me my cane.

"Tell me, Cunningham," I say. "Why does a man like you settle for a job like this?"

That brings him up short, his normally implacable face darkening.

"Life doesn't always leave you a choice in how you live it," he says grimly. "Now, come on. We've a murder to attend."

~ 19 ~

*The evening meal is lit by candelabra, and beneath their flick-*ering glow lies a graveyard of chicken bones, fish spines, lobster shells, and pork fat. The curtains remain undrawn despite the darkness beyond, granting a view toward the forest being whipped by the storm.

I can hear myself eating, the crush and the crack, the squelch and the gulp. Gravy runs down my chins, grease smearing my lips with a ghastly, shimmering shine. Such is the ferocity of my appetite that I leave myself panting between mouthfuls. The other diners are watching this hideous performance from the corner of their eyes, trying to maintain their conversations even as the decorum of the evening crunches between my teeth. How can a man know such hunger? What hollowness must he be trying to fill?

Michael Hardcastle's sitting to the left of me, though we've barely spoken two words since I arrived. He's spent most of his time in hushed conversation with Evelyn, heads bowed close, their affection impenetrable. For a woman who knows herself to be in danger, she seems remarkably unperturbed.

Perhaps she believes herself protected.

"Have you ever traveled to the Orient, my Lord Ravencourt?"

If only the seat to my right was similarly oblivious to my presence. It's filled by Commander Clifford Herrington, a balding former naval officer in a uniform glittering with valor. After an hour spent in his company, I'm struggling to reconcile the man with the deeds. Perhaps it's the weak chin and averted gaze, the sense of imminent apology. More likely it's the scotch sloshing around behind his eyes.

Herrington's spent the evening tossing around tedious stories without bothering to indulge in the courtesy of exaggeration, and now it appears our conversation is washing up on the shores of Asia. I sip my wine to cover my agitation, discovering the taste to be peculiarly piquant. My grimace causes Herrington to lean over conspiratorially.

"I had the same reaction," he says, hitting me full in the face with his warm, alcohol-soaked breath. "I quizzed a servant on the vintage. Might as well have asked the glass I was drinking it out of."

The candelabra gives his face a ghoulish yellow cast, and there's a drunken sheen to his eyes that's repellent. Putting my wine down, I cast about for some distraction. There must be fifteen people around the table, words of French, Spanish, and German seasoning otherwise dull conversational fare. Expensive jewelry clinks against glass, cutlery rattles as waiters remove plates. The mood in the room is somber, the scattered conversations hushed and urgent, spoken across a dozen empty seats. It's an eerie sight, mournful even, and though the absences are notable, everybody seems to be going out of their way to avoid noting them. I can't tell whether it's a matter of good breeding, or there's some explanation I've missed.

I search for familiar faces to ask, but Cunningham's gone to meet Bell and there's no sign of Millicent Derby, Doctor Dickie, or even the repulsive Ted Stanwin. Aside from Evelyn and Michael, the only other person I recognize is Daniel Coleridge, who's sitting near a thin fellow at the far end of the table, the two of them eyeing the other guests from behind their half-filled wineglasses. Somebody's taken exception to that handsome face of Daniel's, adorning it with a split lip and a swollen eye that will be frightful tomorrow, assuming tomorrow ever actually arrives. The injury doesn't appear to be bothering him unduly, though it unsettles me. Until this moment, I'd considered

Daniel immune to the machinations of this place, assuming his knowledge of the future allowed him to simply sidestep misfortune. Seeing him brought so low is like seeing the cards spilling out of a magician's sleeve.

His dining companion thumps the table in delight at one of Daniel's jokes, drawing my attention. I feel as though I know this fellow, but I can't place him.

A future host perhaps.

I certainly hope not. He's a smear of a man with oiled hair and a pale, pinched face, his manner that of somebody who finds everything in the room beneath him. I sense cunning in him, cruelty too, though I can't understand from where I'm gathering these impressions.

"They have such outlandish remedies," says Clifford Herrington, raising his voice slightly to reclaim my attention.

I blink at him in confusion.

"The Orientals, Lord Ravencourt," he says, smiling amiably.

"Of course," I say. "No, I'm afraid I've never visited."

"Incredible place, incredible. They have these hospitals…"

I raise my hand to attract a servant. If I can't be spared the conversation, I can be at least spared the wine. One mercy may yet yield another.

"I was speaking with Doctor Bell last night about some of their opiates," he continues.

Make it end…

"Is the food to your satisfaction, Lord Ravencourt?" says Michael Hardcastle, neatly sidling into the conversation.

I turn my eyes to meet him, gratitude flooding forth.

A glass of red wine is half raised to his lips, mischief sparkling in those green eyes. It's a stark contrast to Evelyn, whose gaze could tear strips from my skin. She's dressed in a blue evening gown and tiara, her blond hair pinned up in curls, exposing the lavish diamond necklace draped around her neck. It's the same outfit, minus an overcoat and

Wellington boots, that she'll be wearing when she accompanies Sebastian Bell into the graveyard later this evening.

Dabbing my lips, I bow my head.

"It's excellent. I'm just sorry there aren't more people to enjoy it," I say, gesturing toward the empty seats scattered around the table. "I was particularly looking forward to meeting Mr. Sutcliffe."

And his plague doctor costume, I think to myself.

"Well, you're in luck," interrupts Clifford Herrington. "Old Sutcliffe's a good friend of mine. Perhaps I can introduce you at the ball."

"Assuming he makes it," says Michael. "He and my father will have reached the back of the liquor cabinet by now. Doubtless Mother's trying to rouse them as we speak."

"Is Lady Hardcastle coming tonight?" I ask. "I hear she hasn't been seen much today."

"Returning to Blackheath has been hard on her," says Michael, lowering his voice as though sharing a confidence. "No doubt she's spent the day exorcising a few ghosts before the party. Rest assured, she'll be here."

We're interrupted by one of the waiters leaning down to whisper in Michael's ear. The young man's expression immediately darkens, and as the waiter retreats, he passes the message to his sister, the gloom washing over her face as well. They look at each other a moment, squeezing hands, before Michael raps on his wineglass with a fork, and gets to his feet. He seems to unfurl as he stands so that he now appears unfeasibly tall, reaching well beyond the dim light of the candelabra, forcing him to speak from the shadows.

The room is silent, all eyes upon him.

"I'd rather hoped my parents might make an appearance and save me from making a toast," he says. "Clearly they're planning some grand entrance at the ball, which knowing my parents will be very grand indeed."

Muted laughter is met with a shy smile.

My gaze skips across the guests, running straight into Daniel's amused stare. Dabbing his lips with a napkin, he flicks his eyes toward Michael, instructing me to pay attention.

He knows what's coming.

"My father wanted to thank you for attending tonight, and I'm sure he'll do so in great detail later," says Michael.

There's a quaver in his voice, the slightest hint of discomfort. "In his stead, I'd like to extend my personal thanks to each of you for coming and to welcome my sister, Evelyn, back home after her time in Paris."

She reflects his adoration, the two of them sharing a smile that has nothing to do with this room, or these people. Even so, glasses are raised, reciprocal thanks washing back along the table.

Michael waits for the commotion to die down, then continues. "She'll soon be embarking on a brand-new adventure, and..." He pauses, eyes on the table. "Well, she's going to be married to Lord Cecil Ravencourt."

Silence engulfs us, all eyes turning in my direction. Shock becomes confusion then disgust; their faces a perfect reflection of my own feelings. There must be thirty years and a thousand meals between Ravencourt and Evelyn, whose hostility this morning is now explained. If Lord and Lady Hardcastle really do blame their daughter for Thomas's death, their punishment is exquisite. They plan to steal all the years from her that were stolen from Thomas.

I look over at Evelyn, but she's fidgeting with a napkin and biting her lip, her former humor having fled. A bead of sweat is rolling down Michael's forehead, the wine shaking in his glass. He can't even look at his sister, and she can't look anywhere else. Never has a man found a tablecloth so engrossing as I do now.

"Lord Ravencourt's an old friend of the family," says Michael mechanically, soldiering on into the silence. "I can't think of anybody who'd take better care of my sister."

Finally, he looks at Evelyn, meeting her glistening eyes.

"Evie, I think you wanted to say something."

She nods, the napkin strangled in her hands.

All eyes are fixed on her, nobody moving. Even the servants are staring, standing by the walls, holding dirty plates and fresh bottles of wine. Finally, Evelyn looks up from her lap, meeting the expectant faces arranged before her. Her eyes are wild, like an animal caught in a trap. Whatever words she prepared, they desert her immediately, replaced with a wretched sob that drives her from the room, Michael chasing after her.

Among the rustle of bodies turning in my direction, I seek out Daniel. The amusement of earlier has passed, his gaze now fixed on the window. I wonder how many times he's watched the slow blush rise up my cheeks; if he even remembers how this shame felt. Is that why he can't look at me now? Will I do any better, when my time comes?

Abandoned at the end of the table, my instinct is to flee with Michael and Evelyn, but I might as well wish for the moon to reach down and pluck me from this chair. Silence swirls until Clifford Herrington gets to his feet, candlelight glinting off his naval medals as he raises his glass.

"To many happy years," he says, seemingly without irony.

One by one, every glass is raised and the toast repeated in a hollow chant.

At the end of the table, Daniel winks at me.

~ 20 ~

The dining hall has long emptied of guests, the servants having finally cleared away the last of the platters when Cunningham comes to collect me. He's been standing outside for over an hour, but every time he tried to enter, I've waved him back. After the humiliation of dinner, having anybody see my valet help me from my seat would be an indignity too far. When he does stroll in, there's a smirk on his face. No doubt word of my shaming has run laps around the house: fat old Ravencourt and his runaway bride.

"Why didn't you tell me about Ravencourt's marriage to Evelyn?" I demand, stopping him in his tracks.

"To humiliate you," he says.

I stiffen, my cheeks reddening, as he meets my gaze.

His eyes are green, the pupils uneven, like splashed ink. I see conviction enough to raise armies and burn churches. God help Ravencourt should this boy ever decide to stop being his footstool.

"Ravencourt is a vain man, easy to embarrass," continues Cunningham in a level voice. "I noticed you'd inherited this quality, and I made sport of it."

"Why?" I ask, stunned by his honesty.

"You blackmailed me," he says, shrugging. "You didn't think I'd take that lying down, did you?"

I blink at him for a few seconds before laughter erupts out of me.

It's a belly laugh, the rolls of my flesh shaking in appreciation at his audacity. I humiliated him, and he handed back an equal weight of that misery, using nothing more than patience. What man wouldn't be charmed by such a feat?

Cunningham frowns at me, his eyebrows knitting together.

"You're not angry?" he asks.

"I suspect my anger is of little concern to you," I say, wiping a tear from my eye. "Regardless, I threw the first stone. I can't complain if a boulder comes back at me."

My mirth prompts an echoing smile in my companion.

"It appears there are some differences between yourself and Lord Ravencourt, after all," he says, measuring each word.

"Not least a name," I say, holding out my hand. "Mine is Aiden Bishop."

He shakes it firmly, his smile deepening.

"Very good to make your acquaintance, Aiden. I'm Charles."

"Well, I have no intention of telling anybody your secret, Charles, and I apologize for threatening it. I wish only to save Evelyn Hardcastle's life and escape Blackheath, and I don't have a lot of time to do either. I'll need a friend."

"Probably more than one," he says, cleaning his glasses on his sleeve. "In all honesty, this tale's so peculiar I'm not sure I could walk away now, even if I wished to."

"Shall we go, then?" I say. "By Daniel's reckoning, Evelyn will be murdered at the party at 11:00 p.m. If we're to save her, that's where we have to be."

The ballroom is on the other side of the entrance hall, Cunningham supporting me at the elbow as we walk there. Carriages are arriving from the village, piling up on the gravel outside. Horses nicker, doormen opening the doors for costumed guests who flutter out like canaries released from their cages.

"Why is Evelyn being compelled to marry Ravencourt?" I whisper to Cunningham.

"Money," he says. "Lord Hardcastle's got an eye for a bad investment, and not nearly enough intelligence to learn from his mistakes. Rumor suggests he's driving the family toward bankruptcy. In return for Evelyn's hand, Lord and Lady Hardcastle will receive a rather generous dowry and Ravencourt's promise to buy Blackheath in a couple of years for a tidy sum."

"So that's it," I say. "The Hardcastles are hard up, and they're pawning their daughter off like old jewelry."

My thoughts flock back to this morning's chess game, the smile on Evelyn's face as I winced out of the sunroom. Ravencourt isn't buying a bride, he's buying a bottomless well of spite. I wonder if the old fool understands what he's getting into.

"And what of Sebastian Bell?" I say, remembering the task I set him. "Did you speak with him?"

"Afraid not. The poor fellow was passed out on his floor when I arrived," he says, genuine pity in his voice. "I saw the dead rabbit. Seems your footman has a twisted sense of humor. I called for the doctor and left them to it. Your experiment will have to wait another day."

My disappointment is drowned out by the music beating at the ballroom's closed doors, the sound tumbling into the hall when a servant sweeps them open for us. There must be at least fifty people inside, whirling through a soft puddle of light cast by a chandelier wreathed in candles. An orchestra is playing with bravado on a stage pressed against the far wall, but the majority of the room has been given over to the dance floor where Harlequins in full livery court Egyptian queens and grinning devils. Jesters leap and mock, dislodging powdered wigs and gold masks held up on long sticks. Dresses, capes, and cowls swoop and swish across the floor, the crush of bodies disorientating. The only space to be found surrounds Michael

Hardcastle in his dazzling sun mask, its pointed rays extending such a distance from his face that it's unsafe to venture anywhere near him.

We're viewing all this from a mezzanine, a small staircase leading down to the dance floor. My fingers are rapping the banister, keeping time with the music. Some part of me, the part that's still Ravencourt, knows this song and is enjoying it. He yearns to pick up an instrument and play.

"Ravencourt's a musician?" I ask Cunningham.

"In his youth," he says. "Talented violinist, by all accounts. Broke his arm riding and could never play as well again. He still misses it, I think."

"He does," I say, surprised by the depth of his longing.

Putting it aside, I return my attention to the matter at hand, but I have no idea how we're going to spot Sutcliffe among the crowd.

Or the footman.

My heart sinks. I hadn't considered that. Amid the noise and the crush of bodies, a blade could do its work and vanish without anybody ever being the wiser.

Such thoughts would have caused Bell to run back to his room, but Ravencourt is made of sterner stuff. If this is where the attempt will be made on Evelyn's life, this is where I must be, come what may. And so with Charles supporting my arm, we descend the stairs, keeping to the shadowy edges of the ballroom.

Clowns slap me on the back, and women swirl in front of me, butterfly masks in hand. I ignore much of it, pushing my way to the couches near the french doors, where I can better rest my weary legs.

Until now, I'd only witnessed my fellow guests in handfuls, their spite spread thin across the house. To be ensnared among them all, as I am now, is something else entirely, and the further I descend into the uproar, the thicker their malice seems to become. Most of the men look to have spent the afternoon soaking in their cups and are staggering instead of dancing, snarling and staring, their conduct savage. Young women throw their heads back and laugh, their makeup running and hair coming loose as they're passed from body to body, goading a small group of wives who've grouped together for safety, wary of these panting, wild-eyed creatures.

Nothing like a mask to reveal somebody's true nature.

Beside me, Charles has grown increasingly tense, his fingers digging deeper into my forearm with every step. All of this is wrong. The celebration is too desperate. This is the last party before Gomorrah fell.

We reach a couch, Charles lowering me onto the cushions. Waitresses are moving through the crowd with trays of drinks, but it's proving impossible to signal them from our position on the fringe of the party. It's too loud to talk, but he points toward the champagne table guests are stumbling away from arm in arm. I nod, dabbing the sweat from my forehead. Perhaps a drink will serve to settle my nerves. As he leaves to fetch a bottle, I feel a breeze on my skin and notice that somebody has opened the french doors, presumably to let a little air circulate. It's pitch-black outside, but braziers have been lit, the flickering flames winding all the way up to a reflecting pool surrounded by trees.

The darkness swirls, taking shape, solidifying as it sweeps inside, candlelight dripping onto a pale face.

Not a face. A mask.

A white porcelain beak mask.

I look around for Charles, hoping he's near enough to lay hands on the fellow, but the crowd has carried him away. Looking back toward the french doors, I see the Plague Doctor slipping through the revelers shoulder first.

Gripping my cane, I heave myself to my feet. Wrecks have been raised from the ocean bed with less effort, but I hobble toward the cascade of costumes shrouding my quarry. I follow glimpses—the glint of a mask, the swirl of a cloak—but he's fog in a forest, impossible to snatch hold of.

I lose him somewhere in the far corner.

I try to catch sight of him, but somebody comes clattering into me. I bellow in a fury, finding myself looking into a pair of brown eyes peering out from behind a porcelain beak mask. My heart leaps and so do I evidently, for the mask is swiftly removed to reveal the pinched boyish face behind.

"Gosh, I'm sorry," he says. "I didn't—"

"Rochester, Rochester, over here!" somebody yells to him.

We turn at the same time, another fellow in a plague doctor costume approaching us. There's another behind him, three more in the crowd. My quarry has multiplied, yet none of them can be my interlocutor. They're too stout and short, too tall and thin; too many imperfect copies of the real thing. They try to drag their friend away, but I catch hold of the nearest arm—any arm, they're all the same.

"Where did you get these costumes?" I ask.

The fellow scowls at me, his gray eyes bloodshot. They're lightless, expressionless. Empty doorways without a coherent thought behind them. Shaking himself loose of my grip, he prods me in the chest.

"Ask me nicely," he slurs drunkenly. He's itching for a fight, and lashing out with my cane, I give it to him. The heavy wood catches him on the leg, a curse detonating on his lips as he drops to one knee. Attempting to steady himself, he places his palm flat on the dance floor, the point of my cane landing on top of his hand, pinning him to the ground.

"The costumes," I shout. "Where did you find them?"

"The attic," he says, his face now as pale as the discarded mask. "There's dozens of them hanging on a rack."

He strains to free himself, but only a fraction of my weight is resting on the cane. I add a little more, pain unsettling his features.

"How did you know about them?" I ask, taking a little pressure off his hand.

"A servant found us last night," he says, tears forming in his eyes. "He was already wearing one, mask and hat, the entire getup. We didn't have costumes, so he took us up to the attic to find some. He was helping everybody, must have been two dozen people up there, I swear."

Seems the Plague Doctor doesn't want to be found.

I watch him squirm for a second or two, balancing the veracity of his story against the pain on his face. Content that the two are of equal weight, I lift my cane, allowing him to stumble away, clutching his aching hand. He's barely out of my sight before Michael emerges from the crowd, spotting me at a distance and driving straight toward me. He's flustered, two red spots on his cheeks. His mouth is moving frantically, but his words are lost in the music and laughter.

Signaling that I cannot understand, he comes closer.

"Have you seen my sister?" he yells.

I shake my head, suddenly fearful. I can see in his eyes that something is wrong, but before I can quiz him further, he's pushing back through the whirling dancers. Hot and giddy, oppressed by a sense of foreboding, I fight my way to my seat, removing my bow tie and loosening my collar. Masked figures drift by, naked arms glittering with perspiration.

I feel nauseous, unable to take pleasure in anything I see. I'm contemplating joining the search for Evelyn when Cunningham returns with a bottle of champagne in a silver bucket crammed with ice, and two long-stemmed glasses tucked under his arm. The metal's sweating, as is Cunningham. It's been so long, I'd quite forgotten what he'd left to do, and I yell into his ear.

"Where have you been?"

"Thought…saw Sutcliffe," he yells back, about half the words carrying through the music. "…costume."

Evidently, Cunningham's had much the same experience I had.

Nodding my understanding, we sit and drink silently, keeping our eyes open for Evelyn, my frustration mounting. I need to be on my feet, searching the house, questioning guests, but Ravencourt's incapable of such feats. This room is too crowded, his body too weary. He's a man of calculation and observation, not action, and if I'm to help Evelyn, these are the skills I must embrace. Tomorrow I'll dash, but today I must watch. I need to see everything that's happening in this ballroom, cataloging every detail, in order to get ahead of this evening's events.

The champagne calms me, but I put my glass down, wary of dulling my faculties. That's when I spot Michael, climbing the few steps that lead to the mezzanine overlooking the ballroom.

The orchestra is silenced, the laughter and chatter slowly dying down as all heads turn toward their host.

"I'm sorry to interrupt," says Michael, gripping the banister. "I feel foolish for asking, but does anybody know where my sister is?"

A ripple of conversation washes over the crowd as heads turn to look at one another. It takes only a minute to determine she's not in the ballroom.

It's Cunningham who spots her first.

Touching my arm, he points toward Evelyn, who's weaving drunkenly as she follows the braziers toward the reflecting pool. She's some distance away already, drifting in and out of the light. A small silver pistol's glinting in her hand.

"Fetch Michael," I cry.

As Cunningham pushes through the crowd, I drag myself to my feet, lurching toward the window. Nobody else has seen her, and the commotion's building again, the temporary fuss of the announcement already fading. The violin player tests a note, the clock showing 11:00 p.m.

I've reached the french doors when Evelyn arrives at the pool.

She's swaying, trembling.

Standing in the trees, only feet away, the Plague Doctor watches passively, the flames of the brazier reflected on his mask.

The silver pistol flashes as Evelyn raises it to her stomach, the gunshot slicing through conversation and music.

And yet, for a moment, all seems well.

Evelyn's still standing on the edge of the water, as though admiring her reflection. Then her legs buckle, the gun dropping from her hand as she topples facefirst into the pool, the Plague Doctor bowing his head and disappearing into the blackness of the trees.

I'm only dimly aware of the screams, or the crowd at my back, surging past me onto the grass as the promised fireworks explode in the air, drenching the pool in colorful light. I'm watching Michael, sprinting into the darkness toward a sister he's too late to save. He's screaming her name, his voice drowned out by the fireworks as he wades into the inky water to scoop up her body. Slipping and stumbling, he tries to drag her from the pool before eventually collapsing, Evelyn still cradled in his arms. Kissing her face, he begs her to open her eyes, but it's a fool's hope. Death's rolled his dice and Evelyn's paid her debt. All that was of value has been taken.

Burying his face in her wet hair, Michael sobs.

He's oblivious as the crowd gathers, as strong arms pry him from his sister's limp body, hoisting her onto the grass so Doctor Dickie can kneel down and make his examination. Not that his skills are required, the hole in her stomach and the silver pistol on the grass tell the story eloquently enough. Despite that, he lingers over her, pressing his fingers to her neck to check for a pulse, before tenderly wiping the dirty water from her face.

Still kneeling, he gestures for Michael to come closer, and taking the weeping man's hand, he bows his head and begins muttering what looks to be a prayer under his breath.

I'm grateful for his reverence.

A few women are crying into accommodating shoulders, but there's something hollow about their performance. It's as though the ball hasn't really ended. They're all still dancing, they've just changed the steps. Evelyn deserves better than to be entertainment for people she despised. The doctor seems to understand this, his every action, no matter how small, restoring some small part of her dignity.

The prayer only takes a minute, and when it's done, he drapes his jacket across Evelyn's face, as though her unblinking stare is of greater offense than the blood staining her dress.

There's a tear on his cheek as he gets to his feet, and placing an arm around Michael, he leads Evelyn's sobbing brother away. To my eyes, they depart older men, slower and more bent, carrying a great weight of sadness across their shoulders.

No sooner are they inside the house than rumors bounce through the crowd. The police are coming, a suicide note's been found, Charlie Carver's spirit has claimed another Hardcastle child. The stories are spun from one mouth to another, and by the time they reach me, they're rich with details and patterns, strong enough to be carried out of here and into society.

I look for Cunningham, but he's nowhere to be seen. I can't imagine what he could be doing, but he's got a quick eye and willing hands so no doubt he's found a purpose—unlike myself. The shot has shattered my nerves.

Taking myself back to the now empty ballroom, I drop onto the couch from earlier, where I sit and tremble, my mind racing.

I know my friend will be alive again tomorrow, but it doesn't change what happened, or the devastation I feel at having witnessed it.

Evelyn took her own life, and I'm responsible. Her marriage to Ravencourt was a punishment, a humiliation designed to push her over the edge, and however unwittingly, I was part of it. It was my face she hated, my presence that drove her to the water's edge with a pistol in her hand.

And what of the Plague Doctor? He offered me freedom in return for solving a murder that wouldn't look like a murder, but I watched Evelyn shoot herself after fleeing a dinner in despair. There can be no doubt about her actions or motivation, which makes me wonder at my captor's. Was his offer just another torment, a sliver of hope to go mad chasing?

What about the graveyard? The gun?

If Evelyn were truly so despondent, why did she seem in such good cheer when she accompanied Bell into the graveyard, less than two hours after dinner? And what about the gun she was carrying? It was a large black revolver, almost too big for her purse. The gun she used to take her life was a silver pistol. Why would she change weapons?

I don't know how long I sit there thinking about it, amid the delighted mourners, but the police never come.

The crowds thin and the candles gutter; the party flickers and goes out.

The last thing I see before falling asleep in my chair is the image of Michael Hardcastle, kneeling on the grass, cradling the dripping-wet body of his dead sister.

~ 21 ~

DAY TWO (CONTINUED)

Pain stirs me, every breath painful. Blinking away the tatters of sleep, I see a white wall, white sheets, and a blossom of crusted blood on the pillow. My cheek is resting on my hand, saliva sticking my top lip to my knuckles.

I know this moment. I saw it through Bell's eyes.

I'm in the butler again, after he was moved to the gatehouse.

Somebody's pacing beside my bed, a maid judging by the black dress and white apron. There's a large book held open in her arms, which she's flipping through furiously. My head's too heavy to see anything above her waist, so I groan to call her over.

"Oh, good, you're awake," she says, halting her pacing. "When's Ravencourt going to be alone? You didn't write it down, but the bloody idiot has his valet nosing around the kitchen—"

"Who are—" My throat is clogged with blood and phlegm.

There's a jug of water on the sideboard, and the maid hurries over to pour me some, placing her book on the counter, while she tips a glass to my lips. I move my head a fraction, trying to look up at her face, but the world immediately starts to spin.

"You shouldn't talk," she says, using her apron to wipe a stray drop of water from my chin.

She pauses.

"I mean you can talk, but only when you're ready."

She pauses again.

"Actually, I really need you to answer my question about Ravencourt, before he gets me killed."

"Who are you?" I croak.

"How hard did that ape... Wait." She lowers her face to my own, her brown eyes searching for something. She's puffy-cheeked and pale with strands of tangled blond hair straying free from her cap. With a start, I realize this is the maid Bell and Evelyn met, the one who was keeping watch on the butler.

"How many hosts have you had?" she asks.

"I don't—"

"How many hosts?" she insists, sitting on the edge of the bed. "How many bodies have you been in?"

"You're Anna," I say, twisting my neck to get a better look at her, the pain setting fire to my bones. Very gently she presses me back down onto the mattress.

"Yes, I'm Anna," she says patiently. "How many hosts?"

Tears of joy prod my eyes, affection washing through me like warm water. Even though I can't remember this woman, I can feel the years of friendship between us, a trust that borders on instinct. More than that, I'm overcome by the simple joy of this reunion. As strange as it is to say about somebody I can't remember, I now realize I've missed her.

Seeing the emotion on my face, answering tears form in Anna's eyes, and leaning down, she hugs me gently.

"I've missed you too," she says, voicing my feeling.

We stay like that for a while, before she clears her throat and wipes the tears away.

"Well, that's enough of that." She sniffs. "Crying on each other isn't going to help. I need you to tell me about your hosts or crying's all we'll do."

"I...I..." I'm struggling to speak through the lump in my throat. "I woke up as Bell, then the butler, Donald Davies, Ravencourt, and now—"

"The butler again," she says thoughtfully. "Third time's a charm, ain't it?"

Stroking a lock of disturbed hair from my forehead, she leans closer.

"I take it we haven't been introduced yet, or at least you haven't been introduced to me," she says. "My name's Anna and you're Aiden Bishop, or have we done that part already? You keep arriving in the wrong order. I never know where we're up to."

"You've met my other selves?"

"They pop in and out," she says, glancing at the door as voices sound somewhere in the house. "Usually with a favor to ask."

"What about your hosts? Are they—"

"I don't have other hosts. It's just me," she says. "No visits from a Plague Doctor. No other days neither. I won't remember any of this tomorrow, which seems a bit of luck given how today's going so far."

"But you know what's happening, you know about Evelyn's suicide?"

"It's murder, and I woke up knowing," she says, straightening my sheets. "Couldn't remember my own name, but I knew yours and I knew there was no escaping until we took the killer's name, and proof of their guilt, to the lake at 11:00 p.m. They're rules, I think. Words scraped onto my brain so I don't forget."

"I didn't remember anything when I woke up," I respond, trying to understand why our torments would be different. "Aside from your name, the Plague Doctor had to tell me everything."

"'Course he did. You're his special project," she says, adjusting my pillow. "Doesn't give a rat's fart about what I'm doing. Haven't heard a peep out of him all day. Won't leave you alone, though. Surprised he's not waiting under that bed."

"He told me only one of us can escape," I say.

"Yeah, and it's pretty bloody obvious he wants it to be you," she says, the anger draining from her voice as quickly as it came. She shakes her head. "Sorry, I shouldn't be taking any of this out on you, but I can't shift the feeling he's up to something, and I don't like it."

"I know what you mean," I say. "But if only one of us can escape—"

"Why are we helping each other?" she interrupts. "Because you've got a plan to get us both out."

"I do?"

"Well, you said you did."

For the first time, her confidence falters, a worried frown appearing on her face, but before I can press the issue, wood creaks in the corridor, steps thumping up the stairs. It feels like the entire house is shaking with their ascent.

"Just a tick," she says, collecting the book from the counter. Only now do I realize it's actually an artist's sketchbook, the brown leather covers filled with sheets of loose-leaf paper, untidily bound by string. Hiding the book under the bed, she comes up instead with a shotgun. Pressing the butt against her shoulder, she stalks over to the door, opening it a crack to better hear the commotion outside.

"Oh hell," says Anna, kicking the door closed with her foot. "It's the doctor with your sedative. Quick, when's Ravencourt going to be alone? I need to tell him to stop searching for me."

"Why? Who's—"

"We don't have time, Aiden," she says, sliding the shotgun back under the bed out of sight. "I'll be here next time you wake up, and we can have a proper talk then, I promise, but for now, tell me about Ravencourt, every detail you can remember."

She's leaning over me, clutching my hand, her eyes pleading.

"He'll be in his parlor at 1:15 p.m.," I say. "You hand him a whiskey, have a chat, and then Millicent Derby arrives. You leave him a card introducing her."

She squeezes her eyes shut, mouthing the time and name over and over again, carving them into her memory. Only now, her features smoothed by concentration, do I realize how young she is; no more than nineteen I'd guess, though hard labor's added a few years to the pile.

"One more thing," she hisses, cupping my cheek, her face so close to mine I can see the amber flecks in her brown eyes. "If you see me out there, pretend you don't know me. Don't even come near me if you can help it. There's this footman... I'll tell you about him later, or earlier. Point is, it's dangerous for us to be seen together. Any talking needs doing, we'll do it in here."

She kisses me on the forehead quickly, offering the room a last glance to make sure everything's in order.

The steps have reached the hall, two sets of voices jumbled up and rolling on ahead. I recognize Dickie, but not the second one. It's deep, urgent, though I can't quite make out what's being said.

"Who's with Dickie?" I ask.

"Lord Hardcastle, most like," she says. "He's been popping in and out all morning to check on you."

That makes sense. Evelyn told me the butler was Lord Hardcastle's batman during the war. Their closeness is the reason Gregory Gold is strung up in the room opposite.

"Are things always like this?" I ask. "The explanations arriving before the questions?"

"I wouldn't know," she says, standing up and smoothing her apron. "Two hours, I've been at this, and all *I've* had are orders."

Doctor Dickie opens the door, his mustache just as preposterous as the first time I saw it. His gaze passes from Anna to myself and back again as he tries to stitch together the torn edges of our hastily severed conversation. No answers forthcoming, he places his black medical bag on the sideboard and comes to stand over me.

"Awake I see," he says, rocking back and forth on his heels, fingers thrust into the watch pockets of his waistcoat.

"Leave us, girl," he says to Anna, who curtsies before exiting the room, casting me a quick glance on her way out.

"So, how are you feeling?" he asks. "No worse for wear from the carriage journey, I hope."

"Not bad—" I begin to say, but he lifts the covers, raising my arm to take my pulse. Even this gentle action is enough to cause spasms of pain, the rest of my response mangled by a wince.

"Little sore, hmmm," he says, lowering my arm once more. "Hardly surprising given the beating you took. Any notion what this fellow Gregory Gold wanted from you?"

"I don't. Must have mistook me for somebody else, sir."

The "sir" isn't my doing. It's an old habit of the butler's, and I'm surprised by how easily it arrived on my tongue.

The doctor's shrewd gaze holds my explanation up to the light, poking a dozen different holes in it. The tight smile he flashes me is one of complicity, both reassuring and a touch threatening. Whatever happened in that hallway, the seemingly benign Doctor Dickie knows more about it than he's letting on.

There's a click as he opens his bag, withdrawing a brown bottle and a hypodermic syringe. Keeping his eyes on me, he pokes the needle through the bottle's wax seal, filling the hypodermic with a clear liquid.

My hand clutches the sheets.

"I'm fine, Doctor. Honestly," I say.

"Yes, that's rather my concern," he says, jabbing the needle into my neck before I have a chance to argue.

A warm liquid floods my veins, drowning my thoughts. The doctor melts, colors blossoming and fading into darkness.

"Sleep, Roger," he says. "I'll deal with Mr. Gold."

～ 22 ～

DAY FIVE

Coughing up a lungful of cigar smoke, I open a new pair of eyes to find myself almost fully clothed on wooden floorboards, one hand lying victorious on an untouched bed. My trousers are around my ankles, a bottle of brandy clutched to my stomach. Clearly an attempt was made at undressing last night, but such a course appears to have been beyond my new host, whose breath stinks like an old beer mat.

Groaning, I claw my way up the side of the bed, dislodging a throbbing headache that nearly knocks me to the floor again.

I'm in a similar bedroom to the one Bell was given, the embers of last night's fire winking at me from the grate. The curtains are open, the sky sagging with early morning light.

Evelyn's in the forest. You need to find her.

Hoisting my trousers up to my waist, I stumble over to the mirror to better inspect this fool I now inhabit.

I nearly run straight into it.

After being shackled to Ravencourt for so long, this new chap feels weightless, a leaf being blown about by a breeze. It's not too surprising when I see him in the glass. He's short and slight, somewhere in his late twenties, with longish brown hair and bloodshot blue eyes above a neatly trimmed beard. I try out his smile, discovering a row of slightly awkward white teeth.

It's the face of a rascal.

My possessions are sitting in a pile on the bedside table, an invitation addressed to Jonathan Derby on top. At least I know who to curse for this hangover. I sift through the items with a fingertip, uncovering a pocketknife, a weathered hip flask, a wristwatch showing 8:43 a.m., and three brown vials with cork stoppers and no labels. Yanking a cork loose, I sniff the liquid within, my stomach twisting at the sickly sweet scent that drifts out.

This must be the laudanum Bell was selling.

I can see why it's so popular. Simply sniffing the stuff has filled my mind with bright lights.

There's a jug of cold water beside a small sink in the corner, and stripping naked, I wash off last night's sweat and grime, digging out the person beneath. What's left of the water I tip to my mouth, drinking until my belly sloshes. Unfortunately, my attempts to drown the hangover only dilute it, aches seeping into every bone and muscle.

It's a foul morning, so I dress in the thickest clothes I can find: hunting tweeds and a heavy black coat that trails along the floor as I leave the bedroom.

Despite the early hour, a drunken couple is squabbling at the top of the stairs. They're in last night's evening wear, drinks still clutched in their hands, accusations passed back and forth in escalating voices, and I give their flailing arms a wide berth as I walk by. Their bickering chases me into the entrance hall, which has been upended by the previous evening's escapades. Bow ties are dangling from the chandelier, leaves and shards of a smashed decanter littering the marble floor. Two maids are cleaning it up, leaving me to wonder what it must have looked like before they started.

I try asking them where Charlie Carver's cottage is located, but they're mute as sheep, lowering their eyes and shaking their heads in response to my questions.

Their silence is maddening.

If Lucy Harper's gossip isn't too far from the mark, Evelyn's going to be somewhere near the cottage with her lady's maid when she's attacked. If I can discover who's threatening her, perhaps I can save her life and escape this house all at the same time—though I have no clue as to how I'm going to help free Anna as well. She's put aside her own schemes to aid me, believing I have some plan that will free us both. For the moment, I can't see how that's anything other than a hollow promise, and judging by her worried frown when we talked in the gatehouse, she's beginning to suspect as much.

My only hope is that my future hosts are a great deal cleverer than my previous ones.

Further questioning of the maids drives them deeper into their silence, forcing me to look around for help. The rooms either side of the entrance hall are deathly quiet, the house still knee-deep in last night, and seeing no other option, I pick my way through the broken glass and head belowstairs toward the kitchen.

The passage to the kitchen is grimier than I remember, the clatter of dishes and smell of roasting meat knocking me sick. Servants eye me as they pass, turning their heads away whenever I open my mouth to ask a question. It's clear they think I shouldn't be here and just as clear they don't know how to get rid of me. This is their place, a river of unguarded conversations and giggling gossip flowing beneath the house. I sully it with my presence.

Agitation rubs me up and down, blood thumping in my ears. I feel tired and raw, the air made of sandpaper.

"Can I help you?" says a voice behind me.

The words are rolled up and flung at my back.

I turn to find the cook, Mrs. Drudge, staring up at me, ample hands on ample hips. Through these eyes she looks like something a child might make out of clay, a small head on a misshapen body, her features pressed into her face by clumsy thumbs. She's stern, no trace of the woman who's going to give the butler a warm scone in a few hours' time.

"I'm looking for Evelyn Hardcastle," I say, meeting her fierce gaze. "She went for a walk in the forest with Madeline Aubert, her lady's maid."

"And what's that to you?"

Her tone is so abrupt I almost recoil. Clenching my hands, I try to keep hold of my rising temper. The servants crane their necks as they scurry by, desperate for theater, but terrified of the star.

"Somebody means her harm," I say through gritted teeth. "If you'll point me toward Charlie Carver's old cottage, I'll be able to warn her."

"Is that what you were doing with Madeline last night? Warning her? Is that how her blouse got torn? Is that why she was crying?"

A vein pulses in her forehead, indignation bubbling beneath every word. She takes a step forward, jabbing a finger into my chest as she speaks.

"I know what—" she says.

White-hot anger explodes out of me. Without thinking, I slap her across the face and shove her backward, advancing on her with the devil's own wrath.

"Tell me where she's gone!" I scream, spittle flying out of my mouth.

Squeezing her bloody lips together, Mrs. Drudge glowers at me.

My hands ball into fists.

Walk away.

Walk away now.

Summoning my will, I turn my back on Mrs. Drudge, stalking up the suddenly silent passage. Servants leap aside as I pass, but my rage can't make sense of anything but itself.

Turning a corner, I slump against a wall and let out a long breath. My hands are trembling, the fog in my mind clearing. For those few terrifying seconds, Derby was utterly beyond my control. That was his poison spilling out of my mouth, his bile coursing through my veins. I can feel it still. Oil on my skin, needles in my bones, a yearning to do something dreadful. Whatever happens today, I need to keep tight hold of my temper or this creature is going to slip loose again, and goodness knows what he'll do.

And that's the truly scary part.

My hosts can fight back.

Mud sucks at my boots as I hurry into the gloom of the trees, desperation tugging me along by a leash. After my failure to glean any information in the kitchen, I'm striking out into the forest in hopes of stumbling upon Evelyn along one of the marked trails. I'm counting on endeavor succeeding where calculation has failed. Even if it doesn't, I need to put some distance between Derby and the temptations of Blackheath.

I've not gone far when the red flags bring me to a stream, water surging around a large rock. A smashed wine bottle is half-encased in sludge, beside a thick black overcoat, Bell's silver compass having fallen out of the pocket. Plucking it from the mud, I turn it over in my palm just as I did that first morning, my fingers tracing the initials *SB* engraved on the underside of the lid. Sebastian Bell's initials. What a fool I felt when Daniel pointed that out to me. Half a dozen cigarette butts lay discarded on the ground, suggesting Bell stood here for a little while, probably waiting for somebody. This must have been where he came after receiving the note at the dinner table, though what could have driven him into the rain and cold at such an hour I cannot fathom. Searching his discarded coat offers no clues, his pockets turning up nothing but a lonely silver key, probably to his trunk.

Wary of losing more time to my former host, I drop the key and compass into my pocket and set out in search of the next red flag, keeping my eyes open for any hint of the footman at my heels. This would be the perfect place for him to strike.

God only knows how long I walk before I finally stumble upon the ruins of what must be Charlie Carver's old cottage. Fire has hollowed it out, consuming most of the roof, leaving only the four blackened walls. Debris crunches underfoot as I step inside, startling some rabbits who flee into the woods, their fur stained with wet ash. The skeletal remnants of an old bed are slumped in the corner, a solitary table leg on the floor, the detritus of a life interrupted. Evelyn told me the cottage burst into flames the day the police hanged Carver.

More likely Lord and Lady Hardcastle threw their memories onto the pyre and lit it themselves.

Who could blame them? Carver stole their son's life by a lake. It seems only fitting they should rid themselves of him with fire.

A rotten fence marks out the garden around the back of the cottage, most of the slats having collapsed after years of neglect. Great piles of purple and yellow flowers run wild in every direction, red berries dangling from stems winding up the fence posts.

A maid emerges from the trees as I kneel to tie my shoelace.

Such terror I hope never to see again.

Color drains from her face, her basket dropping on the floor, spilling mushrooms in every direction.

"Are you Madeline?" I begin, but she's already backing away, looking around for help. "I'm not here to hurt you. I'm trying to—"

She's gone before I can utter another word, bolting into the forest. Snared by weeds, I stagger after her, half falling over the fence.

Picking myself up, I catch sight of her through the trees, glimpses of a black dress moving far more quickly than I would have reckoned. I call out, but if anything my voice is the whip at her back, driving her forward. Even so, I'm faster and stronger, and though I don't wish to frighten the girl, I *cannot* lose sight of her for fear of what will happen to Evelyn.

"Anna!" Bell calls out from somewhere nearby.

"Help me!" Madeline screams back, panicked and sobbing.

She's so close now. I reach out, hoping to tug her back, but my fingers can only brush the material of her dress, and off-balance, I lose ground.

She ducks to avoid a branch, stumbling ever so slightly. I catch hold of her dress, causing her to scream again, before a shot whistles by my face, cracking into a tree behind me.

Surprise loosens my grip on Madeline, who stumbles toward Evelyn as she emerges from the forest. The black revolver she will take to the graveyard is in her hands, but it's not nearly as terrifying as the fury on her face. One wrong step and she'll shoot me dead. I'm certain of it.

"It's not what... I can explain," I pant, hands on my knees.

"Men like you always can," says Evelyn, sweeping the terrified girl behind her with one arm.

Madeline's sobbing, her entire body shaking violently. God help me, but Derby enjoys this. He's aroused by the fear. He's done this before.

"All this...please... It's a misunderstanding," I gasp, taking an imploring step forward.

"Stay back, Jonathan," says Evelyn fiercely, gripping the revolver with both hands. "Stay away from this girl, stay away from all of them."

"I didn't mean to—"

"Your mother's a friend of the family. That's the only reason I'm letting you walk away," interrupts Evelyn. "But if I see you near another woman, if I even hear about it, I swear I'll put a bullet in you."

Taking care to keep the gun trained on me, she removes her coat and wraps it around Madeline's heaving shoulders.

"You're going to stay by my side today," she whispers to the terrified maid. "I'll see no harm comes to you."

They stumble off through the trees, leaving me alone in the forest. Tipping my head to the sky, I suck in cold air, hoping the rain on my face will cool my frustration. I came here to prevent somebody attacking Evelyn, believing I'd unearth a murderer in the process. Instead, I caused the very thing I was trying to stop. I'm chasing my own tail, terrifying an innocent woman in the process. Maybe Daniel was right, maybe the future isn't a promise we can break.

"You're dawdling again," says the Plague Doctor from behind me.

He's standing on the far side of the clearing, little more than a shadow. As always, he seems to have picked the perfect position. Far enough away that I can't possibly reach him, but close enough that we can talk with relative ease.

"I thought I was helping," I say bitterly, still stung by what happened.

"You still can," he says. "Sebastian Bell is lost in the woods."

Of course. I'm not here for Evelyn, I'm here for Bell. I'm here to make sure the loop begins again. Fate's leading me around by the nose.

Removing the compass from my pocket, I hold it in the palm of my hand, remembering the uncertainty I felt as I followed its quivering needle that first morning. Without this, Bell will almost certainly remain lost.

I toss it into the mud at the Plague Doctor's feet.

"This is how I change things," I say, walking away. "Fetch him yourself."

"You misunderstand my purpose here," he says, the sharpness of his tone bringing me up short. "If you leave Sebastian Bell to wander that forest alone, he'll never meet Evelyn Hardcastle. He'll never form the friendship you prize so highly. Abandon him and he won't care about saving her."

"Are you saying I'll forget her?" I ask, alarmed.

"I'm saying you should be careful which knots you unpick," he says. "If you abandon Bell, you'll also be abandoning Evelyn. It will be cruelty without purpose, and nothing I've seen of you so far suggests you're a cruel man."

Perhaps I imagine it, but for the first time, there's a touch of warmth in his tone. It's enough to unbalance me, and I turn to face him once more.

"I need to see this day changed," I say, hearing the desperation in my voice. "I need to see that it can be done."

"Your frustration is understandable, but what use is rearranging the furniture if you burn the house down doing it?"

Bending over, he retrieves the compass from the ground, wiping the mud from its surface with his fingers. The way he groans and the heaviness of his limbs as he rises suggest an older man beneath the costume. Satisfied with his work, he tosses the compass to me, the damn thing nearly slipping from my hands so wet is its surface.

"Take this, and solve Evelyn's murder."

"She committed suicide. I watched her with my own eyes."

"If you think it's that simple, you're much further behind than I thought."

"And you're much crueler than *I* thought," I growl. "If you know what's happening here, why not stop it? Why play these games? Hang the murderer before he harms her."

"An interesting idea, except I don't know who the murderer is."

"How is that possible?" I say, incredulously. "You know every step I'm going to take before I think to take it. How could you be blind to the most important fact in this house?"

"Because it's not my place to know. I watch you, and you watch Evelyn Hardcastle. We both have our roles to play."

"Then I could blame anybody for the crime," I cry, throwing my hands in the air. "Helena Hardcastle did it. There, you see! Free me!"

"You forget that I need proof. Not merely your good word."

"And what if I save her, what then?"

"I don't think it's possible, and I think you'll hamper your investigation trying, but my offer stands regardless. Evelyn was murdered last night and every night prior. Even if you could save her tonight, it doesn't change that. Bring me the name of the person who kills, or is planning to kill, Evelyn Hardcastle, and I'll free you."

For the second time since arriving in Blackheath, I find myself holding a compass and contemplating the instructions of somebody I can't trust. To do as the Plague Doctor asks is to give myself to a day determined to kill Evelyn, but there seems no way to change things without making them worse. Assuming he's telling the truth, I either save my first host, or I abandon Evelyn.

"You doubt my intentions?" he says, prickling at my hesitation.

"Of course I doubt your intentions. You wear a mask and you talk in riddles, and I don't for a minute believe you brought me here just to solve a mystery. You're hiding something."

"And you think stripping me of my disguise will reveal it?" he scoffs. "A face is a mask of another sort. You know that better than most. Though you're right—I am hiding something. If it makes you feel better, I'm not hiding it from you. Should you somehow succeed and tear this mask free, I'd simply be replaced, and your task would remain. I'll let you decide if that's worth the trouble. As for your presence in Blackheath, perhaps it would assuage your doubts to know the name of the man who brought you here."

"And what's that?"

"Aiden Bishop," he says. "Unlike your rivals, you came to Blackheath voluntarily. Everything that's happening today, you brought upon yourself."

His voice suggests regret, but the expressionless white mask makes the statement sinister, a parody of sadness.

"That can't be true," I say stubbornly. "Why would I come here of my own free will? Why would anybody do this to himself?"

"Your life before Blackheath is none of my concern, Mr. Bishop. Solve the murder of Evelyn Hardcastle and you'll have all the answers you require," he says. "In the meantime, Bell needs your help." He points behind me. "He's that way."

Without another word he withdraws into the forest, the dimness swallowing him completely. My mind is clogged up by a hundred small questions, but none of them is going to do me any good in this forest, so I push them to one side and go in search of Bell, finding him bent double and trembling with exertion. He freezes as I approach, catching the sound of twigs cracking beneath my feet.

His timidity revolts me.

Mistaken as she was, at least Madeline had the good sense to flee.

I circle around behind my former self, keeping my face from view. I could try to explain what's happening here, but frightened rabbits make poor allies, especially those already convinced you're a murderer.

All I need from Bell is his survival.

Two more steps and I'm behind him, leaning close enough to whisper into his ear. Sweat pours off his body, the smell like a filthy rag pushed to my face. It's all I can do to speak without gagging.

"East," I say, dropping the compass into his pocket.

Backing away, I head into the trees, toward Carver's burned-out cottage. Bell's going to be lost for another hour or so, giving me plenty of time to follow the flags back to the house without stumbling into him.

Despite my best efforts, everything's happening exactly as I remember it.

~ 24 ~

The looming shape of Blackheath appears through the gaps in the trees. I've come out around the back of the house, which is in an even worse state of disrepair than the front. Several windows are cracked, the brickwork crumbling. A stone balustrade has tumbled from the roof to lodge itself in the grass, thick moss covering it. Clearly, the Hardcastles only repaired the sections of the house their guests would see—little wonder considering the paucity of their finances.

Just as I lingered on the edge of the forest that first morning, I now find myself crossing the garden with similar foreboding. If I came here voluntarily, I must have had a reason, but no matter how hard I strain for the memory, it's beyond reach.

I'd like to believe I'm a good man who came to help, but if that's the case, I'm making a damn mess of things. Tonight, as every night, Evelyn's going to kill herself, and if this morning's actions are any guide, my attempts to paddle away from the disaster may only hurry us toward it. For all I know, my fumbling attempts to save Evelyn are actually the reason she ends up at that reflecting pool with a silver pistol in her hand.

I'm so lost in these thoughts I don't notice Millicent until I'm almost on top of her. The old lady is shivering on an iron bench that looks out across the garden, her arms folded against the wind. Three shapeless coats encase her completely, her eyes peering out over a scarf pulled up above her mouth. She's blue with cold, a hat pulled down over her ears. Hearing my steps, she turns to meet me, surprise showing on her wrinkled face.

"By Jove, you look dreadful," she says, pulling the scarf down from her mouth.

"Good morning to you too, Millicent," I say, taken aback by the sudden surge of warmth her presence stokes within me.

"Millicent?" she says, pursing her lips. "That's rather modern of you, dear. I prefer 'Mother,' if it's all the same to you. I wouldn't want people thinking I picked you up off the street. Though sometimes I wonder if I mightn't have been better off."

My mouth hangs open. I hadn't previously made the connection between Jonathan Derby and Millicent Derby, probably because it's easier to imagine him being delivered onto this earth by a biblical plague.

"Sorry, Mother," I say, stuffing my hands into my pockets and sitting down beside her.

She cocks an eyebrow at me, those clever gray eyes alight with amusement.

"An apology and an appearance before midday. Are you feeling quite all right?" she asks.

"It must be the country air," I say. "What about you? Why are you out on this dreadful morning?"

She grunts, hugging herself even tighter. "I'm supposed to be going for a stroll with Helena, but I've seen neither hide nor hair of the woman. No doubt she's got her times wrong as usual. I know she's meeting Cecil Ravencourt this afternoon. She's probably gone there instead."

"She hasn't," I say. "Ravencourt's still asleep."

Millicent peers at me inquisitively.

"Cunningham told me. Ravencourt's valet," I lie.

"You know him?"

"Vaguely."

"Well, I wouldn't get too friendly," she tuts. "I understand how much you enjoy dubious society, but from what Cecil's told me, this one's most unsuitable, even by your low standards."

That piques my interest. I'm fond of the valet, but he only agreed to help me after I threatened to blackmail him with a secret he's keeping. Until I know what he's hiding, I can't depend on him, and Millicent might be the key to unearthing it.

"How so?" I ask causally.

"Oh, I don't know," she says, waving an airy hand at me. "You know Cecil, secrets tucked between every fold of skin. If you believe the rumors, he only hired Cunningham because Helena asked him to. Now, he's discovered something unsavory about the boy and is thinking of letting him go."

"Unsavory?" I say.

"Well, that's what Cecil said, not that I could get the rest out of him. Blasted fellow has a bear trap for a mouth, but you know how he hates scandal. Given Cunningham's parentage, it must be desperately salacious if he's worried. Wish I knew what it was."

"Cunningham's parentage?" I ask, feeling a quiver of excitement. "I think I've missed a step."

"The boy was raised at Blackheath," she says. "Cook's son, or that's the story at least."

"It's not true?"

The old lady cackles, looking at me slyly.

"Word has it the Honorable Lord Peter Hardcastle used to enjoy himself in London from time to time. Well, on one occasion his enjoyment followed him back to Blackheath with a baby in her arms, which she claimed was his. Peter was ready to send the child to the church, but Helena stepped in and demanded they keep it."

"Why would she do that?"

"Knowing Helena, she probably meant it as an insult," sniffs Millicent, turning her face away from the bitter wind. "She was never very fond of her husband, and inviting his shame into the house would have tickled her. Poor Peter has probably cried himself to sleep every night for the last thirty-three years. Either way, they gave the baby to Mrs. Drudge, the cook, to raise, and Helena made sure everybody knew whose child he was."

"Does Cunningham know any of this?"

"Can't see how he wouldn't; it's one of those secrets people shout at each other," says the old lady, plucking a handkerchief from her sleeve to wipe her running nose. "Anyway, you can ask him yourself seeing as you're so chummy. Shall we walk? I see little point in us freezing on this bench waiting for a woman who isn't coming."

She stands before I have a chance to respond, stamping her boots and blowing warm air into her gloved hands. It really is a dreadful day, the gray sky spitting rain, lathering itself into the fury of a storm.

"Why are you even out here?" I ask, our feet crunching along the gravel path that circles the house. "Couldn't you have met Lady Hardcastle inside?"

"Too many people I'd rather not bump into," she says.

Why was she in the kitchen this morning?

"Speaking of bumping into people, I hear you were in the kitchen this morning," I say.

She bridles. "Who told you that?"

"Well—"

"I haven't been anywhere near the kitchen," she continues, not waiting for a response. "Filthy places. The smell doesn't come out for weeks."

She seems genuinely irritated by the suggestion, which means she probably hasn't done it yet. A moment later she nudges me good-naturedly, her voice suddenly gleeful. "Did you hear about Donald Davies? Apparently he took an automobile last night and ran off back to London. The stable master saw him, said he turned up in the pouring rain, dressed in every color under the sun."

That brings me pause. Surely, I should have returned to Donald Davies by now, as I have done with the butler. He was my third host, and Anna told me I'm obliged to live one full day in each of them, whether I want it or not. It can't have been much past midmorning when I left him asleep on that road, so why haven't I seen him again?

You left him defenseless and alone.

I feel a ripple of guilt. For all I know, the footman has already found him.

"Are you listening to me?" says Millicent, annoyed. "I said Donald Davies took off in an automobile. They're cracked that family, every one of them, and that's an official medical opinion."

"You've been talking to Dickie," I say absently, still thinking about Davies.

"Been talked at, more like," she scoffs. "Thirty minutes I spent trying to keep my eyes off that mustache. I'm surprised sound can penetrate it."

That makes me laugh.

"Do you actually like anybody at Blackheath, Mother?" I say, my good cheer returning.

"Not that I recall, but it's envy I suspect. Society's a dance darling, and I'm too old to take part. Speaking of dancing, here comes the organ grinder himself."

I follow her gaze to see Daniel approaching us from the opposite direction. Despite the cold, he's dressed in a cricket sweater and linen trousers, the same outfit he'll be wearing when he encounters Bell in the entrance hall for the first time. I check my watch. That meeting can't be far off.

"Mr. Coleridge," calls out Millicent with forced bonhomie.

"Mrs. Derby," he says, drawing alongside us. "Broken any hearts this morning?"

"They don't even quiver these days, Mr. Coleridge. More's the pity." There's something cautious in her tone, as if she's crossing a bridge she feels certain will break. "What disreputable business brings you out on such a terrible morning?"

"I've a favor to ask your son, and I assure you, it's entirely aboveboard."

"Well, that's disappointing."

"For you and me both." He looks at me for the first time. "A minute, Derby?"

We step aside, Millicent doing her best to appear uninterested, while shooting us speculative glances from above her scarf.

"What's wrong?" I ask.

"I'm going after the footman," he says, that handsome face of his caught somewhere between fear and excitement.

"How?" I say, immediately taken with the idea.

"We know he's going to be in the dining hall tormenting Ravencourt around 1:00 p.m.," he says. "I propose catching hold of the dog there."

Recalling those ghostly steps and that evil laughter is enough to raise goose bumps on my neck, and the thought of finally laying hands on the devil sets fire to my veins. The ferocity of the feeling isn't far off what Derby felt in the forest, when we were chasing the maid, and it immediately puts me on my guard. I can't give this host an inch.

"What's your scheme?" I say, tempering my enthusiasm. "I was in that room alone. I couldn't even guess at where he was hiding."

"Nor could I, until I got talking to an old friend of the Hardcastles at dinner last night," he says, drawing me a little farther away from Millicent who's managed to sidle onto the edge of our conversation. "Turns out there's a warren of priest tunnels beneath the floorboards. That's where the footman was hiding, and that's where we'll put an end to him."

"How?"

"My new friend tells me there are entrances in the library, drawing room, and gallery. I suggest we each watch an entrance and grab him when he comes out."

"Sounds ideal," I say, struggling to contain Derby's rising excitement. "I'll take the library; you take the drawing room. Who's in the gallery?"

"Ask Anna," he says. "But none of us is strong enough to tackle the footman alone. Why don't you two guard the library, and I'll round up some of our other hosts to help me with the drawing room and gallery?"

"Magnificent," I say, beaming.

If I didn't have a hand on Derby's lead, he'd already be running toward the tunnels with a lantern and a kitchen knife.

"Good," he says, lavishing a smile of such affection upon me it's impossible to imagine how we could ever fail. "Take your position a few minutes before one. With any luck, this will all be over by dinner."

He turns to depart, but I catch his arm.

"Did you tell Anna you'd find a way for both of us to escape if she helped us?" I ask.

He gazes at me steadily, and I quickly withdraw my hand.

"Yes," he says.

"It's a lie, isn't it?" I say. "Only one of us can escape Blackheath."

"Let's call it a potential lie, shall we? I've not given up hope of fulfilling our end of the bargain."

"You're my last host. How much hope do you have?"

"Not a great deal," he says, his expression softening. "I know you're fond of her. Believe me, I haven't forgotten how that felt, but we need her on our side. We won't escape this house if we have to spend the day looking over our shoulder for both the footman *and* Anna."

"I have to tell her the truth," I say, aghast at his callous disregard of my friend.

He stiffens.

"Do that and you make an enemy of her," he hisses, looking around to make sure we're not being overheard. "At which point, any hope of genuinely helping her goes up in smoke."

Puffing out his cheeks, he ruffles his hair and smiles at me, agitation leaking out of him like air from a punctured balloon.

"Do what you think is right," he says. "But at least wait until we've caught the footman." He checks his watch. "Three more hours, that's all I'm asking."

Our eyes meet, mine doubtful and his appealing. I can't help but submit.

"Very well," I say.

"You won't regret it," he says.

Squeezing my shoulder, he waves cheerily at Millicent, before striding back toward Blackheath, a man possessed by purpose.

I turn to find Millicent contemplating me through pursed lips.

"You have some rotten friends," she says.

"I'm a rotten sort of chap," I respond, holding her gaze, until finally she shakes her head and carries on walking, slowing enough for me to fall in step beside her. We come upon a long greenhouse. Most of the windowpanes are cracked, the plants inside so overgrown they're bulging against the glass. Millicent peers inside, but the foliage is much too dense. Gesturing for me to follow, we head to the far end, finding the doors locked with a new chain and padlock.

"Pity," she says, rattling it futilely. "I used to love coming here when I was younger."

"You've visited Blackheath before?"

"I summered here when I was girl. We all did: Cecil Ravencourt, the Curtis twins, Peter Hardcastle, and Helena—that's how they met. When I married, I brought your brother and sister down. They practically grew up with Evelyn, Michael, and Thomas."

She links my arm, continuing our walk.

"Oh, I used to love those summers," she says. "Helena was always frightfully jealous of your sister, because Evelyn was so plain. Michael wasn't much better mind, with that squashed face of his. Thomas was the only one with a dash of beauty and he ended up in that lake, which strikes me as fate kicking the poor woman twice, but there it is. Wasn't a one of them could measure up to you, my handsome lad," she says, cupping my cheek.

"Evelyn turned out all right," I protest. "She's quite striking actually."

"Really?" says Millicent disbelievingly. "Must have blossomed in Paris, not that I'd know. The girl's been avoiding me all morning. Like mother, like daughter, I suppose. Explains why Cecil's circling, though. Vainest man I've ever met, which is saying something after fifty years of living with your father."

"The Hardcastles hate her, you know. Evelyn, I mean."

"Who's filled you head with that rot?" says Millicent, gripping my arm while she shakes her foot, trying to dislodge some mud from her boot. "Michael adores her. He's over in Paris almost every month, and from what I understand, they've been thick as thieves since she got back. And Peter doesn't hate her; he's indifferent. It's only Helena, and she's never been quite right since Thomas died. Still comes up here, you know. Every year on the anniversary of his death, she takes a walk around the lake, even talks to him sometimes. Heard her myself."

The path has brought us to the reflecting pool. This is where Evelyn will take her life tonight, and as with everything at Blackheath, its beauty is dependent on distance. Viewed from the ballroom, the reflecting pool's a magnificent sight, a long mirror conveying all the drama of the house. Here and now, though, it's just a filthy pond, the stone cracked, moss growing thick as carpet on the surface.

Why take her life here? Why not in her bedroom or the entrance hall?

"Are you okay, dear?" asks Millicent. "You look a little pale."

"I was thinking it's a shame they've let the place go," I say, hoisting a smile onto my face.

"Oh, I know, but what could they do?" she says, adjusting her scarf. "After the murder they couldn't live here, and nobody wants these big piles anymore, especially not when they have Blackheath's history. Should have left it to the forest, if you ask me."

It's a maudlin thought, but nothing lingers in Jonathan Derby's mind for too long, and I'm soon distracted by the preparations for tonight's party, which I can see through the ballroom windows beside us. Servants and workmen are scrubbing the floors and painting the walls, while maids balance on teetering stepladders with long feather dusters. At the far end of the hall, bored-looking musicians are scraping semiquavers off the surface of their polished instruments as Evelyn Hardcastle points and gesticulates, arranging things from the center of the room. She's flitting from group to group, touching arms and spreading kindness, making me ache for that afternoon we spent together.

I search for Madeline Aubert, finding her laughing with Lucy Harper—the maid abused by Stanwin and befriended by Ravencourt—the two of them arranging a chaise longue by the stage. That these two mistreated women have found each other brings me a small measure of comfort, though it by no means alleviates my guilt over this morning's events.

"I told you last time I wouldn't clean up another of your indiscretions," says Millicent sharply, her entire body stiff.

She's watching me watching the maids. Loathing and love swirl within her eyes, the shape of Derby's secrets visible in the fog. What I'd only vaguely understood before, now stands in stark relief. Derby's a rapist, more than once over. They're all there, held in Millicent's gaze, every woman he's attacked, every life he's destroyed. She carries them all. Whatever darkness lurks inside Jonathan Derby, Millicent tucked it in at night.

"It's always the weak ones with you, isn't it?" she says. "Always the…"

She falls silent, her mouth hanging open as though the next words simply evaporated on her lips.

"I have to go," she says suddenly, squeezing my hand. "I've had a very strange thought. I'll see you at dinner, darling."

Without another word, Millicent returns back the way we came, disappearing around the corner of the house. Perplexed, I look back into the ballroom, trying to see what she saw, but everybody's moved around except for the band. That's when I notice the chess piece sitting on the window ledge. If I'm not mistaken, it's the same hand-carved piece I found in Bell's trunk, speckled with white paint and looking at me through clumsily whittled eyes. There's a message etched into the dirt on the glass above it.

Behind you.

Sure enough, Anna's waving at me from the edge of the forest, her tiny body shrouded by a gray coat. Pocketing the chess piece, I glance left and right to make sure we're alone, and then follow her deeper into the trees, beyond Blackheath's sight. She looks to have been waiting for some time and is dancing from foot to foot to keep warm. Judging by her blue cheeks, it's not doing the blindest bit of good. Little wonder given her attire. She's draped in shades of gray, her coat threadbare, her knitted hat thin as gossamer. These are clothes passed down and down and down, patched so many times the original material is long gone.

"Don't suppose you've got an apple or something," she says without preamble. "I'm bloody starving."

"I've got a hip flask," I say, holding it out to her.

"Have to do, I suppose," she says, taking it from me and unscrewing the cap.

"I thought it was too dangerous for us to meet outside of the gatehouse."

"Who told you that?" she asks, wincing as she tastes the flask's contents.

"You did," I say.

"Will."

"What?"

"I will tell you it isn't safe for us to meet, but I haven't yet," she says. "I couldn't have. I've only been awake for a few hours and I've spent most of that time keeping the footman from making pin cushions out of your future hosts. Missed breakfast doing it, too."

I blink at her, struggling to stitch together a day being delivered in the wrong order. Not for the first time, I find myself wishing for the speed of Ravencourt's mind. Working within the confines of Jonathan Derby's intellect is like stirring croutons into a thick soup.

Seeing my confusion, she frowns.

"Do you know about the footman yet? I never know where we're up to."

I very quickly tell her about Bell's dead rabbit and the ghostly steps that dogged Ravencourt in the dining hall, her expression darkening with each fresh detail.

"That bastard," she splutters, when I'm finished. She's prowling back and forth, her hands clenched and shoulders rolled forward. "Wait until I get my hands on him," she says, shooting the house a murderous glance.

"You won't have to wait long," I say. "Daniel thinks he's hiding in some tunnels. There are a few entrances, but we're going to guard the library. He wants us in there before one."

"Or we could slit our own throats and save the footman the bother of killing us," she says, her tone frank and unimpressed. She's looking at me as if I've lost my mind.

"What's wrong?"

"The footman's not an idiot," she says. "If we know where he is, it's because we're supposed to know. He's been one step ahead of us since this started. Wouldn't surprise me one bit if he's lying in wait, hoping to trip us up on our own cleverness."

"We have to do something!" I protest.

"We will, but what's the point of doing something stupid when we can do something smart," she says patiently. "Listen to me, Aiden. I know you're desperate, but we've got a deal, you and me. I keep you alive so you can find Evelyn's killer, and then we both get out of here. This is me, doing my job. Now, promise me you won't go after the footman."

Her argument makes sense, but it's weightless against my fear. If there's a chance to put an end to this madman before he finds me, I'm going to take it, no matter the risk. I'd rather die on my feet than cowering in a corner.

"I promise," I say, adding another lie to the pile.

Thankfully, Anna's too cold to notice the catch in my voice. Despite having drunk from the hip flask, she's shivering so hard all the color has abandoned her face. In an attempt to shelter from the wind, she presses against me. I can smell the soap on her skin, forcing me to avert my gaze. I don't want her to see Derby's lust squirming within me.

Sensing my discomfort, she tilts her head to meet my downcast face.

"Your other hosts are better, I promise," she says. "You have to keep hold of yourself. Don't give in to him."

"How do I do that when I don't know where they start and I begin?"

"If you weren't here, Derby would have his hands all over me," she says. "That's how you know who you are. You don't just remember it—you do it, and you keep doing it."

Even so, she takes a step back into the wind, freeing me from my discomfort.

"You shouldn't be out in this weather," I say, removing my scarf and wrapping it around her neck. "You'll catch your death."

"And if you keep this up, people might begin mistaking Jonathan Derby for a human being," she says, tucking the loose ends of the scarf into her coat.

"Tell Evelyn Hardcastle that," I say. "She nearly shot me this morning."

"You should have shot her back," says Anna matter-of-factly. "We could have solved her murder then and there."

"I can't tell if you're joking or not," I say.

"Of course I am," she says, blowing into her chapped hands. "If it were that simple, we'd have been out of here ages ago. Mind you, I'm not sure trying to save her life is a much better plan."

"You think I should let her die?"

"I think we're spending a lot of time not doing the thing we've been asked to do."

"We can't protect Evelyn without knowing who wants her dead," I say. "One thing will give us the other."

"I hope you're right," she says dubiously.

I search for some encouraging platitude, but her doubts have crawled under my skin, and they're beginning to itch. I told her that saving Evelyn's life would deliver us the murderer, but that was an evasion. There's no plan here. I don't even know if I *can* save Evelyn anymore. I'm working at the behest of blind sentiment, and losing ground to the footman as I'm doing it. Anna deserves better, but I have no idea how to give it to her without abandoning Evelyn—and for some reason the thought of doing that is unbearable to me.

There's a commotion on the path, voices carried through the trees by the wind. Taking my arm, Anna pulls me farther into the forest.

"As fun as this has been, I came to ask for a favor."

"Always. What can I do?"

"What's the time?" she says, pulling the artist's sketchbook from her pocket. It's the same one I saw her holding in the gatehouse, crumpled sheets and a cover riddled with holes. She's holding it up so I can't see inside, but, judging by the way she's flicking through the pages, there's something important inside.

I check my watch. "10:08 a.m.," I say, itching with curiosity. "What's in the book?"

"Notes, information. Everything I've managed to learn about your eight hosts and what they're doing," she says absently, running her finger down one of the pages. "And don't ask to see it because you can't. We can't risk you pulling the day down around our ears with what you know."

"I wasn't going to," I protest, though I must admit to trying to catch a peek.

"Right, 10:08 a.m.," says Anna. "Perfect. In a minute, I'm going to put a rock on the grass. I need you standing by it when Evelyn kills herself. You can't move, Aiden. Not an inch. Understand?"

"What's the meaning of all this, Anna?"

"Call it Plan B." She pecks me on the cheek, cold lips meeting numb flesh, as she slides the book back in her pocket.

She's only taken a step when she clicks her fingers and turns back to me, holding out two white tablets in her palm.

"Take these for later," she says. "I filched them from Doctor Dickie's bag when he came to see the butler."

"What are they?"

"Headache pills. I'll trade them for my chess piece."

"This ugly old thing?" I say, handing her the hand-carved bishop. "Why would you want it?"

She smiles at me, watching as I wrap the tablets in a blue pocket handkerchief.

"Because you gave it to me," she says, clutching it protectively in her hand. "It was the first promise you made me. This ugly old thing is the reason I stopped being scared of this place. It's the reason I stopped being scared of you."

"Me? Why would you be afraid of me?" I say, genuinely hurt by the idea of anything coming between us.

"Oh, Aiden," she says, shaking her head. "If we do this right, everybody in this house is going to be afraid of you."

She's carried away on those words, blown through the trees and out onto the grass surrounding the reflecting pool. Perhaps it's her youth, or her personality, or some curious alchemy of all the miserable ingredients surrounding us, but I can't see an ounce of doubt within her. Whatever her plan, she seems extraordinarily confident in it. Maybe dangerously so.

From my position in the tree line, I watch her pick up a large white rock from the flower bed and pace out six steps before dropping it on the grass. Holding an arm straight out from her body, she measures a line to the ballroom's french doors, and then, seemingly satisfied with her work, she wipes the mud from her hands, shoves them in her pockets, and strolls away.

For some reason, this little display makes me uneasy. I came here voluntarily and Anna did not. The Plague Doctor brought her to Blackheath for a reason, and I have no idea what that could be.

Whoever Anna really is, I'm following her blindly.

⌒ 25 ⌒

The bedroom door's locked, no noise coming from within. I'd hoped to catch Helena Hardcastle before she set about her day, but it appears the lady of the house is not one to idle. I rattle the handle again, pressing my ear to the wood. Aside from a few curious glances from passing guests, my efforts are in vain. She's not here.

I'm walking away, when the thought hits me: the room hasn't been broken into yet. Ravencourt will find the door shattered early this afternoon, so it's going to happen in the next few hours.

I'm curious to see who's responsible, and why they're so desperate to get inside. I'd originally suspected Evelyn because she had one of the two revolvers stolen from Helena's bureau, but she nearly killed me with it in the forest this morning. If it's already in her possession, she has no need to break in.

Unless there's something else she wants.

The only other thing that was obviously missing was the appointment page in Helena's day planner. Millicent believed Helena tore it out herself to conceal some suspicious deed, but Cunningham's fingerprints were all over the remaining pages. He refused to explain himself and denied being responsible for the break-in, but if I could catch him with his shoulder to the door, he'd have no choice but to come clean.

My mind made up, I stride into the shadows at the far end of the corridor and begin my vigil.

Five minutes later, Derby is already impossibly bored.

I'm fidgeting, stalking back and forth. I can't calm him.

At a loss, I follow the smell of breakfast toward the drawing room, planning to carry a plate of food and a chair back to the corridor. Hopefully, they'll placate my host for half an hour, after which I'll have to come up with some new amusement.

I find the room smothered in sleepy conversation. Most of the guests are only halfway out of their beds, and they reek of the prior evening, sweat and cigar smoke baked into their skin, spirits curled around every breath. They're talking quietly and moving slowly, porcelain people riddled with cracks.

Taking a plate from the sideboard, I scoop piles of eggs and kidneys onto a large plate, pausing only to eat a sausage from the platter and wipe the grease from my lips with my sleeve. I'm so preoccupied, it takes a little while to realize everybody is silent.

A burly fellow is standing at the door, his gaze passing from face to face, relief coursing through those he slips over. This nervousness is not unwarranted. He's a brutish-looking chap with a ginger beard and sagging cheeks, his nose so mangled it resembles an egg cracked in a frying pan. An old frayed suit strains to contain his width, raindrops sparkling on shoulders you could serve a buffet on.

His gaze lands on me like a boulder in the lap.

"Mr. Stanwin wants to see you," he says.

His voice is coarse, filled with jagged consonants.

"What for?" I ask.

"I expect he'll tell you."

"Well, offer my regrets to Mr. Stanwin, but I'm afraid I'm very busy at present."

"Either you walk or I carry you," he says in a low rumble.

Derby's temper is bubbling nicely, but there's no use making a scene. I can't beat this man; the best I can hope for is to quickly meet Stanwin and return to my task. Besides, I'm curious why he'd want to see me.

Placing my plate of food on the sideboard, I follow Stanwin's thug from the room.

Inviting me to walk ahead of him, the burly fellow guides me up the staircase, telling me to turn right at the top, into the closed-off east wing. Brushing aside the curtain, a damp breeze touches my face, a long corridor stretching out before me. Doors are hanging off their hinges, revealing staterooms covered in dust and four-poster beds collapsed in on themselves. The air scratches my throat as I breathe it.

"Why don't you wait in that room over there like a good gentleman and I'll tell Mr. Stanwin you've arrived," says my escort, jerking his chin toward a room on my left.

Doing as he bids, I enter a nursery, the cheerful yellow wallpaper now hanging limp from the walls. Games and wooden toys litter the floor, a weathered rocking horse put out to pasture by the door. There's a game in progress on a child's chessboard, the white pieces decimated by the black.

No sooner have I set foot inside than I hear Evelyn shrieking in the room beside me. For the first time Derby and I move in concert, sprinting around the corner to find the door blocked by the redheaded thug.

"Mr. Stanwin's still busy, chum," he says, rocking back and forth to keep warm.

"I'm looking for Evelyn Hardcastle. I heard her scream," I say breathlessly.

"Mayhap you did, but doesn't seem like there's much you can do about it, does there?"

I peer over his shoulder into the room behind, hoping to catch sight of Evelyn. It looks to be some sort of reception area, but it's empty. The furniture lies under yellowed sheets, black mold growing up from the hems. The windows are covered in old newspaper, the walls little more than rotting boards. There's another door on the far wall, but it's closed. They must be in there.

I return my gaze to the man, who smiles at me, exposing a row of crooked yellow teeth.

"Anything else?" he says.

"I need to make sure she's all right."

I try to barge past him, but it's a foolish notion. He's three times my weight and half again my height. More to the point, he knows how to use his strength. Planting a flat hand on my stomach, he shoves me backward, barely a flicker of emotion on his face.

"Don't bother," he says. "I'm paid to stand here and make sure nice gentlemen like you don't do themselves a misfortune by wandering places they ain't supposed to go."

They're just words, coals in the furnace. My blood's boiling. I try to dart around him, and, like a fool, I think I've succeeded. Until I'm hoisted backward and tossed bodily back down the corridor.

I scramble to my feet, snarling.

He hasn't moved. He isn't out of breath. He doesn't care.

"Your parents gave you everything but sense, didn't they?" he says, the blandness of the sentiment hitting me like a bucketful of cold water. "Mr. Stanwin's not hurting her if that's your concern. Wait a few minutes and you can ask her all about it when she comes out."

We eye each other for a moment, before I retreat along the corridor into the nursery. He's right; I'm not getting by him. But I can't wait for Evelyn to come out. She won't tell Jonathan Derby anything after this morning, and whatever is happening behind that door could be the reason she takes her life tonight.

Hurrying over to the wall, I press my ear to the boards. If I haven't missed my mark, Evelyn's talking to Stanwin in the room next door, only a few pieces of rotten wood between us. I soon catch the hum of their voices, much too faint to make anything out. Using my pocketknife, I tear the wallpaper from the wall, digging the blade between the loose wooden slats to pry them free. They're so damp they come away without objection, the wood disintegrating in my hands.

"...tell her she best not play any games with me, or it'll be the end of both of you," says Stanwin, his voice poking through the insulating wall.

"Tell her yourself. I'm not your errand girl," says Evelyn coldly.

"You'll be anything I damn well please, so long as I'm footing the bill."

"I don't like your tone, Mr. Stanwin," says Evelyn.

"And I don't like being made a fool of, Miss Hardcastle," he says, practically spitting her name. "You forget I worked here for nearly fifteen years. I know every corner of this place, and everybody in it. Don't mistake me for one of these blinkered bastards you've surrounded yourself with."

His hatred is viscous; it has texture. I could wring it out of the air and bottle it.

"What about the letter?" says Evelyn quietly, her outrage overwhelmed.

"I'll keep hold of that, so you understand our arrangement."

"You're a vile creature, are you aware of that?"

Stanwin swats the insult from the air with a belly laugh.

"At least I'm an honest one," he says. "How many other people in this house can claim the same thing? You can go now. Don't forget to pass along my message."

I hear the door to Stanwin's room open, Evelyn storming past the nursery a few moments later. I'm tempted to follow her, but there'd be little value in another confrontation. Besides, Evelyn mentioned something about a letter that's now in Stanwin's possession. She seemed keen to retrieve it, which means I need to see it. Who knows, perhaps Stanwin and Derby are friends.

"Jonathan Derby's waiting for you in the nursery," I hear the burly fellow tell Stanwin.

"Good," says Stanwin, drawers scraping open. "Let me get changed for this hunt and we'll go have a word with the greasy little bugger."

Or perhaps not.

~ 26 ~

I sit with my feet on the table, the chessboard beside them.
Cupping my chin in my hand, I stare at the game trying to decipher
some strategy from the arrangement of the pieces. It's proving an
impossible task. Derby's too flighty for study. His attention is forever
straying toward the window, toward the dust in the air, and the noises
in the corridor. He's never at peace.

Daniel warned me that each of our hosts thinks differently, but
only now do I comprehend the full extent of his meaning. Bell was a
coward and Ravencourt ruthless, but both possessed focused minds.
That's not the case with Derby. Thoughts come buzzing through his
head like bluebottles, lingering long enough to be distracting but
never settling.

A sound draws my attention to the door, Ted Stanwin shaking out
a match as he surveys me from above his pipe. He's larger than I recall,
a slab of a man spreading sideways like a wedge of melting butter.

"Never took you for a chess man, Jonathan," he says, pushing the
old rocking horse back and forth so that it thumps on the floor.

"I'm teaching myself," I say.

"Good for you. Men should seek to better themselves."

His eyes linger on me before being tugged to the windows. Though
Stanwin hasn't done or said anything threatening, Derby's afraid of
him. My pulse is tapping that out in Morse code.

I glance at the door, ready to bolt, but the burly fellow is leaning against the wall in the corridor with his arms crossed. He offers me a little nod, friendly as two men in a cell.

"Your mother's running a little late on her payments," says Stanwin, his forehead pressed against the window. "I hope all's well?"

"Quite well," I say.

"I'd hate for that to change."

I shift in my seat to catch his eye.

"Are you threatening me, Mr. Stanwin?"

He turns from the window, smiling at the fellow in the corridor, then myself.

"Of course not, Jonathan. I'm threatening your mother. You don't think I'd come all this way for a worthless little sod like yourself, do you?"

Taking a puff on his pipe, he picks up a doll and casually tosses it at the chessboard, sending the pieces scattering across the room. Rage snatches me up by the strings, flinging me at him, but he catches my fist in the air, spinning me around as one of his huge arms crushes my throat.

His breath is on my neck, rotten as old meat.

"Talk to your mother, Jonathan," he sneers, squeezing my windpipe hard enough for black spots to swim in the corners of my eyes. "Otherwise, I might have to pay her a visit."

He lets the words settle, then releases me.

I drop to my knees, clutching my throat and gasping for air.

"You'll come a cropper with that temper," he says, jabbing his pipe in my direction. "I'd get it under control if I were you. Don't worry. My friend here is good at helping people learn new things."

I glare at him from the floor, but he's already on his way out. Passing into the corridor, he nods to his companion who steps into the room. He looks at me without emotion, peeling off his jacket.

"On your feet, lad," he says. "Sooner we get started, sooner it'll be over."

Somehow, he seems even bigger than he did at the door. His chest is a shield, his arms straining the seams of his white shirt. Terror takes hold of me as he closes the distance between us, my fingers searching blindly for a weapon and finding the heavy chessboard on the table.

Without thinking, I hurl it at him.

Time seems to hang as the chessboard turns in the air, an impossible object in flight, my future clinging onto its surface for dear life. Evidently, fate has a soft spot for me because it hits his face with a sickening crunch, sending him reeling backward into the wall with a muffled cry.

I'm on my feet as the blood pours between his fingers, sprinting down the corridor with Stanwin's angry voice at my back. A quick glance behind me reveals Stanwin's halfway out of the reception room, his face red with rage. Fleeing down the staircase, I follow the burble of voices into the drawing room, which is now full of red-eyed guests digging into their breakfasts. Doctor Dickie's guffawing with Michael Hardcastle and Clifford Herrington, the naval officer I met at dinner, while Cunningham piles food onto the silver platter that will greet Ravencourt when he wakes up.

A sudden quieting of chatter tells me Stanwin's approaching, and I slip through into the study, hiding behind the door. I'm half hysterical, my heart beating hard enough to shatter my ribs. I want to laugh and cry, to pick up a weapon and throw myself at Stanwin, screaming. It's taking all my concentration to stand still, but if I don't, I'm going to lose this host and one more precious day.

Peering through the gap between the door and frame, I watch as Stanwin wrenches people around by the shoulder, searching for my face. Men stand aside for him, the powerful mumbling vague apologies as he approaches. Whatever his hold on these people, it's complete enough that nobody takes umbrage at his manhandling of them. He could beat me to death in the middle of the carpet and they wouldn't say a word about it. I'll find no help here.

Something cold touches my fingers, and, looking down, I discover my hand has closed around a heavy cigarette box sitting on the sideboard.

Derby's arming himself.

Hissing at him, I let it go and return my attention to the drawing room, almost crying out in shock.

Stanwin's a few paces away, and he's walking directly toward the study.

I look for places to hide, but there aren't any, and I can't flee into the library without passing the door he's about to walk through. I'm trapped.

Picking up the cigarette box, I take a deep breath, preparing to pounce on him when he walks in.

Nobody appears.

Slipping back to the gap, I peek into the drawing room. He's nowhere to be seen.

I'm shaking, uncertain. Derby isn't built for indecision; he doesn't have the patience. And before I know it, I'm creeping around the door to get a better view.

I immediately see Stanwin.

He has his back to me and is talking to Doctor Dickie. I'm too far away to catch their conversation, but it's enough to propel the good doctor out of the room, presumably to tend to Stanwin's stricken bodyguard.

He has sedatives.

The idea delivers itself fully formed.

I just need to get out of here without being seen.

A voice calls to Stanwin from near the table, and the moment he's out of sight, I drop the cigarette case and flee into the gallery, taking the long way around to reach the entrance hall unseen.

I catch Doctor Dickie as he's leaving his bedroom, his medical case swinging in his hand. He smiles as he sees me, that ridiculous mustache of his leaping about two inches up his face.

"Ah, young Master Jonathan," he says cheerfully, as I fall into step beside him. "Everything well? You seem a little puffed."

"I'm fine," I say, hurrying to keep up with him. "Well, I'm not actually. I need a favor."

His eyes narrow, the cheerful tone dropping out of his voice. "What have you done this time?"

"The man you're going to see. I need you to sedate him."

"Sedate him? Why the devil would I sedate him?"

"Because he's going to harm my mother."

"Millicent?" He stops dead, grabbing me by the arm with a surprising amount of strength. "What's all this about, Jonathan?"

"She owes Stanwin money."

His face falls, his grip loosening. Without his joviality inflating him, he seems a tired old thing, the lines on his face a little deeper, the sorrows less obscure. For a moment, I feel a little guilty about what I'm doing to him, but then I remember the look in his eyes when he sedated the butler, and all my doubts are wiped away.

"So he has dear Millicent under his thumb, does he?" he says, sighing. "Shouldn't be surprised, I suppose; the fiend's got something on the lot of us. Still, I thought…"

He carries on walking, though slower than before. We're at the top of the staircase leading down to the entrance hall, which is flooded with cold. The front door is open, a group of old men departing for a walk, taking their laughter with them.

I can't see Stanwin anywhere.

"So this fellow threatened your mother and you attacked him, eh?" says Dickie, evidently having made up his mind. He beams at me, clapping me on the back. "I see there's some of your father in you after all. But how will sedating this ruffian help?"

"I need a chance to talk with Mother before he gets to her."

For all Derby's faults, he's an accomplished liar, the deceits queuing in orderly fashion on his tongue. Doctor Dickie's silent, rolling the story around his head, kneading it into shape as we cross into the abandoned east wing.

"I've got just the thing, should put the blighter out for the rest of the afternoon," he says, clicking his fingers. "You wait here. I'll signal when it's done."

Squaring his shoulders and puffing out his chest, he strides toward Stanwin's bedroom, the old soldier given one last battle to fight.

It's too exposed in the corridor, and once Dickie's out of sight, I step through the nearest door, my reflection staring back at me from a cracked mirror. Yesterday, I couldn't have imagined anything worse than being stuck inside Ravencourt, but Derby's an entirely different torment—a restless, malevolent imp scurrying between tragedies of his own devising. I can't wait to be free of him.

Ten minutes later, the floorboards creak outside.

"Jonathan," whispers Doctor Dickie. "Jonathan, where are you?"

"Here," I say, poking my head outside.

He's already passed the room and jumps at the sound of my voice.

"Gently, young man. The old ticker, you know," he says, tapping his chest. "Cerberus is asleep and will be for most of the day. Now, I'm going to deliver my prognosis to Mr. Stanwin. I suggest you use this time to hide yourself somewhere he won't find you. Argentina, perhaps. Good luck to you."

He stands to attention, offering me a sharp salute. I throw one back at him, earning a pat on the shoulder before he saunters off down the corridor, whistling tunelessly.

I rather suspect I've made his day, but I have no intention of hiding. Stanwin is going to be distracted by Dickie for a few minutes at least, giving me a chance to search his belongings for Evelyn's letter.

Crossing the reception room previously guarded by Stanwin's bodyguard, I open the door into the blackmailer's bedroom. It's a desolate place, the floorboards barely covered by a threadbare rug, a single iron bed pushed against the wall, flakes of white paint clinging stubbornly to the rust. The only comforts are a starving fire spitting ash and a small bedside table with two dog-eared books on it. As promised, Stanwin's man is asleep on the bed, looking for all the world like a monstrous marionette with all of its strings cut. His face is bandaged and he's snoring loudly, his fingers twitching. I can only imagine he's dreaming of my neck.

Keeping an ear out for Stanwin's return, I quickly open the cupboard, sifting through the pockets of his jackets and trousers, finding only lint and mothballs. His trunk is equally bereft of personal objects, the man seemingly immune to sentiment of any kind.

Frustrated, I check my watch.

I've already been here longer than is safe, but Derby's not easily deterred. My host knows deceit. He knows men like Stanwin and the secrets they keep. The blackmailer could have had the most luxurious room in the house if he'd wanted, but he chose to sequester himself amongst this decay. He's paranoid and clever. Whatever his secrets, he wouldn't carry them with him, not when he's surrounded by enemies.

They're here. Hidden and under guard.

My gaze falls on the fireplace and its anemic flames. Odd, considering how cold the bedroom is. Kneeling down, I stick my hand up the flue, feeling around and finding a small shelf, my groping fingers closing on a book. Withdrawing it, I see that it's a small black journal, its cover bearing the scars of a lifetime's abuse. Stanwin was keeping the fire low to avoid scorching his prize.

Flicking through the tattered pages, I discover it's a ledger of sorts containing a list of dates going back nineteen years alongside entries written in strange symbols.

It must be some sort of code.

Evelyn's letter is stuffed between the last two pages.

Dearest Evelyn,

Mr. Stanwin has informed me of your plight, and I can quite understand your concern. Your mother's behavior is certainly alarming, and you're quite right to be on guard against whatever scheme she's cooking up. I stand ready to help unravel this plot, but I'm afraid Mr. Stanwin's word will not be enough. I require some proof of your agency in these matters. I've often seen you wearing a signet ring, a small castle engraved on its surface. Send me this, and I'll know of your serious intent.

Warmest regards,
Felicity Maddox

Looks like clever old Evelyn didn't accept her fate as easily as I first believed. She brought in somebody called Felicity Maddox to help, and the description of the small castle recalls the one drawn on the note Cunningham found at the well. It may be serving as a signature, a mark of trustworthiness between Evelyn and Felicity, which suggests the message to "stay away from Millicent Derby" came from Felicity.

The bodyguard snores.

Unable to wring any further information from the letter, I replace it in the ledger and slip both in my pocket.

"Thank heavens for devious minds," I mutter, stepping through the door.

"You said it," says somebody behind me.

Pain explodes in my head as I slam into the floor.

DAY TWO (CONTINUED)

I'm coughing blood, red drops spattering my pillow. I'm back in the butler, my aching body screaming as my head jerks upward. The Plague Doctor's sitting in Anna's chair, one leg thrown across the other, his top hat in his lap. He's drumming it with his fingers, coming to a stop when he notices me stirring.

"Welcome back, Mr. Bishop," he says, his voice muffled by the mask.

I stare at him absently, my coughing subsiding as I begin to piece together the pattern of this day. The first time I found myself in this body, it was morning. I answered the door to Bell and was then attacked by Gold after running up the stairs for answers. The second time wasn't more than fifteen minutes later. I was transported to the gatehouse in the carriage with Anna. Must have been midday when I woke up and we were properly introduced, but judging by the light outside the window, it's now early afternoon. It makes sense. Anna told me we get a full day in each of our hosts, but it never occurred to me that I'd experience one in so many fragments.

It feels like a perverse joke.

I was promised eight hosts to solve this mystery, and I've been given them, except that Bell was a coward, the butler was beaten half to death, Donald Davies fled, Ravencourt could barely move, and Derby can't hold a thought.

It's like I've been asked to dig a hole with a shovel made of sparrows.

Shifting in his seat, the Plague Doctor leans closer to me. His clothes are musty, that old attic smell of something long forgotten and badly aired.

"Our last conversation was rather abrupt," he says. "So I thought you might report on your progress. Have you discovered—"

"Why did it have to be this body?" I interrupt, wincing as a hot streak of pain shoots up through my side. "Why trap me in any of these bodies? Ravencourt couldn't walk two steps without tiring, the butler's incapacitated, and Derby's a monster. If you really want me to escape Blackheath, why stack the deck against me? There must be better alternatives."

"More able perhaps, but these men all have some connection to Evelyn's murder," he says. "Making them best placed to help you solve it."

"They're suspects?"

"Witnesses would be a more apt description."

A yawn shakes me, my energy already evaporating. Doctor Dickie must have given me another sedative. I feel as though I'm being squeezed out of this body through the feet.

"And who decides the order?" I say. "Why did I wake up as Bell first and Derby today? Is there any way for me to predict who I'll be next?"

Leaning back, he steeples his fingers and cocks his head. It's a lengthy silence, reevaluating and readjusting. Whether he's pleased by what he finds, or annoyed, I can't tell.

"Why are you asking these questions?" he says eventually.

"Curiosity," I say, and when he doesn't respond to that, "And I'm hoping there's some advantage to be found in the answers," I add.

He makes a small grunt of approval.

"Good to see you're finally taking this seriously," he says. "Very well. Under normal circumstances, you'd arrive in your hosts in the order they woke throughout the day. Fortunately for you, I've been tampering."

"Tampering?"

"We've done this dance many times before, you and I, more than even I can recall. Loop after loop, I've set you the task of solving Evelyn Hardcastle's murder, and it's always ended in failure. At first, I thought the blame for this rested solely on your shoulders, but I've come to realize that the sequence of hosts plays a part. For example, Donald Davies wakes up at 3:19 a.m., which should make him your first host. That doesn't work because his life is so appealing. He has good friends in the house, family. Things you spend the loop trying to return to, rather than seeking to escape. It's for that reason I changed your first host to the more rootless Sebastian Bell," he says, hoisting his trouser leg to scratch his ankle. "In contrast, Lord Ravencourt doesn't stir until 10:30 a.m., which meant you shouldn't have visited him until much deeper in the loop, a period when haste, rather than intellect, is of the essence."

I can hear the pride in his voice, the sense of a watchmaker standing back and admiring the mechanism he's built. "One loop after another, I experimented, making these sorts of decisions for each of your hosts, arriving at the order you're experiencing now," he says, spreading his hands magnanimously. "In my opinion, this is the sequence that gives you the best chance of solving the mystery."

"So why haven't I returned to Donald Davies, the way I keep returning to the butler?"

"Because you walked him down that endless road to the village for almost eight hours and he's exhausted," says the Plague Doctor, a hint of rebuke in his tone. "He's currently sleeping deeply and will be until"—he checks his watch—"9:38 p.m. Until then, you'll continue to be tugged between the butler and your other hosts."

Wood creaks in the corridor. I consider calling for Anna, a thought which must show on my face, because the Plague Doctor tuts at me.

"Come now, how clumsy do you think I am?" he says. "Anna left a little while ago to meet with Lord Ravencourt. Believe me, I know the routines of this house as a director knows those of the actors in his play. If I had any doubt that we might be interrupted, I wouldn't be here."

I have the sense of being a nuisance to him, an errant child in the headmaster's office again. Barely worth a scolding.

A yawn rattles me, long and loud. My brain is clouding over.

"We have a few more minutes to talk before you fall asleep again," says the Plague Doctor, clasping his gloved hands together, the leather squeaking. "If you've any more questions for me, now would be the time."

"Why is Anna in Blackheath?" I say quickly. "You said I chose to come here, and my rivals didn't. That means she was brought against her will. Why are you doing this to her?"

"Any questions aside from that one," he says. "You chose to come to Blackheath, and because of that decision, you have certain advantages. There are also disadvantages, things your rivals instinctively understand, which you do not. I'm here to fill in those blanks, nothing more. Now, how goes the investigation into Evelyn Hardcastle's murder?"

"She's one girl," I say wearily, struggling to keep my eyes open. The drugs are tugging at me with their warm hands. "What makes her death worth all of this?"

"I could ask you the same question," he says. "You're going out of your way to save Miss Hardcastle, despite all the evidence suggesting it's impossible. Why is that?"

"I can't watch her die and do nothing to prevent it," I say.

"That's very noble of you," he says, cocking his head. "Then let me respond in kind. Miss Hardcastle's murder was never solved, and I don't believe such a thing should be allowed to stand. Does that satisfy you?"

"People are murdered every day," I say. "Righting one wrong can't be the only reason for all of this."

"An excellent point," he says, clapping his hands together in appreciation. "But who's to say there aren't hundreds of others like yourself seeking justice for those souls?"

"Are there?"

"Doubtful, but it's a lovely thought, isn't it?"

I'm conscious of the effort of listening, the weight of my eyelids, the way the room is melting around me.

"We don't have much time I'm afraid," says the Plague Doctor. "I should—"

"Wait… I need to… Why did…" My words are sludge, thick in my mouth. "You asked me… You asked… My memory…"

There's a great rustling of material as the Plague Doctor gets to his feet. Picking up a glass of water from the sideboard, he hurls the contents in my face. The water's freezing cold. My body convulses like a cracked whip, dragging me back to myself.

"Apologies, that was most irregular," he says, staring at the empty glass, clearly surprised at his actions. "Normally, I let you fall asleep at this point, but… Well, I'm intrigued." He puts the glass down slowly. "What did you want to ask me? Please choose your words carefully; they're of some import."

Water stings my eyes and drips off my lips, the wetness spreading through my cotton nightshirt.

"When we first met, you asked me what I remembered when I woke up as Bell," I say. "Why would that matter?"

"Each time you fail, we strip your memories and start the loop again, but you always find a way to hold on to something import-ant—a clue, if you will," he says, dabbing the water from my forehead with a handkerchief. "This time, it was Anna's name."

"You told me it was a pity," I say.

"It is."

"Why?"

"Along with the sequence of your hosts, the thing you choose to remember has a significant impact on how the loop plays out," he says. "If you had remembered the footman, you'd have set off chasing him. At least that would have been useful. Instead, you've bound yourself to Anna, one of your rivals."

"She's my friend," I say.

"Nobody has friends in Blackheath, Mr. Bishop, and if you haven't learned that yet, I'm afraid there may be no hope for you."

"Can…" The sedative is dragging at me once again. "Can we both escape?"

"No," he says, folding his damp handkerchief and replacing it in his pocket. "An answer for an exit; that's how this works. At 11:00 p.m., one of you will come to the lake and give me the murderer's name, and that person will be allowed to leave. You're going to have to choose who that is."

He lifts his gold watch from his breast pocket to check the time.

"Time runs away and I have a schedule to keep," he says, retrieving his cane from its spot by the door. "Normally, I remain impartial in these matters, but there's something you should know before you trip over your nobility. Anna remembers more from the last loop than she's telling you."

His gloved hand lifts my chin, his face so close to mine I can hear his breathing through the mask. He has blue eyes. Old, sad, blue eyes.

"She's going to betray you."

I open my mouth to protest, but my tongue's too heavy to move, and the last thing I see is the Plague Doctor disappearing through the door, a great stooped shadow dragging the world behind him.

～ 28 ～

DAY FIVE (CONTINUED)

Life pounds on my eyelids.

I blink, once, twice, but it hurts to keep them open. My head's a shattered egg. A noise escapes my throat. It's somewhere between a groan and a whimper, the low animal gurgle of a creature caught in a trap. I try to heave myself up, but the pain's an ocean, lapping around my skull. I don't have the strength to lift it.

Time passes; I can't say how much. It isn't that sort of time. I watch my stomach rise and fall, and when I'm confident it can do so without my help, I drag myself into a sitting position, resting against the crumbling wall. Much to my dismay I'm back in Jonathan Derby, lying on the floor in the nursery. Pieces of a broken vase are everywhere, including my scalp. Somebody must have hit me from behind when I left Stanwin's bedroom, and then dragged me here out of sight.

The letter, you fool.

My hand leaps to my pocket, searching for Evelyn's letter and the ledger I stole from Stanwin, but they're gone, along with the key to Bell's trunk. All that remains are the two headache pills given to me by Anna, which are still wrapped in the blue handkerchief.

She's going to betray you.

Could this be her doing? The Plague Doctor's warning couldn't have been any clearer, and yet surely an enemy wouldn't provoke such feelings of warmth, or kinship? Perhaps Anna does remember more from our last loop than she admits, but if that information was destined to make us enemies, why would I drag her name from one life into the next, knowing I would chase it like a dog after a burning stick? No, if there's betrayal afoot, it's a result of the empty promises I've made, and that's rectifiable. I need to find the right way of telling Anna the truth.

Swallowing the tablets dry, I claw my way up the wall, staggering back into Stanwin's room.

The bodyguard's still unconscious on the bed, the light fading beyond the window. I check my watch to find it's 6:00 p.m., which means the hunters, including Stanwin, are probably already on their way home. For all I know, they're crossing the lawn or ascending the stairs even now.

I need to leave before the blackmailer comes back.

Even with the tablets, I'm woozy, the world slipping beneath me as I crash through the east wing before pushing aside the curtain to arrive on the landing above the entrance hall. Each step is a battle until I fall through Doctor Dickie's door, nearly vomiting on his floor. His bedroom's identical to all the others on this corridor, with a four-poster bed against one wall and a bath and sink behind a screen opposite. Unlike Bell, Dickie's made himself at home. Pictures of his grandchildren are dotted about the place, a crucifix hanging from one of the walls. He's even laid a small rug down, presumably to keep his feet off the cold wood in the mornings.

This familiarity with oneself is a miracle to me, and I find myself gaping at Dickie's possessions, my wounds momentarily forgotten. Picking up the picture of his grandchildren, I wonder for the first time if I too have a family waiting beyond Blackheath: parents or children, friends who miss me?

Startled by footsteps passing in the corridor, I drop the family picture on the bedside table, accidentally cracking the glass. The steps pass without incident, but awakened to the peril, I move more quickly.

Dickie's medical bag is nestled beneath his bed, and I upend it over his mattress, spilling bottles, scissors, syringes, and bandages onto the covers. The last thing out is a King James Bible, which bounces onto the floor, the pages falling open. Just like the one in Sebastian Bell's bedroom, certain words and paragraphs are underlined in red ink.

It's a code.

A wolf's smile spreads across Derby's face, recognition of another crook. If I had to guess, I'd say Dickie's a silent partner in Bell's drug-peddling business. No wonder he was so concerned for the good doctor's welfare. He was worried about what he'd say.

I snort. It's another secret in a house full of them, and it's not the one I'm after today.

Gathering the bandages and iodine from the pile on the bed, I take them over to the sink and begin my surgery.

It's not a delicate operation.

Every time I pluck one piece loose, blood wells up between my fingers, running down my face and dripping off my chin into the sink. Tears of pain cloud my vision, the world a stinging blur for nearly thirty minutes while I pick apart my porcelain crown. My only consolation is that somewhere within me this is hurting Jonathan Derby almost as much as it's hurting me.

When I'm certain every shard has been removed, I set to work wrapping my head in bandages, securing them with a safety pin, and inspecting my work in the mirror.

The bandages look fine. I look terrible.

My face is pale, my eyes hollow. Blood has stained my shirt, forcing me to strip down to my undershirt. I'm a man undone, coming apart at the seams. I can feel myself unraveling.

"What the devil!" cries Doctor Dickie from the door.

He's fresh from the hunt, dripping wet and shivering, gray as the ashes in the grate. Even his mustache is sagging.

I follow his disbelieving gaze around the room, seeing the devastation through his eyes. The picture of his grandchildren is cracked and smeared with blood, his Bible discarded, his medical bag tossed on the floor, its contents scattered across the bed. Bloody water fills the sink, my shirt in his bathtub. His surgery can't look much worse after an amputation.

Catching sight of me in my undershirt, the bandage trailing loose from my forehead, the shock on his face turns to anger.

"What have you done, Jonathan?" he demands, his voice swelling with rage.

"I'm sorry. I didn't know where else to go," I say, panicked. "After you left, I searched Stanwin's room for something to help Mother and I found a ledger."

"A ledger?" he says in a strangled voice. "You took something from him? You must put it back. Now, Jonathan!" he yells, sensing my hesitation.

"I can't. I was attacked. Somebody smashed a vase across my head and stole it. I was bleeding, and the bodyguard was going to wake up, so I came here."

A dreadful silence swallows the end of the story as Doctor Dickie stands the picture of his grandchildren upright and slowly gathers everything back into his medical bag, sliding it back under the bed.

He moves as though manacled, dragging my secrets behind him.

"It's my fault," he mutters. "I knew you weren't to be trusted, but my affection for your mother..."

He shakes his head, pushing by me to collect my shirt from the bathtub. There's a resignation to his actions that frightens me.

"I didn't mean to—" I begin.

"You used me to steal from Ted Stanwin," he says quietly, gripping the edges of the counter. "A man who can ruin me with a snap of his fingers."

"I'm sorry," I say.

He turns suddenly, his anger thick.

"You've made that word cheap, Jonathan! You said it after we covered up that business in Enderleigh House, and again at Little Hampton. Remember? Now you'd have me swallow this hollow apology as well."

He presses my shirt against my chest, his cheeks flushed red. Tears stand in his eyes. "How many women have you forced yourself upon? Do you even remember? How many times have you wept at your mother's breast, begging her to fix it, promising never to do it again and knowing full well that you would? And now, here you are again, doing the same to me, bloody, stupid Doctor Dickie. Well, I'm done. I can't stomach it anymore. You've been a blight on this world ever since I brought you into it."

I take an imploring step toward him, but he pulls a silver pistol from his pocket, letting it dangle by his side. He's not even looking at me.

"Get out, Jonathan, or by God, I'll shoot you myself."

Keeping one eye on the pistol, I back out of the room, closing the door as I step into the corridor.

My heart's thumping.

Doctor Dickie's gun is the very same one Evelyn will use to take her life tonight. He's holding the murder weapon.

Quite how long I stare at Jonathan Derby in my bedroom mirror, it's impossible to say. I'm looking for the man within, some hint of my real face.

I want Derby to see his executioner.

Whiskey warms my throat, the bottle plundered from the drawing room and already half empty. I need it to stop my hands from shaking as I try to knot my bow tie. Doctor Dickie's testimony confirmed what I already knew. Derby's a monster, his crimes washed away by his mother's money. There's no justice waiting for this man, no trial or punishment. If he's to pay for what he's done, I'll have to march him to the gallows myself, and that's what I intend to do.

First, though, we're going to save Evelyn Hardcastle's life.

My gaze is drawn toward Doctor Dickie's silver pistol, lying harmless on an armchair like a fly swatted out of the air. Stealing it was a simple matter, as easy as sending a servant with an invented emergency to lure the doctor out of his room while I slipped in afterward and took it from his nightstand. For too long I've allowed this day to dictate terms to me, but no longer. If somebody wishes to murder Evelyn with this pistol, they'll have to come through me first. The Plague Doctor's riddle be damned! I don't trust him, and I won't stand idly by while horrors play out in front of me. It's time Jonathan Derby finally did some good on this earth.

Slipping the pistol into my jacket pocket, I take one last mouthful of whiskey and step out into the corridor, following the other guests down the staircase to dinner. Unlike their manners, their taste is impeccable. Evening gowns expose naked backs and pale skin adorned with glittering jewelry. The listlessness of earlier is gone, their charm extravagant. At last, as evening calls, they've come alive.

As always, I keep an eye out for some hint of the footman among these passing faces. He's long overdue a visit, and the longer the day goes on, the more certain I become that something dreadful is coming. At least it'll be a fair fight. Derby has very few laudable qualities, but his anger makes him a handful. I can barely keep hold of him, so I can't imagine what it would be like to see him flying at you, dripping hate.

Michael Hardcastle's standing in the entrance hall with a painted-on smile, greeting the guests coming down the stairs, as though genuinely glad to see every last wretched one of them. I had intended on questioning him about the mysterious Felicity Maddox, and the note at the well, but it will have to wait until later. There's an impregnable wall of taffeta and bow ties between us.

Piano music drags me through the crowds into the long gallery, where guests are mingling with drinks as servants prepare the dining hall on the other side of the doors. Taking a whiskey from one of the passing trays, I keep an eye out for Millicent. I'd hoped to give Derby his goodbyes, but she's nowhere to be seen. In fact, the only person I recognize is Sebastian Bell, who's drifting through the entrance hall on his way to his room.

Stopping a maid, I ask after Helena Hardcastle, hoping the lady of the house might be near at hand, but she hasn't arrived. That means she's been missing all day. Absence has officially become disappearance. It can't be coincidence that Lady Hardcastle is nowhere to be found on the day of her daughter's death, though whether she's a suspect or victim I can't be sure. One way or another, I'm going to find out.

My glass is empty, my head becoming foggy. I'm surrounded

by laughter and conversation, friends and lovers. The good cheer is stirring Derby's bitterness. I can feel his disgust, his loathing. He hates these people, this world. He hates himself.

Servants slip past me with silver platters, Evelyn's last meal arriving in a procession.

Why isn't she afraid?

I can hear her laughter from here. She's mingling with the guests as though all her days lay ahead, yet when Ravencourt brought up the danger this morning, it was clear she knew something was amiss.

Discarding my glass, I make my way through the entrance hall and into the corridor toward Evelyn's bedroom. If there are answers, perhaps that's where I'll find them.

The lamps have been lowered to dim flames. It's quiet and oppressive, a forgotten edge of the world. I'm halfway up the passage when I notice a splash of red emerging from the shadows.

A footman's livery.

He's blocking the passage.

I freeze. Glancing behind me, I try to work out whether I can reach the entrance hall before he's on me. The odds are slim. I'm not even sure my legs will listen when I tell them to move.

"Sorry, sir," says a chirpy voice, the footman taking a step closer and revealing himself to be a short, wiry boy, no more than thirteen, with pimples and a nervous smile. "Excuse me," he adds after a moment, and I realize I'm in his way. Mumbling an apology, I let him pass and blow out an explosive breath.

The footman's made me so afraid, the mere suggestion of his presence is enough to cripple even Derby, a man who'd throw a punch at the sun because it burned him. Was that his intention? The reason he taunted Bell and Ravencourt, rather than killing them? If this continues, he'll be able to pick off my hosts without a shred of resistance.

I'm earning the "rabbit" nickname he's given me.

Proceeding cautiously, I continue to Evelyn's bedroom, finding it locked. Knocking brings no answer, and unwilling to leave without something to show for my efforts, I take a step backward, intending to put my shoulder through it. That's when I notice the door to Helena's bedroom is in exactly the same place as the door into Ravencourt's parlor. Poking my head into both rooms, I find the dimensions are identical. That suggests Evelyn's bedroom was once a parlor. If that's the case, there will be a connecting door from Helena's room, which is useful, because the lock is still broken from this morning.

My guess is proven correct. The connecting door is hidden behind an ornate tapestry on the wall. Thankfully, it's unlocked and I'm able to slip through into Evelyn's room.

Given her fractured relationship with her parents, I'd half expected to find her sleeping in a broom closet, but the bedroom is comfortable enough, if modest. There's a four-poster bed at the center, a bathtub and bowl behind a curtain on a rail. Evidently the maid hasn't been allowed in for some time because the bath is full of cold, dirty water, towels discarded in soggy heaps on the floor, a necklace tossed carelessly on the bedside table next to a pile of scrunched-up tissues, all stained with makeup. The curtains are drawn, Evelyn's fire piled high with logs. Four oil lamps stand in the corners of the room, pinching the gloom between their flickering light and that of the fireplace.

I'm shaking with pleasure, Derby's excitement at this intrusion a warm blush rising through my body. I can feel my spirit trying to recoil from my host, and it's all I can do to hold onto myself as I sift through Evelyn's possessions, searching for anything that might drive her toward the reflecting pool later tonight. She's a messy sort, discarded clothes stuffed wherever they happen to fit, costume jewelry heaped in the drawers, tangled up with old scarves and shawls. There's no system, no order, no hint that she allows a maid anywhere near her things. Whatever her secrets, she's hiding them from more than me.

I catch myself stroking a silk blouse, frowning at my own hand before realizing it's not me that wants this. It's him.

It's Derby.

With a cry, I pull my hand back, slamming the wardrobe shut.

I can feel his yearning. He'd have me on my knees, pawing through her belongings, inhaling her scent. He's a beast, and for a second, he had control.

Wiping the beads of desire from my forehead, I take a deep breath to collect myself before pushing on with the search.

I narrow my concentration to a point, keeping hold of my thoughts, allowing no gap for him to creep through. Even so, the investigation is fruitless. About the only item of interest is an old scrapbook containing curios from Evelyn's life: old correspondence between herself and Michael, pictures from her childhood, scraps of poetry and musings from her adolescence, all combining to present a portrait of a very lonely woman who loved her brother desperately and now misses him terribly.

Closing the book, I push it back under the bed where I found it, departing the room as quietly as I came, dragging a thrashing Derby within me.

～ 30 ～

I'm sitting in an armchair in a dim corner of the entrance hall, the seat arranged to give me a clear view to Evelyn's bedroom door. Dinner's ongoing, but Evelyn will be dead in three hours and I plan to dog her every step to the reflecting pool.

Such patience would normally be beyond my host, but I've discovered that he enjoys smoking, which is handy because it makes me light-headed, dulling the cancer of Derby in my thoughts. It's a pleasant, if unexpected, benefit of this inherited habit.

"They'll be ready when you need them," says Cunningham, appearing through the fog and crouching by my chair. There's a pleased grin on his face I can make neither head nor tail of.

"Who'll be ready?" I say, looking at him.

This grin disappears, embarrassment taking its place as he lurches to his feet.

"I'm sorry, Mr. Derby, I thought you were somebody else," he says hastily.

"I *am* somebody else, Cunningham. It's me, Aiden. I still don't have the foggiest idea what you're talking about, though."

"You asked me to get some people together," he says.

"No, I didn't."

Our confusions must mirror each other, because Cunningham's face has twisted into the same knot as my brain.

"I'm sorry, he said you'd understand," says Cunningham.

"Who said?"

A sound draws my attention to the entrance hall, and turning in my seat, I see Evelyn fleeing across the marble, weeping into her hands.

"Take this. I have to go," says Cunningham, thrusting a piece of paper into my hand with the phrase *all of them* written on it.

"Wait! I don't know what this means," I call after him, but it's too late. He's already gone.

I'd follow him, but Michael is chasing Evelyn into the entrance hall, and this is why I'm here. These are the missing moments that transform Evelyn from the brave, kind woman I met as Bell into the suicidal heiress who'll take her life by the reflecting pool.

"Evie, Evie, don't go. Tell me what I can do," says Michael, catching her arm at the elbow.

She shakes her head, tears sparkling in the candlelight, mirroring the diamonds flashing in her hair.

"I just..." Her voice chokes. "I need to..."

Shaking her head, she shrugs him off, flying past me toward her bedroom. Fumbling the key into the lock, she slips inside, slamming the door shut behind her. Michael watches her go despondently, grabbing a glass of port from the tray Madeline's carrying to the dining hall.

It disappears in one gulp, his cheeks flushing.

Lifting the tray out of her hands, he waves the maid toward Evelyn's bedroom.

"Don't worry about this. See to your mistress," he orders.

It's a grand gesture, somewhat undone by the confusion that follows as he tries to work out what to do with the thirty glasses of sherry, port, and brandy he's inherited.

From my seat, I watch Madeline rap on Evelyn's door, the poor maid becoming increasingly upset with every ignored entreaty. Finally, she returns to the entrance hall, where Michael is still casting around for somewhere to put the tray.

"I'm afraid Mademoiselle is…" Madeline makes a despairing gesture.

"It's fine, Madeline," Michael says wearily. "It's been a difficult day. Why don't you leave her be for now. I'm sure she'll call when she needs you."

Madeline lingers uncertainly, looking back toward Evelyn's bedroom, but after a brief hesitation she does as he asks, disappearing down the servant's staircase toward the kitchen.

Casting left and right for somewhere to dispense with the tray, Michael spots me watching him.

"I must look a damned fool," he says, blushing.

"More like an inept waiter," I say bluntly. "I assume the dinner didn't go as planned?"

"It's this business with Ravencourt," he says, balancing the tray rather precariously across the padded arms of a nearby chair. "Do you have one of those cigarettes spare?"

I emerge from the fog to hand him one, lighting it in his fingers. "Does she really have to marry him?" I ask.

"We're almost broke, old chum," he sighs, taking a long drag. "Father's buying up every empty mine and blighted plantation in the empire. I give it a year or two before our coffers are completely dry."

"But I thought Evelyn and your parents didn't get on? Why would she agree to go through with it?"

"For me," he says, shaking his head. "My parents threatened to cut me off if she doesn't obey them. I'd be flattered if I didn't feel so damn guilty about it all."

"There must be another way."

"Father's wrung every penny he can out of those few banks still impressed by his title. If we don't get this money, well…truth be told, I don't know what will happen, but we'll end up poor, and I'm fairly certain we'll be dreadful at it."

"Most people are," I say.

"Well, at least they've had practice," he says, tapping ash onto the marble floor. "Why is there a bandage on your head?"

I touch it self-consciously, having quite forgotten it was there.

"I got on the wrong side of Stanwin," I say. "I heard him arguing with Evelyn about somebody called Felicity Maddox and tried to intervene."

"Felicity?" he says, recognition showing on his face.

"You know the name?"

He pauses, taking a deep puff of his cigarette, before exhaling slowly.

"Old friend of my sister," he says. "Can't imagine why they'd be arguing about her. Evelyn hasn't seen her in years."

"She's here in Blackheath," I say. "She left a note for Evelyn at the well."

"Are you certain?" he asks skeptically. "She wasn't on the guest list, and Evelyn didn't say anything to me."

We're interrupted by a noise at the doorway, Doctor Dickie hurrying toward me. He places a hand on my shoulder and leans close to my ear.

"It's your mother," he whispers. "You need to come with me."

Whatever's happened, it's dreadful enough for him to have buried his antipathy toward me.

Apologizing to Michael, I run after the doctor, my dread growing with every step, until finally he ushers me into her bedroom.

The window's open, a cold gust snatching at the candle flames lighting the room. It takes my eyes a few seconds to adjust to the dimness, but finally I find her. Millicent's lying on her side in bed, eyes closed and chest still, as though she crawled under the covers for a quick nap. She'd begun dressing for dinner and has combed her usually wild gray hair straight, tying it up away from her face.

"I'm sorry, Jonathan. I know how close you were," he says.

Grief squeezes me. No matter how much I tell myself that this woman isn't my mother, I can't make it let go.

My tears arrive suddenly and silently. Trembling, I sit down in the wooden chair beside her bed, taking her still-warm hand in mine.

"It was a heart attack," says Doctor Dickie in a pained voice. "It would have happened very suddenly."

He's standing on the other side of the bed, the emotion as raw on his face as my own. Wiping away a tear, he pulls the window shut, cutting off the cold breeze. The candles stand to attention, the light in the room solidifying into a warm, golden glow.

"Can I warn her?" I say, thinking of the things I can put right tomorrow.

He looks puzzled for a second, but clearly ascribes the question to grief and answers me in a kind voice.

"No," he says, shaking his head. "You couldn't have warned her."

"What if—"

"It was just her time, Jonathan," he says softly.

I nod. It's all I can manage. He stays a little longer, wrapping me in words I neither hear, nor feel. My grief is a bottomless well. All I can do is fall and hope to hit the bottom. Yet the deeper I go, the more I realize I'm not weeping solely for Millicent Derby. There's something else down here, something deeper than my host's grief, something that belongs to Aiden Bishop. It's raw and desperate, sad and angry, beating at the core of me. Derby's grief has revealed it, but hard as I try, I can't quite pull it up, out of the dark.

Leave it buried.

"What is it?"

A piece of you. Now leave it alone.

A knock at the door distracts me, and looking at the clock, I realize over an hour's passed. There's no sign of the doctor. He must have left without me noticing.

Evelyn pokes her head into the room. Her face is pale, cheeks red with cold. She's still dressed in the blue ball gown, though it's picked up a few creases since I last saw her. The tiara is poking from the pocket of her long beige coat, Wellington boots leaving a trail of mud and leaves on the floor. She must have only just returned from the graveyard with Bell.

"Evelyn…"

I intend to say more, but I choke on my sorrow.

Evelyn gathers the shards of the moment together, then tuts and enters the room, heading straight for a bottle of whiskey on the shelf. The glass has barely touched my lips when she tips it upward, forcing me to drink it down in one swallow.

Gagging, I push the glass away, whiskey running down my chin.

"Why would you—"

"Well, you can hardly help me in your current state," she says.

"Help you?"

She's studying me, turning me over in her mind.

She hands me a handkerchief.

"Wipe your chin. You look atrocious," she says. "I'm afraid sorrow doesn't suit that arrogant face at all well."

"How—"

"It's a very long story," she says. "And I'm afraid we're somewhat pressed for time."

I sit dumbly, struggling to take everything in, wishing for the clarity of Ravencourt's mind. So much has happened, so much I can't quite piece together. I already felt as if I was staring at the clues through a foggy magnifying glass, and now Evelyn's here, tugging a bedsheet over Millicent's face, calm as a summer day. Try as I might, I can't keep up.

Quite clearly, that little tantrum at dinner regarding her engagement was an act, because there's no trace of that crippling sadness about her now. Her eyes are clear, her tone contemplative.

"So I'm not the only one dying tonight," she says, stroking the old lady's hair. "What a miserable thing."

The glass falls from my hand in shock.

"You know about—"

"The reflecting pool, yes. Curious affair, isn't it?"

She has a dreamy tone, as though describing something she once heard and now only half remembers. I'd suspect her mind of having buckled in some way, if it weren't for the hard edge to her words.

"You seem to be taking the news rather well," I say cautiously.

"You should have seen me this morning. I was so angry I was kicking holes in the walls."

Evelyn's running her hand along the edge of the dressing table, opening Millicent's jewelry box, touching the pearl-handled brush. I'd describe her actions as covetous, if there didn't appear to be an equal amount of reverence.

"Who wants you dead, Evelyn?" I ask, unnerved by this curious display.

"I don't know," she says. "There was a letter pushed under my door when I woke up. The instructions were quite specific."

"But you don't know who sent it?"

"Constable Rashton has a theory, but he's kept it rather close to his chest."

"Rashton?"

"Your friend? He told me you were helping him investigate." Doubt and distaste seep out of every word, but I'm too intrigued to take it personally. Could this Rashton be another host? Maybe even the same man who asked Cunningham to deliver that *all of them* message and gather some people together. Either way, he seems to have swept me up into his plan. Whether I can trust it is another matter.

"Where did Rashton approach you?" I ask.

"Mr. Derby," she says firmly. "I'd love nothing more than to sit down and answer all your questions, but we don't really have time. I'm expected at the reflecting pool in ten minutes, and I can't be late. In fact, that's why I'm here. I need the silver pistol you took from the doctor."

"You can't mean to go through with this," I say, jumping up from my seat in alarm.

"As I understand it, your friends are close to unmasking my would-be killer. They simply need a little more time. If I don't go, the killer will know something is wrong, and I can't risk that."

I'm beside her in two steps, my pulse racing.

"Are you saying they know who's behind all of this?" I say excitedly. "Did they give you any indication who it might be?"

Evelyn's holding one of Millicent Derby's cameos up to the light, an ivory face on blue lace. Her hand is shaking. It's the first sign of fear I've seen from her.

"They didn't, but I hope they find out soon. I'm trusting your friends to save me before I'm forced to do something…final."

"Final?" I say.

"The note was specific. Either I take my life out by the reflecting pool at 11:00 p.m., or somebody I care about very deeply dies in my stead."

"Felicity?" I say. "I know she left a note for you at the well and that you wrote to her some time ago asking her for assistance with your mother. Michael said she's an old friend. Is she in danger? Is somebody holding her against her will?"

That would explain why I haven't been able to find her.

The jewelry box clatters shut. Evelyn turns to face me, hands now pressed flat against the dressing table.

"I don't mean to sound impatient, but don't you have somewhere to be?" she says. "I was asked to remind you about a rock that needs watching. Does that make any sense to you?"

I nod, remembering the favor she asked of me earlier this afternoon.

I'm to be standing by it when Evelyn kills herself. I wasn't to move. Not an inch, she'd said.

"In that case my work here is done and I should go," says Evelyn. "Where's the silver pistol?"

Even in her small fingers, it seems an inconsequential thing, more decoration than weapon, an embarrassing way to end a life. I wonder if that's the point, if there's not some quiet rebuke in the instrument of death, as there is in the method. Evelyn isn't merely being murdered, she's being embarrassed, dominated.

Every choice has been taken from her.

"What a pretty way to die," says Evelyn, staring at the pistol. "Please don't be late, Mr. Derby. I suspect my life depends upon it."

After a final glance toward the jewelry box, she's gone.

～ 31 ～

Hugging myself against the cold, I stand over Anna's carefully placed rock, terrified of taking even a small step to my left, where at least I'd be warmed by one of the braziers. I don't know why I'm here, but if it's part of a plan to save Evelyn, I'll stand in this spot until my blood turns to ice.

Glancing toward the trees, I catch sight of the Plague Doctor in his usual location, half hidden by gloom. He's not looking at the reflecting pool as I thought when I witnessed this moment as Ravencourt, but away to his right. The angle of his head suggests he's talking to somebody, though I'm too far away to see who. Either way, it's an encouraging sign. Evelyn suggested she'd found allies among my hosts, and surely, in those bushes, somebody is waiting to come to her aid?

Evelyn arrives at eleven exactly, the silver pistol hanging limp in her hand. Drifting from shadow to flame, she follows the braziers, her blue ball gown trailing in the grass. I long to tear the pistol from her grasp, but somewhere beyond my sight an invisible hand is working, pulling levers I can't possibly understand. Any minute now somebody will call out, I'm certain of it. One of my future hosts will come sprinting into the darkness, telling Evelyn it's over and the murderer is captured. She'll drop the gun and sob her thanks, while Daniel presents his plan for both Anna and me to escape.

For the first time since all this began, I feel myself part of something bigger.

Encouraged by this, I root my feet, hovering over my rock.

Evelyn's come to a stop at the edge of the water, looking around at the trees. For a second, I think she'll spot the Plague Doctor, but she pulls her gaze back before reaching him. She's unsteady, swaying slightly as though moved by some music only she can hear. The flames from the brazier are reflected in the diamonds of her necklace, liquid fire pouring down her throat. She's trembling, desperation mounting on her face.

Something's wrong.

I glance back toward the ballroom to find Ravencourt at the window, looking longingly toward his friend. Words are forming on his lips, but they're too late to do any good.

"God help me," Evelyn whispers to the night.

Tears streaming down her cheeks, she turns the gun toward her stomach and pulls the trigger.

The shot is so loud it cracks the world, drowning out my anguished scream.

In the ballroom, the party holds its breath.

Surprised faces turn toward the reflecting pool, their eyes seeking out Evelyn. She's clutching her stomach, blood seeping out from between her fingers. She looks confused, as though she's been handed something she shouldn't have been, but before she can make sense of it, she buckles, falling forward into the water.

Fireworks explode in the night sky, as guests stream through the french doors, pointing and gasping. Somebody's running toward me, their footsteps pounding the dirt. I turn in time to take their full weight in my chest, sending me sprawling to the ground.

Trying to scramble to their feet, they only succeed in scraping my face with their fingers, a knee jabbing into my stomach. Derby's temper, already clawing to be let out, takes hold of me. With a scream of rage, I begin pounding at this shape in the darkness, clutching their clothing even as they try to wrestle their way free.

Howling in frustration, I'm pulled off the ground, my opponent similarly lofted away, both of us held fast by servants. Lantern light spills across us, revealing a furious Michael Hardcastle desperately trying to break free of Cunningham's strong arms, which are keeping him from Evelyn's stricken form.

I stare at him in astonishment.

It's changed.

The revelation knocks the fight out of me, my body going limp in the servant's arms as I stare at the reflecting pool.

When I saw this event through Ravencourt's eyes, Michael clung to his sister, unable to move her. Now a tall fellow in a trench coat is pulling her out of the water, covering her blood-soaked body with Dickie's jacket.

The servant lets me go, and I drop to my knees in time to see a sobbing Michael Hardcastle led away by Cunningham. Determined to soak up as much of this miracle as possible, my gaze darts this way and that. Up by the reflecting pool, Doctor Dickie's kneeling by Evelyn's body, discussing something with the man in the trench coat, who appears to be in charge. Ravencourt's retreated to a couch in the ballroom and is sitting slumped over his cane, lost in thought. The band is being harangued by drunken guests who, oblivious to the horror outside, want them to carry on playing, while servants stand idle, crossing themselves when they draw closer to the body under the coat.

Heaven knows how long I sit there in the darkness, watching all this unfold. Long enough for everybody else to be ushered into the house by the fellow in the trench coat. Long enough for Evelyn's limp body to be carried away. Long enough to grow cold, to grow stiff.

Long enough for the footman to find me.

He appears around the far corner of the house, a small sack tied to his waist, blood dripping off his hands. Taking out his knife, he begins drawing the blade back and forth across the rim of a brazier. I can't tell whether he's sharpening it, or simply warming it, but I suspect it's irrelevant. He wants me to see it, to hear that unsettling scrape of metal against metal.

He's watching me, waiting for my reaction, and, looking at him now, I wonder how anybody ever mistook him for a servant. Though he's dressed in a footman's red and white livery, he possesses none of the traditional subservience. He's tall and thin, languid in his movements, with dirty blond hair and a teardrop face, dark eyes above a smirk that would be charming if it weren't so empty.

And then there's that broken nose.

It's purple and swollen, distorting his features. By the light of the fire, he looks like a creature dressing up as human, the mask slipping.

The footman holds up the knife to better inspect his work. Satisfied, he uses it to cut the sack from his waist, tossing it at my feet.

It hits the ground with a thud, the material soaked through with blood and tied shut with a drawstring. He wants me to open it, but I have no intention of indulging him.

Getting to my feet, I peel off my jacket and work loose the kinks in my neck.

In the back of my mind, I can hear Anna screaming at me, demanding I run. She's right, I should be afraid, and in any other host, I would be. This is clearly a trap, but I'm tired of fearing this man.

It's time to fight, if only to convince myself I can.

For a moment, we watch each other, the rain falling and the wind swirling. Unsurprisingly, it's the footman who forces the issue, turning on his heel and sprinting into the darkness of the forest.

Bellowing like a lunatic, I charge after him.

Crossing into the forest, the trees huddle around me, branches scratch my face, the foliage thickening.

My legs are tiring, but I keep running until I realize I can't hear him anymore.

Skidding to a halt, I spin on the spot, panting.

He's on me in seconds, covering my mouth to stifle my scream as the blade enters my side and tears up into my ribcage, blood burbling into my throat. My knees buckle, but I'm prevented from falling by his strong arms around me. He's breathing shallowly, eagerly. This isn't the sound of tiredness, it's excitement and anticipation.

A match flares, a tiny point of light held in front of my face.

He's kneeling down directly opposite, his pitiless black eyes boring into me.

"Brave rabbit," he says, slitting my throat.

~ 32 ~

DAY SIX

"Wake up! Wake up, Aiden!"

Somebody's banging on my door.

"You have to wake up, Aiden. Aiden!"

Swallowing my tiredness, I blink at my surroundings. I'm in a chair, clammy with sweat, my clothes twisted tight around me. It's nighttime, a candle guttering on a nearby table. There's a tartan blanket over my lap, old man's hands laid across a dog-eared book. Veins bulge in wrinkled flesh, crisscrossing dry ink stains and liver spots. I flex my fingers, stiff with age.

"Aiden, please!" says the voice in the corridor.

Rising from my chair, I move to the door, old aches stirring throughout my body like swarms of disturbed hornets. The hinges are loose, the bottom corner of the door scraping against the floor, revealing the lanky figure of Gregory Gold on the other side, slumped against the doorframe. He looks much as he will when he attacks the butler, though his dinner jacket's torn and caked with mud, his breathing ragged.

He's clutching the chess piece Anna gave me, and that, together with his use of my real name, is enough to convince me that he's another of my hosts. Normally, I'd welcome such a meeting, but he's in a frightful state, agitated and disheveled, a man dragged to hell and back.

Upon seeing me, he grips my shoulders. His dark eyes are bloodshot, flicking this way and that.

"Don't get out of the carriage," he says, spittle hanging off his lips. "Whatever you do, don't get out of the carriage."

His fear is a disease, the infection spreading through me.

"What happened to you?" I ask, a tremor in my voice.

"He…he never stops…"

"Never stops what?" I ask.

Gold's shaking his head, pounding his temples. Tears stream down his cheeks, but I don't know how to begin comforting him.

"Never stops what, Gold?" I ask again.

"Cutting," he says, drawing up his sleeve to reveal the slices beneath. They look exactly like the knife wounds Bell woke up with that first morning.

"You won't want to, you won't, but you'll give her up, you'll tell, you'll tell them everything, you won't want to, but you'll tell," he babbles. "There's two of them. Two. They look the same, but there's two."

His mind's broken; I can see that now. There isn't an ounce of sanity left to the man. I reach out a hand, hoping to draw him into the room, but he takes fright, backing away until he bumps into the far wall, only his voice remaining.

"Don't get out of the carriage," he hisses at me, wheeling away down the corridor.

I take a step out after him, but it's too dark to see anything, and by the time I return with a candle, the corridor's empty.

～ 33 ～

DAY TWO (CONTINUED)

The butler's body, the butler's pain, heavy with sedative. It's like coming home.

I'm barely awake, and already slipping back toward sleep.

It's getting dark. A man's pacing back and forth across the tiny room, a shotgun in his arms.

It's not the Plague Doctor. It's not Gold.

He hears me stir and turns around. He's in shade. I can't make him out.

I open my mouth, but no words come out of it.

I close my eyes and slip away again.

⌒ 34 ⌒

DAY SIX (CONTINUED)

"Father."

I'm startled to find the freckled face of a young man with red hair and blue eyes inches from my own. I'm old again, still sitting in my chair with the tartan blanket across my lap. The boy is bent at ninety degrees, hands clasped behind his back as though he doesn't trust them in company.

My scowl shoves him a step backward.

"You asked me to wake you at nine fifteen," he says apologetically.

He smells of scotch, tobacco, and fear. It wells up within him, staining the whites of his eyes yellow. They're wary and hunted, like an animal waiting for the shot.

It's light beyond the window, my candle long gone out, and the fire down to ash. My vague memory of being the butler proves I dozed off after Gold's visit, but I don't remember doing so. The horror of what Gold endured—what I must soon endure—kept me pacing into the early hours.

Don't get out of the carriage.

It was a warning and a plea. He wants me to change the day, and while that's exhilarating, it's also disturbing. I know it can be done—I've seen it—but if I'm clever enough to change things, the footman is as well. For all I know, we're running in circles undoing each other's work. This is no longer simply about finding the right answer, it's about holding onto it long enough to deliver it to the Plague Doctor.

I have to speak with the artist at the first opportunity.

I shift in my seat, tugging aside the tartan blanket, bringing the slightest flinch from the boy. He stiffens, looking at me sideways to see if I've noticed. Poor child; he's had all the bravery beaten out of him and now he's kicked for being a coward. My sympathy fares ill with my host, whose distaste for his son is absolute. He considers this boy's meekness infuriating, his silence an affront. He's a failure, an unforgivable failure.

My only one.

I shake my head, trying to free myself of this man's regrets. The memories of Bell, Ravencourt, and Derby were objects in a fog, but the clutter of this current life is scattered around me. I cannot help but trip over it.

Despite the suggestion of infirmity given by the blanket, I rise with only a little stiffness, stretching to a respectable height. My son's retreated to the corner of the room, draping himself in shadows. Though the distance is not great, it's too far for my host, whose eyes falter at half the span. I search for spectacles, knowing it's pointless. This man considers age a weakness, the result of a faltering will. There'll be no spectacles, no walking stick, no aid of any sort. Whatever burdens are heaped upon me, they're mine to endure. Alone.

I can feel my son weighing my mood, watching my face as one watches the clouds for an approaching storm.

"Spit it out," I say gruffly, agitated by his reticence.

"I was hoping I might be excused this afternoon's hunt," he says.

The words are laid at my feet, two dead rabbits for a hungry wolf.

Even this simple request grates upon me. What young man doesn't want to hunt? What young man creeps and crawls, tiptoeing around the edges of the world rather than trampling across the top of it? My urge is to refuse, to make him suffer for the temerity of being who he is, but I bite the desire back. We'll both be happier beyond each other's company.

"Very well," I say, waving him away.

"Thank you, Father," he says, escaping the room before I can change my mind. In his absence my breathing eases, my hands unclench. Anger takes its arms from around my chest, leaving me free to investigate the room for some reflection of its owner.

Books lie three thick on the bedside table, all dealing in the murky details of law. My invitation to the ball is being used as a bookmark and is addressed to Edward and Rebecca Dance. That name alone is enough to make me crumble. I remember Rebecca's face, her smell. The feeling of being near her. My fingers find the locket around my neck, her portrait cradled inside. Dance's grief is a quiet ache, a single tear once a day. It's the only luxury he allows himself.

Pushing aside the grief, I drum the invite with my finger.

"Dance," I murmur.

A peculiar name for such a joyless man.

Knocking perforates the silence, the handle turning, and the door opening seconds later. The fellow who enters is large and shambling, scratching a head full of white hair, dislodging dandruff in every direction. He's wearing a rumpled blue suit below white whiskers and bloodshot red eyes, and would look quite frightful if it weren't for the comfort with which he carries his dishevelment.

He pauses mid-scratch, blinking at me in bewilderment.

"This your room is it, Edward?" asks the stranger.

"Well, I woke up here," I say warily.

"Blast, I can't remember where they put me."

"Where did you sleep last night?"

"Sunroom," he says, scratching an armpit. "Herrington bet me I couldn't finish the last of the port in under five minutes, and that's all I remember until that scoundrel Gold woke me up this morning, ranting and raving like a lunatic."

The mention of Gold takes me back to his rambling warning last night, and the scars on his arm. Don't get out of the carriage, he'd said. Does that suggest I'll be leaving at some point? Or taking a journey? I already know I can't reach the village, so it seems unlikely.

"Did Gold say anything?" I ask. "Do you know where he was going, or what his plans were?"

"I didn't stop and sup with the man, Dance," he says dismissively. "I took his measure and let him know in no uncertain terms I had my eye on him." He glances around. "Did I leave a bottle in here? Need something to quieten this damnable headache."

I've barely opened my mouth to respond when he starts rooting through my drawers, leaving them standing open as he turns his assault upon the wardrobe. After patting down the pockets of my suits, he spins, surveying the room as though he's just heard a lion in the bushes.

Another knock, another face. This one belongs to Commander Clifford Herrington, the boring naval chap who sat next to Ravencourt at dinner.

"Come along, you two," he says, checking his watch. "Old Hardcastle's waiting for us."

Freed from the blight of strong alcohol, he's straight backed and authoritative.

"Any idea what he wants from us?" I ask.

"None whatsoever, but I expect he'll tell us when we get there," he responds briskly.

"I need my walking scotch," says my companion.

"There's sure to be some over at the gatehouse, Sutcliffe," says Herrington, not bothering to hide his impatience. "Besides, you know Hardcastle, he's damned serious these days, probably best if we don't turn up half cut."

Such is the strength of my connection to Dance that the mere mention of Lord Hardcastle causes me to puff out my cheeks in annoyance. My host's presence in Blackheath is a matter of obligation, a fleeting visit lasting only so long as it takes to conclude his business with the family. In contrast, I'm desperate to question the master of the house about his missing wife, and my enthusiasm for our meeting is rubbing up against Dance's agitation like sandpaper on skin.

Somehow, I'm annoying myself.

Badgered once again by the impatient naval officer, the shambling Sutcliffe holds up a hand, begging an extra minute, before turning his desperate fingers loose among my shelves. Sniffing the air, he lurches toward the bed, lifting the mattress to reveal a pilfered bottle of scotch on the springs.

"Lead on, Herrington, old boy," he says magnanimously, unscrewing the cap and taking a hearty slug.

Shaking his head, Herrington gestures us out into the corridor, where Sutcliffe begins telling a lewd joke at the top of his voice, his friend trying unsuccessfully to quieten him.

They're buffoons both, their personalities floating on a sea of arrogance that sets my teeth on edge. My host would happily stride off ahead, but I don't want to walk these corridors alone. As a compromise, I follow two steps behind, far enough away that I don't have to join the conversation, but close enough to give the footman pause should he be lurking nearby.

We're met at the bottom of the stairs by somebody called Christopher Pettigrew, who turns out to be the oily chap Daniel was conferring with at dinner. He's a thin man, built to sneer, with dark greasy hair swept over to one side. He's as stooping and sly as I remember, his gaze running its hands through my pockets before taking in my face. I wondered two nights ago if he might be a future host, but if so, I must have given myself freely to his vices as he's already soft with alcohol, happily taking up the bottle being shared between his chums. It never veers in my direction, meaning I never have to refuse. Clearly,

Edward Dance stands apart from this rabble, and I'm happy it's so. They're a queer bunch; friends certainly, but desperately so, like three men stranded on the same island. Thankfully, their good cheer fades the farther we draw from the house, their laughter whipped away by the wind and rain, the bottle forced into a warm pocket along with the cold hand holding it.

"Did anybody else get yapped at by Ravencourt's poodle this morning?" says the oily Pettigrew, who's little more than a pair of deceitful eyes above a scarf at this point. "What's his name again?"

He clicks his fingers trying to summon the memory.

"Charles Cunningham," I say distantly, only half listening. Farther along the path, I'm certain I saw somebody shadowing us in the trees. Just a flash, enough for doubt, except they appeared to be wearing a footman's livery. My hand goes to my throat, and for an instant, I feel his blade again.

Shuddering, I squint at the trees, trying to wring some use out of Dance's awful eyes, but if it was my enemy, he's gone now.

"That's the one, Charles bloody Cunningham," says Pettigrew.

"Was he asking about Thomas Hardcastle's murder?" says Herrington, his face turned resolutely toward the wind, no doubt a habit of his naval background. "I heard he was up visiting Stanwin this morning, collared him first thing," he adds.

"Damned impertinent," says Pettigrew. "What about you, Dance? Did he come sniffing around?"

"Not that I'm aware," I say, still staring at the forest. We're passing close to the spot where I thought I spotted the footman, but now I see the splash of color is a red trail marker nailed to a tree. My imagination's painting monsters in the woods.

"What did Cunningham want?" I say, reluctantly returning my attention to my companions.

"It's not him," says Pettigrew. "He was asking questions on behalf of Ravencourt, seems the fat old banker's taken an interest in Thomas Hardcastle's murder."

That brings me up short. Of all the tasks I set Cunningham when I was Ravencourt, asking questions about Thomas Hardcastle's murder wasn't one of them. Whatever Cunningham's doing, he's using Ravencourt's name to curry favor. Perhaps this is part of the secret he was so keen to keep me from revealing, the secret which still needs to find its way into an envelope beneath the chair in the library.

"What sort of questions?" I say, my interest kindled for the first time.

"Kept asking me about the second killer, the one Stanwin said he clipped with his shotgun before he escaped," says Herrington, who's tipping a hip flask to his lips. "Wanted to know if there were any rumors about who they were, any descriptions."

"Were there?" I ask.

"Never heard anything," says Herrington. "Wouldn't have told him if I had. Sent him away with a flea in his ear."

"Not surprised Cecil's got Cunningham on it, though," adds Sutcliffe, scratching his whiskers. "He's thick as thieves with every charwoman and gardener who ever took a shilling at Blackheath, probably knows more about this place than we do."

"How's that?" I ask.

"He was living here when the murder happened," says Sutcliffe, glancing over his shoulder at me. "Just a boy back then, of course, bit older than Evelyn, as I remember. Rumor had it he was Peter's bastard. Helena gave him to the cook to raise, or something like that. Never could work out who she was punishing."

His voice is thoughtful, a rather strange sound coming from this shaggy, shapeless creature. "Pretty little thing that cook, lost her husband in the war," he muses. "The Hardcastles paid for the boy's education, even got him the job with Ravencourt when he came of age."

"What's Ravencourt want with a nineteen-year-old murder?" asks Pettigrew.

"Due diligence," says Herrington bluntly, stepping around horse manure. "Ravencourt's buying a Hardcastle. He wants to know what baggage she's bringing along."

Their conversation swiftly frays into trivialities, but my thoughts remain fixed on Cunningham. Last night, he pressed a note into Derby's hand that read *all of them* and told me he was rounding up guests on behalf of a future host. That would suggest I can trust him, but he clearly has his own agenda in Blackheath. I know he's Peter Hardcastle's illegitimate son and that he's asking questions about the murder of his half brother. Somewhere between those two facts is a secret he's so desperate to keep, he's allowed himself to be blackmailed with it.

I grit my teeth. For once, it would be refreshing to find somebody in this place who was exactly what they appeared to be.

Passing the cobbled path toward the stables, we push south along the never-ending road into the village, before finally coming upon the gatehouse. One by one, we fill the narrow corridor of the building, hanging our coats and shaking the rain free of our clothes while complaining about the conditions outside.

"Through here, chaps," says a voice from behind a door on our right.

We follow the voice into a gloomy sitting room lit by an open fire, where Lord Peter Hardcastle sits in an armchair near the window. He has one leg flung across the other, a book flat on his lap. He's somewhat older than his portrait suggested, though still broad chested and fit looking. Dark eyebrows slide toward each other in a V-shape, pointing toward a long nose and mopey mouth curved downward at the edges. A ragged specter of beauty suggests itself, but his stash of splendor has almost run dry.

"Why the hell are we meeting all the way out here?" asks Pettigrew grumpily, dropping into a chair. "You've a perfectly good…" He waves in the direction of Blackheath. "Well, you've got something that resembles a house down the road."

"That damn house has been a curse on this family ever since I was a boy," says Peter Hardcastle, pouring drinks into five glasses. "I won't set foot inside until it's absolutely necessary."

"Perhaps you should have thought of that before throwing history's most tasteless party," says Pettigrew. "Do you really intend on announcing Evelyn's engagement on the anniversary of your own son's murder?"

"Do you think any of this is my idea?" asks Hardcastle, slamming the bottle down and glaring at Pettigrew. "Do you think I want to be here?"

"Easy, Peter," soothes Sutcliffe, shambling over to awkwardly pat his friend's shoulder. "Christopher's grumpy because, well, he's Christopher."

"Of course," says Hardcastle, whose red cheeks suggest anything but understanding. "It's just...Helena's acting damn queer, and now all this. It's been quite trying."

He goes back to pouring drinks, an uneasy silence gagging everything but the rain thumping on the windows.

Personally I'm glad of the quiet, and the chair.

My companions walked quickly and keeping up was a chore. I need to catch my breath, and pride dictates that nobody notice me doing it. In lieu of conversation, I look around the room, but there's little worthy of scrutiny. It's long and narrow, with furniture piled up against the walls like wreckage on a riverbank. The carpet is worn through, the flowery wallpaper gaudy. Age is thick in the air, as though the last owners sat here until they crumbled into dust. It's nowhere near as uncomfortable as the east wing, where Stanwin has sequestered himself, but it's still an odd place to find the lord of the house.

I've not had cause to ask what Lord Hardcastle's role in his daughter's murder might be, but his choice of lodging suggests he's looking to stay out of sight. The question is, what is he doing with that anonymity?

Drinks are deposited before us, Hardcastle resuming his former seat. He's rolling his glass between his palms, gathering his thoughts. There's an endearing awkwardness to his manner that immediately reminds me of Michael.

To my left, Sutcliffe—who's already halfway through his scotch and soda—digs a document from his jacket and hands it to me, indicating that I should pass it along to Hardcastle. It's a marriage contract drafted by the firm Dance, Pettigrew & Sutcliffe. Evidently, myself, the lugubrious Philip Sutcliffe, and the oily Christopher Pettigrew are business partners. Even so, I'm certain Hardcastle hasn't brought us here to talk about Evelyn's nuptials. He's too distracted for that, too fidgety. Besides, why request Herrington's presence if you only needed your solicitors.

Confirming my suspicion, Hardcastle takes the contract from me, offering it the faintest of glances before dropping it on the table.

"Dance and I worked on it ourselves," says Sutcliffe, rising to fetch another drink. "Have Ravencourt and Evelyn put their signatures on the bottom and you're a rich man again. Ravencourt will pay a lump sum upon signing, with the outstanding amount held in trust until after the ceremony. In a couple of years, he'll take Blackheath off your hands as well. Not a bad piece of work if I do say so myself."

"Where is old Ravencourt?" asks Pettigrew, glancing at the door. "Shouldn't he be here for this?"

"Helena's looking after him," says Hardcastle, taking a wooden case from the lintel above the fireplace and opening it to reveal rows of fat cigars that draw childish coos from the party. Declining one, I watch Hardcastle as he offers them around. His smile hides a dreadful eagerness, his pleasure in this display a foundation for other matters.

He wants something.

"How is Helena?" I ask, tasting my drink. It's water. Dance doesn't even allow himself the pleasure of alcohol. "All of this must be hard on her."

"I should hope so. It was her damn idea to come back," snorts Hardcastle, taking a cigar for himself and closing the box. "You know, a chap wants to do his best, be supportive, but dash it all, I've barely seen her since we got here. Can't get two words out of the woman. If I were a spiritual sort of fellow, I'd think her possessed."

Matches are passing from hand to hand, each man indulging his own cigar-lighting ritual. Forgoing Pettigrew's back and forth motion, Herrington's gentle touches, and Sutcliffe's circular theatrics, Hardcastle simply lights it, shooting me an exasperated glance.

A flicker of affection stirs within me, the remnants of some stronger emotion reduced to embers.

Blowing out a long trail of yellow smoke, Hardcastle settles back in his chair.

"Gentlemen, I invited you here today because we all have something in common." His delivery is stiff, rehearsed. "We are all being blackmailed by Ted Stanwin, but I have a way to free us, if you'll hear me out."

He's watching each of us for a reaction.

Pettigrew and Herrington remain quiet, but the lumpen Sutcliffe splutters, taking a hasty gulp of his drink.

"Go on, Peter," says Pettigrew.

"I have something on Stanwin we can exchange for our freedom."

The room is still. Pettigrew is on the edge of his seat, the cigar quite forgotten in his hands.

"And why haven't you used it already?" he asks.

"Because we're in this together," says Hardcastle.

"Because it's damn risky more like," interjects a red-faced Sutcliffe. "You know what happens if one of us moves against Stanwin: he releases what he has on each of us, dropping us all in the pot. Exactly like Myerson's lot."

"He's bleeding us dry," says Hardcastle heatedly.

"He's bleeding *you* dry, Peter," says Sutcliffe, jabbing the table with a thick finger. "You're about to make a pile out of Ravencourt, and you don't want Stanwin getting his hands on it."

"That devil's had his hand in my pocket for nearly twenty years," exclaims Hardcastle, flushing a little. "How much longer can I be expected to let it go on?"

He turns his gaze on Pettigrew.

"Come now, Christopher, surely you're ready to listen to me. Stanwin's the reason…" Storm clouds of embarrassment drift across his gray face. "Well, perhaps Elspeth wouldn't have left if…"

Pettigrew sips at his drink, offering neither rebuke nor encouragement. Only I can see the warmth rising up his neck, or how his fingers are squeezing the glass so tightly the skin behind his nails has turned white.

Hardcastle hurriedly turns his attention toward me.

"We can rip Stanwin's hand from our throat, but we need to confront him together," he says, striking a balled fist into his palm. "Only by showing that we're all ready to act against him will he listen."

Sutcliffe puffs up. "That's—"

"Quiet, Philip," interrupts Herrington, the naval officer's eyes never leaving Hardcastle's. "What have you got on Stanwin?"

Hardcastle flicks a suspicious glance at the door, before lowering his voice.

"He has a child squirreled away somewhere," he says. "He's kept her hidden for fear she may be used against him, but Daniel Coleridge claims to have uncovered her name."

"The gambler?" says Pettigrew. "How's he mixed up in all of this?"

"Didn't seem prudent to ask, old chap," says Hardcastle, swirling his drink. "Some men walk in dark places the rest of us shouldn't tread."

"Word has it he pays half the servants in London for information on their masters," says Herrington, pulling his lip. "I wouldn't be surprised if the same was true of Blackheath, and Stanwin certainly worked here long enough to have let a secret slip. There could be something in this, you know."

Hearing them discuss Daniel gives me an odd tingle of excitement. I've known for some time he's my final host, but he's been operating so far in my future, I've never truly felt connected to him. To see our investigations converging this way is like catching sight of something long sought on the horizon. Finally, there's a road between us.

Hardcastle's on his feet, warming his hands by the heat of the fire. Lit by the flames, it's clear the years have taken more from him than they've given. Uncertainty is a crack through the center of him, undermining any suggestion of solidity or strength. This man's been broken in two and put back together crooked, and if I had to guess, I'd say there was a child-shaped hole right in the middle.

"What does Coleridge want from us?" I ask.

Hardcastle looks at me with flat, unseeing eyes.

"I'm sorry?" he says.

"You said Daniel Coleridge has something on Stanwin, which means he wants something from us in exchange for it. I assume that's why you've called us all together."

"Just so," says Hardcastle, fingering a loose button on his jacket. "He wants a favor."

"Only one?" asks Pettigrew.

"From each of us, with the promise that we'll honor it whenever he calls upon us, no matter what it might be."

Glances are exchanged, doubt handed from face to face. I feel like a spy in the enemy camp. I'm not certain what Daniel's up to, but I'm obviously meant to help sway this argument in his favor. In *my* favor. Whatever this favor turns out to be, hopefully it will help free us and Anna from this dreadful place.

"I'm for it," I say grandly. "Stanwin's comeuppance is long overdue."

"I concur," says Pettigrew, waving cigar smoke from his face. "He's had enough out of me. What about you, Clifford?"

"I agree," says the old sailor.

All heads turn to Sutcliffe, whose eyes are running circuits of the room.

"We're trading devils," says the shaggy lawyer eventually.

"Perhaps," says Hardcastle, "but I've read my Dante, Philip. Not all hells are created equal. Now, what do you say?"

He nods grudgingly, eyes lowered to his glass.

"Good," says Hardcastle. "I'll meet with Coleridge, and we'll confront Stanwin before dinner. All being well, this will be over by the time we announce the wedding."

"And just like that we climb out of one pocket and into another," says Pettigrew, finishing off his drink. "How splendid it is to be a gentleman."

~ 35 ~

Our business settled, Sutcliffe, Pettigrew, and Herrington trail out of the sitting room in a long curl of cigar smoke, as Peter Hardcastle walks over to the gramophone on the sideboard. Wiping the dust from a record with a cotton handkerchief, he lowers the needle and flicks a switch, Brahms blowing out through the flared bronze tube.

Motioning to the others to go on without me, I close the door to the hallway. Peter's taken a seat by the fire, a window opened on his thoughts. He's yet to notice I've stayed behind, and it feels as though some great chasm divides us, though in truth he's only a step or two away.

Dance's reticence in this matter is paralyzing. As a man who despises interruption, he is equally wary of disturbing others, and the personal nature of the questions I must ask is only compounding the problem. I'm mired in my host's manners. Two days ago, this wouldn't have been an obstacle, but every host is stronger than the last, and fighting Dance is like trying to walk into a gale.

Decorum allows a polite cough, Hardcastle turning in his seat to find me by the door.

"Ah, Dance, old man," he says. "Did you forget something?"

"I was hoping we could talk privately."

"Is there some problem with the contract?" he says warily. "I must admit I was worried Sutcliffe's drinking might—"

"It's not Sutcliffe. It's Evelyn," I say.

"Evelyn," he says, wariness replaced by weariness. "Yes, of course. Come, sit by the fire. This damned house is drafty enough without inviting its chill."

Giving me time to settle myself, he hitches his trouser leg, dancing a foot before the flames. Whatever his faults, his manners are meticulous.

"So," he says after a moment, judging the rigors of etiquette to have been adequately obeyed. "What's this about Evelyn? I assume she doesn't want to go through with the wedding?"

Finding no easy way of framing the matter, I decide to simply toss it into his lap.

"I'm afraid it's more serious than that," I say. "Somebody's set their mind to murdering your daughter."

"Murder?"

He frowns, smiling a little, waiting for the rest of the joke to present itself. Undone by my sincerity, he leans forward, confusion wrinkling his face.

"You're serious?" he says, hands clasped.

"I am."

"Do you know who, or why?"

"Only how. She's being compelled to commit suicide, otherwise, somebody she loves will be murdered. The information was relayed in a note."

"A note?" he scoffs. "Sounds damn iffy to me. Probably just a game. You know how these girls can be."

"It's not a game, Peter," I say sternly, knocking the doubt from his face.

"May I ask how you came by this information?"

"The same way I come by all my information, I listen."

He sighs, pinching his nose, weighing the facts and the man bringing them to him.

"Do you believe somebody's trying to sabotage our deal with Ravencourt?" he asks.

"I hadn't considered it," I say, startled by his response. I'd expected him to be concerned for his daughter's well-being, perhaps spurred into making plans to ensure her safety. But Evelyn's incidental. The only loss he fears is that of his fortune.

"Can you think of anybody whose interests would be served by Evelyn's death?" I say, struggling to contain my sudden distaste for this man.

"One makes enemies, old families who'd happily see us ruined, but none of them would resort to this. Whispers are more their thing—gossip at parties, spiteful comments in the *Times*. You know how it is."

He raps the arm of the chair in frustration.

"Dash it all, Dance. Are you sure about this? It seems so outlandish."

"I'm certain, and truth be told, my suspicions lie a little closer to home," I say.

"One of the servants?" he asks, lowering his voice, his gaze leaping to the door.

"Helena," I say.

His wife's name strikes him like a blow.

"Helena, you must be... I mean... My dear man..."

His face is turning red, his words boiling over and spilling out of his mouth. I can feel a similar heat in my own cheeks. This line of questioning is poison to Dance.

"Evelyn suggested the relationship was fractured," I say quickly, laying the words down like stones across a boggy field.

Hardcastle's gone to the window, where he's standing with his back to me. Civility clearly does not allow for confrontation, though I can see his body trembling, his hands clenched behind him.

"I won't deny you Helena has no great fondness for Evelyn, but without her we'll be bankrupt in a couple of years," he says, measuring every word as he struggles to keep his anger in check. "She wouldn't put our future in jeopardy."

He didn't say she's not capable of it.

"But—"

"Damn it, Dance. What's your interest in this slander?" he shouts, yelling at my reflection in the glass so he doesn't have to yell at me.

This is it. Dance knows Peter Hardcastle well enough to know he's at the end of his patience. My next answer will decide whether he opens up, or points me toward the door. I need to choose my words carefully, which means pressing the thing he most cares about. Either I tell him I'm trying to save his daughter's life or...

"I'm sorry, Peter," I say, my voice conciliatory. "If somebody's trying to sabotage this deal with Ravencourt, I must put a stop to it, both as your friend and your legal counsel."

He sags.

"Of course you must," he says, looking at me over his shoulder. "I'm sorry, old friend. It's just...all this talk of murder... Well, it's stirring some old memories... You understand. Naturally, if you think Evelyn's in danger, I'll do everything I can to help, but you're mistaken if you believe Helena would ever harm Evelyn. The relationship is strained, but they do love each other. I'm certain of it."

I allow myself a small sigh of relief. Battling Dance has been exhausting, but finally I'm on the verge of some answers.

"Your daughter contacted somebody called Felicity Maddox, claiming she was worried by Helena's behavior," I continue, obliging my host's need to place the facts in their proper order. "She's not on the guest list, but I believe Felicity came to the house to help, and there's a possibility she's now being held as collateral should Evelyn fail to go through with the suicide. Michael told me she was a childhood friend of your daughter's, but couldn't recall anything more about her. Do you remember this girl? Have you seen her around the house, perhaps? I have reason to believe she was at liberty this morning."

Hardcastle looks bewildered.

"I've never even heard of her, though I must confess Evelyn and I haven't spoken much since her return," he says. "The circumstances of her arrival, the marriage... They've put a barrier between us. It's peculiar Michael wasn't able to tell you more, though. They've been inseparable since she came back, and I know he visited often and wrote frequently while Evelyn was in Paris. I would expect him to know this Felicity, if anybody does."

"I'll talk to him again, but the letter was correct, was it not? Helena has been acting oddly?"

The record catches on the gramophone, the soaring violin solo yanked back to earth over and over again, like a kite in a child's overeager hands.

Peter glances at it, frowning, hoping his dissatisfaction alone will right it. Defeated, he moves to the gramophone, lifting the needle, blowing dust from the record, and holding it up to the light.

"It's scratched," he says with a shake of the head.

He replaces the record, new music taking flight.

"Tell me about Helena," I nudge. "It was her idea to announce the engagement on the anniversary of Thomas's death and throw the party in Blackheath, wasn't it?"

"She's never forgiven Evelyn for abandoning Thomas that morning," he says, watching the record spin. "I confess I thought the years might dull her pain, but"—he spreads his arms—"all this, it's so..." He breathes deeply, composing himself. "Helena means to embarrass Evelyn, I admit. She calls the marriage a punishment, but it's a rather fine match, if you look at the details. Ravencourt won't lay a finger on Evelyn, told me as much himself. 'I'm too old for all that' is what he said. She'll have the run of his homes, nice allowance, any life she chooses, so long as it doesn't embarrass him. In return, he'll get… Well, you know the rumors about his valets. Good-looking chaps coming and going at all hours. Scandalmongering is all it is, but the marriage will put a stop to it." He pauses, his stare defiant. "You see, Dance? Why would Helena arrange all of this if she meant to kill Evelyn? She wouldn't, she couldn't. Beneath it all, she loves Evelyn. Not well, I admit, but well enough. She needs to feel as if Evelyn has been thoroughly punished, and then she'll start making it up to her. You'll see. Helena will come around, and Evelyn will realize this marriage is a blessing in disguise. Believe me, you're barking up the wrong tree."

"I still need to speak with your wife, Peter."

"My organizer's in the drawer; it has her appointments in it." He laughs grimly. "Our marriage is one of overlapping duties these days, but it should tell you where to find her."

I rush to the drawer, unable to contain my excitement.

Somebody in the house, possibly Helena herself, tore these appointments from her day planner to conceal her activities. Whoever did it either forgot, or didn't know, that her husband kept his own copy, and now they're in my hands. Here and now, we might finally discover what was worth all the trouble.

The drawer is stiff, swollen with damp. It comes open grudgingly, revealing a moleskin book held fast with string.

Flipping through the pages, I quickly find Helena's appointments, my ebullience draining out of me immediately. Most of them I already know about. Helena met with Cunningham at 7:30 a.m., though there's no indication why. After that, she arranged to see Evelyn at 8:15 a.m. and Millicent Derby at 9:00 a.m., both of which she missed. She has a meeting with the stable master at 11:30 a.m., which is in an hour's time, and then she's expected in Ravencourt's parlor at 1:30 p.m.

She won't attend.

After that, the planner's blank.

My finger roams the schedule, searching for something suspicious. Evelyn and Ravencourt I know about, and Millicent was an old friend, so that's understandable, but what could be so urgent she'd need to see her husband's bastard son first thing in the morning? He refused to tell me when I asked, but he's the only person who's seen Helena Hardcastle today, which means I can no longer tolerate his evasions. I must have the truth from him.

Before that, I'll need to visit the stables. For the first time, I know where the elusive lady of the house is going to be, and I'm going to be waiting for her when she arrives.

"Do you know why Helena met Charles Cunningham this morning?" I ask Peter, as I replace the organizer in the drawer.

"Likely Helena wanted to say hello," he says, pouring himself another drink. "She was always close to the boy."

"Is Charles Cunningham the reason Stanwin's blackmailing you?" I ask. "Does Stanwin know he's your son?"

"Come now, Dance!" he says, glaring at me.

I meet his gaze, my host's too. Dance is slipping apologies onto my tongue, urging me to flee the room. It's a bloody nuisance. Every time I open my mouth to speak, I have to force aside another man's embarrassment first.

"You know me, Peter, so you know what it takes for me to ask such a thing," I say. "I must have all the pieces of this nasty business to hand."

He considers this, returning to the window with his drink. Not that there's much to see. The trees have grown so close to the house the branches are pressed right up against the glass. Judging by Peter's demeanor, he'd invite them inside right now, if he could.

"Charles Cunningham's parentage isn't why I'm being black-mailed," he says. "That nugget of scandal was on every society page at one time, Helena made sure of it. There's no money in it."

"Then what is it Stanwin knows?"

"I need your word it won't go any further," he says.

"Of course," I say, my pulse quickening.

"Well." He takes a fortifying sip of his drink. "Before Thomas was murdered, Helena was having an affair with Charlie Carver."

"The man who murdered Thomas?" I exclaim.

"They call this sort of thing cuckolding, don't they?" he says, standing stiff at the window. "In my case it's an unusually perfect metaphor. He took my son from me and left his own child in my nest instead."

"His own child?"

"Cunningham isn't my illegitimate child, Dance. He's my wife's. Charlie Carver was his father."

"That blackguard!" I exclaim, temporarily losing control of Dance, whose outrage mirrors my shock. "How on earth did this happen?"

"Carver and Helena loved each other," he says ruefully. "Our marriage was never... I had the name; Helena's family had the money. It was convenient—necessary, one might say—but there was no affection. Carver and Helena grew up together; his father was the gamekeeper on her family's estate. She kept their relationship from me, but brought Carver to Blackheath when we married. I'm sorry to say my indiscretions got back to her, our marriage faltered, and a year or so later, she fell into Carver's bed, becoming pregnant soon after."

"But you didn't raise Cunningham as your own?"

"No, she led me to believe it was mine during the pregnancy but couldn't be certain herself who the real father was, as I'd continued to... Well, a man's needs are... You understand?"

"I believe I do," I say coldly, remembering the love and respect that governed Dance's marriage for so long.

"Anyway, I was out hunting when Cunningham was born, so she had the midwife smuggle him out of the house to be nursed in the village. When I returned, I was told the child died during the delivery, but six months later, when she was certain he didn't look too much like Carver, the baby turned up on our doorstep, carried by some wench I'd had the misfortune to spend time with in London, who was happy enough to take my wife's money and pretend it was mine. Helena played the victim, insisting we take the boy in, and to my shame, I agreed. We handed the child to the cook, Mrs. Drudge, who raised him as her own. Believe it or not, we actually managed to find several peaceful years after that. Evelyn, Thomas, and Michael were born in short order, and for a while we were a happy family."

All through the story I've watched his face for some emotion, but it's been a bland recital of the facts. Once again, I'm struck by the callowness of this man. An hour ago, I'd assumed Thomas's death had reduced his feelings to ash, but now, I wonder if that soil wasn't always infertile. Nothing grows in this man but greed.

"How did you discover the truth?" I ask.

"Sheer chance," he says, laying his hands against the wall either side of the window. "I went for a walk and stumbled upon Carver and Helena arguing over the boy's future. She admitted everything."

"So why not divorce her?" I ask.

"And have everybody know my shame?" he says, aghast. "Bastard children are common currency these days, but imagine the tattle if people discovered Lord Peter Hardcastle had been cuckolded by a common gardener. No, Dance, that won't do."

"What happened after you found out?"

"I let Carver go, gave him a day to get off the estate."

"Was that the same day he killed Thomas?"

"Exactly so. Our confrontation sent him into a rage, and he…he…"

His eyes are blurry, red with drink. He's been emptying and refilling that glass all morning.

"Stanwin came to Helena a few months later with his hand out.

You see, Dance, I'm not being blackmailed directly. It's Helena, and my reputation with her. I simply pay for it."

"And what of Michael, Evelyn, and Cunningham?" I ask. "Do they know any of this?"

"Not to my knowledge. A secret's hard enough to keep without putting it in the mouths of children."

"So how did Stanwin come by it?"

"I've been asking myself that question for nineteen years, and I'm no closer to an answer. Perhaps he was friends with Carver, servants talk, after all. Otherwise, I'm at a loss. All I know is that should word get out, I'll be finished. Ravencourt's sensitive to scandal, and he won't marry into a family on the front pages."

His voice lowers, drunk and mean, his finger pointed directly at me.

"Keep Evelyn alive and I'll give you anything you ask, you hear me? I won't let that bitch cost me my fortune, Dance. I won't allow it."

36

Peter Hardcastle has fallen into a drunken sulk, gripping his glass as though worried somebody will take it from him. Judging his usefulness at an end, I grab an apple from the fruit bowl and slip out of the room on the end of a hollow apology, closing the sitting room's door that I might ascend the stairs without his noticing. I need to speak with Gold, and I'd rather not wade through a cloud of questions to do so.

A draft greets me at the top of the staircase, twisting and curling in the air, sneaking through the cracked windows and beneath the doors to stir the leaves littering the floor. I'm reminded of walking these corridors as Sebastian Bell, searching for the butler with Evelyn at my side. It's odd to think of them here, odder still to remember that Bell and I are the same man. His cowardice makes me cringe, but there's enough distance between us now that it sits apart from me. He feels like an embarrassing story I once overheard at a party. Somebody else's shame.

Dance despises men such as Bell, but I can't be so judgmental. I have no idea who I am beyond Blackheath, or how I think when I'm not wedged inside somebody else's mind. For all I know, I'm exactly like Bell…and would that truly be so bad? I envy him his compassion, as I envy Ravencourt's intelligence, and Dance's ability to see through the shroud to the heart of things. If I carry any of these qualities out of Blackheath, I'll be proud to have them.

Making certain I'm alone in the corridor, I enter the room where

Gregory Gold is hanging from the ceiling by his bound wrists. He's murmuring, jerking in pain, trying to outrun some untiring nightmare. Compassion compels me to cut him down, but Anna wouldn't have left him strung up like this without a very good reason.

Even so, I still need to speak with him, so I shake him gently, then more firmly.

Nothing.

I slap his face, then splash him with water from the nearby jug, but he doesn't stir. This is horrendous. Doctor Dickie's sedative is unyielding, and no matter how hard Gold writhes, he can't free himself of it. My stomach turns, a chill settling on my bones. Until now, the horrors in my future had always been vague, insubstantial things, dark shapes lurking in a fog. But this is me, my fate. Reaching up on my tiptoes, I pull his sleeves down to reveal the slashes on his arms he showed me last night.

"Don't get out of the carriage," I murmur, recalling his warning.

"Step away from him," Anna says from behind me. "And turn around nice and slow. I won't ask twice."

I do as she bids.

She is standing in the doorway with a shotgun pointed at me. Blond hair spills from her cap, her expression fierce. Her aim is steady, her finger pressing against the trigger. One wrong move and I have no doubt she'd kill me to protect Gold. No matter the odds arrayed against me, knowing somebody cares this deeply is enough to make even Dance's cold heart swell.

"It's me, Anna," I say. "It's Aiden."

"Aiden?"

The shotgun lowers a little as she steps close, her face breathing distance from my own as she inspects my newly acquired crags and lines.

"The book mentioned you'd get old," she says, holding the gun in one hand. "Didn't mention you'd end up with a face like a headstone, though."

She nods at Gold.

"Admiring the slashes, are you?" she says. "Doctor reckons he did that to himself. Poor man cut his own arms to ribbons."

"Why?" I ask horrified, trying to imagine any circumstance in which I'd turn a knife on myself.

"You'd know better than me," she sniffs. "Let's talk where it's warm."

I follow her into the room across the corridor, where the butler's sleeping peacefully beneath white cotton sheets. Light is pouring through a high window, and a small fire is crackling in the grate. Dried blood mars the pillow, but otherwise it's a serene scene, affectionate and intimate.

"Has he woken up yet?" I say, nodding to the butler.

"Briefly, in the carriage. We haven't long arrived. Poor sod could barely breathe. What about Dance? What's he like?" asks Anna, hiding the shotgun under the bed.

"Humorless, hates his son, otherwise he's fine. Anything's better than Jonathan Derby," I say, pouring myself a glass of water from the jug on the table.

"I met him this morning," she says, distantly. "Can't imagine it's pleasant being trapped in that head."

"It wasn't." I toss her the apple I took from the sitting room. "You told Derby you were hungry, so I brought you this. I wasn't sure if you'd had a chance to eat yet."

"I haven't," she says, looking pleased as she polishes it on her apron. "Ta!"

My stomach is rumbling, but Dance doesn't eat his first meal of the day until later in the afternoon, believing food dulls the mind. Even if I had brought an apple for myself, I wouldn't be able to eat it. Dance would sooner see me starve than disrupt his routine.

I walk over to the window, clearing a spot of grime away with my sleeve. It looks out over the road, where I'm surprised to see the

Plague Doctor pointing at the gatehouse. Daniel's standing beside him, the two of them conferring.

The scene unsettles me. Thus far, my interlocutor has taken great care to keep a barrier between us. This closeness I see now feels like collaboration, as though I've bowed to Blackheath in some way, accepting Evelyn's death and the Plague Doctor's assertion that only one of us can leave. Nothing could be further from the truth. Knowing I can change this day has given me the belief to keep fighting...so, what on earth are they talking about down there?

"What can you see?" says Anna.

"The Plague Doctor talking with Daniel," I say.

"I haven't met him yet," she says, taking a bite out of her apple. "And what the bloody hell is a Plague Doctor?"

I blink at her. "Meeting you in the wrong order's becoming problematic."

"At least there's only one of me," she says. "Tell me about this doctor of yours."

I quickly fill her in on my history with the Plague Doctor, starting with our meeting in the study when I was Sebastian Bell and recounting how he stopped my car when I tried to escape and, more recently, upbraided me for chasing Madeline Aubert in the forest as Jonathan Derby. It already seems a lifetime ago.

"Sounds like you've made a friend," she says, chewing noisily.

"He's using me," I say. "I just don't know what for."

"Daniel might, they seem chummy enough," she says, joining me at the window. "Any idea what they're talking about? Have you solved Evelyn's murder and forgotten to tell me?"

"If we do this right, there won't be a murder to solve," I say, my attention fixed on the scene below.

"So you're still trying to save her, even after the Plague Doctor said it was almost impossible?"

"As a rule, I ignore half of everything he tells me," I say distantly. "Call it a healthy skepticism of any wisdom delivered through a mask. Besides, I know this day can be changed. I've seen it."

"Christ's sake, Aiden," she says angrily.

"What's wrong?" I ask, startled.

"This, all of this!" she says, spreading her arms exasperatedly. "We had a deal, you and me. I'd sit in this little room and keep these two safe, and you'd use your eight lives to solve this murder."

"That's what I'm doing," I say, confused by her anger.

"No, it's not," she says. "You're running around trying to save the person whose death is our best chance of escape."

"She's my friend, Anna."

"She's *Bell's* friend," Anna counters. "She humiliated Ravencourt, and she nearly killed Derby. Far as I've seen, there's more warmth in a long winter than in that woman."

"She had her reasons."

It's a weak response, intended to bat away the question rather than answer it. Anna's right. Evelyn hasn't been my friend for a long time now, and though the memory of her kindness still lingers, it's not my driving impulse. That's something else, something deeper, something squirming. The idea of leaving her to be slain sickens me. Not Dance, not any of my other hosts. It sickens *me*, Aiden Bishop.

Unfortunately, Anna's building up a head of steam and doesn't give me a chance to dwell on the revelation.

"I don't care about her reasons; I care about yours," she says, pointing at me. "Maybe you don't feel it, but deep down, I know how long I've been in this place. It's *decades*, Aiden, I'm sure of it. I need to leave, I have to, and this is my best chance, with you. You've got eight lives; you'll get out of here eventually. I do all this once, and then forget. Without you I'm stuck, and what happens if next time you wake up as Bell, you don't remember me?"

"I won't leave you here, Anna," I insist, shaken by the desperation in her voice.

"Then solve the damn murder like the Plague Doctor asked you to, and believe him when he says that Evelyn can't be saved!"

"I can't trust him," I say, losing my temper and turning my back on her.

"Why not? Everything he's said has happened. He's—"

"He said you'd betray me," I shout.

"What?"

"He told me you'd betray me," I repeat, shaken by the admission. Until now, I'd never actually voiced the accusation, preferring to dismiss it in the quiet of my thoughts. Now I've said it out loud, it's a real possibility, and it worries me. Anna's right. Everything else the Plague Doctor's said has come true, and as strong as my connection to this woman is, I can't be *completely* certain she won't turn on me.

She reels backward as if struck, shaking her head.

"I'd never... Aiden, I'd never do that, I swear."

"He said you remembered more about our last loop than you were admitting," I say. "Is that true? Is there something you're not telling me?"

She hesitates.

"Is it true, Anna?" I demand.

"No," she says forcefully. "He's trying to get between us, Aiden. I don't know why, but you can't listen to him."

"That's my point," I shoot back. "If the Plague Doctor's telling the truth about Evelyn, he's telling the truth about you. I don't believe he is. I think he wants something, something we don't know about, and I think he's using us to get it."

"Even if that's the case, I don't understand why you're so insistent on saving Evelyn," says Anna, still struggling with what I told her.

"Because somebody's going to kill her," I say haltingly. "And they're not doing it themselves, they're twisting her in knots so she'll do it herself, and they're making sure everybody sees. It's cruel and they're enjoying it, and I can't... It doesn't matter whether we like her, or whether the Plague Doctor is right, you don't get to kill somebody and put them on display. She's innocent, and we can stop it. And we should."

I falter, breathless, teetering on the edge of a memory sprung loose by Anna's questions. It's as though a curtain's been pulled back, the man I used to be almost visible through the gap. Guilt and grief, they're the keys, I'm certain of it. They're what brought me to Blackheath in the first place. They've been driving me to save Evelyn, but that wasn't my purpose here, not really.

"There was somebody else," I say slowly, clutching at the edges of the memory. "A woman, I think. She's the reason I came here, but I couldn't save her."

"What was her name?" says Anna, taking my wrinkled, old hands and looking up into my face.

"I can't remember," I say, my head throbbing in concentration.

"Was it me?"

"I don't know," I say.

The memory's slipping away. There are tears on my cheeks, an ache in my chest. I feel like I've lost somebody, but I have no idea who. I look into Anna's wide, brown eyes.

"It's gone," I say weakly.

"I'm sorry, Aiden."

"Don't be," I say, feeling my strength return. "We're going to get out of Blackheath, I promise, but I have to do it my way. I'll make it work, you just have to trust me, Anna."

I'm expecting an objection, but she confounds me with a smile.

"Then where do we start?" she says.

"I'm going to find Helena Hardcastle," I say, wiping my face with a handkerchief. "Do you have any leads on the footman? He killed Derby last night, and I doubt Dance is far behind."

"Actually, I've been thinking up a plan."

She peers under the bed, bringing out the artist's sketchbook, which she opens and drops on my lap. This is the book that's been guiding her all day, but the intricate spiderweb of cause and effect I'd anticipated is nowhere to be seen.

Its contents are gibberish, far as I can tell.

"I thought I wasn't allowed to see this?" I say, craning my head to read her awkward upside-down writing. "I'm honored."

"Don't be. I'm only letting you see the bit you need," she says.

Circled warnings and sketches of the day's events have been scrawled in an erratic hand, snatches of conversation dashed onto the page, without any context to explain them. I recognize a few of the moments, including a hasty drawing of the butler's beating at the hands of Gold, but most of them are meaningless.

It's only after I've been assaulted by the chaos, that I begin to see Anna's attempt to bring order. Using a pencil, she's diligently written notes for herself near the entries. Guesses have been made, times noted down, our conversations recorded and cross-referenced with those in the book, teasing out the useful information contained within.

"I doubt you'll be able to do much with it," says Anna, watching me struggle. "One of your hosts gave it to me. Might as well be written in another language. A lot of it doesn't make any sense, but I've been adding to it, using it to keep track of your comings and goings. This is everything I know about you. Every host, everything they've done. It's the only way I can keep up, but it's not complete. There are holes. That's why I need you to show me the best time to approach Bell."

"Bell, why?"

"This footman is looking for me, so we're going to tell him exactly where I'll be," she says, flipping to the last page of the book, where a short message is written. "We'll gather some of your other hosts and be waiting for him when he gets his knife out."

"And how are we going to trap him?" I say.

"With this." She tears out the message and hands it to me. "If you tell me about Bell's day, I can make sure to put it somewhere he'll find it. Once I mention it in the kitchen, the meeting will be up and down the house in an hour. The footman's sure to hear of it."

Don't leave Blackheath, more lives than your own are depending on you. Meet me by the mausoleum in the family graveyard at 10:20 p.m., and I'll explain everything.

Love, Anna

I'm transported back to that evening, when Evelyn and Bell stalked into the dank graveyard, revolver in hand, finding only shadows and a shattered compass covered in blood.

As omens go, it's not reassuring, but it's not definitive either. It's another piece of the future come loose from the whole, and until I get there, I'll have no idea what it means.

Anna's waiting for my reaction, but my unease isn't sufficient reason for objection.

"Have you seen how this ends? Does it work?" she asks, fingering the hem of her sleeve nervously.

"I don't know, but it's the best plan we have," I say.

"We're going to need help, and you're running short of hosts."

"Don't worry, I'll find it."

I pull a fountain pen from my pocket, adding one more line to the message, something to spare poor Bell a great deal of frustration.

Oh, and don't forget your gloves. They're burning.

37

I hear the horses before I see them, dozens of shoes clopping along the cobblestones ahead of me. Not far behind is their smell, a musty odor mingled with the stench of manure, a thick rolling mix even the wind can't disturb. Only after I've been assaulted by their impression do I finally come upon the animals themselves, thirty or so being led out of the stables and up the main road toward the village, carriages harnessed to their backs.

Stable hands are guiding them on foot, their uniform flat caps, white shirts, and loose gray trousers rendering them as indistinguishable from each other as the horses in their care.

I'm watching the hooves nervously. In a flash of memory, I recall being thrown from a horse as a boy, the beast's hooves catching me in the chest, my bones cracking...

Don't let Dance get a grip on you.

I tear myself free of my host's memories, lowering the hand that had instinctively gone to the scar on my chest.

It's getting worse.

Bell's personality rarely surfaced at all, but between Derby's lust and Dance's manners and childhood traumas, it's becoming difficult to keep a straight course.

A few horses in the middle of the mass are nipping at those to the side of them, a ripple of agitation passing through the muscular brown tide. It's enough for me to take an ill-advised step off the road, straight into a pile of manure.

I'm flicking the filth free when one of the stable hands peels away from the pack.

"Something I can help you with, Mr. Dance?" he says, tipping his cap at me.

"You know me?" I say, surprised by this recognition.

"Sorry, sir. Name's Oswald, sir. I saddled the stallion you rode yesterday. Fine thing, sir, seeing a gentleman on a horse. Not many know how to ride that way anymore."

He smiles, showing off two rows of gappy teeth stained brown with tobacco.

"Of course, of course," I say, the passing horses nudging him in the back. "Actually, Oswald, I was looking for Lady Hardcastle. She was supposed to be meeting Alf Miller, the stable master."

"Not sure 'bout her ladyship, sir, but you've just missed Alf. Left with somebody about ten minutes gone. Heading to the lake, best I could tell, took the path alongside the paddock. It's on your right as you pass under the arch, sir. You can probably still catch them if you hurry."

"Thank you, Oswald."

"Of course, sir."

Tipping his cap again, he falls in with the pack.

Keeping to the edge of the road, I carry on toward the stables, the loose cobbles slowing me down considerably. In my other hosts, I simply leaped aside when one slid beneath me. Dance's old legs aren't nimble enough for that, and every time one wobbles under my weight, it twists my ankles and knees, threating to tip me over.

Vexed, I pass beneath the arch to find oats, hay, and smashed fruit littering the courtyard, a boy doing his best to sweep the debris into the corners. He'd probably have more luck if he wasn't half the size of the brush. He peeks at me shyly as I pass, trying to doff his cap but only succeeding in losing it to the wind. The last I see of him, he's chasing it across the yard as though all his dreams were stuffed inside.

The path nestled alongside the paddock is little more than a muddy trail rotten with puddles, and my trousers are already filthy by the time I'm halfway along. Twigs are cracking, rain dripping from the plants. I have the sense of being watched, and though there's nothing to suggest it's anything more than nerves, I swear I can feel a presence among the trees, a pair of eyes dogging my steps. I can only hope I'm mistaken, because if the footman does spring onto the path, I'm too weak to fight and too slow to run. The rest of my life will be precisely how long it takes him to pick a way of killing me.

Seeing no sign of the stable master or Lady Hardcastle, I sacrifice my deportment completely, splattering mud up my back as I break into a worried trot.

The trail soon veers away from the paddock and into the forest, that sense of being watched only growing as I move farther away from the stables. Brambles snatch at my clothes as I push through, until finally I hear the murmur of approaching voices and the lapping of water against the shore. Relief overwhelms me, and I realize I've been holding my breath this entire time. We're face-to-face in two steps, though it's not Lady Hardcastle I find accompanying the stable master, but rather Cunningham, Ravencourt's valet. He's wearing a thick coat and the long purple scarf he'll struggle to tug loose when he interrupts Ravencourt speaking with Daniel.

The banker must be asleep in the library.

Surprise silences us, their alarm at bumping into me suggesting they were discussing far more than mere gossip.

It's Cunningham who recovers first, smiling amiably.

"Mr. Dance, what a pleasant surprise," he says. "What brings you out on this foul morning?"

"I was looking for Helena Hardcastle," I say, glancing from

Cunningham to the stable master. "I was under the impression she was taking a walk with Mr. Miller here."

"No, sir," says Miller, kneading his cap between his hands. "Supposed to be meeting at my cottage, sir. I'm on my way there now."

"We three find ourselves in the same boat then," says Cunningham. "I was also hoping to catch her. Perhaps, we can go along together. My business shouldn't take very long, but I'll be happy to stand in line, as it were."

"And what is your business?" I ask, as we begin walking back toward the stables. "It was my understanding you met with Lady Hardcastle before breakfast."

The directness of my question momentarily unsettles his good cheer, a flash of annoyance passing across his face.

"A few matters for Lord Hardcastle," he says. "You know how these things are. One mess soon leads to another."

"But you have seen the lady of the house today?" I say.

"Indeed, first thing."

"How did she seem?"

He shrugs, frowning at me. "I couldn't say. Our talk was very brief. May I ask where these questions are leading, Mr. Dance? I rather feel like I'm facing you in court."

"Nobody else has seen Lady Hardcastle today. That strikes me as strange."

"Perhaps she's wary of being pestered with questions," he says, flaring.

We arrive at the stable master's cottage in an irritated mood, Mr. Miller writhing in discomfort as he invites us inside. It's as neat and orderly as the last time I was here, although much too small for three men and their secrets.

I take the chair by the table, while Cunningham inspects the bookcase, and the stable master frets, doing his best to tidy an already tidy cottage.

We wait for ten minutes, but Lady Hardcastle never arrives.

It's Cunningham who breaks the silence.

"Well, it seems the lady has other plans," he says, checking his watch. "I'd better get off. I'm expected in the library. Good morning to you, Mr. Dance, Mr. Miller," he says, inclining his head before opening the door and departing.

Miller looks up at me nervously.

"What about you, Mr. Dance?" he says. "Will you be waiting longer?"

I ignore this and join him by the fireplace.

"What were you speaking with Cunningham about?" I ask.

He stares at the window, as though his answers are coming by messenger. I snap my fingers in front of his face, drawing his watery eyes toward me.

"At this moment, I'm simply curious, Mr. Miller," I say in a low voice dripping with unpleasant possibilities. "In a minute or so, I'll be annoyed. Tell me what you were speaking about."

"He wanted somebody to show him around," he says, jutting out his lower lip, revealing the pink flesh within. "Wanted to see the lake, he did."

Whatever Miller's skills in this world, lying is not one of them. His elderly face is a mass of wrinkles and overhanging flesh, more than enough material for his emotions to build a stage from. Every frown is a tragedy; every smile, a farce. A lie, sitting as it does somewhere between both, is enough to collapse the entire performance.

Placing my hand on his shoulder, I lower my face to his, watching as his eyes flee mine.

"Charles Cunningham grew up on this estate, Mr. Miller, as well you know. He has no need of a tour guide. Now, what were you discussing?"

He shakes his head. "I promised—"

"I can make promises too, Miller, but you won't enjoy mine."

My fingers press into his collarbone, tight enough to make him wince.

"He was asking about the murdered boy," he says reluctantly.

"Thomas Hardcastle?"

"No, sir, the other one."

"What other one?"

"Keith Parker, the stable boy."

"What stable boy? What are you talking about, man?"

"Nobody remembers him, sir; not important enough," he says, gritting his teeth. "One of mine, he was. Lovely boy, about fourteen. Went missing a week or so before Master Thomas died. Couple of peelers came up to take a look in the forest, but they couldn't find his body, so they said he ran away. I tell you, sir, he never did. Loved his mam, loved his job. He wouldn't have done it. I said as much at the time, but nobody listened."

"Did they ever find him?"

"No, sir. Never did."

"And that's what you told Cunningham?"

"Aye, sir."

"Is that all you told him?"

His eyes shift left and right.

"There's more, isn't there?" I say.

"No, sir."

"Don't lie to me, Miller," I say coldly, my hackles rising. Dance hates people who try to deceive him, considering it a suggestion of gullibility, of stupidity. To even attempt it, liars must believe themselves to be cleverer than the person they're lying to, an assumption he finds grotesquely insulting.

"I'm not lying, sir," protests the poor stable master, a vein bulging on his forehead.

"You are! Tell me what you know!" I demand.

"I can't."

"You will, or I'll destroy you, Mr. Miller," I say, giving my host free rein. "I'll take everything you have, every stitch of clothing and every penny you've squirreled away."

Dance's words pour out of my mouth, each one dripping with poison. This is how he runs his law practice, bludgeoning his opponents with threats and intimidation. In his own way, Dance may be just as vile as Derby.

"I'll dig up every—"

"The story's a lie," Miller blurts out.

His face is ashen, his eyes haunted.

"What does that mean? Out with it!" I say.

"They say Charlie Carver killed Master Thomas, sir."

"What of it?"

"Well, he couldn't have, sir. Charlie and me were friendly like. Charlie had an argument with Lord Hardcastle that morning, been fired he had, so he decided to take severance."

"Severance?"

"A few bottles of brandy, sir, right out of Lord Hardcastle's study. Just walked in and took them."

"So he stole a few bottles of brandy," I say. "How does that prove his innocence?"

"He came to fetch me after I sent Miss Evelyn out riding on her pony. Wanted a last drink with a friend, he said. Couldn't say no, could I? We drank those bottles between us, me and Charlie, but around half an hour before the murder, he said I had to leave."

"Leave, why?"

"He said somebody was coming to see him."

"Who?"

"I don't know, sir. He never said. He just—"

He falters, feeling along the edge of the answer for the crack he's certain he's about to fall through.

"What?" I demand.

The poor fool's wringing his hands together, rucking up the rug with the ball of his left foot.

"He said everything was arranged, sir, said they were going to help him get a good position somewhere else. I thought maybe…"

"Yes."

"The way he was talking, sir… I thought…"

"Spit it out for God's sake, Miller."

"Lady Hardcastle, sir," he says, meeting my gaze for the first time. "I thought maybe he was meeting Lady Helena Hardcastle. They'd always been friendly like."

My hand drops from his shoulder.

"But you didn't see her arrive?"

"I…"

"You didn't leave, did you?" I say, catching the guilt on his face. "You wanted to see who was coming, so you hid somewhere nearby."

"For a minute, sir, just to see, to make sure he was all right."

"Why didn't you tell anybody this?" I say, frowning at him.

"I was told not to, sir."

"By whom?"

He looks up at me, chewing the silence into a desperate plea.

"By whom, dammit?" I persist.

"Well, Lady Hardcastle, sir. That's what made me… Well, she wouldn't have let Charlie kill her son, would she? And if he had, she wouldn't have told me to keep it quiet. Doesn't make no sense, does it? He has to be innocent."

"And you kept this secret all these years?"

"I was afraid, sir. Terrible afraid, sir."

"Of Helena Hardcastle?"

"Of the knife, sir. The one used to kill Thomas. They found it in Carver's cabin, hidden under the floorboards. That's what did for him in the end, sir."

"Why would you be afraid of the knife, Miller?"

"Because it was mine, sir. Horseshoe knife, it was. Went missing from my cottage a couple of days before the murder. That and a nice blanket right off my bed. I thought they might…well, blame me, sir. Like I was in on it with Carver, sir."

The next few minutes pass in a blur, my thoughts far afield. I'm vaguely aware of promising to keep Miller's secrets, just as I'm vaguely aware of leaving the cottage, the rain soaking me as I head back toward the house.

Michael Hardcastle told me somebody had been with Charlie Carver the morning of Thomas's death, somebody Stanwin had clipped with a shotgun before they escaped. Could that person have been Lady Hardcastle? If so, her injuries would have needed tending quietly.

Doctor Dickie?

The Hardcastles were hosting a party the weekend Thomas was murdered, and by Evelyn's account, the same guests were invited back for this ball. Dickie's in the house today, so it's likely he was here nineteen years ago.

He won't talk; he's loyal as a dog.

"He's in the drug-peddling business with Bell," I say, remembering the marked-up Bible I found in his room when I was Derby. "That will be enough leverage to force the truth from him."

My excitement's building. If Dickie confirms that Lady Hardcastle was shot in the shoulder, she'd have to be a suspect in Thomas's death. But why on earth would she take her own son's life, or allow Carver—a man Lord Hardcastle claimed she loved—to take the blame on her behalf?

This is the closest Dance gets to glee, the old lawyer having spent his life following the facts like a hunting dog with the scent of blood in its nose, and it's not until Blackheath lifts itself off the horizon that I finally awake to my surroundings. At this distance, with these weak eyes, the house is smudged, the cracks obscured, and one sees Blackheath as it must formerly have been, back when a young Millicent Derby summered here with Ravencourt and the Hardcastles, when children played in the forest without fear, their parents enjoying parties and music, laughter and singing.

How glorious it must have been.

One could understand why Helena Hardcastle might yearn for those days again, and might even attempt to restore them by throwing another party. One could understand, but only a fool would accept that as the reason any of this is happening.

Blackheath cannot be restored. The murder of Thomas Hardcastle hollowed it out forever, making it fit only for ruin, and yet, despite that, she's invited the same guests to the same party, nineteen years later to the day. The past has been dug up and dressed up, but to what purpose?

If Miller's right and Charlie Carver didn't kill Thomas Hardcastle, chances are it was Helena Hardcastle, the spinner of this dreadful web we're all tangled in, and the woman I'm increasingly convinced is at the center of it.

Chances are she's planning to kill Evelyn tonight, and I still don't have any idea how to find her, let alone stop her.

∽ 38 ∼

A few gentlemen are smoking outside Blackheath, sharing stories of last night's debauchery. Their cheerful greetings follow me up the steps, but I pass by without comment. My legs are aching, my lower back demanding a soak in the bathtub, but I don't have time. The hunt begins in half an hour and I can't miss it. I have too many questions, and most of the answers will be carrying shotguns.

Taking a decanter of scotch from the drawing room, I retire to my room, knocking back a couple of stiff drinks to smother the pain. I can feel Dance's objection, his distaste not only at my acknowledgment of the discomfort, but my need to dim it. My host despises what's happening to him, seeing age as a malignancy, a consumption, and an erosion.

Stripping out of my muddy clothes, I take myself over to the mirror, realizing I still have no idea what Dance looks like. Putting on a new body every day has already become commonplace, and it's only the hope of catching some glimpse of the real Aiden Bishop that compels me to keep looking.

Dance is in his late seventies, as withered and gray on the outside as the inside. Almost bald, his face is a river of wrinkles running off his skull, pinned in place only by a large Roman nose. Either side of that are a small gray mustache and dark, lifeless eyes suggesting nothing of the man within, except, perhaps, that there may not be a man within. Anonymity seems to be a compulsion with Dance, whose clothes—though good quality—come in shades of gray, with only the handkerchiefs and bow ties offering anything in the way of color. Even then, the choice is either dark red or dark blue, giving the impression of a man camouflaged within his own life.

His hunting tweeds are a little tight around the middle, but they'll suffice, and with another glass of scotch warming my throat, I cross the corridor to Doctor Dickie's bedroom, rapping on the door.

Steps approach from the other side, Dickie opening it wide. He's dressed for the hunt.

"I don't work this much at my surgery," he grumbles. "I should warn you, I've already tended knife wounds, memory loss, and a severe beating this morning, so whatever your ailment, it needs to be interesting. And above the waist, preferably."

"You peddle drugs through Sebastian Bell," I say bluntly, watching the smile vanish from his face. "He sells them, you supply them."

White as a sheet, he's forced to steady himself against the doorframe.

Seeing weakness, I press my advantage. "Ted Stanwin would pay handsomely for this information, but I don't need Stanwin. I need to know if you treated Helena Hardcastle, or anybody else, for a gunshot wound the day Thomas Hardcastle was murdered?"

"The police asked me the same question at the time, and I answered honestly," he rasps, loosening his collar. "No, I did not."

Scowling, I turn away from him. "I'm going to Stanwin," I say.

"Damn it, man. I'm telling the truth," he says, catching my arm.

We look each other in the eyes. His are old and dim and lit by fear. Whatever he finds in mine causes him to release me immediately.

"Helena Hardcastle loves her children more than life itself, and she loved Thomas the most," he insists. "She couldn't have harmed him; she wouldn't have been able. I swear to you, on my honor as a gentleman, nobody came to me that day with an injury, and I don't have the first clue who Stanwin shot."

I hold his pleading gaze for a second, searching for some flicker of deceit, but he's telling the truth. I'm certain of it.

Deflated, I let the doctor go and return to the entrance hall where the rest of the gentlemen are gathering, smoking and chatting, impatient for the hunt to begin. I was certain Dickie would confirm Helena's involvement and, in so doing, give me a starting point for Evelyn's death.

I need to get a better picture of what happened to Thomas, and I know precisely the man to ask.

Searching for Ted Stanwin, I step into the drawing room, where I find Philip Sutcliffe in green hunting tweeds, attacking the keys of the pianoforte with a great deal of gusto and very little skill, the almost-music transporting me back to my first morning in the house—a memory currently being lived by Sebastian Bell, who's standing alone and uncomfortable in the far corner, nursing a drink he doesn't even know the name of. My pity for him is balanced by Dance's irritation, the old lawyer having little patience for ignorance of any sort. Given the chance, he'd tell Bell everything, consequences be damned, and I must admit the idea is tempting.

Why shouldn't Bell know that he saw a maid called Madeline Aubert in the forest this morning, and not Anna? And that neither of them died, so his guilt is unnecessary? I could explain the loop, and how Evelyn's murder is the key to escape, preventing him from wasting his day as Donald Davies by trying to flee. Cunningham is Charlie Carver's son, I'd say, and it looks like he's trying to prove Carver didn't kill Thomas Hardcastle. When the time comes, this is the information you'll blackmail Cunningham with, because Ravencourt abhors scandal and would almost certainly get rid of his valet if he found out. I'd tell him to find the mysterious Felicity Maddox, and, most importantly, Helena Hardcastle, because every road leads back to the missing lady of the house.

It wouldn't work.

"I know," I mutter ruefully.

Bell's first thought would be that I'd escaped from the madhouse, and when he finally realized it was all true, his investigation would change the day completely. Much as I want to help him, I'm too close to my answer to risk unraveling this loop.

Bell will have to do this alone.

An arm catches my elbow, Christopher Pettigrew appearing beside me with a plate in his hand. I've never been this near to him before, and if it weren't for Dance's impeccable manners, my disgust would be plain on my face. Up close, he looks like something recently dug up.

"Soon be rid of him," says Pettigrew, nodding over my shoulder toward Ted Stanwin, who's picking at the cold cuts on the dining table, while watching his fellow guests through narrowed eyes. His disgust is obvious.

Until this moment, I'd always taken him for a simple bully, but it's more than that I see now. His business is blackmail, which means he knows every secret and hidden shame, every possible scandal and perversity lapping around this house. Worse, he knows who got away with what. He despises everybody in Blackheath, including himself for protecting their secrets, so he spends every day picking fights to make himself feel better.

Somebody pushes by me, a confused Charles Cunningham arriving from the library with Ravencourt's letter in his hand, while the maid Lucy Harper clears away plates, oblivious to the events brewing around her. With a pang, I realize that she looks a little like my dead wife Rebecca. In her younger days, of course. There's a similarity of movement, a gentleness of action, as though...

Rebecca wasn't your wife.

"Damn it, Dance," I say, shaking myself free of him.

"Sorry, didn't catch that, old man," says Pettigrew, frowning at me.

Flushing with embarrassment, I open my mouth to respond, but I'm distracted by poor Lucy Harper as she tries to squeeze past Stanwin to fetch an empty plate. She's prettier than I recall, freckled and blue-eyed, trying to tuck her wild red hair back under her cap.

"'Scuse me, Ted," she says.

"Ted?" he says angrily, grabbing her wrist and squeezing hard enough to make her wince. "Who the hell do you think you're talking to, Lucy? It's Mr. Stanwin to you. I'm not downstairs with the rats anymore."

Shocked and afraid, she searches our faces for help.

Unlike Sebastian Bell, Dance is a keen observer of human nature, and watching this scene play out before me, I'm struck by something queer. When I first witnessed this moment, I'd taken note only of Lucy's fear at being manhandled, but she isn't merely afraid, she's surprised. Upset even. And rather oddly, so is Stanwin.

"Let her go, Ted," says Daniel Coleridge from the doorway.

The rest of the confrontation goes as I remember, Stanwin retreating, Daniel collecting Bell and taking him through into the study to meet Michael, offering me a small nod of acknowledgement along the way.

"Shall we go?" asks Pettigrew. "I suspect our entertainment is at an end."

I'm tempted to search for Stanwin, but I have no desire to climb those stairs and make my way into the east wing when I know for certain he's coming on this hunt. Better to wait for him here, I decide.

Shouldering our way through the scandalized throng, we pass through the entrance hall and out onto the driveway to find Sutcliffe already waiting, along with Herrington and a couple of other chaps I don't recognize. Dark clouds are clambering atop one another, pregnant with a storm I've now seen batter Blackheath half a dozen times. The hunters are huddled in a pack, holding onto their hats and jackets as the wind tugs at them with a thousand thieving hands. Only the dogs seem eager, straining at their leads and barking into the gloom. It's going to be a miserable afternoon, and the knowledge that I'm going to be striding into it only makes things worse.

"What ho?" says Sutcliffe upon our approach, the shoulders of his jacket dusted with dandruff.

Herrington nods at us, trying to scrape something unpleasant off his shoes. "Did you see Daniel Coleridge's little showdown with Stanwin?" he asks. "I think we've backed the right horse after all."

"We'll see," says Sutcliffe darkly. "Where's Daniel gone, anyway?"

I look around, but Daniel's nowhere to be seen and all I can offer in reply is a shrug.

Gamekeepers are handing out shotguns to those who haven't brought their own, including me. Mine's been polished and oiled, the barrels are cracked open to display the two red shells stuffed in the cylinders. The others seem to have some experience with firearms, immediately checking the sights by aiming at imaginary targets in the sky, but Dance does not share their enthusiasm for the pursuit, leaving me somewhat at a loss. After watching me fiddle with the shotgun for some minutes, the impatient gamekeeper shows me how to settle it across my forearm, handing me a box of shells and moving on to the next man.

I must admit the gun makes me feel better. All day I've felt eyes upon me, and I'll be glad of a weapon when the forest surrounds me. No doubt the footman's waiting to catch me alone, and I'll be damned if I'm going to make it easy for him.

Appearing out of nowhere, Michael Hardcastle is by our side, blowing warm breaths into his hands.

"Sorry for the delay, gentlemen," he says. "My father sends his apologies, but something's come up. He's asked us to press on ahead without him."

"And what should we do if we spot Bell's dead woman?" asks Pettigrew sarcastically.

Michael scowls at him. "A little Christian charity, please," he says. "The doctor's been through a lot."

"Five bottles at least," says Sutcliffe, bringing guffaws from everybody except Michael. Catching the younger man's withering look, he throws his hands up in the air. "Oh, come, Michael, you saw the state he was in last night. You can't believe we're actually going to find anything? Nobody's missing; the man's raving."

"Bell wouldn't make this up," says Michael. "I saw his arm. Somebody cut him to ribbons out there."

"Probably fell over his own bottle," snorts Pettigrew, rubbing his hands together for warmth.

We're interrupted by the gamekeeper, who hands Michael a black revolver. Aside from a long scratch down the barrel, it's identical to the gun Evelyn will carry into the graveyard tonight, one of the pair taken from Helena Hardcastle's bedroom.

"Oiled it for you, sir," says the gamekeeper, tipping his cap and moving off.

Michael slips the weapon into the holster at his waist, resuming our conversation, quite oblivious to my interest.

"I don't see why everybody's taking it so hard," he continues. "This hunt's been arranged for days. We're merely going in a different direction than originally intended, that's all. If we spot something, very well. If not, we've lost nothing in setting the doctor's mind at rest."

A few expectant glances are cast my way, Dance usually being the deciding voice in these matters. I'm spared having to comment by the barking dogs, who've been given a little lead by the gamekeepers and are now tugging our company across the lawn toward the forest.

Looking back toward Blackheath, I search out Bell. He's framed by the study window, his body half obscured by the red velvet drapes. In this light, at this distance, there's something of the specter about him, though in this case I suppose the house is haunting him.

The other hunters are already entering the forest, the group having fractured into smaller knots by the time I finally catch up. I need to talk to Stanwin about Helena, but he's moving quickly, holding himself apart from us. I can barely keep sight of him, let alone talk with him, and eventually I give up, deciding to corner him when we stop to rest.

Wary of encountering the footman, I join Sutcliffe and Pettigrew, who are still pondering the implications of Daniel's deal with Lord Hardcastle. Their good cheer doesn't last. The forest is oppressive, bludgeoning every utterance down to a whisper after an hour, and crushing all conversation twenty minutes after that. Even the dogs have gone quiet, sniffing at the ground as they tug us deeper into the murk. The shotgun is a comforting weight in my arms, and I cling to it fiercely, tiring quickly, but never letting myself fall too far behind the group.

"Enjoy yourself, old man," Daniel Coleridge calls out from behind me.

"I'm sorry?" I stir sluggishly from my thoughts.

"Dance is one of the better hosts," says Daniel, drawing closer. "Good mind, calm manner, able-enough body."

"This able-enough body feels like it's walked a thousand miles, not ten," I say, hearing the weariness in my voice.

"Michael's arranged for the hunting party to split," he says. "The older gents will take a breather, while the younger lot continue on. Don't worry. You'll have a chance to rest your legs soon."

Thick bushes have sprung up between us, forcing us to carry on our conversation blind, like two lovers in a maze.

"It's a damn nuisance being tired all of the time," I say, seeing glimpses of him through the leaves. "I'm looking forward to Coleridge's youth."

"Don't let this handsome face of his fool you," he muses. "Coleridge's soul is black as pitch. Keeping hold of him is exhausting. Mark my words, when you're wearing this body, you'll look back on Dance with a great deal of fondness, so enjoy him while you can."

The bushes recede, allowing Daniel to fall into step beside me. He has a black eye and is walking with a slight limp, every step accompanied by a wince of pain. I remember seeing these injuries at dinner, but the gentle candlelight made them look far less severe. Shock must show on my face, because he smiles weakly.

"It's not as bad as it looks," he says.

"What happened?"

"I chased the footman through the passages," he says.

"You went without me?" I say, surprised by his recklessness. When we made the plan to corner the footman beneath the house, it was evident that it required six people to be successful, a pair to watch each of the three exits. Once Anna refused to help and Derby was knocked unconscious, I assumed Daniel would drop it. Evidently, Derby isn't the last of my bullheaded hosts.

"No choice, old chap," he says. "Thought I had him. Turns out I was mistaken. Luckily, I managed to fight him off before he loosed his knife."

Anger sizzles in every word. I can only imagine how it must feel to be so preoccupied by the future that you're blindsided by the present.

"Have you found a way to free Anna yet?" I ask.

With a painful groan, Daniel hitches his shotgun up his arm. Even limping at my slow pace, he's barely able to stand up straight.

"I haven't, and I don't think I'm going to," he says. "I'm sorry, hard as it is to hear, only one of us can leave, and the closer we get to 11:00 p.m., the more likely it is Anna will betray us. We can only trust each other from here on."

She'll betray you.

Is this the moment behind the Plague Doctor's warning? Friendship is a simple matter when everybody stands to benefit, but now...how will she react knowing Daniel's giving up on her?

How will you react?

Sensing my hesitation, Daniel lays a comforting hand on my shoulder. With a start, I realize that Dance admires this man. He finds his sense of purpose exhilarating, his single-mindedness resonating with a quality my host values in himself. Perhaps that's why Daniel approached me with this information rather than any of our other hosts. These two are reflections of each other.

"You didn't tell her, did you?" he says anxiously. "About our offer being hollow?"

"I was distracted."

"I know it's difficult, but you must keep all of this to yourself," says Daniel, sweeping me into his confidence as one would a child entrusted with a secret. "If we're to outfox the footman, we'll need Anna's help. We won't get that if she knows we can't hold up our end of the bargain."

Heavy steps sound behind us, and, looking over my shoulder, I see Michael advancing on us, his customary grin replaced by a scowl.

"Heavens," says Daniel. "You look like somebody kicked your dog. What on earth's wrong?"

"It's this damnable search," he says irritably. "Belly saw a girl murdered out here, and yet I can't get a single person to take it seriously. I'm not asking much, just that they look around as they walk. Maybe knock over a pile of leaves, that sort of thing."

Daniel coughs, shooting Michael an embarrassed glance.

"Oh dear," says Michael, frowning at him. "This is bad news, isn't it?"

"Good news, really," says Daniel hastily. "There's no dead girl. It was a misunderstanding."

"A misunderstanding," says Michael slowly. "How on earth could it be a misunderstanding?"

"Derby was out here," says Daniel. "He frightened a maid, things got heated, and your sister took a shot at him. Bell mistook it for a murder."

"Blast Derby!" Michael turns abruptly for the house. "I'll not have it. He can go to the devil under somebody else's roof."

"It wasn't his fault," interrupts Daniel. "Not this time at least. Hard as it is to believe, Derby was trying to help. He simply got the wrong end of the stick."

Michael stops, eyeing Daniel suspiciously.

"Are you certain?" he asks.

"I am," says Daniel, putting an arm around his friend's tense shoulders. "It was a dreadful misunderstanding. Nobody's fault."

"That's a first for Derby."

Michael lets out a rueful sigh, the fury evaporating from his face. He's a man of fleeting emotions, this one. Quick to anger, easily amused, and just as easily bored, I shouldn't wonder. I briefly imagine what it would be like to inhabit that mind. Dance's coldness has its drawbacks, but it's undoubtedly preferable to Michael's mood hopscotch.

"All morning I've been telling the chaps there's a dead body out here, and they should be ashamed of being so jolly," says Michael, abashed. "As if this weekend wasn't already miserable enough for them."

"You were helping a friend." Daniel offers him a fatherly smile. "You have nothing to be ashamed of."

I'm taken aback by Daniel's kindness, and more than a little pleased. While I admire his commitment to escaping Blackheath, I'm alarmed by his ruthless pursuit of it. Suspicion is already my first emotion, and fear binds me tighter every minute. It would be easy to mistake everybody for enemies and treat them accordingly, and I'm heartened to see Daniel is still capable of rising above such thoughts.

As Daniel and Michael walk close together, I take my opportunity to question the young man. "I couldn't help but notice your revolver," I say, pointing to his holster. "It's your mother's, isn't it?"

"Is it?" He seems genuinely surprised. "I didn't even know Mother kept a gun. Evelyn gave it to me this morning."

"Why would she give you a revolver?" I ask.

Michael flushes with embarrassment.

"Because I don't like hunting very much," he says, kicking at some leaves in his path. "All that blood and thrashing, it makes me feel damn queer. I wasn't even supposed to be out here, but between the search and Father's absence, I didn't have a great deal of choice. I was in a dreadful state about it, but Evelyn's a clever old stick. She gave me this." He taps the gun. "Said it was impossible to hit anything, but I'd look very dashing trying."

Daniel's trying to suppress laughter, drawing a good-natured smile from Michael.

"Where are your parents, Michael?" I say, ignoring the teasing. "I thought this was their party, but the burden of it seems to have fallen solely on your shoulders."

He scratches the back of his neck, looking gloomy.

"Father's locked himself in the gatehouse, Uncle Edward. He's brooding as usual."

Uncle?

Snatches of Dance's memory surface, fleeting glimpses of a lifelong friendship with Peter Hardcastle that made me an honorary part of the family. Whatever we had has long since faded, but I'm surprised by the affection I still feel for this boy. I've known him his entire life. I'm proud of him. Prouder than of my own son.

"As for Mother," continues Michael, oblivious to my momentary confusion. "To tell you the truth, she's been acting strangely since we got here. Actually, I was hoping you'd speak with her privately. I think she's avoiding me."

"And me," I counter. "I haven't managed to catch hold of her all day."

He pauses, making his mind up on something. Lowering his voice, he continues confidentially, "I'm worried she's gone off the deep end."

"Deep end?"

"It's like she's somebody else entirely," he says, worried. "Happy one minute, angry the next. It's impossible to keep track, and the way she looks at us now, it's as if she doesn't recognize us."

Another rival?

The Plague Doctor said there were three of us: the footman, Anna, and myself. I can't see what purpose would be served by lying. I steal a glance at Daniel, trying to gauge whether he knows anything more about this, but his attention is riveted on Michael.

"When did this behavior start?" I ask casually.

"I couldn't tell you, feels like forever."

"But when was the first time you noticed it?"

He chews his lip, cycling back in his memories.

"The clothes!" he says suddenly. "That would be it. Did I tell you about the clothes?" He's looking at Daniel, who shakes his head blankly. "Come now, I must have? Happened about a year ago?"

Daniel shakes his head again.

"Mother had come up to Blackheath for her annual morbid pilgrimage, but when she got back to London, she burst into my place in Mayfair and started ranting about finding the clothes," says Michael, telling the story as though expecting Daniel to leap in at any moment. "That's all she'd say, that she'd found the clothes, and did I know anything about them."

"Whose clothes were they?" I say, humoring him.

I'd been excited to hear about Helena's altered personality, but if she changed a year ago, it's unlikely she's another rival. And while there's certainly something strange about her, I don't see how laundry can help me decipher what it is.

"Damned if I know," he says, throwing his hands up. "I couldn't get a sensible thing out of her. In the end, I managed to calm her down, but she wouldn't keep quiet about the clothes. Kept saying everybody would know."

"Know what?" I say.

"She never did say, and she left shortly after, but she was adamant."

Our group is thinning out as the dogs draw the hunters in a different direction, Herrington, Sutcliffe, and Pettigrew waiting for us a little farther ahead. They're obviously hanging back for further directions, and after saying his goodbyes, Michael jogs ahead to point the way.

"What did you make of that?" I ask Daniel.

"I haven't yet," he says vaguely.

He's preoccupied, his gaze dragging behind Michael. We continue in silence until we reach an abandoned village at the bottom of a cliff. Eight stone cottages are arranged around a dirt junction, the thatched roofs rotted away, the logs that once supported them collapsed. Echoes of old lives linger still; a bucket among the rubble, an anvil tipped over by the side of the road. Some might find them charming, but I see only relics of former hardships, happily deserted.

"Nearly time," Daniel mutters, staring at the village.

There's a look on his face I can't quite place, married to a tone that's impatient, excited, and a little afraid. It makes my skin prickle. Something of note is about to happen here, but for the life of me I can't see what it could be. Michael's showing Sutcliffe and Pettigrew one of the old stone houses, while Stanwin leans against a tree, his thoughts far afield.

"Be ready," Daniel says enigmatically, disappearing into the trees before I have the chance to question him further. Any other host would follow him, but I'm exhausted. I need to sit down somewhere.

Settling myself on a crumbling wall, I rest while the others talk, my eyelids drooping. Age is coiling around me, its fangs in my neck, drawing my strength when I need it most. It's an unpleasant sensation, perhaps even worse than the burden of Ravencourt's bulk. At least the initial shock of being Ravencourt waned, allowing me to become accustomed to his physical limitations. Not so with Dance, who still thinks of himself as a vigorous young man, waking up to his age only when he catches sight of his wrinkled hands. Even now, I can feel him frowning at my decision to sit down, to give in to my tiredness.

I pinch my arm, struggling to stay awake, irritated at my vanishing energy.

It makes me wonder how old I am outside of Blackheath. It's not something I've allowed myself to dwell on before, time being short enough without indulging pointless musing, but here and now, I pray for youth, for strength, good health, and a sound mind. To escape all this only to find myself permanently trapped in—

~ 39 ~

DAY TWO (CONTINUED)

I wake abruptly, stirring the Plague Doctor who's staring at a gold pocket watch, his mask painted a sickly yellow color by the candle in his hand. I'm back in the butler, swaddled in cotton sheets.

"Right on time," says the Plague Doctor, snapping the watch shut.

It looks to be dusk, the room mired in a gloom only partially beaten back by our small flame. Anna's shotgun is lying on the bed beside me.

"What happened?" I say, my voice hoarse.

"Dance is dozing on his wall." The Plague Doctor chuckles, placing his candle on the floor and dropping into the small chair by the bed. It's far too small for him, his greatcoat swallowing the wood completely.

"No, I meant the shotgun. Why do I have it?"

"One of your hosts left it for you. Don't bother calling for Anna," he says, noticing that I'm eyeing the door. "She's not here. I came to warn you that your rival has almost solved the murder. I'm expecting him to find me at the lake tonight. You must work quickly from this point onward."

I try to straighten out, but the pain in my ribs immediately puts an end to my efforts.

"Why are you so interested in me?" I ask, letting the agony settle into its familiar spots.

"I'm sorry?"

"Why do you keep coming here for these talks? I know you don't bother with Anna, and I'd wager you don't see much of the footman either."

"What's your name?"

"Why does—"

"Answer the question," he says, rapping the floor with his cane.

"Edward Da…no, Derby. I…" I flounder for a moment. "Aiden… something."

"You're losing yourself to them, Mr. Bishop," he says, crossing his arms and leaning back in his chair. "It's been happening for a while now. That's why we only allow you eight hosts. Any more than that and your personality wouldn't be able to rise above theirs."

He's right. My hosts are getting stronger, and I'm getting weaker. It's been happening incrementally, insidiously. It's as though I fell asleep on a beach and now find myself cast out to sea.

"What do I do?" I say, feeling a surge of panic.

"Hold on," he says with a shrug. "It's all you can do. There's a voice in your mind, you must have heard it by now. Dry, slightly distant? It's calm when you're panicked, fearless when you're afraid."

"I've heard it."

"That's what's left of the original Aiden Bishop, the man who first entered Blackheath. It's not much more than a fragment anymore, a little piece of his personality clinging on from one loop to the next, but if you begin to lose yourself, heed that voice. It's your lighthouse. Everything that remains of the man you once were."

With a great rustling of clothing, he gets to his feet, the candle flame snapping in the breeze. Stooping down, he lifts the candle from the floor and heads to the door.

"Wait," I say.

He pauses, his back to me. The candlelight forms a warm halo around his body.

"How many times have we done all of this?" I ask.

"Thousands, I suspect. More than I could possibly count."

"So why do I keep failing?"

He sighs, looking over his shoulder at me. There's a sense of weariness in his bearing, as though every loop is sediment, pressing down on him.

"It's a question I've pondered myself from time to time," he says, melting wax running down the side to stain his glove. "Chance has played its part, stumbling when being surefooted would have saved you. Mostly, though, I think it's your nature."

"My nature?" I ask. "You think I'm destined to fail?"

"Destined? No. That would be an excuse, and Blackheath is intolerant of excuses," he says. "Nothing that's happening here is inevitable, much as it may appear otherwise. Events keep happening the same way day after day, because your fellow guests keep making the same decisions day after day. They decide to go hunting; they decide to betray each other; one of them drinks too much and skips breakfast, missing a meeting that would change his life forever. They cannot see another way, so they never change. You are different, Mr. Bishop. Throughout the loops, I've watched you react to moments of kindness and cruelty, random acts of chance. You make different decisions, and yet repeat the same mistakes at crucial junctures. It's as though some part of you is perpetually pulled toward the pit."

"Are you saying I have to become somebody else to escape?"

"I'm saying every man is in a cage of his own making," he says. "The Aiden Bishop who first entered Blackheath." He sighs, as if the memory troubles him. "The things he wanted and his way of getting them were…unyielding. That man could never have escaped Blackheath. This Aiden Bishop before me is different. I think you're closer than you've ever been, but I've thought that before and been fooled. The truth is you've yet to be tested, but that's coming, and if you've changed, truly changed, then who knows, there may be hope for you."

Ducking under the doorframe, he disappears into the corridor with the candle.

"You have four hosts after Edward Dance, including what's left of the days of the butler and Donald Davies. Be cautious, Mr. Bishop, the footman isn't going to rest until they're all dead, and I'm not sure you can afford to lose a single one of them."

With that, he closes the door.

～40～

DAY SIX (CONTINUED)

Dance's years fall on me like a thousand small weights.

Michael and Stanwin are speaking behind me, Sutcliffe and Pettigrew laughing uproariously with a drink in their hand.

Rebecca hovers over me with a silver tray, one last glass of brandy for the taking.

"Rebecca," I say fondly, almost reaching out a hand to touch my wife's cheek.

"No, sir. It's Lucy, sir, Lucy Harper," says the maid, concerned. "Sorry to wake you. I was worried you were going to fall off the wall."

I blink away the memory of Dance's dead wife, cursing myself for a fool. What a ridiculous mistake to make. Thankfully, the remembrance of Lucy's kindness toward the butler tempers my irritation at being caught in a moment of such sentiment.

"Would you like a drink, sir?" she asks. "Something to warm you up?"

I look past her to see Evelyn's lady's maid, Madeline Aubert, packing dirty glasses and half-empty brandy bottles into a hamper. The two of them must have carried it over from Blackheath, arriving while I slept. I seem to have dozed for longer than I suspected, as they're already readying themselves to leave.

"I think I'm unsteady enough," I say.

Her gaze flickers over my shoulder toward Ted Stanwin, whose hand is gripping Michael Hardcastle's shoulder. Uncertainty writes itself in large letters across her face, which is little wonder considering his treatment of her at lunchtime.

"Don't worry, Lucy. I'll take it over to him," I say, rising and removing the glass of brandy from the tray. "I need to speak with him anyway."

"Thank you, sir," she says with a wide smile, departing before I can change my mind.

Stanwin and Michael are quiet when I come upon them, but I can hear the things not being said and the unease that stands in its place.

"Michael, may I have a private word with Mr. Stanwin?" I ask.

"Of course," says Michael, inclining his head and withdrawing.

I hand Stanwin the drink, ignoring the suspicion with which he glances at the glass.

"Rare that you'd lower yourself to come talk with me, Dance," says Stanwin, sizing me up the way a boxer might an opponent in the ring.

"I thought we could help each other," I say.

"I'm always interested in making new friends."

"I need to know what you saw on the morning of Thomas Hardcastle's murder."

"It's an old story," he says, tracing the edge of his glass with a fingertip.

"But worth hearing from the horse's mouth, surely," I say.

He's looking over my shoulder, watching Madeline and Lucy depart with their hamper. I have the sense he's searching for a distraction. Something about Dance puts him on edge.

"No harm in it, I suppose," he says with a grunt, returning his attention to me. "I was Blackheath's gamekeeper back then. I was on my rounds around the lake, same as every morning, when I saw Carver and another devil with his back to me stabbing the little boy. I took a shot at him, but he escaped into the woods while I was wrestling with Carver."

"And for that Lord and Lady Hardcastle gave you a plantation?" I say.

"They did, not that I asked," he sniffs.

"Alf Miller, the stable master, says Helena Hardcastle was with Carver that morning, a few minutes before the attack. What do you say to that?"

"That he's a drunk and a damned liar," says Stanwin smoothly.

I search for some tremor, some hint of unease, but he's an accomplished deceiver this one, his fidgeting put away now he knows what I want. I can feel the scales tipping in his direction, his confidence growing.

I've misjudged this.

I believed I could bully him as I did the stable master and Dickie, but Stanwin's nervousness wasn't a symptom of fear. It was the unease of a man finding a lone question in his pile of answers.

"Tell me, Mr. Dance," he says, leaning close enough to whisper into my ear. "Who's the mother of your son? I know it wasn't your dearly departed Rebecca. Don't get me wrong, I've got a few ideas, but it would save me the cost of confirming them if you'd tell me up front. I might even discount your monthly payment afterward, for services rendered."

My blood freezes. This secret sits at the core of Dance's being. It's his greatest shame, his only weakness, and Stanwin's just closed his fist around it.

I couldn't respond even if I wanted to.

Stepping away from me, Stanwin tosses the untouched brandy into the bushes with a flick of his wrist.

"Next time you come to trade, make sure you have something—"

A shotgun explodes behind me.

Something splashes my face, Stanwin's body jolting backward before hitting the ground in a mangled heap. My ears are ringing and, touching my cheek, I find blood on my fingertips.

Stanwin's blood.

Someone shrieks, others gasp and cry out.

Nobody moves, then everybody does.

Michael and Clifford Herrington race toward the body, hollering for somebody to fetch Doctor Dickie, but it's obvious the blackmailer's dead. His chest is broken open, the malice that drove him flown the coop. One good eye is pointed in my direction, an accusation held within. I want to tell him this wasn't my fault, that I didn't do this. Suddenly, that seems like the most important thing in the world.

It's shock.

Bushes rustle, Daniel stepping out, smoke rising from the barrel of his shotgun. He's looking down at the body with so little emotion, I could almost believe him innocent of the crime.

"What did you do, Coleridge?" cries Michael, checking Stanwin for a pulse.

"Exactly what I promised your father I would do," he says flatly. "I've made sure Ted Stanwin will never blackmail any of you again."

"You murdered him!"

"Yes," says Daniel, meeting his shocked gaze. "I did."

Reaching into his pocket, Daniel hands me a silk handkerchief.

"Clean yourself up, old man," he says.

I take it unthinkingly, even thanking him. I'm dazed, bewildered. Nothing about this feels real. Wiping Stanwin's blood off my face, I stare at the crimson smear on the handkerchief, as if it can somehow explain what's happening. I was speaking with Stanwin, and then he was dead, and I don't understand how that could be. Surely, there should be more? A chase, fear, warning of some sort. We shouldn't simply die. It feels like a swindle. So much paid, too much asked.

"We're ruined," wails Sutcliffe, slumping against a tree. "Stanwin always said that if anything happened to him, our secrets would be made common knowledge."

"That's your concern?" yells Herrington, wheeling on him. "Coleridge murdered a man in front of us!"

"A man we all hated," Sutcliffe shoots back. "Don't pretend you weren't thinking the same thing. Don't any of you pretend! Stanwin bled us dry in life, and he's going to destroy us in death."

"No, he won't," says Daniel, resting the shotgun across his shoulder.

He's the only one who's calm, the only one who isn't acting like an entirely different person. None of this means anything to him.

"Everything he has on us—" says Pettigrew.

"Is written in a book that I now own," interrupts Daniel, retrieving a cigarette from his silver case.

His hand's not even shaking. My hand. What the hell does Blackheath make me?

"I commissioned somebody to steal it for me," he continues casually, lighting his cigarette. "Your secrets are my secrets, and they'll never see the light of day. Now, I believe each of you owes me a promise. It's this: you won't mention this to anybody for the rest of the day. Is that understood? If anybody asks, Stanwin stayed behind when we left. He didn't say why, and that was the last you saw of him."

Blank faces find each other, everybody too stunned to speak. I can't tell whether they're aghast at what they've witnessed or simply overcome by their good fortune.

For my part, the shock is fading, the horror of Daniel's actions finally sinking in. Half an hour ago, I was praising him for showing a modicum of kindness to Michael. Now I'm covered in another man's blood, realizing how deeply I've underestimated his desperation.

My desperation. This is my future I'm seeing, and it makes me sick.

"I need to hear the words, gentleman," says Daniel, blowing smoke from the corner of his mouth. "Tell me you understand what happened here."

Assurances arrive in a jumble, muted but sincere. Only Michael seems upset.

Meeting his gaze, Daniel speaks coldly.

"And don't forget, I have all of your secrets in my hands." He lets that settle. "Now, I think you should head back before anybody comes looking for us."

The suggestion is met with a murmur of agreement, everybody disappearing back into the forest. Signaling for me to remain behind, Daniel waits until they're out of earshot before speaking.

"Help me go through his pockets," he says, rolling up his sleeves. "The other hunters will be coming back this way soon, and I don't want them to see us with the body."

"What have you done, Daniel?" I hiss.

"He'll be alive tomorrow," he says, waving his hand dismissively. "I've knocked over a scarecrow."

"We're supposed to be solving a murder, not committing one."

"Give a little boy an electric train set and he'll immediately try to derail it," he says. "The act does not speak to his character, nor do we judge him for it."

"You think this is a game?" I snap, pointing at Stanwin's body.

"A puzzle, with disposable pieces. Solve it and we get to go home." He frowns at me, as if I'm a stranger who's asked directions to a place that doesn't exist. "I don't understand your concern."

"If we solve Evelyn's murder in the manner you're suggesting, we don't deserve to go home! Can't you see? These masks we wear betray us. They reveal us."

"You're babbling," he says, searching Stanwin's pockets.

"We are never more ourselves than when we think people aren't watching. Don't you realize that? It doesn't matter if Stanwin's alive tomorrow; you murdered him today. You murdered a man in cold blood, and that will blot your soul for the rest of your life. I don't know why we're here, Daniel, or why this is happening to us, but we should be proving that it's an injustice, not making ourselves worthy of it."

"You're misguided," he says, contempt creeping into his voice. "We can no more mistreat these people than we could their shadow cast upon the wall. I don't understand what you're asking of me."

"That we hold ourselves to a higher standard," I say, my voice rising. "That we be better men than our hosts! Murdering Stanwin was Daniel Coleridge's solution, but it shouldn't be yours. You're a good man. You can't lose sight of that."

"A good man," he scoffs. "Avoiding unpleasant acts doesn't make a man good. Look at where we are, what's been done to us. Escaping this place requires that we do what is necessary, even if our nature compels us otherwise. I know this makes you squeamish, that you don't have the stomach for it. I was the same, but I no longer have the time to tiptoe around my ethics. I can end this tonight and I mean to, so don't measure me by how tightly I cling to my goodness, measure me by what I'm willing to sacrifice that you might cling to yours. If I fail, you can always try another way."

"And how will you live with yourself when you're done?" I demand.

"I'll look at the faces of my family and know that what I lost in this place was not nearly as important as my reward for leaving it."

"You can't believe that," I say.

"I do, and so will you after a few more days in this place," he says. "Now, please, help me search him before the hunters find us here. I have no intention of wasting my evening answering a policeman's questions."

It's no use arguing with him. Shutters have come down behind his eyes.

I sigh, taking myself over to the body.

"What am I looking for?" I ask.

"Answers, same as always," he says, unbuttoning the blackmailer's bloody jacket. "Stanwin collected every lie in Blackheath, including the last piece of our puzzle, the reason for Evelyn's murder. Every scrap of knowledge he holds is contained in a book written in code, with a separate book of ciphers required to read it. I have the first. Stanwin keeps the latter on him at all times."

That was the book Derby stole from Stanwin's bedroom.

"Did you take it from Derby?" I ask. "I was coshed on the head almost as soon as I got my hands on it."

"Of course not," he says. "Coleridge had already commissioned somebody to retrieve the book before I took control of him. I didn't even know he was interested in Stanwin's blackmail business until the book was delivered to me. If it's any consolation, I did consider warning you."

"So, why didn't you?"

He shrugs. "Derby's a rabid dog. It seemed better for everybody to let him sleep for a few hours. Now, come along. We're short of time."

Shuddering, I kneel beside the body. This is no way for a man to die, even one such as Stanwin. His chest is mincemeat and blood has soaked through his clothing. It oozes around my fingers when I delve inside his trouser pockets.

I work slowly, barely able to look.

Daniel has no such qualms, patting down Stanwin's shirt and jacket, seemingly impervious to the tattered flesh showing through. By the time we're finished, we've uncovered a cigarette case, pocket-knife, and lighter, but no codebook.

We glance at each other.

"We have to roll him over," says Daniel, voicing my thoughts.

Stanwin was a large man, and it takes a great deal of effort to push him onto his front. It's worth it. I'm much more comfortable searching a body that isn't looking up at me.

As Daniel runs his hands along Stanwin's trouser legs, I lift his jacket, spotting a bulge in the lining surrounded by haphazard stitching.

A ripple of excitement shames me. The last thing I want is to justify Daniel's methods, but now we're on the verge of a discovery, I'm growing more elated.

Using the dead man's pocketknife, I slice the stitches, letting the codebook slide into my palm. No sooner has it come free when I notice there's something else in there. Reaching inside, I pull out a small silver locket, its chain removed. There's a painting inside, and though it's old and cracked, it's obviously of a little girl, around seven or eight with red hair.

I hold it out to Daniel, but's he too busy flipping through the codebook to pay attention.

"This is it," he says excitedly. "This is our way out."

"I certainly hope so," I say. "We paid a high price for it."

He looks up from the book a different man to the one who started reading it. This is neither Bell's Daniel, nor Ravencourt's. It's not even the man of a few minutes ago, arguing the necessity of his actions. This is a man victorious, one foot already out the door.

"I'm not proud of what I did," he says. "But we couldn't have done this any other way. You must believe that."

He may not be proud, but he's not ashamed either. That much is evident, and I'm reminded of the Plague Doctor's warning.

The Aiden Bishop who first entered Blackheath…the things he wanted and his way of getting them were unyielding. That man could never have escaped Blackheath.

In his desperation, Daniel's making the same mistakes I always have, exactly as the Plague Doctor warned me I would. Whatever happens, I can't let myself become this.

"Are you ready to go?" says Daniel.

"Do you know the way home?" I say, searching the forest and realizing I have no idea how we arrived here.

"It's east," he says.

"And which way is that?"

Thrusting a hand into his pocket, he brings out Bell's compass.

"I borrowed it from him this morning," he says, laying it flat in his palm. "Funny how things repeat, isn't it?"

~ 41 ~

We come upon the house rather unexpectedly, the trees giving way to the muddy lawn, its windows burning bright with candlelight. I must admit I'm glad to see it. Despite the shotgun, I've spent the entire journey glancing over my shoulder for the footman. If the codebook is as valuable as Daniel believes, I must assume our enemy is also in pursuit of it.

He'll be coming for us soon.

Silhouettes are passing back and forth in the upper windows, hunters trudging up the steps into the golden glow of the entrance hall where caps and jackets are wrenched loose and discarded, filthy water pooling on the marble. A maid moves among us with a tray of sherry, from which Daniel plucks two glasses, handing me one.

Clinking my glass, he throws his drink down his throat as Michael arrives at our side. As with the rest of us, he looks to have crawled off the ark, his dark hair plastered to his pale face by the rain. Glancing at his watch, I discover it's 6:07 p.m.

"I've sent a couple of trustworthy servants to collect Stanwin's body," he whispers. "I told them I stumbled on his body coming back from the hunt and instructed them to inter him in one of the old potting sheds. Nobody will find him, and I won't summon the police until early tomorrow morning. I'm sorry, but I won't leave him to rot in the forest any longer than I have to."

He clutches a half-empty glass of sherry, and though the drink has put a little color in his cheeks, it's not nearly enough.

The crowd in the hall is thinning out now. A couple of maids have already appeared with buckets of sudsy water and are waiting in the wings with their mops and their frowns, trying to shame us into leaving so they can get to work.

Rubbing his eyes, Michael looks at us directly for the first time.

"I'm going to honor my father's promise," he says. "But I don't like it."

"Michael—" says Daniel, reaching out a hand, but Michael steps away.

"No, please," he says, his sense of betrayal palpable. "We'll speak another day, but not now, not tonight."

He turns his back on us, heading up the stairs toward his bedroom.

"Never mind him," says Daniel. "He thinks I acted from greed. He doesn't understand how important this is. The answers are in the ledger, I know it!"

He's excited, like a boy with a new slingshot.

"We're almost there, Dance," he says. "We're almost free."

"And then what happens?" I say. "Do *you* walk out of here? Do *I*? We can't both escape; we're the same man."

"I don't know," he says. "Presumably Aiden Bishop wakes up again, his memories intact. Hopefully he won't remember either of us. We're bad dreams, best forgotten." He checks his watch. "Let's not think about that now. Anna has arranged to meet Bell in the graveyard this evening. If she's right, the footman's heard about it and is sure to show. She'll need us to help capture him. That gives us about four hours to dig what we need out of this book. Why don't you get changed and come up to my room? We'll do it together."

"I'll be right along," I say.

His giddiness is a rare fillip. Tonight we'll deal with the footman and deliver the Plague Doctor's answer. Somewhere in the house, my other hosts are surely refining their plan to save Evelyn's life, which means I simply need to work out how to save Anna as well. I cannot believe she's been lying to me this whole time, and I cannot imagine leaving this place without her by my side, not after everything she's done to help me.

Floorboards echo as I return to my room, the house grumbling under the weight of the returned. Everybody will be getting ready for dinner.

I envy them their evening, for a darker purpose lies ahead of me.

Much darker, the footman will not go quietly.

"There you are," I say, glancing around to make sure nobody's listening. "Is it true you're what's left of the original Aiden Bishop?"

Silence greets my question, and somewhere within I can feel Dance sneering at me. I can only imagine what the stiff old solicitor would say about a man talking to himself in this fashion.

Aside from the dim light of the fire, my bedroom is shrouded, the servants having forgotten to light the candles ahead of my arrival. Suspicion pricks me. I raise the shotgun to my shoulder. A gamekeeper tried to collect it when we came inside, but I brushed him off, insisting it was part of my personal collection.

Sparking the lantern beside the door, I see Anna standing in the corner of the room, arms by her sides, expression blank.

"Anna," I say, surprised, lowering the shotgun. "What's the—"

Wood creaks behind me, pain flares in my side. A rough hand yanks me backward, covering my mouth. I'm spun around, bringing me face-to-face with the footman. There's a smirk on his lips, his eyes scratching at my face, as though digging for something buried beneath.

Those eyes.

I try to scream, but he clamps my jaw shut.

He holds his knife up. Very slowly he runs the point down my chest, before ramming it into my stomach, the pain of each blow eclipsing the one before until pain is all there is.

I've never been so cold, never felt so quiet.

My legs buckle, his arms taking my weight, lowering me carefully to the floor. He keeps his eyes on mine, soaking up the life slipping out of them.

I open my mouth to scream, but no sound comes out.

"Run, rabbit," he says, his face close to mine. "Run."

~ 42 ~

DAY TWO (CONTINUED)

I scream, lurching up from the butler's bed only to be pressed back down by the footman.

"This him?" he says, looking over his shoulder at Anna, who's standing by the window.

"Yes," she says, a tremor in her voice.

The footman leans close, his voice hoarse, ale-thick breath warm on my cheek.

"Didn't leap far enough, rabbit," he says.

The blade slips into my side, my blood spilling onto the sheets, taking my life with it.

43

DAY SEVEN

I scream into suffocating darkness, my back against a wall, my knees tucked under my chin. Instinctively I grab the spot where the butler was stabbed, cursing my stupidity. The Plague Doctor was telling the truth. Anna betrayed me.

I feel sick, my mind scrambling for a reasonable explanation, but I saw her myself. She's been lying to me this whole time.

She isn't the only one guilty of that.

"Shut up," I say angrily.

My heart is racing, my breathing shallow. I need to calm down, or I'll be no use to anybody. Taking a minute, I try to think of anything but Anna, but it's surprisingly difficult. I hadn't realized how often my mind has reached for her in the quiet.

She was safety, and comfort.

She was my friend.

Shifting position, I try to work out where I've woken up and whether I'm in any immediate danger. At first blush, it doesn't appear so. My shoulders are touching walls on either side of me, a sliver of light piercing a crack near my right ear, dusting cardboard boxes on my left and bottles down by my feet.

I move my wristwatch to the light, discovering that it's 10:13 a.m. Bell hasn't even reached the house yet.

"It's still morning," I say to myself, relieved. "I still have time."

My lips are dry, my tongue cracked, the air so thick with mildew it feels like a dirty rag's been stuffed down my throat. A drink would be nice, something cold, anything with ice. It seems a long time since I've woken up beneath cotton sheets, the day's torments queuing patiently on the other side of a warm bath.

I didn't know when I was well off.

My host must have slept in this position all night because it's agony to move. Thankfully, the panel to the right of me is loose and pushes open without too much effort, my eyes watering as they're exposed to the harsh brightness of the room beyond.

I'm in a long gallery stretching the length of the house, cobwebs dangling from the ceiling. The walls are dark wood, the floor littered with dozens of pieces of old furniture that are thick with dust and almost hollowed out by woodworm. Brushing myself off, I get to my feet, shaking some life into my iron limbs. Turns out my host spent the night in a storage cupboard beneath a small flight of stairs leading up to a stage. Yellowed sheet music sits open in front of a dusty cello, and looking at it, I feel like I've slept through some great calamity, judgment having come and gone while I was stuffed in that cupboard.

What the hell was I doing under there?

Aching, I stagger over to one of the windows lining the gallery. It's shrouded with grime, but wiping a spot clear with my sleeve reveals Blackheath's gardens below. I'm on the top floor of the house.

Out of habit, I begin searching my pockets for some clue as to my identity, but realize I don't need it. I'm Jim Rashton. I'm twenty-seven, a constable in the police force, and my parents Margaret and Henry beam with pride whenever they tell anybody. I have a sister, I have a dog, and I'm in love with a woman called Grace Davies, who's the reason I'm at this party.

Whatever barrier used to exist between myself and my hosts is almost completely knocked through. I can barely tell Rashton's life from my own. Unfortunately, my recollection of how I came to end up in the cupboard is clouded by the bottle of scotch Rashton was drinking last night. I remember telling old stories, laughing and dancing, barreling recklessly through an evening that had no other purpose than pleasure.

Was the footman there? Did he do this?

I strain for the memory, but last night's a drunken smear. Agitation instinctively sends my hand to the leather cigarette case Rashton keeps in his pocket, but there's only one cigarette left inside. I'm tempted to light it to calm my nerves, but given the circumstances, a frayed temper might serve me better, especially if I have to fight my way out of here. The footman tracked me from Dance into the butler, so it's doubtful I'll find safe harbor in Rashton.

Caution will be my truest friend now.

Casting around for a weapon, I find a bronze statue of Atlas. I creep forward with it held above my head, picking my way through walls of armoires and giant webs of interlocking chairs until I arrive at a faded black curtain stretching the length of the room. Cardboard trees are propped against the walls, near clothes racks stuffed with costumes. Among them are six or seven plague doctor outfits, the hats and masks piled in a box on the floor. It appears the family used to put on plays up here.

A floorboard creaks, the curtain twitching. Somebody's shuffling around back there.

I tense. Raising Atlas above my head, I—

Anna bursts through, her cheeks red.

"Oh, thank God," she says, catching sight of me.

She's out of breath, dark circles surrounding bloodshot brown eyes. Her blond hair is loose and tangled, her cap scrunched up in her hand. The artist's sketchbook chronicling each of my hosts bulges in her apron.

"You're Rashton, right? Come on, we only have half an hour to save the others," she says, lunging forward to take hold of my hand.

I step back, the statue still raised, but the breathlessness of the introduction has knocked me off balance, as has the lack of guilt in her voice.

"I'm not going anywhere with you," I say, gripping Atlas a little tighter.

Confusion paints her face, followed by a dawning realization.

"Is this because of what happened to Dance and the butler?" she asks. "I don't know anything about that, about anything really. I've haven't been up long. I just know you're in eight different people and a footman's killing them, and we need to go save the ones that are left."

"You expect me to trust you?" I say, stunned. "You distracted Dance while the footman murdered him. You were standing in the room when he killed the butler. You've been helping him. I've seen you!"

She shakes her head.

"Don't be an idiot," she cries. "I haven't done any of that yet, and even when I do, it won't be because I'm betraying you. If I wanted you dead, I'd pick off your hosts before they ever woke up. You wouldn't see me, and I certainly wouldn't work with a man guaranteed to turn on me once we'd finished."

"Then what were you doing there?" I demand.

"I don't know. I haven't lived that part yet," she snaps back. "You—another you, I mean—was waiting for me when I woke up. He gave me a book that told me to find Derby in the forest, then come here and save you. That's my day. That's everything I know."

"It's not enough," I say bluntly. "I haven't done any of that, so I don't know if you're telling the truth." Putting the statue down, I walk past her, heading for the black curtain she emerged through. "I can't trust you, Anna."

"Why not?" she says, catching my trailing hand. "I'm trusting *you*."

"That's not—"

"Do you remember anything from our previous loops?"

"Only your name," I say, looking down at her fingers intertwined with mine, my resistance already crumbling. I want to believe her so badly.

"But you don't remember how any of them ended?"

"No," I say impatiently. "Why are you asking me this?"

"Because I do," she says. "The reason I know your name is because I remember calling for you in the gatehouse. We'd arranged to meet there. You were late, and I was worried. I was so happy to see you, and then I saw the look on your face."

Her eyes find mine, the pupils wide and dark and daring. They're guileless. Surely, she couldn't have...

Everybody in this house is wearing a mask.

"You murdered me right where I stood," she says, touching my cheek, studying the face I still haven't seen. "When you found me this morning, I was so scared I almost ran away, but you were so broken... so scared. It was like all your lives had crashed down on top of you. You couldn't tell one from another, you didn't even know who you were. You pushed this book into my hands and said you were sorry. You kept repeating it. You told me you weren't that man anymore and that we couldn't get out of this by making the same mistakes all over again. It was the last lucid thing you said."

Memories are stirring slowly and so far away that I feel like a man reaching across a river to trap a butterfly between his fingers.

She presses the chess piece into my palm, curling my fingers around it.

"This might help," she says. "We used these pieces in the last loop to identify ourselves. A bishop for you, Aiden Bishop, and a knight for me. The protector, like now."

I remember the guilt, the sorrow. I remember the regret. There aren't images, there isn't even a memory. It doesn't matter. I can feel the truth of what she's saying, as I felt the strength of our friendship the first time we met, and the agony of the grief that brought me to Blackheath.

She's right. I murdered her.

"Do you remember now?" she says.

I nod, ashamed and sick to my stomach. I didn't want to hurt her, I know that. We'd been working together like today, but something changed… I became desperate. I saw my escape slipping away, and I panicked. I promised myself I'd find a way to get her out after I'd left. I couched my betrayal in noble intentions, and I did something awful.

I shudder, waves of revulsion washing over me.

"I don't know which loop the memory is from," says Anna. "But I think I held onto it as a warning to myself. A warning not to trust you again."

"Why didn't you tell me the truth when we first met?" I say, still ashamed.

"Because you already knew," she says, wrinkling her forehead. "From my perspective, we met two hours ago, and you knew everything about me."

"The first time I met you, I was Cecil Ravencourt," I respond. "It was early afternoon."

"Then we're meeting in the middle, because I don't know who that is yet," she says. "It doesn't matter, though. I won't tell him, or any of the others, because it doesn't matter. It wasn't us in any of those previous loops. Whoever they were, they made different choices, different mistakes. I'm choosing to trust you, Aiden, and I need you to trust me, because this place is…you know how it works. Whatever you think I was doing when the footman killed you, it wasn't everything. It wasn't the truth."

She'd seem confident if it weren't for the nervous throb in her throat, the way her foot worries at the floor. I can feel her hand trembling against my cheek, the strain in her voice. Beneath all the bravado, she's still afraid of me, of the man I was, of the man who may still be lurking within.

I can't imagine the courage it took to bring her here.

"I don't know how to get us both out of here, Anna."

"I know."

"But I will. I won't leave without you, I promise."

"I know that too."

And that's when she slaps me.

"That's for murdering me," she says, standing on her tiptoes to plant a kiss on the sting. "Now, let's go and make sure the footman doesn't murder any more of you."

～ 44 ～

Wood creaks, the narrow, twisting staircase darkening the farther down we get, until finally we sink beneath the gloom.

"Do you know why I was in that cupboard?" I ask Anna, who's ahead of me and moving fast enough to outrun a falling sky.

"No idea, but it saved your life," she says, glancing back at me over her shoulder. "The book said the footman would be coming for Rashton around this time. If he'd slept in his bedroom last night, the footman would have found him."

"Maybe we should *let* him find me," I say, feeling a rush of excitement. "Come on, I've got an idea."

I push past Anna and begin leaping down the steps two at a time.

If the footman's coming for Rashton this morning, there's every chance he'll still be lurking around the corridors. He'll be expecting a man asleep in his bed, which means I've got the upper hand for once. With a little luck, I can put an end to this here and now.

The steps end abruptly at a whitewashed wall. Anna's still halfway up and calling for me to slow down. A police officer of considerable skill—as he'd freely admit himself—Rashton's no stranger to hidden things. My fingers expertly locate a disguised catch allowing me to tumble into the dark hallway outside. Candles flicker behind sconces, the sunroom standing empty on my left. I've emerged on the first floor, the door I came through already blending into the wall.

The footman is less than twenty yards away. He's on his knees, jimmying the lock to what I instinctively know is my bedroom.

"Looking for me, you bastard," I spit, hurling myself at him before he has a chance to grab his knife.

He's on his feet quicker than I could have imagined, leaping backward and kicking out to catch me in the chest, knocking the wind from me. I land awkwardly, clutching my ribs, but he doesn't move. He's standing there waiting, wiping saliva from the corner of his mouth with the back of his hand.

"Brave rabbit," he says, grinning. "I'm going to gut you slow."

Rising and dusting myself off, I raise my fists in a boxer's stance, suddenly aware of how heavy my arms feel. That night in the cupboard's done me no favors, and my confidence is eking away by the second. This time I approach him slowly, feinting left and right, working an opening that never comes. A jab catches my chin, rocking my head back. I don't even see the second punch that smashes into my stomach, or the third that puts me on the floor.

I'm disorientated, dizzy, struggling for breath as the footman looms over me, dragging me up by my hair and stretching for his knife.

"Hey!" shouts Anna.

It's the slightest of distractions, but it's enough. Slipping free of the footman's hold, I kick his knee, then launch my shoulder up into his face, breaking his nose, blood splattering my shirt. Reeling backward down the corridor, he grabs hold of a bust and hurls it at me one-handed, forcing me to leap aside as he flees around the corner.

I want to go after him, but I don't have the strength. I slide down the wall until I'm sitting on the floor, clutching my aching ribs. I'm shaken and unnerved. He was too fast, too strong. If that fight had gone on any longer, I'd be dead, I'm certain of it.

"You bloody idiot!" yells Anna, glowering at me. "You almost got yourself killed."

"Did he catch sight of you?" I say, spitting out the blood in my mouth.

"I don't think so," she says, reaching out a hand to help me up. "I kept to the shadows, and I doubt he was seeing much after you broke his nose."

"I'm sorry, Anna," I say. "I honestly thought we could catch hold of him."

"You damn well should be," she says, surprising me with a fierce hug, her body trembling. "You have to be careful, Aiden. Thanks to that bastard, you've only got three hosts left. If you make a mistake, we're going to be stuck here."

Realization hits me like a rock.

"I only have three hosts left," I repeat, stunned.

Sebastian Bell fainted after seeing the dead rabbit in the box. The butler, Dance, and Derby were slain, and Ravencourt fell asleep in the ballroom after watching Evelyn commit suicide. That leaves Rashton, Donald Davies, and Gregory Gold. Between the split days and leaping back and forth, I lost count.

I should have seen it immediately.

Daniel claimed he was the last of my hosts, but that can't be true.

A warm blanket of shame pulls itself over my body. I can't believe I was so easily deceived. So willingly deceived.

It wasn't entirely your fault.

The Plague Doctor warned me Anna would betray me. Why would he do that when it was Daniel who was lying to me? And why would he tell me there were only three people trying to escape this house, when there are four? He's gone out of his way to conceal Daniel's duplicity.

"I've been so blind," I say hollowly.

"What's wrong?" says Anna, pulling away and looking at me with concern.

I falter, my mind clicking into gear as embarrassment gives way to cold calculation. Daniel's lies were elaborate, but their purpose remains obscure. I could understand him trying to earn my trust if he wanted to profit from my investigation, but that's not the case. He's barely asked about it. Quite the contrary; he gave me a head start by telling me it was Evelyn who would be murdered at the ball, and he warned me about the footman.

I can no longer call him a friend, but I can't be certain he's an enemy either. Until I'm certain where he stands, I have to maintain the illusion of ignorance, beginning with Anna. God help us if she let anything slip to Derby, or Dance. Their first reaction to a problem is to run at it, and that won't work with Daniel.

Anna's watching me, waiting for an answer.

"I know something," I say, meeting her eyes. "Something important that matters to both of us, but I can't tell you what it is."

"You're worried about changing the day," she says, as if it's the most obvious thing in the world. "Don't worry, this book's full of things I'm not allowed to tell you." She smiles, her concern washing away. "I trust you, Aiden. I wouldn't be here, if I didn't."

Holding out a hand, she helps me off the floor.

"We can't stay in this corridor," she says. "I'm only alive because the footman doesn't know who I am. If he sees us together, I won't live long enough to help you." She smooths her apron and straightens her cap, dropping her chin enough to appear diffident. "I'll go ahead. Meet me outside Bell's bedroom in ten minutes and keep your eyes open. Once the footman's healed up, he'll be looking for you."

I agree, but I have no intention of waiting in this drafty corridor. Everything that's happening today has Helena Hardcastle's fingerprints on it. I need to speak with her, and this might be my last chance.

Still nursing my injured pride and ribs, I look for her in the drawing room, finding only a few early risers gossiping about how Derby was hauled off by Stanwin's thug. Sure enough, his plate of eggs and kidneys is sitting on the table, where he discarded it. It's still warm. He can't have long departed.

Nodding to them, I make my way to Helena's bedroom, but knocking on her door brings only silence. Running short of time, I kick it open, shattering the lock.

That's the mystery of who broke in solved.

The curtains are drawn, the tangled sheets on the four-poster bed trailing off the mattress onto the floor. The room has the soiled atmosphere of a troubled sleep, the sweat of nightmares as yet unwashed by fresh air. The wardrobe is open, a vanity table covered in spilled powder from a large tin, cosmetics torn open and pushed aside, suggesting Lady Hardcastle attended her toilet in something of a hurry. Laying my hand on the bed, I find it cold. She's already been gone some time.

Just as when I visited this room with Millicent Derby, the roll-down bureau stands open, today's page torn from Helena's day planner and the lacquered gun case emptied of the two revolvers it should contain. I saw Evelyn with one of them in the forest this morning, so she must have taken them very early, possibly after receiving the note compelling her to commit suicide. She would have had no trouble slipping through the connecting door from her bedroom after her mother left.

But if she intends on shooting herself with the revolver, why does she end up using the silver pistol Derby stole from Doctor Dickie instead? And why would she take both revolvers from the case? I know she gives one to Michael to use on the hunt, but I can't imagine that was foremost in her mind after discovering her own life, and that of her friend, was being threatened.

My eyes drift toward the day planner and its torn-out page. Is this also Evelyn's work, or is somebody else responsible? Millicent suspected Helena Hardcastle.

Running my fingertip along the torn edge, I let myself worry.

I've seen Helena's appointments in Lord Hardcastle's planner, so I know the missing page refers to her meetings with Cunningham, Evelyn, Millicent Derby, the stable master, and Ravencourt. The only one of those I can be certain Helena Hardcastle kept is with Cunningham. He admitted it himself.

I slam the book closed in agitation. Behind every answer there's ten more questions, and I'm running short of time.

Ideas gnaw at me as I head upstairs to Anna who's pacing back and forth outside Bell's bedroom, examining the sketchbook in her hands. I can hear muffled voices on the other side of the door. Daniel must be talking to Bell in there. The butler is down in the kitchen with Mrs. Drudge. He should be along shortly.

"Have you seen Gold? He should already be here," says Anna, staring into the shadows, perhaps hoping to carve him out of the gloom with the sharpness of her glare.

"I haven't," I say, looking around. "Why are we here?"

"The footman will kill the butler and Gold this morning, unless we get them somewhere safe, where I can protect them," she says.

"Like the gatehouse," I say.

"Exactly. Only it can't look like that's what we're doing. If it does, the footman will know who I am and kill me, as well. If he thinks I'm just a nursemaid, and they're too hurt to be a threat, he'll leave us be for a little while, and that's what we want. The book reckons they've still got a role to play in all this, assuming we can keep them alive."

"So what do you need me for?"

"Damned if I know. I'm not exactly sure what *I'm* supposed to be doing. The book says to bring you here at this time, but"—she sighs, shaking her head—"that was the only clear instruction; everything else is gibberish. It's like I said, you weren't exactly lucid when you gave it to me. I've spent most of the last hour trying to decipher it, knowing if I read it wrong, or arrive too late, you'll die."

I shiver, unnerved by this brief glimpse at my future.

The book must have been given to Anna by Gregory Gold, my final host. I can still remember him raving at Dance's door about the carriage. I remember thinking how pitiable he was, how frightening. Those dark eyes wild and lost.

I'm not looking forward to tomorrow.

Or whatever happens to make me like that.

Folding my arms, I lean against the wall next to Anna, our shoulders touching. I'm trying to offer some comfort, but knowing you've killed somebody in a previous life tends to narrow possible avenues of affection.

"You've done a better job than I did," I say. "The first time somebody handed me the future, I ended up chasing a maid called Madeline Aubert halfway across the forest thinking I was saving her life," I say. "I nearly frightened the poor girl to death."

"This day should come with instructions," she says glumly.

"Do whatever comes naturally."

"I'm not sure running and hiding would help us," she says, her frustration punctured by the sound of hurried steps on the staircase.

Without a word we scatter out of sight, Anna disappearing around the corner, while I duck into an open bedroom. Curiosity compels me to keep the door open a crack, allowing me to see the butler limping down the corridor toward us, his burned body even more wretched in motion. He looks balled up and tossed away, a collection of sharp angles under a ratty brown dressing gown and pajamas.

Having relived so many of these moments since that first morning, I would have thought I'd become numb, but I can feel the butler's frustration and fear as he races to confront Bell about this new body he's trapped within.

Gregory Gold is stepping out of a bedroom, the butler too preoccupied to notice. At this distance, with his back to me, the artist seems oddly shapeless, less a man, more a long shadow thrown up the wall.

There's a poker in his hand, and without any warning, he begins striking the butler with it.

I remember this attack, this pain.

Pity takes me, a sickening sense of helplessness as blood is sent flying by the poker, freckling the walls.

I'm with the butler as he shrivels up on the floor, begging for mercy and reaching for help that isn't coming.

And that's when reason washes its hands of me.

Snatching a vase from the sideboard, I burst out into the corridor, advancing on Gold with hell's own wrath, and smashing it over his head, shards of porcelain falling around him as he collapses to the floor.

Silence congeals in the air as I clutch the broken rim of the vase while staring at the two unconscious men at my feet.

Anna appears behind me.

"What happened?" she says, feigning surprise.

"I—"

There's a crowd gathering at the end of the corridor, half-dressed men and startled women, roused from their beds by the commotion. Their eyes travel from the blood on the walls to the bodies on the floor, latching onto me with an unbecoming curiosity.

Doctor Dickie is rushing up the stairs, and unlike the other guests, he's already dressed, that huge mustache expertly oiled, his balding head gleaming with some lotion.

"What the devil happened here?" he exclaims.

"Gold went mad," I say, bringing a tremor of emotion to my voice. "He started attacking the butler with the poker, so I—"

I wave the rim of the vase at him.

"Fetch my medical bag, girl," says Dickie to Anna, who's positioned herself in his eyeline. "It's near my bed."

Doing as she's bid, Anna begins deftly sliding pieces of the future into place without ever appearing to take control. The doctor requires somewhere warm and quiet to tend the butler, so Anna recommends the gatehouse while volunteering to administer his medications. By simple expedient of having nowhere else to lock him up, it's decided Gold should be taken over to the gatehouse as well, with sedatives to be administered regularly until a servant can bring a policeman back from the village—a servant Anna volunteers to find.

They descend the staircase with the butler on a makeshift stretcher, Anna offering me a relieved smile as she goes. I meet it with a perplexed frown. All this effort, and I'm still not certain what we've truly accomplished. The butler will be consigned to bed, making him easy pickings for the footman this evening, and Gregory Gold is going to be sedated and strung up. He'll live, but his mind is broken.

That's hardly a reassuring thought considering it's his instructions we're following. Gold gave Anna that book, and while he's the last of my hosts, I have no idea what he's trying to accomplish. I can't even be certain *he* knows. Not after everything he's suffered.

I dig through my memories, searching for the pieces of the future I've glimpsed, but not yet lived. I still need to know what the *"all of them"* message Cunningham delivers to Derby means, and why he tells him he's gathered some people together. I don't know why Evelyn takes the silver pistol from Derby when she already has the black revolver from her mother's room, or why he ends up guarding a rock while she takes her own life.

It's frustrating. I can see the breadcrumbs laid out ahead of me, but for all I know, they're leading me toward a cliff edge.

Unfortunately, there's no other path to follow.

～ 45 ～

Freed of Edward Dance's advanced years, I'd also hoped to shed his niggling pains, but my night in the cupboard has wrapped my bones in brambles. Every stretch, every bend and twist brings a jolt of pain and a wince, piling some new complaint atop the mound. The journey to my bedroom has proven unexpectedly taxing. Evidently, Rashton made quite an impression last night, because my passage through the house is punctuated by hearty handshakes and backslaps. Greetings lie scattered in my wake like tossed rocks, their goodwill bringing me out in bruises.

Upon reaching my bedroom, I throw off my forced smile. There's a white envelope on the floor, something bulky sealed inside. Somebody must have slipped it under my door. Tearing it open, I look up and down the corridor for any sign of the person who left it.

You left it

begins the note inside, which is wrapped around a chess piece that's almost identical to the one Anna carries around with her.

Take amyl nitrite, sodium nitrite, and sodium thiosulfate. KEEP HOLD OF THEM.

GG

"Gregory Gold." I sigh, reading the initials.

He must have left it before attacking the butler.

Now I know how Anna feels. The instructions are barely legible, and incomprehensible even once I'm able to untangle his terrible handwriting.

Throwing the note and chess piece on the sideboard, I lock my door and bar it with a chair. Normally I'd go immediately to Rashton's possessions or a mirror to inspect this new face, but I already know what's in his drawers and how he looks. I need only stretch my thought toward a question to find its answer, which is why I know a set of brass knuckles is hidden in the sock drawer. He confiscated them from a brawler a few years back, and they've come in handy more than once. I slip them on, thinking only of the footman and how he lowered his face to mine, breathing in my last breath, and sighing with pleasure as he added me to some private tally.

My hands are shaking, but Rashton isn't Bell. Fear motivates, rather than cripples. He wants to seek the footman out and put an end to him, to take back whatever dignity was lost in our previous confrontation. Looking back at our fight this morning, I'm certain it was Rashton who sent me down the stairs and into the corridor. That was his anger, his pride. He had control, and I didn't even notice.

It can't happen again.

Taking off the brass knuckles, I fill the sink and begin washing in front of the mirror.

Rashton's a young man—though not quite as young as he pictures himself—tall, strong, and remarkably handsome. Freckles are splashed across his nose, honey-colored eyes and short blond hair suggesting a face spun out of sunlight. About the only note of imperfection is an old bullet scar on his shoulder, the ragged line long faded. The memory would give itself to me if I asked, but I've enough pain without inviting another man's misery into my mind.

I'm wiping my chest when the door handle rattles.

"Jim, are you in there? Somebody's locked the door."

It's a woman's voice, husky and dry.

Putting on a fresh shirt, I pull away the chair and unlock the door to find a confused-looking young woman on the other side, her fist raised for another knock. Blue eyes peer at me from beneath long eyelashes, a dash of red lipstick the only color on a glacial face. She's in her early twenties with thick black hair tumbling over a crisp white shirt tucked into jodhpurs, her presence immediately setting Rashton's blood racing.

"Grace..." My host shoves the name onto my tongue, and plenty more besides. I'm boiling in a stew of adoration, elation, arousal, and inadequacy.

"Have you heard what that damn fool brother of mine has done?" she says, barging past me.

"I suspect I'm about to."

"He borrowed one of the cars last night," she says, flinging herself onto the bed. "Woke the stable master at two in the morning dressed like a rainbow and took off for the village."

She's got it all wrong, but I have no way of salvaging her brother's good name. It was my decision to take the car, to flee the house, and make for the village. At this moment, poor Donald Davies is asleep on a dirt road where I abandoned him, and my host is trying to drag me out the door after him.

His loyalty is almost overpowering, and searching for a reason, I'm immediately beset by horrors. Rashton's affection for Donald Davies was molded amid the mud and blood of the trenches. They went to war as fools and came back brothers, each of them broken in places only the other could see.

I can feel his anger at my treatment of his friend.

Or perhaps I'm just angry at myself.

We're so jumbled together, I can no longer tell.

"It's my fault," says Grace, crestfallen. "He was going to buy more of that poison from Bell, so I threatened to tell Daddy. I knew he was angry with me, but I didn't think he'd run off." She sighs helplessly. "You don't think he's done something foolish, do you?"

"He's fine," I say reassuringly, sitting down next to her. "He's got the wind up, that's all."

"I wish we'd never met that damn doctor," she says, smoothing the creases from my shirt with the flat of her hand. "Donald hasn't been the same since Bell turned up with his trunk of tricks. It's that damnable laudanum; it's got hold of him. I can barely talk to him anymore. I wish there was something we could…"

Her words run smack bang into an idea. I can see her standing back from it wide-eyed, following it from start to finish like a horse she's backed in the derby.

"I need to go see Charles about something," she says abruptly, kissing me on the lips before darting into the corridor.

She's gone before I can respond, the door hanging open in her wake.

I stand up to close it, hot, bothered, and not a little confused. On the whole, things were simpler when I was in that cupboard.

~ 46 ~

Step by slow step, I proceed down the corridor, poking my head into every empty bedroom before allowing myself to walk past it. I'm wearing the brass knuckles and jumping at every noise and shadow, wary of the assault I'm certain is coming, knowing I can't beat the footman should he catch me unawares.

Pushing aside the velvet curtain blocking the corridor, I pass into Blackheath's abandoned east wing, a sharp wind stirring drapes that slap the wall like slabs of meat hitting a butcher's counter.

I don't stop until I reach the nursery.

Derby's unconscious body isn't immediately obvious, as it's been dragged into the corner of the room, out of sight of the door and behind the rocking horse. His head is a mess of congealed blood and broken pottery, but he's alive and well hidden. Considering he was attacked coming out of Stanwin's bedroom, whoever was responsible obviously had enough of a conscience to keep the blackmailer from finding and killing him, but not enough time for anything more thorough.

I quickly rifle through his pockets, but everything he took from Stanwin has been stolen. I didn't expect otherwise, but as the architect of so many of the house's mysteries, it was worth a try.

Leaving him sleeping, I continue on to Stanwin's rooms at the end of the passage. Surely only fear could have pushed him into this misbegotten corner of the house, so far from the meager comforts afforded by the rest of Blackheath. By that criteria, though, he's chosen well.

The floorboards are his spies, screaming my approach with every step, and the long corridor offers only one way in and out. The blackmailer clearly believes himself surrounded by enemies, a fact which I may be able to exploit.

Passing through the reception room, I knock on Stanwin's bedroom door. A strange silence greets me, the din of somebody trying to be quiet.

"It's Constable Jim Rashton," I call through the wood, putting the brass knuckles away. "I need to speak with you."

The declaration is met with a flurry of sounds. Steps go lightly across the room, a drawer scrapes, something is lifted and moved, before finally a voice creeps around the doorframe.

"Come in," says Ted Stanwin.

He's sitting on a chair, a hand stuck inside his left boot, which he's polishing with a soldier's vigor. I shiver a little, rocked by a powerful sense of the uncanny. The last time I saw this man, he was dead on a forest floor and I was going through his pockets. Blackheath's picked him up and dusted him off, winding his key so he can do it all again. If this isn't hell, the devil is surely taking notes.

I look past him. His bodyguard is sleeping deeply on the bed, breathing nosily through his bandaged nose. I'm surprised Stanwin hasn't moved him, and more surprised to see how the blackmailer's angled his chair to face the bed, much as Anna has done with the butler. Clearly, Stanwin feels some affection for this chap.

I wonder how he'd react knowing Derby's been next door this whole time.

"Ah, the man at the center of it all," says Stanwin, the brush pausing while he regards me.

"I'm afraid you have me at a loss," I say, confused.

"I wouldn't be a very good blackmailer if I didn't," he says, gesturing toward a rickety wooden chair by the fire. Accepting his invitation,

I drag the chair closer to the bed, making sure to avoid the dirty newspaper and boot polish strewn on the floor.

Stanwin's wearing a rich man's approximation of a stable hand's livery, which is to say the white cotton shirt is pressed and the black trousers are spotless. Looking at him now, dressed plainly, scrubbing his own boots, and squatting in a crumbling corner of a once-grand house, I fail to see what nineteen years of blackmail have bought him. Burst blood vessels riddle his cheeks and nose, while sunken eyes, red raw and hungry for sleep, keep watch for the monsters at his door.

Monsters he invited there.

Behind all his bluster is a cowering soul, the fire that once drove him long extinguished. These are the ragged edges of a man defeated, his secrets the only warmth left to him. At this point, he's as much afraid of his victims as they are of him.

Pity pricks me. Something about Stanwin's situation feels terribly familiar, and deep down, beneath my hosts, where the real Aiden Bishop resides, I can feel a memory stirring. I came here because of a woman. I wanted to save her, and I couldn't. Blackheath was my chance to... What? Try again?

What did I come here to do?

Leave it alone.

"Let's state facts plainly," says Stanwin, looking at me steadily. "You're in league with Cecil Ravencourt, Charles Cunningham, Daniel Coleridge, and a few others; the lot of you fishing around a murder that happened nineteen years ago."

My prior thoughts scatter.

"Oh, don't look so shocked," he says, inspecting a dull spot on his boot. "Cunningham came asking questions early this morning on behalf of that fat master of his, and Daniel Coleridge was sniffing around a few minutes after that. Both of them wanted to know about the man I shot when I chased Master Hardcastle's murderer off. Now here you are. Too much of a coincidence to be a coincidence, I reckon. Ain't hard to see what you're up to, not if you've two eyes and a brain behind them."

He glances at me, the facade of nonchalance slipping to reveal the calculation at its foundation. Aware of his eyes upon me, I dig for the right words, anything to repudiate his suspicion, but the silence stretches, growing taut.

"Wondered how you'd take it," grunts Stanwin, putting his boot down on the newspaper and wiping his hands clean with a rag.

When he speaks again, it's low and soft, the voice of somebody telling stories. "Seems to me this sudden lust for justice probably has one of two causes," he says, digging at the dirt beneath his fingernails with a penknife. "Either Ravencourt's caught the whiff of scandal and he's paying you to look into it for him, or you think there's a big case waiting to be solved that will put you in the papers and make your name."

He sneers at my silence.

"Look, Rashton, you don't know me or my business, but it knows men like you. You're a working-class plod walking out with a rich woman you can't afford. Nothing wrong with climbing, done it myself, but you're going to need money to get on the ladder and I can help. Information is valuable, which means we can help each other."

He's holding my gaze, but not comfortably. A pulse throbs violently in his neck, sweat gathering on his forehead. There's danger in this approach, and he knows it. Even so, I can feel the lure of his offer. Rashton would love nothing more than to pay his way with Grace. He'd like to buy finer clothes and pay for dinner more than once a month.

Thing is, he loves being a copper more.

"How many people know that Lucy Harper is your daughter?" I say blandly.

Now it's my turn to watch *his* face fall.

My suspicions were raised when I watched him bully Lucy at the lunch table, all because she had the temerity to use his first name when asking him to move out of the way. I didn't think much of it when I saw it through Bell's eyes. Stanwin is a brute and a blackmailer, so it seemed only natural. It was only when I witnessed it again as Dance that I caught the affection in Lucy's voice, and the fear on his face. A roomful of men who'd happily stick a knife in his ribs and there she is, all but telling them that she cares about him. She might as well have painted a target on her back. No wonder he lashed out. He needed her out of that room as quickly as possible.

"Lucy who?" he says, the rag twisting tight in his hands.

"Don't insult me by denying it, Stanwin," I interrupt. "She has your red hair and you keep a locket with her picture in your jacket, along with a codebook detailing your blackmailing business. Odd things to keep together, except they're the only things you care about. You should have heard how she defended you to Ravencourt."

Each fact out of my mouth is a hammer blow.

"It isn't hard to figure out," I say. "Not for a man with two eyes and a brain behind them."

"What do you want?" he asks quietly.

"I need to know what really happened the morning Thomas Hardcastle was murdered."

His tongue roams his lips as his mind gets to work, cogs and gears lubricated by lies.

"Charlie Carver and another man took Thomas out to the lake, then stabbed him to death," he says, picking up the boot once again. "I stopped Carver, but the other one got away. Any other old stories you want to hear?"

"If I was interested in lies, I'd have asked Helena Hardcastle," I say, leaning forward with my hands clasped between my knees. "She was there, wasn't she? Like Alf Miller said. Everybody believes the family gave you a plantation for trying to save the little boy, but I know that's not what happened. You've been blackmailing Helena Hardcastle for nineteen years, ever since the boy died. You saw something that morning, something you've held over her all this time. She told her husband the money was to keep Cunningham's real parentage secret, but that's not it, is it? It's something bigger."

"And if I don't tell you what I saw, what then?" he snarls, throwing the boot aside. "You spread word that Lucy Harper's old man is the infamous Ted Stanwin and wait to see who kills her first?"

I open my mouth to respond, only to be confounded when no words come out. Of course that was my plan, but sitting here, I'm reminded of that moment on the staircase when Lucy led a confused butler back into the kitchen, so he wouldn't get into trouble. Unlike her father, she's got a good heart, knotted with tenderness and doubt—perfect for men like me to step on. No wonder Stanwin stayed out of sight, letting her mother raise her. He probably funneled his family a little money over the years, intending to make them comfortable until he could put them permanently beyond the reach of his powerful enemies.

"No," I say, as much to myself as Stanwin. "Lucy was kind to me when I needed kindness. I won't put her in danger, even for this."

He surprises me with a smile, and the regret lurking behind it.

"You won't get far in this house with sentiment," he says.

"Then what about common sense?" I ask. "Evelyn Hardcastle is going to be murdered tonight, and I think it's because of something that happened nineteen years ago. Seems to me it's in your interest to keep Evelyn alive so she can marry Ravencourt, and you can keep getting paid."

He whistles. "If that's true, there's better coin to be made in knowing who was responsible, but you're coming at this crooked," he says emphatically. "I don't need to keep getting paid. This is it for me. I've got a big payout coming, then I'm selling the business and getting out. That's why I came to Blackheath in the first place, to pick up Lucy and finish the deal. She's coming with me."

"Who are you selling it to?"

"Daniel Coleridge."

"Coleridge is planning to murder you during the hunt in a few hours. How much information is that worth?"

Stanwin looks at me with a bright suspicion.

"Murder me?" he says. "We've got a square deal, him and me. We're going to finish our business out in the forest."

"The business is in two books, isn't it?" I say. "All the names, crimes, and payments in one, written in code, of course. And the cipher to decrypt it in another. You keep them separate and think that keeps you safe, but it doesn't, and square deal or not, you'll be dead in"—I pull up my sleeve to check my watch—"four hours, at which point Coleridge will have both of the books without parting with a shilling."

For the first time, Stanwin looks uncertain.

Reaching over to the drawer in his bedside table, he removes a pipe and a small pouch of tobacco, which he packs into the pipe's bowl. Scraping away the excess, he circles the burning match across the leaves, taking a few puffs to draw the flame. By the time his attention returns to me, the tobacco is burning, smoke forming a halo above his ill-deserving head.

"How's he going to do it?" asks Stanwin, out of the corner of his mouth, his pipe gripped between his yellow teeth.

"What did you see the morning of Thomas Hardcastle's death?" I ask.

"That's it, is it? A murder for a murder?"

"Square deal," I say.

He spits on his hand.

"Shake then," he says.

I do as he asks, then light my last cigarette. The need for tobacco has come upon me slowly, the way the tide nudges up a riverbank, and I let the smoke fill my throat, my eyes watering in pleasure.

Scratching his stubble, Stanwin begins speaking, his voice thoughtful.

"It was a funny day that, strange from the off," he says, adjusting the pipe in his mouth. "The guests had arrived for the party, but there was already a bad atmosphere around the place. Arguments in the kitchen, fights in the stables, even the guests were at it; couldn't walk past a closed door without hearing raised voices behind it."

There's a wariness to him now, the sense of a man unpacking a trunk filled with sharp objects.

"It weren't much of a surprise when Charlie got fired," he says. "He'd been carrying on with Lady Hardcastle long as anybody could remember. Secret at first. Obvious later, too obvious if you ask me. They wanted to be caught, I reckon. Don't know what got 'em in the end, but news went around the kitchen like a pox when Charlie was dismissed by Lord Hardcastle. We thought he'd come downstairs, say goodbye, but we didn't hear a peep, then a couple of hours later, one of the maids fetches me, tells me she's just seen Charlie drunk as a lord, wandering around the children's bedrooms."

"The children's bedrooms, you're sure?"

"That's what she said. Poking his head in the doors one after another, like he was looking for something."

"Any idea what?"

"She thought he was trying to say goodbye, but they were all out playing. Either way, he left with a big leather bag over his shoulder."

"And she didn't know what was in it?"

"Not a clue. Whatever it was, nobody begrudged him. He was popular, Charlie, we all liked him."

Stanwin sighs, tipping his face to the ceiling.

"What happened next?" I prod, sensing his reluctance to continue.

"Charlie was my friend," he says heavily. "So I went looking for him, to say goodbye more than anything else. Last anybody saw he was heading to the lake so that's where I went, only he wasn't there. Nobody was, at least that's what it looked like at first. I would have left except I saw the blood in the dirt."

"You followed the blood?" I say.

"Aye, to the edge of the lake…that's when I saw the boy."

He gulps, drawing his hand across his face. The memory's lurked in the darkness of his mind for so long I'm not surprised he's having trouble dragging it into the light. Everything he's become has grown out of this poisonous seed.

"What did you see, Stanwin?" I ask.

Dropping his hand from his face, he looks at me as though I'm a priest demanding confession.

"At first, just Lady Hardcastle," he says. "She was kneeling in the mud, sobbing her heart out. There was blood everywhere. I didn't see the boy; she was cradling him so tight…but she turned when she heard me. She'd stabbed him through the throat, almost taken his head off, she had."

"She confessed?" I say.

I can hear the excitement in my voice. Looking down, I notice that my hands are clenched, my body tense. I'm on the edge of my seat, my breath held in my throat.

I'm immediately ashamed of myself.

"More or less," says Stanwin. "Just kept saying it was an accident. That was it, over and over again. It was an accident."

"So where does Carver come into this?" I ask.

"He arrived later."

"How much later?"

"I don't know…"

"Five minutes, twenty minutes?" I ask. "It's important, Stanwin."

"Not twenty, ten maybe, can't have been too long."

"Did he have the bag?"

"The bag?"

"The brown leather bag the maid saw him take from the house? Did he have it with him?"

"No, no bag." He points the pipe at me. "You know something, don't you?"

"I think so, yes. Finish your story, please."

"Carver came, took me to one side. He was sober, dead sober, the way a man is when he's had a shock. He asked me to forget everything I'd seen, to tell everybody he'd done it."

"I said I wouldn't, not for her, not for the Hardcastles, but he said he loved her, that it'd been an accident and it was the only thing he could do for her, the only thing he could give her. He reckoned he had no future anyway, not after being dismissed from Blackheath and having to move away from Helena. He made me swear to keep her secret."

"Which you did, except you made her pay for it," I say.

"And you'd have done different, would you, copper?" he says furiously. "Clapped her in irons then and there, betraying a promise to your friend. Or would you have let her get away with it, scot-free?"

I shake my head. I don't have an answer for him, but I'm not interested in his pitying self-justification. There's only two victims in this story: Thomas Hardcastle and Charlie Carver, a murdered child and a man who walked to the gallows to protect the woman he loved. It's too late for me to help either of them, but I'm not going to let the truth stay buried any longer.

It's done enough damage already.

~ 47 ~

Bushes rustle, twigs cracking underfoot. Daniel's moving through the forest quickly, making no attempt at stealth. He has no need. My other hosts are all occupied, and nearly everybody else is either on the hunt or in the sunroom.

My heart is racing. He slipped out of the house after speaking with Bell and Michael in the study, and I've been following him for the last fifteen minutes, picking my way silently through the trees. I remember him missing the start of the hunt and having to catch up with Dance, and I'm curious what kept him. Hopefully, this errand will shed more light on his plans.

The trees break suddenly, giving way to an ugly clearing. We're not far from the lake, and I can just about see the water away to my right. The footman's pacing in circles like a caged animal, and I have to duck behind a bush to keep from being seen.

"Make it quick," says Daniel, approaching him.

The footman punches him in the chin, staggering him backward. Daniel straightens, inviting a second blow with a nod of his head. This one crunches into his stomach and is followed by a cross that knocks him to the ground.

"More?" asks the footman, looming over him.

"That's enough," says Daniel, dabbing his split lip. "Dance needs to believe we fought, not that you nearly killed me."

They're working together.

"Can you catch them?" says the footman, helping Daniel off the ground. "The hunters have a good head start."

"Lot of old legs. They won't have gone far. Any luck snatching up Anna?"

"Not yet. I've been busy."

"Well, hurry up. Our friend's getting impatient."

So that's what this was all about. They want Anna.

That's why Daniel told me to find her when I was Ravencourt, and why he asked Derby to bring her to the library, when he laid out his plan to trap the footman. I was supposed to deliver her to them. A lamb to slaughter.

My head spinning, I watch them exchange a few final words, before the footman makes for the house. Daniel's wiping the blood from his face, but he doesn't move, and a second later I see why. The Plague Doctor's entering the clearing. This must be the "friend" Daniel mentioned.

It's as I feared. They're working together. Daniel's formed a partnership with the footman, and they're hunting Anna on the Plague Doctor's behalf. I can't imagine what's fueling this enmity, but it explains why the Plague Doctor's spent the day pouring scorn on our partnership. Trying to turn me against her.

Placing a hand on Daniel's shoulder, he leads him into the trees, beyond my sight. The intimacy of this gesture throws me. I can't recall a single time when the Plague Doctor has touched me, or even come close enough for that to happen.

Keeping low, I hurry after them, stopping at the tree line to listen for their voices, but I can't hear anything. Cursing, I press deeper into the forest, stopping periodically, hoping to catch some sign of them. It's no use. They're gone.

Feeling like a man in a dream, I return the way I came.

Everything I saw that first day, how much of it was real? Was anybody who they claimed to be? I believed Daniel and Evelyn were

my friends, the Plague Doctor was a madman, and that I was a doctor
called Sebastian Bell, whose biggest problem was memory loss. How
could I know those were merely starting positions in a race nobody
had told me I was running?

It's the finish line you should be concerned with.

"The graveyard," I say out loud.

Daniel believes he'll capture Anna there, and I have no doubt he'll
have the footman with him when he tries. That's where this will end,
and I need to be ready.

I've arrived at the wishing well, where Evelyn received the note
from Felicity that first morning. I'm eager to put my plan into action,
but instead of heading for the house, I turn left, toward the lake. This
is Rashton's doing. It's instinct. A copper's instinct. He wants to see the
scene of the crime while Stanwin's testimony is still fresh in my mind.

The trail is overgrown, trees leaning in on either side, their roots
writhing up through the ground. Brambles snag my trench coat, rain
spilling off leaves, until finally I emerge on the lake's muddy banks.

I've only ever seen it at a distance, but it's much bigger up close,
with water the color of mossy stone, and a couple of skeletal rowboats
tethered to a boathouse that's crumbling to firewood on the far-right
bank. A bandstand sits on an island at the center, the peeling turquoise
roof and wooden frame battered by the wind and rain.

No wonder the Hardcastles chose to leave Blackheath. Something
evil happened here, and it haunts the lake still. Such is my unease I
almost turn on my heel, but a greater part of me needs to make sense of
what happened here nineteen years ago, and so I walk the length of the
lake, circling it twice, much as a coroner might circle a body on his slab.

An hour passes. My eyes are busy, but they stick to nothing.

Stanwin's story seems cut and dry, but it doesn't explain why the
past is reaching up to claim another Hardcastle child. It doesn't
explain who's behind it, or what they hope to gain. I thought coming

here would bring some clarity, but whatever the lake remembers, it has little interest in sharing. Unlike Stanwin, it cannot be bartered with, and unlike the stable master, it cannot be bullied.

Cold and wet, I might be tempted to give up, but Rashton is already tugging me toward the reflecting pool. The policeman's eyes aren't soft like my other hosts. They seek the edges, the absences. My memories of this place aren't enough for him; he needs to see it all afresh. And so, hands deep in my pockets, I arrange myself at the edge of the water, which is high enough to touch the bottom of my shoes. A light rain is rippling the surface, plinking against thick patches of floating moss.

At least the rain is constant. It's tapping Bell's face as he walks with Evelyn, and the windows of the gatehouse where the butler sleeps and Gold is strung up. Ravencourt's listening to it in his parlor, wondering where Cunningham has got to, and Derby...well, Derby's still unconscious, which is the best thing for him. Davies is collapsed on the road, or maybe walking back. Either way, he's getting wet. As is Dance, who's traipsing through the forest, a shotgun slung over his arm, wishing he was anywhere else.

As for me, I'm standing exactly where Evelyn will stand tonight, where she'll press a silver pistol to her stomach and pull the trigger.

I'm seeing what she'll see.

Trying to understand.

The murderer found a way to force Evelyn to commit suicide, but why not have her shoot herself in her bedroom out of sight? Why bring her out here during the middle of the party?

So everybody would see.

"Then why not the middle of the dance floor, or the stage?" I mutter.

All this, it's too theatrical.

Rashton's worked on dozens of murders. They aren't stage-managed; they're immediate, impulsive acts. Men crawl into their cups after a hard day's work, stirring the bitterness settled at the bottom. Fights break out; wives grow tired of their black eyes and pick up the nearest kitchen knife. Death happens in alleys and quiet rooms with doilies on the tables. Trees fall, people are crushed, tools slip. People die the way they've always died, quickly, impatiently, or unluckily; not here, not in front of a hundred people in ball gowns and dinner jackets.

What kind of mind makes theater of murder?

Turning back toward the house, I try to recall Evelyn's route to the reflecting pool, remembering how she drifted from flame to darkness, wobbling as if drunk. I remember the silver pistol glinting in her hand, the shot, the silence, and then the fireworks as she tumbled into the water.

Why take two guns when one will do?

A murder that doesn't look like a murder.

That's how the Plague Doctor described it...but what if... My mind gropes at the edges of a thought, teasing it forward out of the dimness. An idea emerges, the queerest of ideas.

The only one that makes sense.

I'm startled by a tap on my shoulder, almost sending me stumbling into the reflecting pool. Thankfully, Grace catches hold of me, pulling me back into her arms. It's not, I must admit, an unpleasant predicament, especially when I turn around to meet those blue eyes, looking up at me with a mixture of love and bemusement.

"What on earth are you doing out here?" she asks. "I've been searching for you all over. You missed lunch."

There's concern in her voice. She holds my gaze, searching my eyes, though I have no idea what she's looking for.

"I came for a walk," I say, trying to slip free of her worry. "And I started imagining what this place must have been like in its pomp."

Doubt flickers on her face, but it vanishes in a blink of her glorious eyes as she slips an arm through mine, the heat of her body warming me up.

"It's difficult to remember now," she says. "Every memory I have of this place, even the happy ones, are stained by what happened to Thomas."

"Were you here when it happened?"

"Have I never told you this?" she says, resting her head on my shoulder. "I suppose I wouldn't have. I was only young. Yes, I was here, nearly everybody here today was."

"Did you see it?"

"Thank heavens, no," she says, aghast. "Evelyn had arranged a treasure hunt for the children. I can't have been more than seven, same for Thomas. Evelyn was ten. She was all grown up, so we were her responsibility for the day."

She grows distant, distracted by a memory taking flight.

"Of course, now I know she just wanted to go riding and not have to look after us, but at the time we thought her terribly kind. We were having a jolly time chasing each other through the forest looking for clues, when all of a sudden Thomas bolted off. We never saw him again."

"Bolted? Did he say why he was leaving, or where he was going?"

"You sound like the policeman who questioned me," she says, hugging me closer. "No, he didn't hang around for questions. He asked after the time and left."

"He asked the time?"

"Yes, it was like he had somewhere to be."

"And he didn't tell you where he was going?"

"No."

"Was he acting strangely? Did he say anything odd?"

"Actually, we could barely get a word out of him," she says. "He'd been in a strange mood all week come to think of it, withdrawn, sulky, not like him at all."

"What was he normally like?"

She shrugs. "A pest most of the time. He was at that age. He liked to tug our ponytails, and scare us. He'd follow us through the woods, then jump out when we least expected it."

"But he'd been acting strangely for a week?" I say. "Are you certain that's how long it had been?"

"Well, that's how long we were at Blackheath before the party, so yes." She's shivering now, peering up at me. "What's that mind of yours got hold of, Mr. Rashton?" she asks.

"Got hold of?"

"I can see the little crease"—she taps the spot between my eyebrows—"you get when something's bothering you."

"I'm not sure yet."

"Well, try not to do it when you meet grandmother."

"Crease my forehead?"

"Think, silly."

"Why the heavens not?"

"She doesn't take kindly to young men who think too much. She believes it's a sign of idleness."

The temperature is dropping quickly. What little color was left to the day is fleeing the dark storm clouds bullying the sky.

"Shall we go back to the house?" says Grace, stamping her feet to warm up. "I dislike Blackheath as much as the next girl, but not so much that I'm willing to freeze to death to avoid going back inside it."

I glance at the reflecting pool a little forlornly, but I can't press my idea without speaking to Evelyn first, and she's out walking with Bell. Whatever my mind's got hold of—to use Grace's phrase—it'll have to keep until she returns in a couple of hours. Besides, the idea of spending time with somebody who isn't mired in today's many tragedies is appealing.

Our shoulders pressed together, we make our way back to the house, arriving in the entrance hall in time to see Charles Cunningham trotting down the steps. He's frowning, lost in thought.

"Are you quite all right, Charles?" says Grace, drawing his attention.

"Honestly, what is it with the men in this house today? You're all on a cloud."

A grin cracks his face, his joy at seeing us quite at odds with the seriousness with which he normally greets me.

"Ah, my two favorite people," he says grandly, leaping from the third step to clap us both on the shoulder. "I'm sorry. I was miles away."

Affection draws a huge smile on my face.

Until now, the valet was simply somebody who flitted in and out of my day, occasionally helpful, but always pursuing some purpose of his own, making him impossible to trust. Seeing him through Rashton's eyes is like watching a charcoal outline get colored in.

Grace and Donald Davies summered at Blackheath, growing up side by side with Michael, Evelyn, Thomas, and Cunningham. Despite being raised by the cook, Mrs. Drudge, everybody believed he was Peter Hardcastle's son by birth, and this elevated him beyond the kitchen. Encouraging this perception, Helena Hardcastle instructed the governess to educate Cunningham with the Hardcastle children. He may have become a servant, but neither Grace nor Donald would ever see him as such, no matter what their parents might say. The three of them are practically family, which is why Cunningham was one of the first people Donald Davies introduced Rashton to when they returned from the war. The three of them are as close as brothers.

"Is Ravencourt being a nuisance?" asks Grace. "You didn't forget his second helping of eggs again, did you? You know how disagreeable that makes him."

"No, no, it's not that." Cunningham shakes his head thoughtfully. "You know how sometimes your day starts as one thing, and then, just like that, it's something else? Ravencourt told me something rather startling, and to tell you the truth, I still haven't wrapped my head around it."

"What did he say?" asks Grace, cocking her head.

"That he's not…" He trails off, pinching his nose. Thinking better of it, he sighs, dismissing the entire line of conversation. "Best I tell you this evening over a brandy, when everything's shaken out. Not sure I have the words just yet."

"It's always the same with you, Charles," she says, stamping her foot. "You always start juicy stories but never finish them."

"Well, maybe this will improve your mood."

From his pocket he produces a silver key, a cardboard tag identifying it as Sebastian Bell's. The last time I saw that key, it was in the vile Derby's pocket, shortly before somebody coshed him over the head outside Stanwin's bedroom and stole it.

I can feel myself being slotted into place, a cog in a massive ticking clock, propelling a mechanism I'm too small to understand.

"You found it for me?" says Grace, clapping her hands together.

He beams at me. "Grace asked me to snatch a spare key to Bell's bedroom from the kitchen so we could steal his drugs," he says, dangling the key from his finger. "I went one better and found the key to his trunk."

"It's childish, but I want Bell to suffer the way Donald is suffering," she says, her eyes glittering viciously.

"And how on earth did you come by the key?" I ask Cunningham.

"In the course of my duties," he says a little uneasily. "I've got his bedroom key in my pocket. All those little vials dropped in the lake, can you imagine?"

"Not the lake," says Grace, making a face. "It's bad enough coming back to Blackheath, but I won't go anywhere near that awful place."

"There's the well," I say, remembering the spot out past the gatehouse where Evelyn collected the note from Felicity. "Old and deep. If we drop the drugs down there, nobody will ever find them."

"Perfect," says Cunningham, rubbing his hands together gleefully. "Well, the good doctor has gone for a walk with Miss Hardcastle, so I should say this is as good a time as any. Who's up for a little daylight robbery?"

~ 48 ~

Grace keeps watch by the door as Cunningham and I slip into Bell's bedroom, nostalgia painting everything in cheerful colors. After wrestling with the domineering natures of my other hosts, my attitude toward Bell has softened considerably. Unlike Derby, Ravencourt, or Rashton, Sebastian Bell was a blank canvas, a man in retreat, even from himself. I poured into him, filling the empty spaces so completely I didn't even realize he was the wrong shape.

In an odd way, he feels like an old friend.

"Where do you think he keeps the stuff?" Cunningham asks, closing the door behind us.

Though I know perfectly well where Bell's trunk is, I feign ignorance, giving myself the opportunity to wade about in his absence for a little while, enjoying the sensation of walking back into a life I once inhabited.

Cunningham uncovers the trunk soon enough, though, engaging my help to drag it out of the wardrobe, making a terrible racket as he scrapes it on the wooden floorboards. It's as well everybody's hunting as the noise could wake the dead.

The key fits perfectly, the latch springing open on well-oiled hinges to reveal an interior stuffed to bursting with brown vials and bottles arranged in neat rows.

Cunningham has brought a cotton sack, and kneeling either side of the trunk, we begin filling it with Bell's stash. There are tinctures and concoctions of every sort and not merely those designed to put a foolish smile on the face. Among the dubious pleasures is a half-empty flask of strychnine, the white grains looking for all the world like large chunks of salt.

Now what's he doing with that?

"Bell will sell anything to anyone, won't he?" says Cunningham with a tut, plucking the flask from my hand and dropping it into the sack. "Not for much longer, though."

Picking the bottles from the trunk, I remember the note Gold pushed under my door, and the three things it demanded I pilfer. Thankfully, Cunningham's so enraptured by his task he doesn't notice me slipping the bottles into my pocket, or the chess piece I drop into the trunk. Amid all the plots, it seems an inconsequential thing to bother with, but I can still remember how much comfort it brought me, how much strength. It was a kindness when I needed one most, and it cheers me to be the one delivering it.

"Charles, I need you to tell me the truth about something," I begin.

"I've told you, I'm not getting between you and Grace," he says distantly, carefully filling his sack. "Whatever you're arguing about this week, admit you're wrong and be grateful when she accepts your apology."

He flashes me a grin, but it evaporates when he sees my grim expression.

"What's wrong?" he asks.

"Where did you get the key to the trunk?" I reply.

"If you must know, one of the servants gave it to me," he says, avoiding my gaze as he continues to pack.

"No, they didn't," I say, scratching my neck. "You took it off Jonathan Derby's body after you coshed him over the head. Daniel Coleridge hired you to steal Stanwin's blackmail ledger, didn't he?"

"Th…that's nonsense," he says.

"Please, Charles," I say, my voice rough with emotion. "I've already spoken with Stanwin."

Rashton has counted on Cunningham's friendship and counsel many times over the years, and watching him squirm under the spotlight of my questioning is unbearable.

"I…I didn't mean to hit him," says Cunningham, shamefaced. "I'd just put Ravencourt into his bath and was going for my breakfast when I heard a commotion on the stairs. I saw Derby hare into the study with Stanwin on his tail. I thought I could slip into Stanwin's room while everybody was distracted and grab the ledger, but the bodyguard was in there, so I hid in one of the rooms opposite, waiting to see what would happen."

"You saw Dickie give the bodyguard a sedative, and then Derby find the ledger," I say. "You couldn't let him walk out of there with it. It was too valuable."

Cunningham nods eagerly.

"Stanwin knows what happened that morning. He knows who really killed Thomas," he says. "He's been lying all this time. It's in that ledger of his. Coleridge is going to decipher it for me, and then everybody will know my father, my real father, is innocent."

Fear swells in his eyes.

"Does Stanwin know about the bargain I struck with Coleridge?" he asks suddenly. "Is that why you met with him?"

"He doesn't know anything," I say gently. "I went to ask about Thomas Hardcastle's murder."

"And he told you?"

"He owed me for saving his life."

Cunningham is still on his knees, his hands gripping my shoulders. "You're a miracle worker, Rasher," he says. "Don't leave me in suspense."

"He saw Lady Hardcastle covered in blood and cradling Thomas's body," I say, watching him closely. "Stanwin drew the obvious conclusion, but Carver arrived some minutes later and insisted Stanwin place the blame on him."

Cunningham stares through me as he tries to pick holes in an answer long sought. When he speaks again, there's bitterness in his voice.

"Of course," he says, sagging to the floor. "I've spent years trying to prove my father was innocent, so naturally I find out that my mother's the murderer instead."

"How long have you known who your real parents are?" I say, doing my best to sound consoling.

"Mother told me when I turned twenty-one," he says. "She said my father wasn't the monster he was accused of being, but would never explain why. I've spent every day since then trying to work out what she meant."

"You saw her this morning, didn't you?"

"I took her tea," he says gently. "She drank it in bed while we spoke. I used to do the same thing when I was a child. She'd ask after my happiness, my education. She was kind to me. It was my favorite time of the day."

"And this morning? I assume she didn't mention anything suspicious?"

"About murdering Thomas? No, it didn't come up," he says sarcastically.

"I meant anything out of character, unusual."

"Out of character," he snorts. "She's barely been in character for a year, or more. Can't keep up with her. One minute she's giddy, the next she's in tears."

"A year," I say thoughtfully. "Ever since she visited Blackheath on the anniversary of Thomas's death?"

It was after that visit she turned up on Michael's doorstep raving about clothes.

"Yes…maybe," he says, tugging an earlobe. "I say, you don't think it all got on top of her, do you? The guilt I mean. That would explain why she's been acting so queer. Maybe she's been building up her courage to finally confess. It would certainly make sense of her mood this morning."

"Why? What did you speak about?"

"She was calm, actually. A touch distant. She talked about putting things right, and how she was sorry I'd had to grow up ashamed of my father's name." His face falls. "That's it, isn't it? She means to confess at the party tonight. That's why she's gone to all this trouble to reopen Blackheath and invite the same guests back."

"Maybe," I say, unable to keep my doubt from surfacing. "Why were your fingerprints all over her planner? What were you looking for?"

"When I pressed her for more information, she asked me to look up what time she was meeting the stable master. She said she'd be able to tell me more after that, and I should come by the stables. I waited, but she never arrived. I've been looking for her all day, but nobody's seen her. Maybe she's gone to the village."

I ignore that.

"Tell me about the stable hand who went missing," I say. "You asked the stable master about him."

"Nothing to tell really. A few years back, I got drunk with the inspector who investigated Thomas's murder. He never believed my father—Carver, I mean—did it, mainly because this other boy, Keith Parker, had gone missing a week earlier while my father was in London with Lord Hardcastle, and he didn't like the coincidence. The inspector asked around after the boy, but nothing came of it. By all accounts, Parker up and left without a word to anybody and never came back. They never found a body, so couldn't disprove the rumor that he'd run away."

"Did you know him?"

"Vaguely. He used to play with us sometimes, but even the servants' children had jobs to do around the house. He worked in the stables most of the time. We rarely saw him."

Catching my mood, he looks at me inquisitively.

"Do you really think my mother's a murderer?" he says.

"That's what I need your help to find out," I say. "Your mother entrusted Mrs. Drudge to raise you, yes? Does that mean they were close?"

"Very close. Mrs. Drudge was the only other person who knew about my real father before Stanwin found out."

"Good. I'm going to need a favor."

"What sort of favor?"

"Two favors actually," I say. "I need Mrs. Drudge to… Oh!"

I've just caught up to my past. The answer to a question I was about to ask has already been delivered to me. Now I need to make sure it happens again.

Cunningham waves a hand in front of my face. "You quite all right, Rasher? You seem to have come over a bit queer."

"Sorry, old chap, I got distracted," I say, batting away his confusion. "As I was saying, I need Mrs. Drudge to clear something up for me, and then I need you to gather a few people together. When you're done, find Jonathan Derby and tell him everything you've discovered."

"Derby? What's that scoundrel got to do with this?"

The door opens, Grace poking her head inside the room.

"For heaven's sake, what's taking so long?" she asks. "If we wait any longer, we're going to have to run Bell a bath and pretend we're servants."

"One more minute," I say, laying my hand on Cunningham's arm. "We're going to put this right, I promise you. Now listen closely, this is important."

The cotton sack clinks as we walk, its weight conspiring with the uneven ground to continually trip me up, Grace wincing in sympathy at each stumble.

Cunningham's run off to do my favor, Grace meeting his sudden departure with puzzled silence. I feel the urge to explain, but Rashton knows this woman well enough to know it's not expected. Ten minutes after Donald Davies introduced his grateful family to the man who'd saved his life during the war, it was clear to anybody with eyes and a heart that Jim Rashton and Grace Davies would one day be married. Undaunted by their different backgrounds, they spent that first dinner building a bridge out of affectionate barbs and probing questions, love blossoming across a table littered with cutlery Rashton couldn't identify. What was born that day has only grown since, the two of them coming to inhabit a world of their own making. Grace knows I'll tell the story when it's finished, when it's shored up with facts strong enough to support the telling. In the meantime, we walk together in a companionable silence, happy just to be in each other's company.

I'm wearing my brass knuckles, having vaguely mentioned a threat from Bell and Doctor Dickie's confederates. It's a weak lie, but it's enough to keep Grace on her toes, the young woman whipping her head toward every dripping leaf. So it is, we come upon the well, Grace pushing aside a tree branch that I might emerge into the clearing without becoming snagged. I immediately drop the sack into the well, where it hits the bottom with a tremendous crash.

Waggling my arms, I try to shake the ache from my muscles, as Grace peers into the well's darkness.

"Any wishes?" she asks.

"That I don't have to carry the sack back," I say.

"Oh, my heavens, it really works," she says. "Do you think I can wish for more wishes?"

"Sounds like cheating to me."

"Well, nobody's used it for years, there's probably a few going spare."

"May I ask you a question?" I reply.

"Never known you to be shy about them," she says, leaning so far into the well her feet are in the air.

"The morning of Thomas's murder, when you went on the scavenger hunt, who was with you?"

"Come on, Jim, it was nineteen years ago," she says, her voice muffled by the stone.

"Was Charles there?"

"Charles?" She removes her head from the well. "Yes, probably."

"Probably, or actually? It's important, Grace."

"I can see that," she says, pulling herself clear and wiping her hands. "Has he done something wrong?"

"I really hope not."

"So do I," she says, mirroring my concern. "Let me think. Wait a tick. Yes, he was there! He stole an entire fruitcake from the kitchen. I remember him giving me and Donald some. Must have driven Mrs. Drudge wild."

"What about Michael Hardcastle, was he there?"

"Michael? Why, I don't know…"

A hand goes to a curl of hair, twisting it around her finger while she thinks. It's a familiar gesture, one that fills Rashton with such an overpowering love it's almost enough to push me aside completely.

"He was in bed, I think," she says eventually. "Sick with something or other, one of those childish things."

She takes my hand in both of her own, holding me fast in those beautiful blue eyes.

"Are you doing something dangerous, Jim?" she asks.

"Yes," I say.

"Are you doing it for Charles?"

"Partly."

"Will you ever tell me about it?"

"Yes, when I know what needs to be said."

Standing on her tiptoes, she kisses me on the nose.

"Then you better get going," she says, rubbing her lipstick off my skin. "I know what you're like when you've got a bone to dig up, and you won't be happy until you have it."

"Thank you."

"Say it with the story, and say it soon."

"I will," I say.

It's Rashton who kisses her now. When I do wrestle this body back from him, I'm flushed and embarrassed, Grace grinning at me with a wicked glint in her eye. It's all I can do to leave her there, but for the first time since this began, I have my hands around the truth, and unless I dig my fingers in, I'm worried it'll slip free. I need to talk to Anna.

I make my way along the cobbled path around the rear of the gatehouse, shaking the rain from my trench coat before hanging it on the rack in the kitchen. Footsteps echo through the floor, heartbeats in the wood. A commotion's coming from the sitting room on my right, the place where Dance and his cronies met Peter Hardcastle this morning. My first assumption is that one of them has returned, but opening the door, I find Anna standing over Peter Hardcastle, who's slumped in the same chair I found him in earlier.

He's dead.

"Anna," I say quietly.

She turns to greet me, shock on her face.

"I heard a noise and came down…" she says, gesturing at the body. Unlike myself, she's not spent the day wading through blood and finding a body has hit her hard.

"Why don't you go splash some water on your face?" I say, touching her lightly on the arm. "I'll have a nose around."

She nods at me gratefully, offering the body one last lingering look before hurrying out of the room. I can't say I blame her. His once handsome features are frightfully twisted, his right eye barely open, his left eye fully exposed. His hands are gripping the arms of the chair, his back arched in pain. Whatever happened here took his dignity and his life at the same time.

My first thought would be heart attack, but Rashton's instincts make me cautious.

I reach out to close his eyes, but can't bring myself to touch him. With so few hosts left, I'd rather not tempt Death's gaze back toward me.

There's a folded letter sticking out of his top pocket, and plucking it free, I read the message inside.

I couldn't marry Ravencourt and I couldn't forgive my family for making me do so. They brought this on themselves.

Evelyn Hardcastle

A draft is blowing in through an open window. Mud smears the frame, suggesting somebody made their escape through it. About the only note of disturbance I can see is a drawer that's been left hanging open. It's the one I rifled through as Dance, and sure enough, Peter's organizer is missing. First, somebody tore a page out of Helena's planner, and now they've taken Peter's. Something Helena did today is worth killing to cover up. That's useful information. Horrific, but useful.

Putting the letter in my pocket, I poke my head out of the window, looking for some evidence of the murderer's identity. There's not much to see, aside from a few footsteps in the dirt, already washing away in the rain. From their shape and size, whoever fled the gatehouse was a woman in pointed boots, which might give the note some credence except that I know Evelyn is with Bell.

She couldn't have done this.

I take a seat opposite Peter Hardcastle, as Dance did this morning. Despite the late hour, the memory of that gathering is still about the room. The glasses we drank from haven't been removed from the table, and the cigar smoke still hangs in the air. Hardcastle's wearing the same clothes I last saw him in, meaning he never got changed for the hunt, so it's likely he's been dead for a couple of hours. One by one I dab my finger into the dregs of the drinks, tasting each of them with the tip of my tongue. They're all fine, except for Lord Hardcastle's. Behind the charred whiskey lays a subtle bitter taste.

Rashton recognizes it immediately.

"Strychnine," I say, staring into the victim's twisted, smiling face. He looks delighted by the news, as though he's sitting here all this time waiting for somebody to tell him how he died. He'd probably also want to know who killed him. I have an idea about that, but for the moment an idea's all it is.

"Is he telling you anything?" asks Anna, passing me a towel.

She's still a little pale, but her voice is stronger, suggesting she's recovered from her initial shock. Even so, she keeps her distance from the body, arms wrapped tightly around herself.

"Somebody poisoned him with strychnine," I say. "Bell supplied it."

"Bell? Your first host? You think he's tied up in all of this?"

"Not willingly," I say, drying my hair. "He's too much of a coward to tangle himself up in murder. Strychnine is often sold in small quantities as rat poison. If the killer was part of the household, they could have requested a significant amount under the guise of getting Blackheath up and running. Bell would have no reason to be suspicious until the bodies started appearing. That probably explains why somebody tried to kill him."

"How do you know all of this?" says Anna, astonished.

"Rashton knows it," I say, tapping my forehead. "He worked on a strychnine case a few years back. Nasty business. Matter of inheritance."

"And you can just...remember it?"

I nod, still thinking through the implications of the poisoning.

"Somebody lured Bell out to the forest last night, intending to silence him," I say to myself. "But the good doctor managed to escape with only the injuries to his arms, losing his pursuer in the darkness. Lucky fellow."

Anna's looking at me strangely.

"What's wrong?" I say, frowning.

"It's the way you were speaking..." She falters. "It wasn't... I didn't recognize you. Aiden, how much of *you* is still in there?"

"Enough," I say impatiently, handing her the letter I found in Hardcastle's pocket. "You should see this. Somebody wants us to believe this is Evelyn's doing. The murderer's trying to wrap it all up in a nice little bow."

She drags her gaze away from me and reads the letter.

"What if we've been looking at this all wrong?" she says, after she's finished. "What if somebody means to knock off the entire Hardcastle family, and Evelyn is just the first."

"You think Helena's hiding?"

"If she's got any sense, that's exactly what she's doing."

I let my mind bat the idea around for a while, trying to see it from every angle. Or at least, I try. It's too heavy. Too ponderous. I can't see what could be on the other side.

"What should we do next?" she asks.

"I need you to tell Evelyn that the butler's awake and that he needs to speak with her, privately," I say, getting to my feet.

"But the butler isn't awake, and he doesn't want to speak with her."

"No, but I do, and I'd rather stay out of the footman's crosshairs if I can."

"I'll take any excuse to leave this room, but you need to watch the butler and Gold in my place," she says.

"I will."

"And what are you going to say to Evelyn when she gets here?"

"I'm going to tell her how she dies."

~ 50 ~

It's 5:42 p.m., and Anna hasn't returned.

It's been over three hours since she left. Three hours of fidgeting and worrying, the shotgun laid across my lap, leaping into my hands at the slightest noise, making it a near-constant presence in my arms. I don't know how Anna did it.

This place is never at rest. The wind claws its way through the cracks in the windows, howling up and down the corridor. Timbers creak, floorboards stretch, shifting under their own weight as though the gatehouse were an old man trying to rise out of his chair. Time and again I heard steps approaching, only to open the door and find I'd been tricked by the banging of a loose shutter or a tree branch rapping on the window.

But these noises have stopped provoking any reaction in me, because I no longer believe my friend is coming back. An hour into my vigil, I reassured myself she was simply struggling to locate Evelyn following her walk with Bell. After two hours, I reasoned she might be running errands—a theory I tried to confirm by piecing together her day from our previous encounters. By her own account, she met Gold first, Derby in the forest, and then Dance, before collecting me from the attic. After that, she talked with the butler for the first time in the carriage on the way here, left the note for Bell in the stable master's cottage, and sought out Ravencourt in his parlor. There was another conversation with the butler after that, but it wasn't until the footman attacked Dance in the evening that I saw her again.

For six days she's been disappearing every afternoon, and I haven't noticed.

Now, passing my third hour in this room, darkness pressing against the glass, I'm certain she's in trouble and that the footman's lurking somewhere behind it. Having seen her with our enemy, I know she's alive, though that's cold comfort. Whatever the footman did to Gold broke his mind, and I cannot bear the thought of Anna undergoing similar torment.

Shotgun in hand, I pace the room, trying to stay one step ahead of my dread long enough to come up with a plan. The easiest thing would be to wait here, knowing the footman will come for the butler eventually, but in doing so I'd waste the hours I need to solve Evelyn's murder. And what use is saving Anna if I can't free her from this house? As desperate as I feel, I must first attend to Evelyn and trust Anna to take care of herself while I do so.

The butler whimpers, his eyes fluttering open.

For a moment, we simply stare at each other, trading guilt and confusion.

By leaving him and Gold unguarded, I'm condemning them to madness and death, but I can see no other way.

As he falls asleep, I lay the shotgun on the bed by his side. I've seen him die, but I don't have to accept it. My conscience demands I give him a fighting chance, at the very least.

Snatching my coat off the chair, I depart for Blackheath, where I find Evelyn's messy bedroom exactly as I left it, the fire burned so low there's barely any light to see by. Adding a few logs, I begin my search.

My hand is shaking, though this time it's not Derby's lust at work; it's my own excitement. If I find what I'm looking for, I'll know who's responsible for Evelyn's death. Freedom will be within touching distance.

Derby may have searched this room earlier, but he had neither Rashton's training nor experience. The constable's hands immediately seek out hiding spots behind cabinets and around the bedframe, my feet tapping the floorboards in the hope of locating a loose panel. Even so, after a thorough search, I come up empty.

There's nothing.

Turning on the spot, my eyes sweep the furnishings, searching for something I've missed. I can't be wrong about the suicide; no other explanation makes sense. That's when my gaze alights on the communicating door into Helena's bedroom. Taking an oil lamp, I pass through, repeating my search.

I've almost given up hope when I lift the mattress off the bed and find a cotton bag tied to one of the bars. Unpicking the drawstring, I find two guns inside. One is a harmless starting pistol, the stalwart of village fetes everywhere. The other is the black revolver Evelyn took from her mother's room, the one she had in the forest this morning and will carry into the graveyard this evening. It's loaded. A single bullet missing from the chamber.

There's also a vial of blood and a small syringe filled with a clear liquid.

My heart is racing.

"I was right," I mutter.

It's the stirring of the curtains that saves my life.

The breeze from the opened door touches my neck an instant before a step sounds behind me. Throwing myself to the floor, I hear a knife slashing through the air. Rolling onto my back, I bring the revolver up in time to see the footman fleeing into the corridor.

Letting my head drop onto the floorboards, I rest the gun on my stomach and thank my lucky stars. If I'd noticed the curtains a second later, this would all be over.

I give myself a chance to recover my breath, then get to my feet, replacing the two weapons and the syringe in the bag, but taking the vial of blood. Cautiously departing the bedroom, I ask around for Evelyn until somebody points me toward the ballroom, which is echoing with loud banging, a stage being finished by builders. The french doors have been thrown open in hopes of evacuating the paint fumes and dust, maids scrubbing their youth away on the floor.

I spot Evelyn by the stage, speaking with the bandleader. She's still in the green dress she wears during the day, but Madeline Aubert is standing behind her with a mouthful of pins, hurriedly jabbing them into escaping locks of hair, trying to fashion the style she'll wear tonight.

"Miss Hardcastle," I call out, crossing the room.

Dismissing the bandleader with a friendly smile and a squeeze of the arm, she turns toward me.

"Evelyn, please," she says, holding out her hand. "And you are?"

"Jim Rashton."

"Ah, yes, the policeman," she says, her smile vanishing. "Is everything well? You look a little flushed."

"I'm not used to the hustle and bustle of polite society," I say.

I shake her hand lightly, surprised by how cold it is.

"How can I help you, Mr. Rashton?" she asks.

Her voice is distant, almost annoyed. I feel like a squashed insect she's discovered on the bottom of her shoe.

As with Ravencourt, I'm struck by the disdain with which Evelyn armors herself. Of all Blackheath's tricks, being exposed to every unpleasant side of a person you once considered a friend is surely the cruelest.

The thought brings me pause.

Evelyn was kind to Bell, and the memory of that kindness has driven me ever since, but the Plague Doctor said he'd experimented with different combinations of hosts over many different loops. If Ravencourt had been my first host, as he surely was at some point, I'd have known nothing of Evelyn beyond her contempt. Derby drew only anger, and I doubt she'd have spared any kindness for servants like the butler, or Gold. That means there were loops where I watched this woman die and felt almost nothing about it, my only concern being to solve her murder, rather than desperately trying to prevent it.

I almost envy them.

"May I speak with you?" I glance at Madeline. "Privately?"

"I really am awfully busy," she says. "What's this about?"

"I'd prefer to speak privately."

"And I'd prefer to finish getting this ballroom ready before fifty people arrive and find there's nowhere for them to dance," she says sharply. "You can imagine which preference I'm giving greater weight to."

Madeline smirks and pins another lock of Evelyn's loose hair into place.

"Very well," I say, producing the vial of blood I found in the cotton sack. "Let's talk about this."

I might as well have slapped her, but the shock slides off her face so quickly, I have trouble believing it was ever there.

"We'll finish this later, Maddie," says Evelyn, fixing me with a cool, level stare. "Go down to the kitchen and get yourself some food."

Madeline's gaze is equally misgiving, but she drops the pins into her apron pocket before curtsying and leaving the room.

Taking me by the arm, Evelyn leads me toward the corner of the ballroom, far from the ears of the servants.

"Is it your habit to root through people's personal possessions, Mr. Rashton?" she asks, taking a cigarette from her case.

"Lately, yes," I say.

"Maybe you need a hobby."

"I have a hobby. I'm trying to save your life."

"My life doesn't need saving," she says coolly. "Perhaps you should try gardening instead."

"Or perhaps I should fake a suicide so I don't have to marry Lord Ravencourt?" I say, pausing to enjoy the collapse of her supercilious expression. "That seems to be keeping you busy lately. It's very clever.

Unfortunately, somebody's going to use that fake suicide to murder you, which is a great deal cleverer."

Her mouth hangs open, her blue eyes sick with surprise.

Averting her gaze, she tries to light the cigarette held between her fingers, but her hand is trembling. I take the match from her and light it myself, the flame singeing my fingertips.

"Who put you up to this?" she hisses.

"What are you talking about?"

"My plan," she says, snatching the vial of blood from my hand. "Who told you about it?"

"Why? Who else is involved?" I ask. "I know you invited somebody called Felicity Maddox to the house, but I don't know who that is yet."

"She's..." She shakes her head. "Nothing. I shouldn't even be talking to you."

She turns for the door, but I catch her by the wrist, pulling her back rather more forcefully than I'd intended. Anger flashes on her face, and I immediately release her, raising my hands.

"Ted Stanwin told me everything," I say desperately, trying to keep her from storming out of the room.

I need a plausible explanation for the things I know, and Derby overheard Stanwin and Evelyn arguing this morning. If I'm very lucky, the blackmailer has a hand in all of this. It's not much of a stretch. He has a hand in everything else that's happening today.

Evelyn's still, watchful, like a deer in the woods that's just heard a branch snap.

"He said you were planning to kill yourself by the reflecting pool this evening, but that made no sense," I press on, trusting to Stanwin's formidable reputation to sell the story. "Forgive me for being blunt, Miss Hardcastle, but if you were serious about ending your life, you'd already be dead, not playing the dutiful hostess to people you despise. My second idea was that you wanted everybody to see it happen, but then why not do it in the ballroom, during the party? I couldn't make sense of it until I stood on the edge of the reflecting pool and realized how dark it was, how easily it could conceal something dropped into it."

Scorn glitters in her eyes.

"And what is it you want, Mr. Rashton? Money?"

"I'm trying to help you," I insist. "I know you intend to go to the reflecting pool at 11:00 p.m., press a black revolver to your stomach, and collapse into the pool. I know you won't actually pull the trigger of the black revolver, and a starting pistol will make the sound of the gunshot everybody hears, just as I know you plan to drop the starting pistol into the water when you're done. The vial of blood will be hung from a long cord around your neck and will crack open when you hit it with the revolver, providing the gore.

"I'm guessing the syringe I found in the sack is filled with some combination of muscle relaxant and sedative to help you play dead, making it easy for Doctor Dickie—who I assume is being paid handsomely for his trouble—to make it official on the death certificate, forgoing the need for an unpleasant inquest. One would imagine that a week or so after your death, you'll be back in France enjoying a nice glass of white."

A couple of maids are carrying slopping buckets of dirty water toward the doors, their gossip coming to an abrupt halt as they notice us. They pass by with uncertain dips, Evelyn steering me farther into the corner.

For the first time, I see fear on her face.

"I admit I didn't want to marry Ravencourt, and I knew I couldn't keep my family from forcing me into it unless I disappeared, but why would anybody want to kill me?" she asks, the cigarette still trembling in her hand.

I study her face for a lie, but I might as well be turning a microscope on a patch of fog. This woman has been lying to everybody for days. I wouldn't recognize the truth even if it did manage to escape her lips.

"I have certain suspicions, but I need proof," I say. "That's why I need you to go through with your plan."

"Go through with it, are you mad?" she exclaims, lowering her voice as all eyes turn toward us. "Why would I go through with it after what you've just told me?"

"Because you won't be safe until we draw the conspirators out, and for that they need to believe their plan has succeeded."

"I'll be safe when I'm a hundred miles from here."

"And how will you get there?" I ask. "What happens if the carriage driver is part of the plot, or a servant? Whispers carry in this house, and when the murderers get word you're trying to leave, they'll push forward with their plan and kill you. Believe me, running will only delay the inevitable. I can put a stop to it here and now, but only if you go along with it all. Point a gun at your stomach and play dead for half an hour. Who knows, you may even get to stay dead and escape Ravencourt as you planned."

She has her hand pressed to her forehead, eyes squeezed shut in concentration. When she speaks again, it's in a quieter voice, somehow emptier.

"I'm caught between the devil and the deep, blue sea, aren't I?" she says. "Very well, I'll go through with it, but there's something I need to know first. Why are you helping me, Mr. Rashton?"

"I'm a policeman."

"Yes, but you're not a saint, and only a saint would put themselves in the middle of all this."

"Then consider it a favor to Sebastian Bell," I say.

Surprise softens her expression. "Bell? What on earth has the dear doctor got to do with this?"

"I don't know yet, but he was attacked last night, and I doubt it's a coincidence."

"Perhaps, but why is that your concern?"

"He wants to be a better person," I say. "That's a rare thing in this house. I admire it."

"As do I," she says, pausing to weigh up the man in front of her. "Very well, tell me your plan, but first I want your word that I'll be safe. I'm putting my life in your hands, and that's not something I submit to without guarantee."

"How do you know my word is worth anything?"

"I've been around dishonorable men my entire life," she says simply. "You're not one of them. Now, give me your word."

"You have it."

"And a drink," she continues. "I'm going to need a little courage to see this through."

"More than a little," I say. "I want you to befriend Jonathan Derby. He has a silver pistol we'll be needing."

51

Dinner's being served, the guests taking their seats at the table, as I crouch in the bushes near the reflecting pool. It's early, but my plan depends on being the first person to reach Evelyn when she emerges from the house. I can't risk the past tripping me up.

Rain drips from the leaves, icy cold on my skin.

The wind stirs, my legs cramping.

Shifting my weight, I realize I haven't eaten or taken a drink all day, which isn't ideal preparation for the evening ahead. I'm light-headed, and without anything to distract me, I can feel every one of my hosts pressed up against the inside of my skull. Their memories crowd the edges of my mind, the weight of them almost too much to bear. I want everything they want. I feel their aches and am made timid by their fears. I'm no longer a man, I'm a chorus.

Oblivious to my presence, two servants spill out of the house, their arms laden with wood for the braziers, oil lamps hanging from their belts. One by one they ignite the braziers, drawing a line of fire into the pitch-black evening. The last one is next to the greenhouse, the flames reflecting on the glass panels so that the entire thing seems to be ablaze.

As the wind howls and the trees drip, Blackheath flickers and changes, following the guests as they make their way from the dining hall to their bedrooms and finally into the ballroom, where the band has taken to the stage, and the evening guests await. Servants open the french doors, music exploding outward, tumbling across the ground and into the forest.

"Now you see them as I do," says the Plague Doctor, in a low voice. "Actors in a play, doing the same thing night after night."

He's standing behind me, mostly obscured by trees and bushes. In the uncertain light of the brazier, his mask appears to float in the gloom like a soul trying to tug free of its body.

"Did you tell the footman about Anna?" I hiss.

It's taking every ounce of self-control I have not to leap up and throttle him.

"I have no interest in either of them," he says flatly.

"I saw you outside the gatehouse with Daniel, then again near the lake, and now Anna's missing," I say. "Did you tell him where to find her?"

For the first time, the Plague Doctor sounds uncertain.

"I assure you, I wasn't at either of those locations, Mr. Bishop."

"I saw you," I growl. "You spoke with Daniel."

"It wasn't…" When he speaks again, it's with a spark of understanding. "So that's how he's been doing it. I wondered how he knew so much."

"He lied to me from the start, and you kept his secret."

"It wasn't my place to interfere. I knew you'd see through him eventually."

"So why warn me about Anna?"

"Because I worried that you wouldn't."

The music stops sharply, and checking my watch, I discover it's a few minutes before eleven. Michael Hardcastle has silenced the orchestra to ask if anybody's seen his sister. There's movement by the side of the house, darkness stirred by darkness as Derby takes his position by the rock, following Anna's instructions.

"I wasn't in that clearing, Mr. Bishop. I promise you," says the Plague Doctor. "I'll explain everything soon, but for the moment, I have my own investigation to undertake."

He departs quickly, leaving only questions in his wake. If this were any other host, I'd run after him, but Rashton's a subtler creature, slow to startle, quick to think. For the moment, Evelyn's my only concern. I put the Plague Doctor out of my thoughts and creep closer to the reflecting pool. Thankfully, the leaves and twigs are so demoralized by the earlier rain they don't have the heart to cry out beneath my feet.

Evelyn's approaching, sobbing, looking for me in the trees. Whatever her involvement in all this, she's clearly afraid, her entire body shaking. She must have already taken the muscle relaxant because she's swaying slightly, as though moved by some music only she can hear.

I rustle a nearby bush to let her know I'm here, but the drug's doing its work. She can barely see, let alone find me in the darkness. Even so, she keeps on walking, the silver pistol glinting in her right hand, and the starting pistol in her left. It's pressed against her leg, out of sight.

She has courage; I'll give her that.

Reaching the edge of the reflecting pool, Evelyn hesitates, and knowing what comes next, I wonder if perhaps the silver pistol is too heavy for her now, the weight of the plan too much.

"God help us," she says quietly, turning it toward her own stomach and pulling the trigger of the starting pistol by her leg.

The shot is so loud it cracks the world, the starting pistol slipping from Evelyn's hand into the inky blackness of the reflecting pool, as the silver pistol hits the grass.

Blood spreads across her dress.

She watches it, bemused, then topples forward into the pool.

Anguish paralyzes me, some combination of the gunshot and Evelyn's expression before she fell nudging an old memory loose.

You don't have time for this.

It's so close. I can almost see another face, hear another plea. Another woman I failed to save, who I came to Blackheath to…what?

"Why did I come here?" I gasp out loud, struggling to pull the memory up from the darkness.

Save Evelyn. She's drowning!

Blinking, I look at the reflecting pool, where Evelyn's floating facedown. Panic washes away the pain, and I scramble to my feet, leaping through the bushes and into the icy water. Her dress has spread across the surface, as heavy as a sodden sack, and the base of the reflecting pool is covered in slippery moss.

I can't get any purchase on her.

There's a commotion by the ballroom. Derby is fighting with Michael Hardcastle, drawing almost as much attention as the dying woman in the pool.

Fireworks explode overhead, staining everything in red and purple, yellow and orange lights.

I hook my arms around Evelyn's midriff, wrestling her out of the water and onto the grass.

Slumped in the mud, I catch my breath, checking to make sure Cunningham's taken firm hold of Michael as I asked him to.

He has.

The plan's working. No thanks to me. The old memory the gunshot stirred almost paralyzed me. Another woman, and another death. It was the fear on Evelyn's face. That's what did it. I recognized that fear. It's what brought me to Blackheath, I'm certain of it.

Doctor Dickie runs up to me. He's flushed, panting, a fortune going up in flames behind his eyes. Evelyn told me he'd been paid to fake the death certificate. The jovial old soldier's got quite the criminal empire up and running.

"What happened?" he says.

"She shot herself," I respond, watching the hope blossom on his face. "I saw the entire thing, but I couldn't do anything."

"You mustn't blame yourself." He clasps me by the shoulder. "Listen here, why don't you go and get a brandy while I look her over. Leave it to me, eh?"

As he kneels beside the body, I scoop the silver pistol off the ground and make my way to Michael, who's still being held fast by Cunningham. Looking at the two of them, I wouldn't have thought it possible. Michael's short and stocky, a bull ensnared by Cunningham's rope-like arms. Even so, Michael's writhing is only tightening Cunningham's grip. A pry bar and a chisel couldn't free him at this point.

"I'm terribly sorry, Mr. Hardcastle," I say, placing a sympathetic hand on the struggling man's arm. "Your sister took her own life."

The fight goes out of him immediately, tears building in his eyes as his anguished gaze goes out toward the pool.

"You can't know that," he says, straining to see past me. "She might still be—"

"The doctor has confirmed it. I'm so sorry," I say, taking the silver pistol from my pocket and pressing it into his palm. "She used this gun. Do you recognize it?"

"No."

"Well, you should keep hold of it for the moment," I suggest. "I've asked a couple of footmen to carry her body into the sunroom, away from..." I gesture toward the gathered crowds. "Well, everybody. If you'd like a few minutes alone with your sister, I can arrange it."

He's staring at the silver pistol dumbly, as though he's been delivered some object from the far future.

"Mr. Hardcastle?"

Shaking his head, his empty eyes find me.

"What... Yes, of course," he says, his fingers closing around the gun. "Thank you, Inspector."

"Just a constable, sir," I say, waving Cunningham over. "Charles, would you mind escorting Mr. Hardcastle to the sunroom? Keep him away from the crowds, would you?"

Cunningham meets my request with a curt nod, placing a hand on Michael's lower back and gently guiding him toward the house. Not for the first time, I'm glad the valet is on my side. Watching him depart, I feel a pang of sadness that this will probably be the last time we meet. For all the mistrust and lies, I've grown fond of him this last week.

Dickie's finished his examination, the old man getting slowly to his feet. Under his watchful eye, the footmen drag Evelyn's body onto a stretcher. He wears his sadness like a secondhand suit. I don't know how I didn't see it before. This is murder as pantomime, and everywhere I look the curtain is rustling.

As Evelyn is lifted off the ground, I race through the rain toward the sunroom, on the far side of the house, slipping inside through the french doors I unlocked earlier and concealing myself behind a screen. Evelyn's grandmother watches me from the painting above the fireplace. In the flickering candlelight, I could swear she's smiling. Perhaps she knows what I know. Maybe she's always known and has been forced to watch day after day as the rest of us blundered through here oblivious to the truth.

No wonder she was scowling before.

Rain raps the windows as the footmen arrive with their stretcher. They move slowly, trying not to jostle the body, which is now draped in Dickie's jacket. In no time at all, they're inside, transferring the body onto the sideboard, pressing their flat caps to their chests in respect before departing, closing the french doors behind them.

I watch them go, catching sight of myself in the glass, my hands stuffed into my pockets, Rashton's quietly competent face suggesting nothing but certainty.

Even my reflection is lying to me.

Certainty was the first thing Blackheath took from me.

The door swings open, the draft from the corridor swiping at the candle flames. In the gaps between the screen's panels, I can see

Michael, pale and shaking, gripping the doorframe for support, tears in his eyes. Cunningham's behind him, and after flashing a covert glance toward the screen where I'm hiding, he closes the door on us.

The instant he's alone, Michael springs out of his grief, his shoulders straightening and eyes hardening, his sorrow transformed into something altogether more feral. Hurrying over to Evelyn's body, he searches her bloodied stomach for a bullet hole, murmuring to himself when he doesn't find one.

Frowning, he removes the magazine from the gun I gave him outside, finding it loaded.

Evelyn was supposed to take a black revolver to the pool, not this silver pistol. He must be wondering what caused her to change the plan, and whether she actually carried through on the plot.

Satisfied that she's still alive, he backs away, fingers drumming his lips as he weighs the pistol. He appears to be in communion with it, frowning and biting his lip as though navigating a series of tricky questions. I lose sight of him momentarily when he strides off into the corner of the room, forcing me to lean out a little from my hiding place to get a better look. He's picked up an embroidered pillow from one of the chairs and he brings it to Evelyn, pressing it against her stomach, presumably to muffle the sound of the pistol jammed up against it.

There isn't even a pause, any sort of goodbye. Turning his face away, he pulls the trigger.

The pistol clicks impotently. He tries again and again, until I step out from behind the screen, putting an end to this charade.

"It won't work," I say. "I filed down the firing pin."

He doesn't turn around. He doesn't even let go of the pistol. "I'll make you a rich man if you let me kill her, Inspector," he says, a quiver in his voice.

"I can't do that, and as I told you outside, I'm a constable."

"Oh, not for very much longer with a mind like yours, I'm sure."

He's trembling, the pistol still held firm against Evelyn's body. Sweat is trickling down my spine, the tension in the room thick enough to scoop up in handfuls.

"Drop the weapon and turn around, Mr. Hardcastle. Slowly, if you please."

"You don't need to fear me, Inspector," he says, dropping the pistol into a plant pot and turning around with his hands in the air. "I have no desire to hurt anybody."

"No desire?" I say, surprised by the sorrow on his face. "You tried to put five bullets into your own sister."

"And every one of them would have been a kindness, I assure you."

Hands still raised, he angles a long finger toward an armchair near the chessboard where I first met Evelyn.

"Mind if I sit down?" he asks. "I'm feeling a little light-headed."

"Be my guest," I say, watching him closely as he drops into the chair. Part of me worries he's going to make a dash for the door, but truth be told he looks like a man who's had all the fight wrung out of him. He's pale and twitchy, arms hanging limp by his sides, legs splayed out before him. If I had to guess, I'd say it took all his strength to decide to pull the trigger.

Murder didn't come easy to this man.

I let him settle, then drag a wingback chair over from the window to sit opposite him.

"How did you know what I was planning to do?" he asks.

"It was the revolvers," I say, sinking a little deeper into the cushion.

"The revolvers?"

"Two matching black revolvers were taken from your mother's room, early this morning. Evelyn had one, and you the other. I couldn't understand why."

"I'm not following."

"The only obvious reason Evelyn had to steal a gun was because she thought herself in danger—a rather redundant explanation for somebody about to commit suicide—or because she planned to use it in the suicide. The latter being more likely, what reason could she possibly have for taking both of the revolvers? Surely one was up to the task."

"And where did these thoughts lead you?"

"Nowhere, until Dance noticed you carrying the second revolver on the hunt. What had been odd, was now damn peculiar. A woman contemplating suicide, at her lowest ebb, has enough forethought to remember her brother's aversion to hunting and steal the second weapon for him?"

"My sister loves me a great deal, Inspector."

"Perhaps, but you told Dance that you didn't know you were going hunting until midday, and the revolvers disappeared from your mother's room early in the morning, well before that decision was made. Evelyn couldn't possibly have taken the second gun for the reason you suggested. Once I heard about your sister's fake suicide scheme, I realized you were lying, and from there everything became clear. Evelyn didn't take the revolvers from your mother's room. You did. You kept one, and gave Evelyn the other to use as a prop."

"Evelyn told you about the fake suicide?" he asks, his tone dubious.

"Partially," I say. "She explained how you'd agreed to help her by running up to the reflecting pool and dragging her onto the grass, as a grieving brother naturally would. That's when I saw how you could commit the perfect crime, and why you needed two matching revolvers. Before pulling her out of the pool, all you had to do was shoot her in the stomach using the fireworks as cover for the second shot. The murder weapon would disappear into the murky water, and the bullet would match the identical gun she'd just dropped on the grass. Murder by suicide. It was quite brilliant, really."

"Which is why you made her use the silver pistol instead," he says, understanding coming into his voice. "You needed me to change my plan."

"I had to bait the trap."

"Very clever," he says, miming applause.

"Not clever enough," I say, surprised by his calmness. "I still don't understand how you could go through with it. Time and again today I've been told how close you and Evelyn are. How much you care for her. Was that all a lie?"

Anger brings him upright in his chair.

"I love my sister more than anything in this world," he says, glaring at me. "I would do anything for her. Why else do you think she came to me for help? Why else would I have said yes?"

His passion has thrown me. I set this plan in motion believing I knew the story Michael would be telling, but this isn't it. I expected to hear how his mother had put him on this path while she orchestrated events elsewhere. Not for the first time, I have the unmistakable feeling of having misread the map.

"If you love your sister, why betray her?" I ask, confused.

"Because her plan wasn't going to work!" he says, slapping his palm down on the arm of the chair. "We couldn't pay the amount Dickie wanted for the fake death certificate. He agreed to assist us anyway, but yesterday Coleridge found out that Dickie was planning to sell our secret to Father later this evening. Do you see? After all this, Evelyn would have woken up in Blackheath trapped in the same life she was so desperate to escape."

"Did you tell her this?"

"How could I?" he asks miserably. "This plan was her one chance to be free, to be happy. How could I take that away from her?"

"You could have killed Dickie."

"Coleridge said the same thing, but when? I needed him to confirm Evelyn's death, and he intended on meeting my father directly afterward." He shakes his head. "I made the only decision I could."

There are two glasses of scotch beside his chair, one halfway full and smeared with lipstick, the other unmarked, a little alcohol left at the bottom. He reaches toward the lipstick-smeared one slowly, keeping his eyes on me.

"Mind if I have a drink?" he asks. "It's Evelyn's. We had a toast in here before the ball began. Best of luck and all that."

There's a catch in his throat. Any other host might think him repentant, but Rashton can spot fear a mile away.

"Of course."

He picks it up gratefully and takes a stiff belt. If nothing else, it serves to steady his trembling hands.

"I know my sister, Inspector," he says, his voice hoarse. "She's always hated being forced into things, even when we were children. She couldn't bear the humiliation of a life with Ravencourt, knowing people were laughing behind her back. Look at what she was willing to do to avoid it. Slowly but surely that marriage would have destroyed her. I wanted to spare her that suffering."

His cheeks are flushed, his green eyes glazed. They're filled with such a sweet, sincere sorrow that I almost believe him.

"And I suppose money had nothing to do with it?" I say flatly.

A scowl mars his sadness.

"Evelyn told me that your parents threatened to cut you from the will if she didn't do as they asked," I say. "You were leverage, and it worked. That threat was the reason she obeyed their summons in the first place, but who knows if she'd have done the same thing again if her escape plan was gone? With Evelyn dead, that uncertainty is laid to rest."

"Look around you, Inspector," he says, gesturing around the room with his glass. "Do you really think any of this is worth killing for?"

"Now your father can't squander what's left of the family fortune, I imagine your prospects have improved immeasurably."

"Squandering the fortune is all my father's good for," he snorts, finishing his drink.

"Is that why you killed him?"

His scowl deepens. He's tight lipped, pale.

"I found his body, Michael. I know you poisoned him, probably when you went to fetch him for the hunt. You left a note blaming Evelyn. The boot print outside the window was particularly devious." His expression flickers uncertainly. "Or was that somebody else's?" I say slowly. "Felicity, perhaps? I'll admit, I still haven't untangled that knot. Or was it your mother's? Where is she, Michael? Or did you kill her, as well?"

His eyes widen as his face crumples in shock, his glass slipping from his hand onto the floor.

"You deny it?" I ask, suddenly unsure.

"No... I...I..."

"Where's your mother, Michael? Did she put you up to this?"

"She... I..."

At first, I mistake his floundering for remorse, his gasping for the shallow breaths of a man searching for the right words. It's only when his fingers grip the arm of the chair, white foam running down his lips that I realize he's been poisoned.

I spring to my feet in alarm, but I have no idea what to do.

"Somebody help us," I yell.

His back arches, his muscles tense, his eyes turning red as the blood vessels pop. Gurgling, he falls forward onto the floor. From behind me I hear rattling. Swinging around, I find Evelyn convulsing on the sideboard, the same white foam bubbling up between her lips.

The door bursts open, Cunningham taking in the scene with an open mouth.

"What's happening?" he asks.

"They've been poisoned," I say, looking from one to the other. "Fetch Dickie."

He's gone before the words have fallen from my lips. Hand to my forehead, I stare helplessly at them. Evelyn is writhing on the sideboard as if possessed, while Michael's clenched teeth crack in his mouth.

The drugs, you fool.

My hand dives into my pocket, retrieving the three vials I was instructed to steal from Bell's trunk when Cunningham and I ransacked it this afternoon. Unwrapping the note, I search for instructions I know aren't on it. Presumably, I mix everything together, but I don't know how much to give them. I don't even know if I have enough for two doses.

"I don't know who to save," I cry, looking from Michael to Evelyn.

Michael knows more than he's told us.

"But I gave Evelyn my word I'd protect her," I say.

Evelyn spasms on the table so violently she falls to the floor, as Michael continues to thrash, his eyes now rolled so far back in his head only the whites can be seen.

"Damn it," I say, running over to the bar.

Emptying the three vials into a scotch glass, I add water from a jug and stir it all together until it foams. Evelyn's back is arched, her fingers biting into the thick weave of a rug. Tilting her head back, I pour the entire filthy creation down her throat, even as Michael chokes behind me.

Evelyn's seizures end as abruptly as they started. Blood weeping from her eyes, she sucks in deep, hoarse breaths. Letting out a sigh of relief, I touch my fingers to her neck, checking for a pulse. It's frantic, but it's strong. She's going to live. Unlike Michael.

I cast a guilty glance at the body of the young man. He looks exactly as his father did in the sitting room. They've clearly been poisoned by the same strychnine Sebastian Bell smuggled into the house. It must have been in the scotch he drank. Evelyn's scotch. Her glass was half full. Judging by how long it took to affect her, she can only have taken a sip or two. Michael, by contrast, finished the lot in under a minute. Did he know it was poisoned? The alarm I saw on his face suggests not.

This was somebody else's work.

There's another killer in Blackheath.

"But who?" I demand, angry with myself for allowing this to happen. "Felicity Maddox? Helena Hardcastle? Who could Michael have been working with? Or was it somebody he knew nothing about?"

Evelyn's stirring, the color already returning to her cheeks. Whatever was in that concoction it's working fast, though she's still weak. Her fingers paw at my sleeve, her lips forming empty sounds.

I lower my ear to her mouth.

"I'm not…" She swallows. "Millicent was…murder."

Very weakly she tugs at her throat, pulling out the chain which was concealed by her dress. There's a signet ring on the end of it, bearing the Hardcastle family seal if I'm not very much mistaken.

I blink at her, not understanding.

"I hope you got everything you needed," says a voice from the french doors. "It's not going to do you much good, though."

Looking over my shoulder, I see the footman emerging out of the darkness, his knife glinting in the candlelight as he taps the point against his thigh. He's wearing his red and white livery, the jacket dotted with grease spots and dirt, as though the essence of him is somehow leaking through. A clean, empty hunting sack is tied to his waist, and with mounting horror I remember how he tossed a full sack at Derby's feet, the material so blood soaked it hit the ground with a wet slap.

I check the clock. Derby will be out there now, sitting in the warmth of a brazier, watching the party dissolve around him. Whatever the footman's going to put in the bag, he plans to carve off Rashton.

The footman smiles at me, his eyes glittering in anticipation.

"You'd think I'd get bored of killing you, wouldn't you?" he asks.

The silver pistol's still in the plant pot where Michael discarded it. It won't fire, but the footman doesn't know that. If I could reach it, I might be able to bluff him into fleeing. It will be a close-run thing, but there's a table in his way. I should be able to get there before him.

"I'm going to do it slow," he says, touching his broken nose. "I owe you for this."

Fear doesn't come easily to Rashton, but he's afraid now, and so am I. I have two hosts left after today, but Gregory Gold is going to spend most of his day strung up in the gatehouse and Donald Davies is stranded on a dirt road, miles from here. If I die now, there's no telling how many more chances I'll get to escape Blackheath.

"Don't worry about the gun," says the footman. "You won't need it."

Mistaking his meaning, hope flares in my chest, fizzling again when I see his smirk.

"Oh, no, my handsome lad. I'm going to kill you," he says, wagging the knife at me. "I just mean you ain't going to fight me," he adds, coming closer. "See, I've got Anna, and if you don't want her to die messy, you're going to give yourself to me, and then you're going to bring whoever's left to the graveyard tonight."

Opening his palm, he reveals Anna's chess piece, spotted with blood. With a flick of his wrist, he tosses it into the fire, the flames consuming it immediately.

Another step closer.

"What's it to be?" he asks.

My hands are clenched by my sides, my mouth dry. For as long as he can remember, Rashton expected to die young. In a dark alley, or on a battlefield, a place beyond light and comfort, beyond friendship, his situation hopeless. He knew how sharp the edges of his life had become, and he'd made peace with it, because he knew he'd die fighting. Futile as it may have been, weak as it may have been, he expected to wade into the darkness with his fists in the air.

And now, the footman has taken even that away. I'm to die without a struggle, and I feel ashamed.

"What's the answer?" says the footman, his impatience growing.

I can't bring myself to say the words, to admit how thoroughly defeated I am. Another hour in this body and I'd have solved it, and that knowledge makes me want to scream.

"Your answer!" he demands.

I manage to nod as he looms over me, his stench wrapping itself around me when he sinks the blade into the familiar spot beneath my ribs, blood filling my throat and mouth.

Gripping my chin, he lifts my face, looking me in the eyes.

"Two to go," he says, and with that, he twists the blade.

52

DAY THREE (CONTINUED)

Rain thumps the roof, horses clip-clopping along the cobbles. I am in a carriage, two women in evening wear wedged onto the seat opposite me. They're talking under their breath, their shoulders bumping together as the carriage sways from side to side.

Don't get out of the carriage.

Fear prickles my spine. This is the moment Gold warned me about. The moment that drove him mad. Out there in the dark, the footman's waiting with his knife.

"He's awake, Audrey," says one of them, noticing me stirring.

Perhaps believing my hearing to be defective, the second lady leans close.

"We found you asleep near the road," she says loudly, laying one hand on my knee. "Your automobile was a few miles farther up. The driver tried to get it running, but it was beyond him."

"I'm Donald Davies," I say, feeling a surge of relief.

The last time I was this man, I drove a car through the night until morning dawned, abandoning it when the fuel ran out. I walked for hours along that never-ending road toward the village, collapsing in exhaustion no nearer my destination. He must have slept the entire day away, saving him from the footman's wrath.

The Plague Doctor told me I'd be returned to Davies when he woke up again. I never could have imagined he'd have been rescued and returned to Blackheath when it happened.

Finally, some good luck.

"You sweet, beautiful woman," I say, cupping my savior's cheeks and kissing her soundly on the lips. "You don't know what you've done."

Before she can respond, I poke my head out the window. It's evening, the carriage's swaying lanterns gently illuminating the darkness rather than banishing it. We're in one of three carriages rolling toward the house from the village, twelve or so others parked either side of the road, their drivers snoring or chatting in small groups, passing a solitary cigarette among themselves. I can hear music from the direction of the house, shrill laughter climbing high enough to puncture the distance between us. The party is in full swing.

Hope surges through me.

Evelyn hasn't made her way to the reflecting pool, which means there may still be time for me to question Michael and discover if he was working with anybody. Even if I'm too late for that, I can still ambush the footman when he comes for Rashton and find out where he's keeping Anna.

Don't get out of the carriage.

"Blackheath in a few minutes, m'lady," the driver shouts down from somewhere above us.

I glance out the window again. The house is directly in front of us, and the stables down the road on our right. That's where they keep the shotguns, and I'd have to be a fool to tackle the footman without one.

Unlocking the door, I leap from the carriage, landing in a painful heap on the wet cobbles. The ladies are shrieking, the coach driver yelling after me as I pick myself up and stagger toward the distant lights. The Plague Doctor told me the pattern of this day was dictated by the character of those living it. I can only hope that's true and fate is in a charitable mood, because if it's not I've damned both myself and Anna.

Within the glow of the braziers, stable boys are undoing the harnesses connecting the horses and carriages, leading the whinnying beasts to shelter. They're working quickly, but they look done in, barely able to speak. I approach the nearest chap who, despite the rain, is wearing only a cotton shirt with the sleeves rolled up.

"Where do you keep the shotguns?" I ask.

He's tightening a harness, gritting his teeth as he pulls the taut strap toward the last buckle. He peers at me suspiciously, his eyes narrowed beneath his flat cap.

"Bit late for hunting, ain't it?" he says.

"And far too early for impertinence," I snap, overwhelmed by my host's upper-class disdain. "Where are the damn shotguns, or do I need to bring Lord Hardcastle down here to ask you himself?"

After looking me up and down, he gestures over his shoulder toward a small redbrick building, a dim light seeping through the window. The shotguns are arranged on a wooden rack, boxes of shells stored in a nearby drawer. I take one down and load it carefully, dropping a handful of spare shells into my pocket.

The gun is heavy, a cold slab of courage that propels me across the yard and up the road toward Blackheath. The stable hands exchange looks as I approach, standing aside to let me pass. Doubtless they think me some rich lunatic with a score to settle, a piece of gossip to add to the pile tomorrow morning. Certainly not somebody worth risking bodily harm for. I'm glad of that. If they were to creep closer, they might notice how crowded my eyes are, how all my previous hosts are jostling for a better view. In some way or another, the footman's harmed every one of them, and they've all turned up for his execution. I can barely think through their clamor.

Halfway along the road I notice a light bobbing toward me, and my grip tightens around the shotgun's trigger.

"It's me," yells Daniel over the din of the storm.

There's a storm lantern in his hand, the waxy light running down his face and upper body. He looks like a genie spilled out of a bottle.

"We have to hurry, the footman's in the graveyard," says Daniel. "He has Anna with him."

He still thinks we're fooled by his act.

My finger strokes the shotgun as I stare back toward Blackheath, trying to decide the best course of action. Michael could be in the sunroom as we speak. But I'm certain Daniel knows where Anna's being kept, and I won't have a better opportunity to get the information from him. Two roads and two ends, and somehow I know that one of them leads to failure.

"This is our chance," yells Daniel, wiping the rain from his eyes. "This is what we've been waiting for. He's in there, right now, lying in wait. He doesn't know we've found each other. We can spring his trap, and we can finish this together."

For so long I fought to change my future, to alter the day. Now I have, I'm undone, racked with the futility of my choices. I saved Evelyn and thwarted Michael, two things which only matter if Anna and I live long enough to tell the Plague Doctor at 11:00 p.m. Past this point, I'm making every decision blind, and with only one host left after today, every decision matters.

"What if we fail?" I shout back, my words barely making it to his ears. The clatter of rain on stone is almost deafening, the wind ripping and tearing at the forest, screaming through the trees like some feral creature slipped loose of its cage.

"What choice do we have?" Daniel yells, clutching the back of my neck. "We have a plan, which means for the first time we have the advantage over him. We must pursue it."

I remember the first time I met this man, how calm he seemed, how patient and reasonable. None of that is in him now. It's all been washed away in Blackheath's endless storms. He has the eyes of a fanatic, eager and imploring, wild and desperate. He has as much riding on the outcome of this moment as I do.

He's right, though. We need to put an end to this.

"What time is it?" I ask.

He frowns. "Why does that matter?"

"I never know until afterward," I say. "The time, please?"

He checks his watch, impatiently. "Nine forty-six," he says. "Can we go now?"

Nodding, I follow him across the lawn into the slanting rain.

The stars are cowards, closing their eyes as we creep closer to the graveyard, and by the time Daniel pushes open the gate, our only light's the flickering glow of his storm lantern. We're shielded by the trees back here, muting the storm which makes its way through to us in sharp gusts, daggers of wind slipping through the cracks in the armor of the forest.

"We should hide out of sight," whispers Daniel, hanging the lantern on the angel's arm. "We'll call to Anna when she arrives."

Lifting the shotgun to my shoulder, I press both barrels to the back of his head.

"You can drop the act, Daniel. I know we're not the same man," I say, my eyes flicking across the woods, searching for some sign of the footman. Unfortunately, the lantern's so bright it obscures much of what it should reveal.

"Hands in the air, turn around," I say.

He does as I ask, staring at me, pulling me apart, looking for something broken. I don't know whether he finds it or not, but after a long silence a charming smile breaks out on his handsome face.

"Couldn't last forever, I suppose," he says, gesturing to his breast pocket. I motion for him to continue, and he slowly withdraws a cigarette case, tapping one out against his palm.

I followed this man into the graveyard, knowing that if I didn't confront him, I'd always be looking over my shoulder, waiting for him to strike again, but now I'm here, faced with his calmness, my certainty is wavering.

"Where is she, Daniel? Where's Anna?" I say.

"Why, that was to be my question to you," he says, placing the cigarette between his lips. "That was it exactly, where *is* Anna? I've been trying to get you to tell me all day, even thought I'd succeeded when Derby agreed to help me flush the footman out from under the house. You should have seen your face, so eager to please."

Shielding his cigarette from the wind, he finally lights it at the third try, illuminating a face that's as hollow-eyed as those of the statues beside him. I have a gun pointed at him, and somehow he still has the upper hand.

"Where's the footman?" I say, the shotgun growing heavy in my arms. "I know you're partners."

"Oh, it's nothing like that. I'm afraid you've got the wrong end of the stick entirely," he says, dismissing the fellow with a wave of his hand. "He's not like you, me, or Anna. He's one of Coleridge's associates. There's actually a few of them in the house. Unsavory chaps the lot of them, but then Coleridge is in an unsavory business. The footman, as you call him, was the brightest of them, so I explained what was happening in Blackheath. I don't think he believed me, but killing's rather his specialty, so he didn't bat an eyelid when I pointed him at your hosts. Probably enjoyed it, truth be told. Helps enormously that I've made him a very rich man, of course."

Blowing smoke out through his nostrils, he grins as though we've shared some private joke. He's moving with assurance, the confidence of a man living in a world of premonitions. A dispiriting contrast to my shaking hands and thudding heart. I just wish he'd hurry up and play his cards. Until I know what he's planning, I can't do anything except wait.

"You're like Anna, aren't you?" I say. "One day, and then you forget everything and start again."

"Hardly seems fair, does it? Not when you have eight lives and eight days. All the gifts were given to you. Now why was that?"

"I see the Plague Doctor didn't tell you everything about me."

He grins again. It's like ice rolling down my spine.

"Why are you doing this, Daniel?" I ask, surprised by my misery. "We could have helped each other."

"But my dear fellow, you *have* helped me," he says. "I have both of Stanwin's blackmail books in my possession. Without Derby poking around his bedroom, I might only have found the one, and I'd be no nearer an answer than I was this morning. In two hours, I'll take what I've learned to the lake and be free of this place, and it's your doing. Surely you can take some comfort in that."

Behind me, wet steps sound. A shotgun is cocked, cold metal pressed into my back. A thug brushes past me, taking a spot in the light beside Daniel. Unlike his friend behind me, he isn't armed, though he doesn't need to be by the looks of things. He has the face of a barroom brawler, his nose broken, his cheek decorated by an ugly scar. He's rubbing his knuckles, his tongue roaming his lips in anticipation. Neither action makes me feel terribly confident about what's coming.

"Be a dear and drop the weapon," says Daniel.

Sighing, I let the shotgun fall on the ground, raising my hands in the air. Foolish as it may be, my overriding thought is to wish they weren't trembling so.

"You can come out now," says Daniel in a louder voice.

There's a rustling in the bushes to my left, the Plague Doctor stepping into the pool of light cast by the lantern. I'm about to hurl some insult at him, when I notice a single silver tear painted on the left side of his mask. It's glittering in the light, and now that I take stock, I realize there are other differences. This coat is finer, darker, the edges not so frayed. Embroidered roses twist up the gloves, and now I see this person is shorter, more erect in their posture.

This isn't the Plague Doctor at all.

"You were the one talking to Daniel by the lake," I say.

Daniel whistles, flicking a glance at his companion.

"How on earth did he see that?" he asks Silver Tear. "Didn't you pick that spot so nobody would find us together?"

"I saw you outside the gatehouse as well," I say.

"Curiouser and curiouser," says Daniel, enjoying himself immensely at his confederate's expense. "I thought you knew every second of his day?" He adopts a pompous tone. "Nothing happens here that is beyond my sight, Mr. Coleridge," he huffs.

"If that were true, I wouldn't need your help capturing Annabelle," says Silver Tear. Her voice is stately, a far cry from the put-upon Plague Doctor. "Mr. Bishop's actions have disrupted the usual course of events. He's changed Evelyn Hardcastle's fate and contributed to the death of her brother, unpicking the threads that hold this day together in the process. He's maintained his alliance with Annabelle far longer than he ever has before, which means things are happening out of order, running long or short, if they happen at all. Nothing's quite where it's supposed to be."

The mask turns toward me.

"You should be commended, Mr. Bishop," she says. "I haven't seen Blackheath in this much disarray for decades."

"Who are you?" I say.

"I could ask the same of you," she says, waving my question away. "I won't because you don't know yourself, and there are more pressing questions. Suffice to say, I'm here to rectify my colleague's mistake. Now, please tell Mr. Coleridge where he might find Annabelle."

"Annabelle?"

"He calls her Anna," says Daniel.

"What do you want with Anna?" I ask.

"That's not your concern," says Silver Tear.

"It's getting to be," I say. "You must want her very badly if you're willing to make a deal with somebody like Daniel to bring her to you."

"I'm redressing the balance," she snaps. "Do you think it's a coincidence that you inhabit the hosts you do, the men closest to Evelyn's
murder? Are you not curious why you woke up in Donald Davies
precisely when you needed him most? My colleague has been playing
favorites from the beginning and that is forbidden. He was supposed
to watch without interfering, to appear at the lake and wait for an
answer. Nothing more. Worse, he's opened the door to a creature who
must never be allowed to leave this house. I cannot let this continue."

"So that's why you're here," says the Plague Doctor, emerging from
the shadows, rainwater running in rivulets down his mask.

Daniel tenses, watching the interloper warily.

"Apologies for not announcing myself earlier, Josephine," continues the Plague Doctor, his attention fixed on Silver Tear. "I wasn't
certain you'd tell me the truth if I asked directly, given how hard
you've worked to stay hidden. I would never have known you were in
Blackheath if Mr. Rashton hadn't spotted you."

"Josephine?" interrupts Daniel. "You two are acquainted?"

Silver Tear ignores him.

"I hoped it wouldn't come to this," she says, addressing the Plague
Doctor. Her tone has softened, warmed. It ripples with regret. "My
intention was to complete my task and depart without you knowing."

"I fail to see why you're here, at all. Blackheath is my watch, and
everything is well in hand."

"You can't believe that!" she says, becoming exasperated. "Look at
how close Aiden and Annabelle have become, how near they are to
escape. He's willing to sacrifice himself for her. Do you see that? If we
let this continue, before long, she'll stand before you with an answer,
and then what will you do?"

"I'm confident it won't come to that."

"I'm confident it will," she snorts. "Tell me truthfully, will you let
her leave?"

The question knocks him silent a moment, a slight tilt of his head conveying his indecision. My eyes slip toward Daniel, who's watching them, his face rapt. I imagine he feels as I do, like a child watching his parents argue, understanding only half of the things being said.

When the Plague Doctor speaks again, his voice is firm, though rehearsed. His conviction born of repetition rather than faith.

"The rules of Blackheath are very clear, and I'm beholden to them, as you are," he says. "If she brings me the name of Evelyn Hardcastle's murderer, I can't refuse to hear her case."

"Rules or not, you know what our superiors will do to you if Annabelle escapes Blackheath."

"Have they sent you to replace me?"

"Of course they haven't." She sighs, sounding hurt. "Do you think their reaction would be so temperate? I came as your friend, to clean up this mess before they ever find out how close you came to blundering. I'm going to quietly remove Annabelle, ensuring you won't have to make a choice you'll regret."

She signals to Daniel. "Mr. Coleridge, could you please persuade Mr. Bishop to reveal Annabelle's location. I trust you understand what's at stake."

Crushing his cigarette underfoot, Daniel nods at the brawler, who takes hold of my arms, pinning me in place. I try to struggle, but he's much too strong.

"This is forbidden, Josephine," says the Plague Doctor, shocked. "We do not take direct action. We do not give orders. We certainly don't feed them information they aren't supposed to know. You're breaking every rule we've promised to uphold."

"You dare lecture *me*?" says Silver Tear scornfully. "All you've done is interfere."

The Plague Doctor shakes his head vehemently.

"I explained Mr. Bishop's purpose here and encouraged him when he faltered. Unlike Daniel and Anna, he didn't wake up with the rules burned into him. He was free to doubt, to veer from his purpose. I never gave him knowledge he hadn't earned, as you have done with Daniel. I sought to bring balance, not offer advantage. I'm begging you, don't do this. Let events follow their natural course. He's so close to solving it."

"And because of that, so is Annabelle," she says, her voice hardening. "I'm sorry, I must choose between Aiden Bishop's well-being and your own. Proceed, Mr. Coleridge."

"No!" yells the Plague Doctor, holding out a placating hand.

The thug with the shotgun points it at him. He's nervous, his finger gripping the trigger a little too tightly. I don't know if the Plague Doctor can be hurt by these weapons, but I can't let him risk it. I need him alive.

"Just leave," I say to him. "There's nothing else you can do here."

"This is wrong," he protests.

"Then make it right. My other hosts need you." I pause meaningfully. "I don't."

I don't know if it's my intonation, or whether he's simply watched this moment play out before, but finally, grudgingly, he relents, staring at Josephine, before disappearing from the graveyard.

"Selfless, as always," says Daniel, walking toward me. "I want you to know that I've admired that quality, Aiden. The way you've fought to save the woman whose death would set you free. Your fondness for Anna, who would have undoubtedly betrayed you if I hadn't done so first. In the end, though, I'm afraid it's all been for nothing. Only one of us can leave this house, and I have no interest in it being you."

Crows are gathering in the branches above me. They arrive as if by invitation, gliding in on silent wings, their feathers slick with recent rain. There are dozens of them, pressed together like mourners at a funeral, watching me with a curiosity that makes my skin crawl.

"Up until an hour ago, we had Anna in our custody," continues

Daniel. "Somehow she's managed to escape. Where would she go, Aiden? Tell me where she's hiding and I'll instruct my men to make your death quick. There's only you and Gold left now. Two gunshots and you'll wake up in Bell, knock on Blackheath's door, and start everything again without me getting in your way. You're a clever fellow. I'm certain you'll solve Evelyn's murder in no time."

His face is ghoulish in the lantern light, twisted by need.

"How frightened are you, Daniel?" I say slowly. "You've killed my future hosts, so I'm not a threat, but you have no idea where Anna is. It's been eating away at you all day, hasn't it? The fear that she's going to solve this before you."

It's my smile that scares him, the faintest sense that I might not be quite so trapped as he first believed.

"If you don't give me what I want, I'll start cutting," says Daniel, drawing a line across my cheek with his fingertip. "I'll take you apart an inch at a time."

"I know. I've met myself after you're done," I say, staring at him. "You break my mind so badly, I carry my madness into Gregory Gold. He slashes his own arms and babbles warnings at Edward Dance. It's horrific. And my answer is still no."

"Tell me where she is," he says, raising his voice. "Coleridge has half the servants in this house on his payroll, and I have a pocketbook thick enough to buy the other half if necessary. I can surround the lake twice over. Don't you see? I've already won. What's the use of being stubborn now?"

"Practice," I snarl. "I'm not going to tell you anything, Daniel. Every minute I frustrate you is another minute Anna has to reach the Plague Doctor with the answer. You'd need a hundred men to guard that lake on a pitch-black night like this, and I doubt even Silver Tear can help with that."

"You'll suffer," he hisses.

"One hour until 11:00 p.m.," I say. "Which one of us do you think can hold out the longer?"

Daniel hits me hard enough to rip the air from my lungs and knock me to my knees. When I look up, he's looming over me, rubbing his grazed knuckles. Anger flickers at the edges of his face like a storm creeping across a cloudless sky. Gone is the suave gambler of earlier, replaced by a scrappy con man, his body twisted by red-hot anger.

"I'm going to kill you slowly," he growls.

"I'm not the one who dies here, Daniel," I say, letting loose a shrill whistle. Birds scatter from the trees, the underbrush rustling with movement. In the inky blackness of the forest, a lantern flares into life. It's followed by another a few feet away, and then another.

Daniel spins on the spot, following the lanterns. He hasn't spotted Silver Tear, who's backing toward the forest, looking unsure of herself.

"You've hurt a lot of people," I say, as the lights come closer. "And now you get to face them."

"How?" he stammers, confounded by the reversal in his fortunes. "I killed all your future hosts."

"You didn't kill their friends," I say. "When Anna told me her plan to lure the footman here, I decided we'd need more bodies to capture him. Once I realized you and the footman were in league together, I expanded my recruiting drive. It wasn't hard to find enemies of yours."

Grace Davies appears first, shotgun raised. Rashton nearly bit his tongue off to prevent me from asking for her help, but I was short of options. The rest of my hosts are busy, or dead, and Cunningham is at the ball with Ravencourt.

The second light belongs to Lucy Harper, who was easily swayed to my cause by the revelation that Daniel murdered her father, and finally comes Stanwin's bodyguard, his head completely bandaged, aside from those cold, hard eyes. Though they're all armed, none of them looks very confident, and I wouldn't trust a single one to hit

anything they're aiming at. It doesn't matter. At this stage, it's the
numbers that count, and they're enough to rattle Daniel and Silver
Tear, whose mask is sweeping back and forth, searching for an escape.

"It's over, Daniel," I say, my voice steely. "Surrender, and I'll let you
go back to Blackheath unharmed."

He glares at me desperately, then at my friends.

"I know what this place can do to us," I continue. "But you were
kind to Bell that first morning, and I saw your affection for Michael
on the hunt. Be a good man one more time, and call off the footman.
Let me and Anna go with your blessing."

His expression wavers, torment showing on his face, but it's not
enough. Blackheath has poisoned him completely.

"Kill them," he says savagely.

A shotgun explodes behind me, and I instinctively throw myself to
the ground. My allies scatter as Daniel's man advances on them, firing
shot after shot into the darkness. The unarmed man is cutting left,
keeping low as he tries to take them by surprise.

I can't tell whether it's my anger, or my host's, which drives me to
lash out at Daniel. Donald Davies is raging, although his fury is one of
class rather than crime. He's aggrieved that anybody should presume
to treat him so shabbily.

My anger is altogether more personal.

Daniel has blocked my way ever since that first morning. He
sought to escape Blackheath by climbing out over me, undoing my
plans in service of his own. He came to me as a friend, smiling as he
lied, laughing as he betrayed me, and it's this that causes me to hurl
myself like a spear at his midriff.

He slips aside, catching me in the stomach with an uppercut.
Doubled over, I punch him in the groin and then grab his neck,
dragging him to the ground.

I see the compass too late.

He smashes it into my cheek, the glass splintering, blood dripping off my chin. My eyes are watering, sodden leaves squelching beneath my palms. Daniel advances, but a shot whistles past him, catching Silver Tear who screams, clutching her shoulder and falling in a heap.

Glancing at the trembling gun in Lucy Harper's hand, Daniel sprints off toward Blackheath. Picking myself up, I give chase.

We run like a hound and fox across the lawn in front of the house and down the driveway, flying past the gatehouse. I'm almost convinced he's fleeing to the village when, finally, he turns left, following the trail to the well and, beyond that, the lake.

The moon is prowling the clouds like a dog behind an old wooden fence, and bereft of its light, I soon lose sight of my quarry. Fearing an ambush, I slow my pursuit, listening intently. Owls hoot, rain drips through the leaves of the trees. Branches snatch at me as I duck and weave, emerging upon Daniel, doubled over by the edge of the water with his hands on his knees, panting for breath, a storm lantern at his feet.

There's nowhere left for him to run.

My hands are shaking, fear squirming in my chest. Anger gave me courage, but it's also made a fool of me. Donald Davies is short and slight, softer than the beds he lies in. Daniel is taller, stronger. He preys on these people. Whatever numerical advantage I had in the graveyard I've left far behind, which means that for the first time since I arrived in Blackheath, neither of us knows what's coming next.

Spotting my approach, Daniel waves me back, gesturing for a minute to catch his breath. I give it to him, using the time to select a heavy rock I can use as a weapon. After the compass, we're beyond fighting fair.

"Whatever you do, they're not going to let Anna leave," he says, forcing out the words between breaths. "Silver Tear told me everything about you in exchange for a promise that I'd find and kill Anna. She told me about your hosts, where they woke up, and when. Don't you understand? None of this matters. I'm the only one who can escape."

"You could have told me this earlier," I say. "It didn't have to end like this."

"I have a wife and a son," he says. "That's the memory I brought with me. Can you imagine how that feels? Knowing they're out there, waiting for me. Or, they were."

I take a step toward him, the rock by my side.

"How will you face them, knowing what you did to escape this place?" I ask.

"I'm only what Blackheath has made me," he pants, spitting phlegm into the mud.

"No, Blackheath's what we made it," I say, advancing a little more. He's still buckled, still tired. A couple more steps and this will all be over. "Our decisions led us here, Daniel. If this is hell, then it's one of our making."

"And what would you have us do?" he says, looking up at me. "Sit here and repent until somebody sees fit to open the doors?"

"Help me save Evelyn and we can take what we know to the Plague Doctor together," I say passionately. "All of us—you, me, and Anna. We have a chance to walk out of this place better men than we arrived."

"I can't risk it," he says in a flat, dead voice. "I won't let this opportunity to escape pass me by. Not for guilt, and not to help people long past helping."

Without warning, he kicks the storm lantern over.

Night floods my eyes.

I hear the splash of his steps before his shoulder drives into my stomach, knocking the wind from me.

We hit the ground with a thud, the rock dropping from my hands.

It's all I can do to throw my arms up to protect myself, but they're thin and frail, and his punches easily break through. Blood fills my mouth. I'm numb, inside and out, but the blows keep coming until his knuckles slip off my bloody cheeks.

His weight recedes as he lifts himself free of me.

He's panting, his sweat dripping onto me.

"I tried to avoid this," he says.

Strong fingers grip my ankle, dragging me through the mud toward the water. I reach for him, but his assault has driven the strength from me and I collapse back.

He pauses, wiping the sweat from his brow. Moonlight hammers through the clouds, bleaching his features. His hair is silver, his skin white as fresh snow. He's looking down at me with the same pity he showed Bell the first morning I arrived.

"We don't…" I say, coughing up blood.

"You should have stayed out of my way," he says, yanking me forward once again. "That's all I ever asked of you."

He splashes into the lake, pulling me with him, the cold water rushing up my legs, soaking my chest and head. The shock of it stirs some fight within me, and I try to claw my way back up the bank, but Daniel grabs my hair, pushing my face into the freezing water.

I scratch at his hand, kicking my legs, but he's too strong.

My body convulses, desperate for a breath.

Still, he holds me down.

I see Thomas Hardcastle, dead these last nineteen years, swimming toward me out of the murk. He's blond-haired and wide-eyed, lost down here, but he takes my hand and squeezes my fingers, urging me to be brave.

Unable to hold my breath any longer, my mouth springs open, gulping in cold, muddy water.

My body spasms.

Thomas pulls my spirit clear of this dying flesh, and we float side by side in the water, watching Donald Davies drown.

It's peaceful and still. Surprisingly quiet.

Then something crashes into the water.

Hands plunge through the surface, gripping the body of Donald Davies, tearing him upward, and a second later I follow him.

The dead boy's fingers are still entwined in mine, but I can't pull him clear of the lake. He died here and so he's trapped here, watching sorrowfully as I'm dragged to safety.

I'm lying in the mud coughing water, my body made of lead.

Daniel is floating facedown in the lake.

Somebody slaps me.

Then again harder.

Anna's hovering above me, but everything's blurry. The lake's holding its hands over my ears, tugging me back.

Darkness is calling me.

She leans closer, a smudge of a person.

"...find me," screams Anna, the words faint. "7:12 a.m. in the entrance hall..."

Beneath the lake, Thomas beckons me back, and closing my eyes, I join the drowned boy.

～ 53 ～

DAY EIGHT

My cheek is resting against the curve of a woman's back. We're naked, tangled in sweat-soaked sheets on a dirty mattress, rain wriggling through the rotten window frames to run down the wall and collect on the bare floorboards.

She stirs as I do, Madeline Aubert rolling over to meet me. The maid's green eyes shine with a sickly need, her dark hair stuck to her damp cheeks. She looks much as Thomas Hardcastle did in my dream, drowned and desperate, clinging to whatever's at hand.

Finding me lying beside her, she drops her head on the pillow with a disappointed sigh. Such obvious disdain should make me uncomfortable, but any ruffled feathers are smoothed by the remembrance of our first meeting; the shame of our mutual need and the eagerness with which she came into my arms when I pulled one of Bell's laudanum vials from my pocket.

My eyes lazily search the cottage for more drugs. My work for the Hardcastles is complete, their new portraits hung in the long gallery. I'm not invited to the party, and I'm not expected at the house, leaving me a free morning on this mattress, the world circling me like paint down a plughole.

My gaze snags on Madeline's cap and apron, which are hanging off a chair.

As if slapped, I immediately return to myself, the uniform summoning Anna's face, her voice and touch, the peril of our situation.

Clinging to this memory, I manage to elbow Gold's personality to one side.

I'm so filled with his hopes and fears, lusts and passions, that Aiden Bishop had felt like a dream in the morning light.

I believed I was no more than this.

Edging off the mattress, I knock over a pile of empty laudanum vials, which roll away across the floor like fleeing mice. Kicking them aside, I go to the fire where a single flame licks the embers, swelling as I add more tinder and wood from the pile. Chess pieces line the mantel, each of them handcrafted, a few painted, though splashed in color might describe them better. They're only half-finished, and lying beside them is the small knife Gold is using to carve them. These are the chess pieces Anna will spend the day carrying around, and the blade is a perfect match for the slashes I saw on Gold's arms yesterday.

Fate is lighting signal fires again.

Madeline's retrieving her clothes, which are scattered across the floor. Such haste speaks of an unruly passion, though there's only shame at work within her now. She dresses with her back to me, eyes on the wall opposite. Gold's gaze is not so chaste, gorging on the sight of her pale flesh, her hair spilling down her back.

"Do you have a mirror?" she asks, doing up her dress, the lightest touch of a French accent in her words.

"I don't believe so," I say, enjoying the warmth of the fire on my bare skin.

"I must look terrible," she says absently.

A gentleman would disagree out of respect, but Gold is no gentleman and Madeline is no Grace Davies. I've never seen her without powder and makeup, and I'm surprised by how sickly looking she appears. Her face is desperately thin, with yellow, pockmarked skin and tired eyes rubbed raw.

Skirting along the far wall in order to stay as far away from me as possible, she opens the door to leave, cold air stealing the warmth from the room. It's early, still hours until dawn, and there's fog on the ground. Blackheath is framed by trees, night still draped around its shoulders. Given the angle I'm seeing it from, this cottage must be somewhere out by the family graveyard.

I watch Madeline hurrying along the path toward the house, a shawl pulled tight across her shoulders. If events had followed their original course, it would be me stumbling into the night. Driven mad by the footman's torture, I'd have taken the carving knife to my own flesh before climbing Blackheath's stairs to bang on Dance's door, screaming my warning. By seeing through Daniel's betrayal, and overwhelming him in the graveyard, I've avoided that fate. I've rewritten the day.

Now I have to make sure it has a happy ending.

Closing the door behind Madeline, I light an oil lamp, pondering my next move as the darkness slinks into the corners. Ideas claw at the inside of my skull, one last half-formed monster still waiting to be dragged into the brightness. To think, when I woke up that first morning as Bell, I fretted about possessing too few memories. Now I must contend with an overabundance. My mind is a stuffed trunk that needs unpacking, but for Gold the world only makes sense on canvas, and it's there I must find my answer. If Rashton and Ravencourt have taught me anything, it's to value my host's talents, rather than lament their limitations.

Picking up the lamp, I head toward the studio at the back of the cottage to search for some paint. Canvases are stacked against the walls, the paintings half-finished or slashed in a fury. Bottles of wine have been kicked over, spilling across the floor onto hundreds of pencil sketches, scrunched up and tossed aside. Turpentine drips down the wall, blurring a landscape Gold seems to have begun in a flurry and abandoned in a rage.

Stacked at the center of the squalor like a pyre awaiting the torch are dozens of old family portraits, their woodworm-riddled frames ripped off and tossed aside. Most of the portraits have been destroyed by turpentine, though a few pale limbs have managed to survive the purge. Evelyn told me Gold had been commissioned to touch up the art around Blackheath. Seems he wasn't terribly impressed with what he found.

Staring at the pile, an idea begins to form.

Rummaging through the shelves, I snatch up a charcoal stick and return to the front room, placing the lamp on the floor. There's no canvas to hand so I dash my thoughts across the wall instead, working within the small pool of dancing light cast by the lantern. They arrive in a frenzy, a lurch of knowledge that wears the stick down to a nub in minutes, forcing me into the gloom to scavenge another.

Working downward from a canopy of names clustered near the ceiling, I feverishly sketch a trunk of everybody's actions over the course of the day, the roots stretching back nineteen years, burrowing into a lake with a dead boy at the bottom. At some point, I accidentally reopen an old cut on my hand, smearing my tree red. Tearing the sleeve from my shirt, I bandage the wound as best I can before returning to my labor. The first rays of the new dawn creep over the horizon as I step back, the charcoal stick dropping from my hand and shattering on the bare floorboards. Exhausted, I sit down in front of it, my arm trembling.

Too little information and you're blind, too much and you're blinded.

I squint at the pattern. There are two knots in the tree representing two swirling holes in the story. Two questions that will make sense of everything: What did Millicent Derby know, and where is Helena Hardcastle?

The cottage door opens, bringing the smell of dew.

I'm too tired to look around. I'm melted candle wax, formless and spent, waiting for somebody to scrape me off the floor. All I want to do is sleep, to close my eyes and free myself of all thought, but this is my last host. If I fail, everything starts over again.

"You're here?" says the Plague Doctor, startled. "You're never here. By this time, you're usually raving. How did... What is that?"

He sweeps by me, his greatcoat swishing. The costume is utterly ridiculous by the light of a new day, the nightmarish bird revealed as a theatrical tramp. No wonder he makes most of his house calls at night.

He stops inches from the wall, running his gloved hand along the curve of the tree, smudging the names.

"Remarkable," he says under his breath, looking it up and down.

"What happened to Silver Tear?" I ask. "I saw her shot in the graveyard."

"I trapped her in the loop," he says sadly. "It was the only way to save her life. She'll wake up in a few hours thinking she's just arrived and repeat everything she did yesterday. My superiors will notice her absence eventually and come to free her. I'm afraid I have some difficult questions ahead of me."

As he stands in communion with my painted tree, I open the front door, sunlight drawing across my face, warmth spreading down my neck and bare arms. Squinting into the glare, I breathe in its golden light. I've never been awake this early before, never seen the sun rise over this place.

It's miraculous.

"Does this painting say what I think it says?" asks the Plague Doctor, his voice tight with expectation.

"What do you believe it says?"

"That Michael Hardcastle tried to murder his own sister."

"Then, yes, that's what it says."

Birds are singing, three rabbits hopping around the cottage's small garden, their fur made rust-colored by the sunlight. If I'd known paradise was on the far side of a sunrise, I'd never have wasted a single night on sleep.

"You've solved it, Mr. Bishop. You're the first one to solve it," he says, his voice rising in excitement. "You're free! After all this time, you're finally free!" He removes a silver hip flask from the folds of his robe and presses it into my hand.

I can't identify the liquid in the flask, but it sets fire to my bones, jolting me awake.

"Silver Tear was right to worry," I say, still watching the rabbits. "I'm not leaving without Anna."

"That's not your choice," he says, standing back to better see the tree.

"What are you going to do, drag me out to the lake?" I ask.

"I won't need to," he says. "The lake was simply a meeting place. The answer was all that ever mattered. You've solved Evelyn's murder and convinced me of the solution. Now that I've accepted it, even Blackheath can't keep hold of you. Next time you sleep, you'll be freed!"

I want to be angry, but I can't rouse myself to it. Sleep is tugging at me with soft hands, and every time I close my eyes, it becomes that much harder to open them again. Returning to the open door, I slide my back down the frame until I'm sitting on the floor, half of my body in gloom, the other half in sunshine. I can't bring myself to abandon the warmth and birdsong, the blessings of a world so long denied.

I take another sip from the flask, forcing myself awake.

I've still got so much to do.

So much you can't be seen to be doing.

"It wasn't a fair competition," I say. "I had eight hosts whereas Anna and Daniel only had one. I could remember the week and they couldn't."

He pauses, considering me.

"You had those things because you chose to come to Blackheath," he says quietly, as if afraid of being overheard. "They did not, and that's all I can say on the matter."

"If I chose to come here once, I can choose to come again," I say. "I won't leave Anna behind."

He begins to pace, glancing between me and the painting.

"You're afraid," I say, surprised.

"Yes, I'm afraid," he snaps. "My superiors, they're not... You shouldn't defy them. I promise you, after you leave, I'll offer Anna all the assistance it's in my power to grant."

"One day, one host. She'll never escape Blackheath; you know she won't," I say. "I couldn't have done this without Ravencourt's intelligence and Dance's cunning. It was only because of Rashton that I started looking at the clues like evidence. Hell, even Derby and Bell played their part. She'll need all of their skills, just as I did."

"Your hosts will still be in Blackheath."

"But I won't be controlling them!" I insist. "They won't help a maid. I'll be abandoning her to this place."

"Forget about her! This has already gone on long enough," he says, swinging around to confront me, swiping his hand through the air.

"What's gone on long enough?"

He's looking at his gloved hand, startled by his own loss of control.

"Only you can make me this angry," he says in a quieter voice. "It's always been the same. Loop after loop, host after host. I've seen you betray friends, make alliances, and die on principle. I've seen so many versions of Aiden Bishop, you'd probably never recognize yourself in them, but the one thing that's never changed is your stubbornness. You pick a path, and you walk down it until the end, no matter how many holes you fall down along the way. It would be impressive if it weren't so intensely irritating."

"Irritating or not, I have to know why Silver Tear went to such lengths to try to kill Anna."

He offers me a long, appraising look and then sighs.

"Do you know how you can tell if a monster's fit to walk the world again, Mr. Bishop?" he says contemplatively. "If they're truly redeemed and not just telling you what you want to hear?" He takes another slug from the hip flask. "You give them a day without consequences, and you watch to see what they do with it."

My skin prickles, my blood running cold.

"This was all a test?" I say slowly.

"We prefer to call it rehabilitation."

"Rehabilitation…" I repeat, understanding rising within me like the sun over the house. "This is a prison?"

"Yes, except instead of leaving our prisoners to rot in a cell, we give them a chance to prove themselves worthy of release every single day. Do you see the beauty of it?" exclaims the Plague Doctor. "The murder of Evelyn Hardcastle was never solved, and probably never would have been. By locking prisoners inside the murder, we give them a chance to atone for their own crimes by solving somebody else's. It's as much a service, as a punishment."

"Are there other places like this?" I say, trying to wrap my head around it.

"Thousands," he says. "I've seen a village that wakes up each morning with three headless bodies in the square, and a series of murders on an ocean liner. There must be fifteen prisoners attempting to solve that one."

"Which makes you, what? A warden?"

"An assessor. I decide if you're worthy of release."

"But you said I chose to come to Blackheath? Why would I choose to come to a prison?"

"You came for Anna, but you got trapped, and loop after loop Blackheath picked you apart until you forgot yourself, as it was designed to." His voice is tight with anger, his gloved hands clenched. "My superiors should never have let you inside. It was wrong. For the longest time, I thought the innocent man who'd entered here was lost, sacrificed in some futile gesture, but you've found your way back. *That's* why I've been helping you. I gave you control of different hosts, searching for those who were best equipped to solve her murder, finally settling on the eight of today. I experimented with their order to ensure you got the best out of them. I even arranged to have Mr. Rashton hidden in that cupboard to keep him alive. I'm bending every rule possible so that you can escape. Do you see now? You must leave while you're still the person you wish to be."

"And Anna…?" I say haltingly, hating the question I'm about to ask.

I've never allowed myself to believe that Anna belonged here, preferring to think of this place as the equivalent of being shipwrecked or struck by lightning. By assuming her to be a victim, I took away the niggling doubt of whether this was deserved, but without that comfort, my fear is growing.

"What did Anna do to deserve Blackheath?" I ask.

He shakes his head, passing me the flask. "That's not for me to say. Just know that the weight of the punishment is equal to the crime. The prisoners I told you about in the village and on the boat received lighter sentences than either Anna or Daniel. Those places are much less harrowing than here. Blackheath was built to break devils, not petty thieves."

"You're saying Anna's a devil?"

"I'm saying thousands of crimes are committed every day, but only *two* people have been sent to this place." His voice is rising, racked with emotion. "Anna's one of them, and yet you risked your life to help her escape. It's madness."

"Any woman who can inspire that loyalty has to be worth something."

"You're not hearing me," he says, his fists balled.

"I'm hearing you, but I won't leave her here," I say. "Even if you make me go today, I'll find my way back in tomorrow. I did it once. I'll do it again."

"Stop being such a bloody fool!" He thumps the doorframe hard enough to bring dust down on our heads. "It wasn't loyalty that brought you to Blackheath; it was vengeance. You didn't come here to *rescue* Anna; you came for your pound of flesh. She's safe in Blackheath. Caged, but safe. You didn't want her to be caged; you wanted her to suffer—so many people out there wanted her to suffer, but none of them was willing to do what you were, because nobody hated this woman as much as you did. You followed her into Blackheath, and for the last thirty years, you've dedicated yourself to torturing her, just as the footman tortures you today."

Silence presses down on us.

I open my mouth to respond, but my stomach's in my shoes, my head spinning. The world has upended itself, and even though I'm sitting on the floor, I can feel myself falling and falling.

"What did she do?" I whisper.

"My superiors—"

"Opened Blackheath's doors to an innocent man intent on murder," I say. "They're as guilty as anybody in here. Now tell me what she did."

"I can't," he says weakly, his resistance all but spent.

"You've helped me this far."

"Yes, because what happened to you is wrong," he says, taking a long swig from the flask, his Adam's apple bouncing up and down in his throat. "Nobody objected to my helping you escape because you weren't supposed to be here anyway, but if I start telling you things you shouldn't know, there'll be repercussions. For both of us."

"I can't leave without knowing why I'm going, and I can't promise not to come back until I'm certain of why I came in the first place," I say. "Please, this is how we end this."

The beak mask turns toward me slowly, and for a full minute, he stands there, deep in thought. I can feel myself being measured, my qualities weighed and set aside, my flaws held up to the light that they might be better judged.

It's not you he's measuring.

What does that mean?

He's a good man. This is when he finds out how good.

Bowing his head, the Plague Doctor surprises me by taking off his top hat, revealing the brown leather straps holding the beak mask in place. One by one, he begins undoing them, grunting with the effort as his thick fingers pry at the catches. As the last clasp comes loose, he removes his mask and pulls down his hood, revealing the bald head beneath. He's older than I would have imagined, closer to sixty than fifty certainly, his face that of a decent, overworked man. His eyes are bloodshot, his skin the color of old paper. If my tiredness could take a shape, it would look like this.

Oblivious to my concern, he tilts his face to catch the early morning light seeping through the window.

"Well, that's done it," he says, tossing the mask onto Gold's bed. Freed from the porcelain, his voice is almost, but not quite, the one I know.

"I don't imagine you were supposed to do that." I nod toward the mask.

"It's getting to be quite a list," he replies, sitting down on a step outside the door, positioning himself so that his entire body is bathed in sunlight.

"I come here every morning, before I start work," he says, taking a deep breath. "I love this time of the day. It lasts for seventeen minutes, then the clouds gather and two footmen resume a quarrel from the evening prior, ending in a fistfight at the stables." He's peeling his gloves off, finger by finger. "It's a shame this is the first time you've been able to enjoy it, Mr. Bishop."

"Aiden," I say, extending my hand.

"Oliver," he says as he shakes it.

"Oliver," I repeat thoughtfully. "I never thought of you having a name."

"Perhaps I should tell it to Donald Davies when I confront him on the road," he says, a faint smile on his lips. "He'll be very angry. It might calm him."

"You're still going out there? Why? You have your answer."

"Until you escape, it remains my duty to shepherd those that follow you, to give them the same chance you had."

"But you know who killed Evelyn Hardcastle now," I say. "Won't that change things?"

"Are you suggesting I'll find my task difficult because I know more than them?" He shakes his head. "I've always known more than them. I knew more than you. Knowledge was never my problem. Ignorance is the condition I struggle with."

His face hardens again, the levity slipping from his tone. "That's why I've taken my mask off, Aiden. I need you to see my face and hear my voice, and know that what I'm telling you is the absolute truth. I can't have you doubting me anymore."

"I understand," I say. It's all I can manage. I feel like a man waiting for the fall.

"The name Annabelle Caulker, the woman you know as Anna, is a curse in every language in which it is spoken," he says, pinning me in place with his gaze. "She was the leader of a group that sowed destruction and death across half the nations of the world and would surely still be doing so if she hadn't been caught, over thirty years ago. That's who you're trying to free."

I should be surprised. I should be shocked, or angry. I should protest, but I don't feel any of those things. This doesn't feel like a revelation, more the voicing of facts I've long been familiar with. Anna's fierce and fearless, even brutal when she needs to be. I saw her expression in the gatehouse when she came at Dance with the shotgun, not realizing it was me. She would have pulled the trigger without any regret at all. She killed Daniel when I could not and casually suggested murdering Evelyn ourselves as a way of answering the Plague Doctor's question. She said it was a joke, but even now, I'm not certain.

And yet, Anna only killed those people to protect me, buying time so that I could solve this mystery. She's strong, she's kind, and she stayed loyal even when my desire to save Evelyn threatened to undermine our investigation into her murder.

Of all the people in the house, she's the only one who never hid who she truly was.

"She's not that person anymore," I argue. "You said Blackheath was meant to rehabilitate people, to break down their old personalities and test the new ones. Well, I've seen Anna up close this last week. She's helped me, saved my life more than once. She's my friend."

"She murdered your sister," he says bluntly.

My world empties.

"She tortured her, humiliated her, and made the world watch," he continues. "That's who Anna is, and people like that don't change, Aiden."

I drop to my knees, clutching my temples as old memories erupt.

My sister was called Juliette. She had brown hair and a bright smile. She was charged with capturing Annabelle Caulker, and I was so proud of her.

Every recollection feels like a shard of glass tearing through my mind.

Juliette was driven and clever, and thought justice was something that had to be defended and not simply expected. She made me laugh. She thought that was worth doing.

Tears roll down my cheeks.

Annabelle Caulker's men came in the night and took Juliette from her home. They executed her husband with a single bullet to the head. He was lucky. Juliette's bullet didn't come for seven days. They tortured her and let everybody watch.

They called it justice for their persecution.

They said we should have expected this.

I don't know anything more about myself, or the rest of my family. I didn't keep hold of my happy memories. Only those that could help me, only hate and grief.

It was Juliette's murder that brought me to Blackheath. It was the weekly phone calls that stopped coming. The stories we stopped sharing. It was the space where she should have been and would never be again. It was the way Annabelle was eventually caught.

Bloodlessly. Painlessly.

Entirely without incident.

And they sent her to Blackheath, where my sister's murderer would spend a lifetime solving the death of a murdered sister. They called it justice. They patted themselves on the back for their ingenuity, thinking I'd be as pleased as they were. Thinking it was enough.

They were wrong.

The injustice tore into me at night and stalked me during the day. It whittled me down until Annabelle Caulker was the only thing I could think about.

I followed her through the gates of hell. I pursued, terrified, and tortured her, until I forgot the reasons why. Until I forgot Juliette. Until Annabelle became Anna, and all I saw was a terrified girl at the mercy of monsters.

I became the thing I hated and made Annabelle into the thing I loved.

And I blamed Blackheath.

I look up at the Plague Doctor through eyes raw with tears. He's looking me full in the face, weighing my reaction. I wonder what he sees, because I have no idea what to think. All of this is happening to me because of the person I'm trying to save.

This is Anna's fault.

Annabelle.

"What?" I ask, surprised by how insistent the voice in my head sounds.

It's Annabelle Caulker's fault, not Anna's. That's who we hated.

"Aiden?" asks the Plague Doctor.

And Annabelle Caulker's dead.

"Annabelle Caulker's dead," I repeat slowly, meeting the Plague Doctor's startled gaze.

He shakes his head. "You're wrong."

"It took thirty years," I say. "And it wasn't done with violence and it wasn't done with hatred. It was done with forgiveness. Annabelle Caulker is dead."

"You're mistaken."

"No, you are," I say, building in confidence. "You asked me to listen to the voice in my head, and I am. You asked me to believe Blackheath could rehabilitate people, and I have. Now you need to do the same, because you're so blinded by who Anna used to be, you're ignoring who she's become, and if you're not willing to accept she's changed, then what good is any of this?"

Frustrated, he kicks at the dirt with the toe of his boot.

"I should never have taken the mask off," he growls, getting to his feet and striding into the garden, scattering the rabbits eating the grass. Hands on hips, he stares at Blackheath in the distance, and for the first time, I realize it's as much his master as mine. While I was free to tinker and change, he's been forced to watch as we murdered and raped and committed suicide. He's had to accept whatever the day brought him, no matter how horrific. And unlike me, he wasn't allowed to forget. A man could go mad. Most men would, unless they had faith. Unless they believed the ends justified the means.

As if privy to my thoughts, the Plague Doctor turns toward me.

"What is it you're asking of me, Aiden?"

"Only that you do your job," I say firmly. "Come to the lake at eleven. There'll be a monster there, and I guarantee it won't be Anna. Watch her, give her a chance to prove herself. You'll see who she really is, and you'll see I'm right."

He looks uncertain.

"How can you know that?" he asks.

"Because I'll be in danger."

"Even if you convince me she's rehabilitated, you've already solved the mystery of Evelyn's death," he says. "The rules are clear; the first prisoner to explain who killed Evelyn Hardcastle will be released. That's you. Not Anna. What's your solution to that?"

Getting to my feet, I stumble over to my sketch of the tree, jabbing at the knots, the holes in my knowledge.

"I haven't solved everything," I say. "If Michael Hardcastle planned to shoot his sister in the reflecting pool, why would he also poison her? I don't think he did. I don't think he knew there was poison in the drink that killed him. I think somebody else put it there in case Michael failed."

The Plague Doctor's followed me inside.

"That's thin reasoning, Aiden."

"We still have too many questions for anything else," I say, recalling Evelyn's pale face after I saved her in the sunroom, and the message she worked so hard to deliver. "If this was finished, why would Evelyn tell me Millicent Derby was murdered? What does that achieve?"

"Perhaps Michael killed her also?"

"And what was his motive? No, we're missing something."

"What sort of something?" he asks, his conviction wavering.

"I think Michael Hardcastle was working with somebody else, somebody who's kept out of sight all along," I say.

"A second killer," he says, taking a second to consider it. "I've been here for a long time, and I've never suspected... Nobody ever has. It can't be, Aiden. It's impossible."

"Everything about today is impossible," I say, thumping my

charcoal tree. "There's a second killer, I know there is. I have an idea who it may be, and if I'm right, they killed Millicent Derby to cover their tracks. They're as implicated in Evelyn's murder as Michael, and that means you need two answers. If Anna delivers Michael's partner, will that be enough to set her free?" I ask.

"My superiors do not want to see Annabelle Caulker leave Blackheath," he says. "And I'm not certain they can be convinced she's changed. Even if they can, they'll be looking for any excuse to keep her imprisoned, Aiden."

"You helped me because I don't belong here," I say. "If I'm right about Anna, the same is now true for her."

Running his hand across his scalp, he paces back and forth, casting anxious glances between myself and the sketch.

"I can only promise I'll be at the lake tonight with an open mind," he says.

"It's enough," I say, clapping him on the shoulder. "Meet me by the boathouse at eleven, and you'll see I'm right."

"And may I ask what you'll be doing in the meantime?"

"I'm going to find out who murdered Millicent Derby."

~ 54 ~

Keeping to the trees, I approach Blackheath unseen, my shirt damp with fog, my shoes caked in mud. The sunroom lies a few paces away, and crouching among the dripping bushes, I look for any movement within.

It's still early, but I don't know when Daniel wakes up, or when he's recruited by Silver Tear. For safety's sake, I must assume Daniel and his spies are still a threat until he's lying facedown in the lake, all of his plots drowned with him.

After the sun's early foray, it's abandoned us to the gloom, the sky a muddle of grays. I search the flower beds for splashes of red, hints of purple, pink, or white. I search for the brighter world behind this one, imagining Blackheath alight, wearing a crown of flames and a cape of fire. I see the gray sky burning, black ash falling like snow. I imagine the world remade, if only for an instant.

I come to a halt, suddenly uncertain of my purpose. I look around, not recognizing anything, wondering why I left the cottage without my brushes and easel. Surely I came to paint, but I'm not a fan of the morning light here. It's too dreary, too quiet, a gauze across the landscape.

"I don't know why I'm here," I say to myself, looking down at my charcoal-stained shirt.

Anna. You're here for Anna.

Her name shakes me loose of Gold's confusion, my memories returning in a flood.

It's getting worse.

Taking a deep breath of cold air, I clutch the chess piece from the mantel in my hand, building a wall between myself and Gold by using every memory I have of Anna. I make bricks of her laughter, her touch, her kindness and warmth, and only when I'm content my wall is high enough, do I resume my study of the sunroom, letting myself inside when I'm satisfied the house sleeps.

Dance's drunken friend, Philip Sutcliffe, is asleep on one of the couches, his jacket drawn up over his face. He stirs briefly, smacking his lips and peering at me blearily. He murmurs something, shifts his weight, and then falls asleep again.

I wait, listening. Dripping. Breathing heavily.

Nothing else moves.

Evelyn's grandmother watches me from the portrait above the fireplace. Her lips are pursed, the artist capturing her exactly at the moment of rebuke.

My neck prickles.

I find myself frowning at the painting, dismayed by how gently she's been rendered. My mind repaints it, the curves as harsh as scars, the oil piled like mountains. It becomes a mood smeared on canvas. A black one at that. I'm certain the old battle-ax would have preferred its honesty.

A peal of shrill laughter sounds through the open door, a dagger driven into somebody's story. The guests must have started drifting down to breakfast.

I'm running out of time.

Closing my eyes, I try to remember what Millicent spoke with her son about, what drove her to hurry off so quickly and come here, but everything's a clutter. There are too many days, too many conversations.

A gramophone springs into life down the corridor, slashing at the quiet with random notes. There's a crash, the music screeching to a halt, hushed voices bickering and blaming.

We were standing outside the ballroom, that's where it started. Millicent was sad, wrapped in memory. We talked of the past; how she'd visited Blackheath as a child and brought her own children when they were old enough. She was disappointed in them, then angry with me. She caught me looking through the ballroom window at Evelyn and mistook my concern for lust.

"It's always the weak ones with you, isn't it?" she said. "Always the..."

Something she saw caused her to lose her train of thought.

Squeezing my eyes shut, I try to recall what it was.

Who else was in there with Evelyn?

Half a second later, I'm sprinting into the corridor toward the gallery.

A single oil lamp's burning on the wall, its sickly flame encouraging the shadows rather than diminishing them. Snatching it off the hook, I hold it up to the family oil paintings, inspecting them one by one.

Blackheath shrinks around me, shriveling like a spider touched to the flame.

In a few hours, Millicent will see something in the ballroom that so startles her, she'll leave her son standing on the path and rush to this gallery. Wrapped in scarves and armed with her suspicions, she'll spot Gold's new paintings among the older ones. Any other time she might have walked past. Maybe she has during a hundred other loops, but not on this occasion. This time, the past will hold her hand and squeeze.

Memory will murder her.

55

It's 7:12 a.m. and the entrance hall is a mess. Smashed decant-
ers litter the marble floor, portraits hang at odd angles, lipstick kisses
planted on the mouths of long-dead men. Bow ties dangle from the
chandelier like sleeping bats, and at the center of it all stands Anna,
barefoot in her white cotton nightgown, staring at her hands as
though they're a riddle she can't make sense of.

She hasn't noticed me, and for a few seconds, I watch her, trying
to reconcile my Anna with the Plague Doctor's stories of Annabelle
Caulker. I wonder if Anna's hearing Caulker's voice right now, the way
I heard Aiden Bishop's that first morning. Something dry and distant,
a part of her, yet apart at the same time, impossible to ignore.

To my shame, my faith in my friend wavers. After working so hard
to convince the Plague Doctor of Anna's innocence, now I'm the one
looking at her askew, questioning whether any part of the monster
who murdered my sister has survived, waiting to surface again.

Annabelle Caulker's dead. Now, help her.

"Anna," I say softly, suddenly wary of my own appearance. Gold
spent most of his evening in a laudanum-fueled fug, my only conces-
sion to hygiene being a splash of water on his face before I came
charging out of the cottage. Goodness knows how I must appear to
her, or smell.

She looks up at me, startled.

"Do I know you?" she asks.

"You will," I say. "This might help."

I toss her the chess piece I took from the cottage, which she catches in one hand. Opening her palm, she stares down at it, memory setting light to her face.

Without warning, she flings herself into my arms, wet tears seeping through my shirt.

"Aiden," she says, her mouth against my chest. She smells of milky soap and bleach, her hair catching in my whiskers. "I remember you, I remember..."

I feel her stiffen, her arms falling loose.

Disentangling herself, she pushes me away, grabbing a piece of shattered glass from the floor to use as a weapon. It trembles in her hand.

"You murdered me," she snarls, gripping the glass tight enough to draw blood.

"Yes, I did," I say, the knowledge of what she did to my sister hanging on my lips.

Annabelle Caulker's dead.

"And I'm sorry about that," I continue, stuffing my hands into my pockets. "I promise it won't happen again."

For a second all she can do is blink at me.

"I'm not the man you remember anymore," I say. "It was a different life, a different set of choices. A lot of mistakes I've tried not to make again, and haven't, because of you, I think."

"Don't..." she says, thrusting the glass shard at me when I take a step toward her. "I can't... I remember things. I *know* things."

"There are rules," I say. "Evelyn Hardcastle is going to die, and we're going to save her together. I have a way we can both get out of here."

"We can't both escape, it's not allowed," she insists. "That's one of the rules, isn't it?"

"Allowed or not, we're going to do it," I say. "You have to trust me."

"I can't," she says fiercely, wiping a stray tear from her cheek with her thumb. "You killed me. I remember it. I can still feel the shot. I was so excited to see you, Aiden. I thought we were finally leaving. You and me together."

"We are."

"You killed me!"

"It wasn't the first time," I say, my voice cracked by regret. "We've both hurt each other, Anna, and we've both paid for it. I'm never going to betray you again, I promise. You can trust me. You already *have* trusted me; you just can't remember it."

Raising my hands as if surrendering, I move slowly toward the staircase. Brushing away a broken pair of glasses and some confetti, I sit down on the red carpet. Every host is pressing down upon me, their memories of this room crowding the edges of my mind, their weight almost too much to bear. Clear as the morning it happened—

This is the morning it happened.

—I recall Bell's conversation with the butler at the door and how afraid they both were. My hand throbs from the pain of Ravencourt's cane as he struggled toward the library, shortly before Jim Rashton heaved a sack of stolen drugs out through the front door. I hear the light steps of Donald Davies on the marble, as he fled the house after his first meeting with the Plague Doctor, and the laughter of Edward Dance's friends, even as he stood silent.

So many memories and secrets, so many burdens. Every life has such weight. I don't know how anybody carries even one.

"What's wrong with you?" asks Anna, creeping closer, the glass shard held a little looser in her hand. "You don't look well."

"I've got eight different people rattling around in here," I say, tapping my temple.

"Eight?"

"Eight versions of today as well," I say. "Every time I wake up, I'm in a different guest. This is my last one. Either I solve this today, or I start all over again tomorrow."

"That's not... The rules won't let you. We only get one day to solve the murder, and you can't be anybody else. That's... It's not right."

"The rules don't apply to me."

"Why?"

"Because I chose to come here," I say, rubbing my tired eyes. "I came here for you."

"You're trying to rescue me?" she says incredulously, the glass shard dangling by her side, forgotten.

"Something like that."

"But you murdered me."

"I never said I was very good at it."

Perhaps it's my tone, or the way I'm slouching on the step, but Anna lets the glass shard drop to the floor and sits beside me. I can feel the warmth of her, the solidity. She's the only real thing in a world of echoes.

"Are you still trying?" she asks, peering up at me through big brown eyes, her skin pale and puffy, streaked with tears. "To rescue me, I mean."

"I'm trying to rescue us both, but I can't do it without your help," I say. "You have to believe me, Anna. I'm not the man who hurt you."

"I want to..." She falters, shaking her head. "How can I trust you?"

"You just have to start," I say, shrugging. "We don't have time for anything else."

She nods, taking that in. "And what would you need me to do, if I could start to trust you?"

"A lot of small favors and two big ones," I say.

"What are the big ones?"

"I need you to save my life. Twice. This will help."

From my pocket I take out the artist's sketchbook, a battered old thing filled with crumpled pieces of loose-leaf paper, the leather covers bound with string. I found it in Gold's jacket when I left the cottage. After tossing away Gold's somewhat anarchic sketches, I wrote down everything I could remember about my hosts' schedules, leaving notes and instructions dotted throughout.

"What is it?" she asks, taking it from me.

"It's the book of me," I say. "And it's the only advantage we have."

56

"Have you seen Gold? He should already be here."

I'm sitting in Sutcliffe's empty bedroom, the door opened a crack. Daniel is busy speaking with Bell in the room opposite, and Anna's outside, pacing furiously.

It's not my intention to make her fret, but after I finished scattering letters across the house, including the one in the library revealing Cunningham's parentage, I retired here with a decanter of whiskey from the drawing room. I've been drinking solidly for an hour, trying to wash away the shame of what's coming, and though I'm drunk, I'm not nearly drunk enough.

"What's our plan?" I hear Rashton say to Anna.

"We need to keep the footman from killing the butler and Gold this morning," she says. "They've still got a role to play in all this, assuming we can keep them alive long enough."

I take another belt of the whiskey, listening to them talk.

Gold doesn't have a drop of violence in him, and it would take a great deal of convincing to make him hurt an innocent man. I don't have time for that, so I'm hoping to numb him instead.

I'm not having any luck so far.

Gold beds other men's wives, cheats at dice, and generally carries on as though the sky is going to fall any minute, but he wouldn't crush a wasp that stung him. He loves life too much to bring pain to anybody else's, which is unfortunate, because pain is the only thing that will keep the butler alive long enough to meet Anna in the gatehouse.

Hearing his dragging steps outside the door, I take a breath and stride into the corridor, obstructing his path. Through Gold's strange eyes, he's a beautiful sight, his burned face a joy, so much more engaging than the bland symmetry of most people.

He tries to back away from me with a hurried apology, but I snatch his wrist. He looks up at me, mistaking my mood. He sees anger when all I feel is anguish. I have no desire to hurt this man, yet I must.

He tries to move around me, but I block his path.

I despise what I must do, wishing I could explain, but there isn't time. Even so, I can't bring myself to raise the poker and strike an innocent man. I keep seeing him lying in bed, swaddled in white cotton sheets, beaten black and blue, struggling to breathe.

If you don't do this, Daniel wins.

Just his name is enough to stir my hate, my fists balling by my sides. I think of his duplicity, fanning the flames of my rage by remembering every lie he told me, drowning all over again with the little boy in the lake. I remember the feeling of the footman's knife as it slipped between Derby's ribs and slashed Dance's throat. The surrender he forced on Rashton.

With a roar I vent my anger, striking the butler with the poker I took from the fireplace, catching him across the back of the shoulders, sending him crashing into the wall and down onto the floor.

"Please," he says, trying to slide away from me. "I'm not—"

He wheezes for help, holding out an imploring hand. It's the hand that pushes me over the edge. Daniel did something similar by the lake, turning my own pity upon me. Now it's Daniel I see on the floor, and my anger catches fire, boiling in my veins.

I kick him.

Once, then again and again and again. Reason deserts me, rage pouring into the void. Every betrayal, every pain and sorrow, every regret, every disappointment, every humiliation, every anguish, every hurt…all of them, they're filling me up.

I can barely breathe, barely see. I'm sobbing, as I kick him over and over.

I pity this man.

I pity myself.

I hear Rashton an instant before he hits me with the vase. The crash echoes inside my skull as I fall and fall, the ground catching me in its hard arms.

⌒ 57 ⌒

DAY TWO (CONTINUED)

"Aiden!"

The voice is distant, washing over my body like water lapping a beach.

"God, wake up. Please wake up."

Wearily, ever so wearily, my eyes flicker open.

I'm staring at a cracked wall, my head resting on a white pillowcase spattered with red blood. Tiredness reaches for me, threatening to drag me back under.

Much to my surprise, I'm the butler again, lying in that bed in the gatehouse.

Stay awake. Stay still. We're in trouble.

I move my body a fraction, the pain in my side leaping as far as my mouth before I bite it back, trapping a scream in my throat. If nothing else, it's enough to wake me up.

Blood has soaked the sheets where the footman stabbed me earlier. The agony must have been enough to knock me unconscious, but not enough to kill me. Surely that's no accident. The footman has ushered a lot of people into the afterlife, and I doubt he got lost this time. The idea chills me. I thought nothing was more frightening than somebody trying to kill me. Turns out, it's more a matter of who's doing the killing, and when that's the footman, being left alive is far more terrifying.

"Aiden, are you awake?"

I turn over painfully to see Anna in the corner of the room, legs and hands tied by a length of rope, which is knotted around an old radiator. Her cheek is swollen, a black eye blossoming on her face like a flower in the snow.

Night shows through the window above her, but I don't have any clue what time it is. For all I know, it's already eleven and the Plague Doctor is waiting for us by the lake.

Seeing me awake, Anna lets out a sob of relief.

"I thought he'd killed you," she says.

"That makes two of us," I croak.

"He grabbed me outside the house, told me he'd kill me if I didn't come with him," she says, struggling against her bonds. "I knew Donald Davies was safely asleep on that road, and that he couldn't reach him, so I did what he asked. I'm so sorry, Aiden, but I couldn't think of another way."

She'll betray you.

This is what the Plague Doctor warned me about, the decision Rashton mistook for evidence of Anna's duplicity. That lack of trust nearly sabotaged everything we've been working for throughout the day. I wonder if the Plague Doctor knew the circumstances of Anna's "betrayal," hiding them for his own ends, or whether he genuinely believed this woman had turned against me.

"It's not your fault, Anna," I say.

"I'm still sorry." She flicks a frightened glance at the door, then lowers her voice. "Can you reach the shotgun? He put it on the sideboard."

I glance across toward it. It's only a few feet away, but it might as well be on the moon. I could barely roll over, let alone stand up to get it.

"Awake are you?" interrupts the footman, who emerges through the door, slicing chunks off an apple with his pocketknife. "That's a shame. I was looking forward to waking you up again."

There's another man behind him. It's the thug from the graveyard, the one who held my arms while Daniel tried to beat Anna's location out of me.

The footman approaches the bed.

"Last time we met, I let you live," he says. "Had to be done, but still…it was unsatisfying." Clearing his throat, I feel a wet splat of saliva hit my cheek. Disgust echoes through me, but I haven't the strength to lift my arm and wipe it away.

"Won't happen a second time," he says. "I don't like people waking up again. Feels like a job half done. I want Donald Davies, and I want you to tell me where I can lay my hands on him."

My mind whirls, connecting the giant jigsaw pieces of my life.

Daniel found me on the road after I jumped out of the carriage and convinced me to follow him into the graveyard. I never questioned how he knew where I'd be, but here is my answer anyway. In a few minutes, I'm going to tell the footman.

If I wasn't so afraid, I'd smile at the irony.

Daniel believes I'm betraying Davies to his death, but without their confrontation in the graveyard, I'll never find out Silver Tear is in Blackheath, or fight Daniel by the lake, allowing Anna to finally finish him off.

It's a trap all right. One built by Rashton, sprung by Davies, and baited by me. It's as neat as you'd like, except that when I tell the footman what he wants to know, he'll butcher Anna and me like cattle.

Placing his knife and the apple on the sideboard beside the shotgun, the footman picks up the sleeping tablets, the jar rattling as he shakes a pill into his hand. I can almost hear him frowning at it, his thoughts thudding back and forth. His companion is still at the door, arms folded and expressionless.

The jar rattles again. Once, twice, three times.

"How many of these things does it take to kill a burned cripple like you, eh?" he asks, gripping my chin with his hand and forcing my face toward his own.

I try to turn away, but his grip hardens, his eyes fastening on mine. I can feel the heat of him; his malice a prickly, hot thing crawling along my skin. I could have woken up behind that gaze. I could have shared that rat's warren of a brain, wading through memories and impulses I'd never have been able to shake off.

Maybe I did in a past loop.

Suddenly, even the loathsome Derby seems like a blessing.

His iron fingers release me, my head lolling to one side, beads of perspiration welling on my forehead.

I don't know how much longer I have.

"Judging by those burns, you've had a hard life," he says, withdrawing a little. "Hard life deserves an easy death, I reckon. That's what I'm offering. Fall asleep with a belly full of pills, or writhe around for a couple of hours while I keep missing the important bits with my knife."

"Leave him alone!" Anna screams from the corner, the wood creaking as she strains to break free.

"Better yet," he says, waving his knife at her. "I could take my blade to the girl here. I need her alive. Doesn't mean she can't scream a bit first."

He takes a step toward her.

"Stables," I say quietly.

He stops dead, looking at me over his shoulder.

"What did you say?"

He walks back over to me.

Close your eyes. Don't let him see your fear. That's what he craves. He won't kill you until you open your eyes.

Squeezing them shut, I feel the bed sag as he sits down. A few seconds later, the edge of his blade caresses my face.

Fear tells me to open my eyes, to see the harm coming.

Just breathe. Wait for your moment.

"Donald Davies will be at the stables?" he hisses. "Is that what you said?"

I nod, trying to ward off panic.

"Leave him alone!" Anna screams again from the corner, pounding the floorboards with her heels and pulling violently against the ropes restraining her.

"Shut up!" the footman screams at her, before returning his attention to me. "When?"

My mouth is so dry I'm not even sure I can still speak.

"When?" he insists, the blade biting my cheek, drawing blood.

"Twenty to ten," I say, remembering the time Daniel gave me.

"Go! That's ten minutes from now," he tells the man at the door, fading steps charting the thug's departure down the corridor.

The blade wanders along the edge of my lips, tracing the contours of my nose until I feel the slightest pressure on my closed eyelid.

"Open your eyes," he hisses.

I wonder if he can hear my heart beating. How could he not? It's pounding like mortar fire, wearing down what little bravery remains to me.

I begin to tremble, ever so slightly.

"Open your eyes," he repeats, spittle hitting my cheeks. "Open your eyes, little rabbit. Let me see inside."

Wood snaps and Anna screams.

I can't help but look.

She's managed to rip the radiator from one of its brackets, freeing her hands in the process, though not her legs. The knife withdraws as the footman leaps to his feet, the bedsprings squeaking as they're relieved of his weight.

Now. Move now!

I throw myself at him. There's no skill in it, no strength, just desperation and momentum. A hundred other times I fail and my body hits him like a blown rag, but there's something about the angle he's standing at and the way he's holding the knife. I catch the handle perfectly, turning it and pushing the blade into his stomach, blood welling up between my fingers as we hit the floor in a tangled pile.

He's gasping, stunned, hurt even, but not fatally so. Already he's gathering himself.

I look down at the knife in my hand, only the hilt now visible, and I know it's not going to be enough. He's too strong and I'm too weak.

"Anna!" I yell, ripping the knife free and skimming it across the floor toward her, watching in despair as it comes to a halt a few inches from her straining fingertips.

The footman claws at me, nails raking across my cheeks as he scrabbles desperately for my throat. The weight of my body pins his right hand, my shoulder crushing his face, blinding him. He's writhing, grunting, trying to shake me off.

"I can't hold him!" I scream at Anna.

His hand finds my ear, and he wrenches at it, my eyes filled with blinding white pain. I jerk away, banging into the sideboard, knocking the shotgun to the floor.

The footman's hand breaks free from underneath me. He pushes me off him, and as I hit the floorboards, I see Anna reaching for the shotgun, the freshly severed rope still trailing from her wrist. Our eyes meet, fury gathered on her face.

The footman's hands wrap themselves around my neck and tighten.

I strike at his broken nose, causing him to howl in pain, but he doesn't let go. He squeezes harder, choking the breath from me.

The shotgun explodes, and so does the footman, his headless body collapsing beside me, blood pouring from his neck and spreading across the floor.

I stare at the shotgun trembling in Anna's hands. If it hadn't fallen when it did...if the knife hadn't reached her, or she'd been a few seconds later freeing herself...

I shiver, horrified at the margins between life and death.

Anna's talking to me, worrying about me, but I'm so exhausted I only hear half of what's she saying, and the last thing I feel before the darkness takes me is her hand in mine, and the soft touch of her lips as they kiss my forehead.

～ 58 ～

DAY EIGHT (CONTINUED)

Fighting through the thick fog of sleep, I announce myself with a cough, startling Anna, who's standing on her tiptoes, her body pressed against mine as she tries to cut me loose with a kitchen knife. I'm back in Gold, strung up from the ceiling by my wrists.

"I'll have you down in a tick," says Anna.

She must have come straight from the room next door, because her apron is covered in the footman's blood. Brow furrowed, she saws at the rope, her haste making her clumsy. Swearing, she slows down, but after a few minutes my bonds are slack enough for me to wriggle my hands free.

I drop like a stone, hitting the floor with a thud.

"Easy," says Anna, kneeling beside me. "You've been tied up all day, there's no strength left in you."

"What…" A hacking cough overtakes me, but there's no water in the jug to ease it. The Plague Doctor wasted it all trying to keep me awake earlier. My shirt's still wet from where he splashed me.

I wait for the coughing to ease, then try speaking again.

"What time…" I force out, feeling as though I'm pushing stones up through my throat.

"Nine forty-five," says Anna.

If you've killed the footman, he can't kill Rashton or Derby. They're alive. They can help.

"Don't need them," I rasp.

"Need who?" says Anna.

I shake my head, gesturing for her to help me up. "We have to..."

Another painful cough, another look of sympathy from Anna.

"Sit a second for pity's sake," she says, handing me a folded piece of paper that's fallen from my breast pocket.

If she looked inside, she'd see the phrase *all of them* written in Gold's dreadful handwriting. Those words are the key to everything that's happening, and they've been following me around since Cunningham delivered the message to Derby three days ago.

Tucking the note back into my pocket, I gesture for Anna to help me stand.

Somewhere in the darkness, the Plague Doctor is making his way toward the lake, where he'll be expecting Anna to give him an answer she doesn't yet have. After eight days of asking questions, we now have a little over an hour to make our case.

I have to hope it's enough.

With my arm around Anna's shoulders and hers around my waist, we stumble through the door drunkenly, almost falling down the stairs. I'm very weak, but the greater problem lies in how numb my limbs are. I feel like a wooden puppet on the end of twisted strings.

We depart the gatehouse without a backward glance, smacking straight into the cold night air. The quickest route to the lake would take us past the wishing well, but there's too great a chance of bumping into Daniel and Donald Davies by going that way. I have no desire to upset whatever delicate balance we've arrived at by blundering into an event that's already been settled in my favor.

We'll have to go the long way around.

Prickly with sweat, lead-footed, and gasping, I stagger up the driveway toward Blackheath. My chorus comes with me—Dance, Derby, and Rashton out ahead, with Bell, Collins, and Ravencourt struggling behind. I know they're figments of my fracturing mind, but I can see them as clearly as reflections, their individual gaits, their eagerness and disdain for the task before us.

Veering off the driveway, we follow the cobbled road to the stables.

It's quiet there, now the party's in full swing, a few stable hands warming themselves around the braziers, waiting for the last of the carriages to arrive. They look done in, but uncertain of who's in Daniel's employ, I tug Anna away from the light and toward the paddock, following the small trail leading up to the lake. A dying flame flickers at the end of the path, its warm glow breaking through the gaps in the trees. Creeping closer, I see that it's Daniel's fallen lantern, burning its last breaths in the dirt.

Squinting into the darkness, I spot its owner in the lake, holding Donald Davies facedown beneath the water, the younger man thrashing his legs as he tries to escape.

Scooping a rock off the ground, Anna takes a step toward them, but I catch her arm.

"Tell him…7:12 a.m.," I croak, hoping the intensity of my gaze can carry a message my throat is unfit to elaborate on.

She bounds toward Daniel, raising the rock above her head as she goes.

Turning my back, I pick up the fallen storm lantern, stoking the sickly flame with a hoarse breath. I have no urge to watch somebody else die, no matter how much they may deserve it. The Plague Doctor claimed Blackheath was meant to rehabilitate us, but bars can't build better men and misery can only break what goodness remains. This place pinches out the hope in people, and without that hope, what use is love or compassion or kindness? Whatever the intention behind its creation, Blackheath speaks to the monster in us, and I have no intention of indulging mine any longer. It's had free rein long enough.

Lifting the lantern into the air, I peel away toward the boathouse. All day I've been looking for Helena Hardcastle, believing her responsible for the events in the house. Strange to think I was probably right, though not in the way I imagined.

Whether she intended it or not, she's the reason all of this is happening.

The boathouse is little more than a shed overhanging the water, the stilts along the right-hand side collapsed, twisting the entire building out of shape. The doors are locked, but the wood is so rotten it crumbles beneath my touch. They'll open with the slightest of force, but still I hesitate. My hand is shaking, the light bouncing. It's not fear that gives me pause, Gold's heart is still as a stone. It's expectation. Something long sought is about to be found, and when that happens, all this will be over.

We'll be free.

Taking a deep breath, I push the doors open, disturbing some bats that flee the boathouse in a chorus of indignant squeaks. A couple of skeletal rowboats are tethered inside. Only one of them is covered in a moldy blanket, though.

Kneeling down, I pull it aside, revealing Helena Hardcastle's pale face. Her eyes are open, the pupils as colorless as her skin. She seems surprised, as though death arrived with flowers in its hand.

Why here?

"Because history repeats," I mutter.

"Aiden?" Anna yells, a slight note of panic in her voice.

I try to shout back, but my throat is still hoarse, forcing me outside into the rain. I tip my mouth to the falling rain, swallowing the freezing cold drops.

"Over here," I call out. "In the boathouse."

Stepping back inside, I run my lantern up and down Helena's body. Her long coat is unbuttoned, revealing a rust-colored woolen jacket and skirt, with a white cotton blouse beneath. Her hat has been tossed into the boat beside her. She was stabbed in the throat, long enough ago for the blood to have coagulated.

If I'm right, she's been dead since this morning.

Anna arrives behind me, gasping as she catches sight of the body in the boat.

"Is that…"

"Helena Hardcastle," I say.

"How did you know she'd be here?" she asks.

"This was the last appointment she kept," I explain.

The gash in her neck isn't large, but it's large enough, exactly the size of a horseshoe knife I shouldn't wonder. The same weapon used to kill Thomas Hardcastle nineteen years ago. Here, finally, is what this is all about. Every other death was an echo of this one. A murder nobody heard.

My legs are aching with the strain of crouching, so I stand up and stretch them out.

"Did Michael do this?" asks Anna, clutching my coat.

"No, this wasn't Michael," I say. "Michael Hardcastle was afraid. He became a killer out of desperation. This murder was something else; it took patience and pleasure. Helena was lured here and stabbed at the door so she'd collapse inside, out of sight. The killer picked a spot not twenty feet from where Thomas Hardcastle was killed on the very anniversary of his death. What does that tell you?"

As I speak, I imagine Lady Hardcastle falling, hearing the crack of wood as she lands in the boat. A shadowy figure looms in my thoughts, drawing the blanket across the body before wading into the water.

"The killer was covered in blood," I say, sweeping the lantern across the room. "They washed themselves in the water, knowing they were concealed by the walls of the boathouse. They had fresh clothes waiting…"

Sure enough there's an old carpetbag in the corner, and undoing the catch, I discover a mound of bloody women's clothes inside. The murderer's clothes.

This was planned...

...A long time ago, for another victim.

"Who did this, Aiden?" asks Anna, fear rising in her voice.

I step out of the boathouse, searching the darkness until I spot a storm lantern on the far side of the lake.

"Expecting company?" she asks, her gaze fixed on the growing light.

"It's the murderer," I say, feeling oddly calm. "I had Cunningham spread a rumor we were coming out here to...well, use the boathouse, so to speak."

"Why?" says Anna, terrified. "If you know who helped Michael, tell the Plague Doctor!"

"I can't," I say. "You have to explain the rest of it."

"What?" she hisses, offering me a sharp glance. "We had a deal: I keep you alive; you find Evelyn's murderer."

"The Plague Doctor has to hear it from you," I say. "He won't let you go otherwise. Trust me, you have all the pieces, you just need to put them together. Here, take this."

Reaching into my pocket, I hand her the piece of paper. Unfolding it, she reads it aloud.

"All of them," she says, wrinkling her forehead. "What does that mean?"

"It's the answer to a question I had Cunningham ask Mrs. Drudge."

"What question?"

"Were any of the other Hardcastle children Charlie Carver's. I wanted to know who he'd give his life for."

"But they're all dead now."

The mysterious lantern bobs in the air, coming closer and closer. The person holding it is hurrying, making no attempt at stealth. The time for subterfuge has passed.

"Who is that?" asks Anna, shielding her eyes and squinting at the approaching light.

"Yes, who am I?" says Madeline Aubert, lowering the lantern to reveal the gun pointed directly at us.

She's discarded her maid's uniform in favor of trousers and a loose linen shirt, a beige cardigan thrown over her shoulders. Her dark hair's wet, her pockmarked skin thick with powder. The mask of servitude removed, she has the look of her mother, the same oval eyes and freckles swirling into a milky white complexion. I can only hope Anna sees it.

Anna looks from me to Madeline and back again, confusion giving way to panic on her face.

"Aiden, help me," she pleads.

"It has to be you," I say, searching out her cold hand in the darkness. "All the pieces are in front of you. Who was in a position to kill Thomas Hardcastle and Lady Hardcastle in exactly the same way, nineteen years apart? Why did Evelyn say 'I'm not' and 'Millicent murder' after I saved her? Why did she have a signet ring she'd given to Felicity? What did Millicent Derby know that got her killed? Why was Gregory Gold hired to paint new portraits of the family when the rest of the house was crumbling? Who would Helena Hardcastle and Charlie Carver have lied to protect?"

Clarity arrives on Anna's face like a sunrise, her eyes widening as she looks from the note to Madeline's expectant expression.

"Evelyn Hardcastle," she says quietly. Then louder, "You're Evelyn Hardcastle."

Quite what reaction I'd expected from Evelyn I'm not sure, but she surprises me by clapping her hands in delight, jumping up and down as though we're pets performing a new trick.

"I knew it would be worth following you two," she says, placing her lantern on the ground, stitching its glow to ours. "People don't trek all the way into the darkness without a little knowledge to light the way. Though I must confess, I'm at a loss as to how this is any of your concern."

She's shed her French accent and with it any trace of the dutiful maid she was hiding behind. Shoulders that once slouched straighten immediately, her neck stiffening, pushing her chin into the air so that she seems to survey us from atop some lofty cliff.

Her questioning gaze passes between us, but my attention is fixed on the forest. This will all be for nothing if the Plague Doctor isn't here to hear it, but beyond the puddle of light cast by our two lanterns, it's pitch-black. He could be standing ten yards away and I'd never know.

Mistaking my silence for obstinacy, Evelyn offers me a wide smile. She's enjoying us. She's going to savor us.

We have to keep her entertained until the Plague Doctor arrives.

"This was what you had planned for Thomas all those years ago, wasn't it?" I say, pointing toward Helena's body in the boathouse. "I questioned the stable master, who told me you'd gone out riding on the morning of his death, but that was just an alibi. You'd arranged to meet Thomas here, so all you had to do was ride past the gatehouse, tie up the horse, and cut directly through the forest. I timed it myself. You could have arrived in under half an hour without anybody seeing, giving you plenty of time to murder Thomas quietly in the boathouse, wash in the water, change clothes, and be back on your horse before anybody knew he was missing. You'd stolen the murder weapon from the stable master and the blanket you were going to cover the body in. He was supposed to take the blame once Thomas was found, only the plan went wrong, didn't it?"

"Everything went wrong," she says, clicking her tongue. "The boathouse was a backup, in case my first idea went awry. I intended to daze Thomas with a rock and then drown him, leaving him floating in the lake for somebody to find. A tragic accident, and we'd all go about our lives. Sadly, I didn't get a chance to use either plan. I hit Thomas over the head, but not nearly hard enough. He started screaming and I panicked, stabbing him out here in the open."

She sounds irritated, though not unduly so. It's as though she's describing nothing more serious than a picnic spoiled by bad weather, and I catch myself staring at her. I'd deduced most of the story before coming here, but to hear it relayed so callously, without regret of any sort, is horrifying. She's soulless, conscienceless. I can barely believe she's a person.

Noticing me floundering, Anna takes up the conversation.

"And that's when Lady Hardcastle and Charlie Carver stumbled upon you." She's considering every word, laying them ahead of her onrushing thoughts. "Somehow, you managed to convince them Thomas's death was an accident."

"They did most of the work themselves," muses Evelyn. "I thought it was all over when they appeared on that path. I got halfway through telling them I was trying to get the knife away from Thomas when Carver filled in the rest for me. Accident, children playing, that sort of thing. He handed me a story gift wrapped."

"Did you know Carver was your father?" I ask, regaining my composure.

"No, but I was a child. I simply accepted my good fortune and went riding, as I was told. It wasn't until I'd been shipped off to Paris that Mother told me the truth. I think she wanted me to be proud of him."

"So Carver sees his daughter covered in blood on the lake bank," continues Anna, speaking slowly, trying to put everything in order. "He realizes you're going to need some clean clothes, and he goes to the house to fetch them while Helena stays with Thomas. That's what Stanwin saw when he followed Carver to the lake; that's why he believed Helena killed her own son. It's why he let his friend take the blame."

"That and a great deal of money," says Evelyn, her lip curling, revealing the tips of her teeth. Her green eyes are glassy, blank. Utterly without empathy, intolerant of remorse. "Mother paid him handsomely over the years."

"Charlie Carver didn't know you'd planned the murder beforehand and already had a change of clothes waiting in the boathouse," I say, struggling not to look for the Plague Doctor among the trees. "The clothes stayed there, hidden, for eighteen years until your mother found them when she visited Blackheath last year. She knew what they meant immediately. She even told Michael about them, probably to test his reaction."

"She must have thought he knew about the murder," says Anna pityingly. "Can you imagine… She couldn't trust either of her children."

A breeze is stirring, rain plinking against our lanterns. There's a noise from the forest, indistinct and distant but enough to draw Evelyn's attention for an instant.

Stall her, I mouth to Anna, as I remove my coat and lay it across her thin shoulders, earning a grateful smile.

"It must have been terrible for Lady Hardcastle," says Anna, drawing the coat tighter. "Realizing the daughter she let her lover go to the gallows to protect had murdered her own brother in cold blood." Her voice drops. "How could you do that, Evelyn?"

"I think the better question is why she did it," I say, looking at Anna. "Thomas liked to follow people around. He knew he'd get into trouble if he was caught, so he got very good at being quiet. One day he followed Evelyn into the forest, where she met a stable boy. I don't know why they were meeting, or even if it had been planned. Maybe it was a coincidence, but I think there was an accident. I hope it was an accident," I say, shooting a glance at Evelyn, who's appraising me like a moth that's landed on her jacket. Our entire future's written in the creases around her eyes; that pale face is a crystal ball with only horrors in the fog.

"Doesn't matter really," I carry on, realizing she isn't going to answer me. "Either way, she killed him. Likely, Thomas didn't understand what he'd seen, or he'd have run back and told his mother, but at some point Evelyn realized he knew. She had two choices: silence Thomas before he told somebody, or confess to what she'd done. She chose the first option and set about her work methodically."

"That's very good," says Evelyn, her face lighting up. "Aside from a detail or two, it's almost as if you were there in the flesh. You're a delight, Mr. Gold. You know that? Far more entertaining than the dull creature I mistook you for last night."

"What happened to the stable boy?" asks Anna. "The stable master said he was never found."

Evelyn considers her for a long while. At first I think it's because she's deciding whether to answer the question, and then I realize the truth. She's summoning the memory. She hasn't thought about it in years.

"It was the most curious thing," says Evelyn distantly. "He took me to see some caves he'd found. I knew my parents wouldn't approve, so we went in secret, but he was very tedious company. We were exploring, and he fell into a deep hole. Nothing too serious, I could easily have fetched help. I told him I was going to, and then it dawned on me. I didn't have to fetch help. I didn't have to do anything at all. I could leave him there. Nobody knew where he'd gone, or that I was with him. It seemed like fate."

"You just abandoned him," says Anna, aghast.

"And you know, I rather enjoyed it. He was my thrilling little secret until Thomas asked me why I'd gone to the caves that day." Keeping her gun trained on us, she lifts her lantern out of the mud. "And the rest you know. Pity, really."

She cocks the hammer, but Anna steps in front of me.

"Wait!" she says, stretching out a hand.

"Please, don't beg," says Evelyn, exasperated. "I hold you in such high regard. Really, you have no idea. Aside from my mother, nobody's thought twice about Thomas's death in nearly twenty years, and then, out of the blue, you two appear with almost the entire thing wrapped up in a nice little bow. It must have taken a great deal of determination, and I admire that, but nothing is so unbecoming as a lack of pride."

"I'm not going to beg, but the story's not done," says Anna. "We deserve to hear the rest of it."

Evelyn smiles, her expression beautiful and brittle and utterly mad.

"You think me a fool," she says, wiping the rain from her eyes.

"I think you're going to kill us," says Anna calmly, speaking as one would to a small child. "And I think if you do it out in the open, lots of people will hear. You need to move us somewhere quieter, so why not let us talk on the way."

Evelyn takes a few steps toward her, holding the lantern close to her face so that she might better inspect her. Her head is cocked, lips slightly parted.

"Clever girl," says Evelyn, purring in admiration. "Very well, turn around and start walking."

I listen to this exchange with increasing panic, desperately hoping the Plague Doctor will appear out of the gloom and finally put an end to this. He must surely have enough evidence to support Anna's freedom by now.

Unless he's been delayed.

The thought fills me with dread. Anna's trying to keep us alive, but it will all be for nothing if the Plague Doctor doesn't know where to find us.

I reach for our lantern, but Evelyn kicks it away, motioning us into the forest with the point of her gun.

We walk side by side with Evelyn a couple of paces behind, humming softly. I risk a look over my shoulder, but she's far enough back to make snatching the gun an impossible endeavor. Even if I could, it wouldn't be any use. We're not here to capture Evelyn. We're here to prove Anna's not like her, and the best way of doing that is to be in danger.

Heavy clouds blot out the stars, and with only Evelyn's dim flame to guide us, we're having to move cautiously to avoid tripping. It's like trying to navigate through ink, and still there's no sign of the Plague Doctor.

"If your mother knew a year ago what you'd done, why didn't she tell everybody then?" asks Anna, glancing back at Evelyn. "Why arrange this party? Why invite all these people?"

There's genuine curiosity in her tone. If she's afraid, she's keeping it in a pocket somewhere I can't see. Evidently, Evelyn's not the only actress in the house. I can only hope I'm doing as well. My heart's thumping hard enough to crack a rib.

"Greed," says Evelyn. "My parents needed money more than my mother needed to see me hang. I can only assume the marriage took some time to arrange, because Mother sent me a letter last month telling me that unless I allowed myself to be wed to that odious Ravencourt, they'd turn me in. The humiliation of today's party was a parting shot, a sliver of justice for Thomas."

"So you killed them in revenge?" asks Anna.

"Father was my gift to Michael. My brother wanted his inheritance while there still was one. He's buying Stanwin's blackmail business with Coleridge."

"Then it really was your boot print I saw outside the gatehouse window," I say. "And you left the note claiming responsibility."

"Well, I couldn't have poor Michael being blamed, that would defeat the point entirely," she says. "I don't intend on using my name once I leave here, so why not put it to some use?"

"And your mother?" asks Anna. "Why kill her?"

"I was in Paris," says Evelyn, anger heating her words for the first time. "If she hadn't bartered me to Ravencourt, she'd never have seen me again. As far as I'm concerned, she committed suicide."

The trees break suddenly, revealing the gatehouse. We've come out around the back of the building, opposite the latched door into the kitchen the fake Evelyn showed Bell that first morning.

"Where did you find the other Evelyn?" I ask.

"Her name was Felicity Maddox," says Evelyn vaguely. "She was some sort of con artist, from what I understand. Stanwin arranged everything. Michael told him the family wanted Felicity to marry Ravencourt in my place, at which point they'd pay him half of the dowry to keep quiet."

"Did Stanwin know what you planned to do?" asks Anna.

"Perhaps, but why would he care?" shrugs Evelyn, gesturing for me to open the door. "Felicity was an insect. Some policeman or other tried to help her this afternoon, and you know what she did? Instead of admitting everything to him, she ran straight to Michael and asked for more money to keep quiet. Really, a person like that is a stain upon the world. I consider her murder an act of public service."

"And Millicent Derby, was her death a public service?"

"Oh, Millicent," says Evelyn, brightening at the memory. "You know, back in the day, she was as bad as her son. She just didn't have the energy for it in her later years."

We're passing through the kitchen, into the hallway. The house is silent, all of its occupants dead. Despite that, a lamp burns brightly on the wall, suggesting Evelyn always intended on coming back here.

"Millicent recognized you, didn't she?" I say, dragging my fingertips along the wallpaper. I can feel myself coming unstuck. None of this feels real anymore. I need to touch something solid so I know I'm not dreaming. "She spotted you in the ballroom alongside Felicity," I continue, remembering how the old lady hurried away from Derby. "She had watched you grow up and wasn't going to be fooled by a maid's outfit and Gold's new portraits on the wall. Millicent knew immediately who you were."

"She came down to the kitchen, demanding to know what I was up to," says Evelyn. "I told her it was a prank for the ball, and the silly old dear believed me."

I glance around, hoping for some hint of the Plague Doctor's presence, but my hope is fading. There's no reason for him to know we're here, so he will have no idea how courageous Anna's being, or that she's solved his riddle. A madwoman's taking us to our death, and it's all for nothing.

"How did you kill her?" I ask, frantically trying to keep Evelyn talking while I come up with a new plan.

"I stole a bottle of veronal from Doctor Dickie's bag and crushed a few tablets into her tea," she says. "When she passed out, I held a pillow over her face until she stopped breathing and then fetched Dickie."

There's joy in her voice, as if this is some happy old story being shared among friends at the dinner table. "He saw the veronal from his bag on her nightstand and immediately realized he was implicated," she says. "That's the beauty of corrupt men, you can always rely on them to be corrupt."

"So he took the bottle away and claimed it was a heart attack to cover his own tracks," I say, letting out a little sigh.

"Oh, don't fret, lover," she says, prodding me in the back with the barrel of the gun. "Millicent Derby died as she lived, with elegance and calculation. It was a gift, believe me. We should all be so lucky to meet such a meaningful end."

I worry she's leading us into the room where Lord Hardcastle sits twisted in his chair, but instead she shepherds us through the door opposite. It's a small dining room, four chairs and a square table at its center. Evelyn's lantern light scatters across the walls, illuminating two canvas bags in the corner, each of them stuffed to bursting with jewelry, clothing, and whatever else she could steal from Blackheath.

Her new life will begin where ours ends.

Ever the artist, Gold can at least appreciate the symmetry.

Placing her lantern on the table, Evelyn gestures for us to kneel on the floor. Her eyes are glittering, her face flushed.

A window faces the road, but I can see no sign of the Plague Doctor.

"I'm afraid you're out of time," she says, raising the gun.

One move left to play.

"Why did you kill Michael?" I ask quickly, hurling the accusation at her.

Evelyn tenses, her smile evaporating. "What are you talking about?"

"You poisoned him," I say, watching the confusion sketch itself on her face. "Every day, all I've heard is how close you two were, how much you loved him. He didn't even know that you'd killed Thomas, or your mother, did he? You didn't want him thinking ill of you. And yet when the time came, you killed him as easily as the rest of your victims."

Her gaze is flicking between myself and Anna, the gun wavering in her hand. For the first time, she seems afraid.

"You're lying. I'd never hurt Michael," she says.

"I watched him die, Evelyn," I say. "I stood over him as—"

She strikes me with the gun, blood oozing from my lip.

I'd intended on snatching the gun from her, but she was too fast, and she's already taken a step away from us.

"Don't lie to me," she wails, eyes ablaze, rapid breaths escaping her mouth.

"He's not," protests Anna, wrapping her arms around my shoulders protectively.

Tears roll down Evelyn's cheeks, her lip trembling. Her love is rabid, pulsing and rotten, but it's sincere. Somehow that only makes her more monstrous.

"I didn't..." She's clutching her hair, pulling hard enough to tear it from the roots. "He knew I couldn't marry... He wanted to help." She looks at us pleadingly. "He killed her for me, so I could be free... He loved me..."

"You had to be certain, didn't you?" I say. "You couldn't risk him losing his nerve, and Felicity waking up again, so you gave her a glass of poisoned scotch before she walked out to the reflecting pool. Michael didn't know, though. He drank what was left, while Rashton was questioning him."

Evelyn's gun has dipped, and I tense, readying myself to spring for it, but Anna tightens her grip around me.

"He's here," she whispers into my ear, nodding toward the window.

A single candle burns on the road, illuminating a porcelain beak mask. Hope stirs, but withers immediately. He isn't moving. He can't even hear what's being said.

What's he waiting for?

"Oh no," says Anna, sounding sick to her stomach.

She's staring at the Plague Doctor as well, except instead of my confusion, there's horror. She's gone pale, her fingers clutching at my sleeve.

"We haven't solved it," she says, speaking under her breath. "We still don't know who kills Evelyn Hardcastle, the *real* Evelyn Hardcastle. And our suspect pool is down to two."

A cold weight settles on me.

I'd hoped Anna's unmasking of Evelyn would be enough to earn her freedom, but she's right. For all the Plague Doctor's talk of redemption and rehabilitation, he still needs one more life to pay the piper, and he expects one of us to deliver it.

Evelyn's still pacing, still tearing at her hair, still distracted by Michael's death, but she's too far away to ambush. Maybe Anna or I could wrestle the gun from her hand, but not before the other one was shot dead.

We've been tricked.

The Plague Doctor stayed away on purpose so he wouldn't have to hear Anna's answer and confront the good woman she's become. He doesn't know I was wrong about Michael.

Or he doesn't care.

He's got what he wanted. If I die, he'll free me. If she dies, she's trapped here, just like his superiors wanted. They're going to keep her forever, no matter what she does.

Unable to hold in my despair any longer, I run to the window and bang on the glass.

"It's not fair!" I scream at the distant shape of the Plague Doctor.

My fury startles Anna who jumps away in fright. Evelyn advances on me with her gun raised, mistaking my anger for panic.

Desperation claws at me.

I told the Plague Doctor I wouldn't abandon Anna, that I'd find a way back into Blackheath if they released me, but I can't spend another day in this place. I can't let myself be slaughtered again. I can't watch Felicity's suicide, or be betrayed by Daniel Coleridge. I can't live any of this over, and part of me, a much larger part than I'd ever have believed possible, is ready to rush Evelyn and be done with it all, regardless of what happens to my friend.

Blinded by my misery, I don't notice Anna come to me. Ignoring Evelyn, who's watching her the way an owl might a dancing mouse, Anna takes both my hands and stands on her tiptoes, kissing me on the cheek.

"Don't you dare come back for me," she says, pressing her forehead to mine.

She acts fast, turning on her heel and leaping at Evelyn in one fluid motion.

The gunshot is deafening, and for a few seconds its fading echo is all there is. Crying out, I rush to Anna's side, even as the gun clatters to the floor, blood seeping through Evelyn's shirt above her hip.

Her mouth opens and closes as she drops to her knees, a silent plea held in those hollow eyes.

Felicity Maddox is standing in the doorway, a nightmare come to life. She's still wearing her blue ball gown, now dripping wet and covered in mud, her makeup running down pale cheeks scratched by her hurried flight through the trees. Her lipstick is smeared, her hair wild, the black revolver steady in her hand.

She throws us a quick glance, but I doubt she sees us. Rage has left her half mad. Pointing the revolver at Evelyn's stomach, she pulls the trigger, the shot so loud I have to cover my ears as blood splashes across the wallpaper. Not satisfied, she fires again, Evelyn collapsing on the floor.

Walking over to her, Felicity empties the last of her bullets into Evelyn's lifeless body.

～60～

Anna's face is pressed against my chest, but I can't look away from Felicity. I don't know if this is justice or not, but I'm desperately grateful for it all the same. Anna's sacrifice would have set me free, but the guilt would never have let me go.

Her death would have made me a stranger to myself.

Felicity saved me.

Her revolver's empty, but she's still pressing the trigger, burying Evelyn in a chorus of hollow clicks. I think she would go on forever, but she's interrupted by the Plague Doctor's arrival. He gently takes the weapon from her hand, and as if a spell's been broken, her eyes clear, life coming into her limbs. She looks bone-tired and emptied out, pushed beyond thought.

With a last lingering look at Evelyn's body, she nods to the Plague Doctor, before brushing by him and disappearing outside, not even a lantern to guide her way. A moment later, the front door opens, the sound of pounding rain filling the air.

I let Anna go and slump onto the carpet, holding my head in my hands.

"You told Felicity we were here, didn't you?" I say through my fingers.

It comes out as an accusation, though I'm certain I'd meant to signal my gratitude. At this point, with all that's happened, perhaps there's no untangling the two.

"I gave her a choice," he says, kneeling down to close Evelyn's still-open eyes. "Her nature took care of the rest, as did yours."

He's looking at Anna as he says this, but his gaze soon passes over her, roaming the blood-splattered walls, before returning to the body lying at his feet. Part of me wonders if he isn't admiring his own work, the indirect ruin of a human being.

"How long have you known who the real Evelyn was?" asks Anna, who's looking the Plague Doctor up and down, examining him with a child's wonder.

"At precisely the same moment you did," he says. "I came to the lake as requested and witnessed her unmasking firsthand. When it became apparent where she was leading you, I returned to Blackheath to relay the information to the actress."

"But why help us?" asks Anna.

"Justice," he says simply, the beak mask turning in her direction. "Evelyn deserved to die, and Felicity deserved to kill her. You two have proven that you deserve your freedom, and I would not have you falter at the final hurdle."

"Is this it? Are we really done?" I ask, my voice trembling.

"Almost," he says. "I still need Anna to formally answer the question of who killed Evelyn Hardcastle."

"And what about Aiden?" she asks, placing a hand on my shoulder. "He blamed Michael."

"Mr. Bishop solved the murders of Michael, Peter, and Helena Hardcastle, and the attempted murder of Felicity Maddox, a crime so cleverly concealed it was entirely unknown to myself and my superiors," says the Plague Doctor. "I cannot fault him for answering questions we never thought to ask, nor will I punish a man who risked so much to save somebody else's life. His answer stands. Now I need yours. Who killed Evelyn Hardcastle, Anna?"

"You didn't say anything about Aiden's other hosts," she says, stubbornly. "Will you let them go, as well? Some of them are still alive. If we go now, we can probably still save the butler. And what about poor Sebastian Bell. He only woke up this morning. What will he do without me to help him?"

"Aiden *is* the Sebastian Bell who woke up this morning," says the Plague Doctor, kindly. "They were never anything more than a trick of the light, Anna. Shadows on a wall. Now you get to walk away with the flame that casts them, and once that happens, they'll vanish."

She blinks at him.

"Trust me, Anna. Tell me who killed Evelyn Hardcastle and everybody is freed. One way or another."

"Aiden?" Anna glances at me uncertainly, waiting for my approval. I can only nod. A flood of emotion is welling up inside of me, waiting for release.

"Felicity Maddox," she declares.

"You're free," he says, standing up. "Blackheath won't cling to either of you any longer."

My shoulders are shaking. Unable to hold it in, I begin sobbing wretchedly, eight days of misery and fear pouring out like poison. Anna takes hold of me, but I can't stop. I'm on the edge of my nerves, relieved and exhausted, terrified we're being tricked.

Everything else in Blackheath was a lie, why not this as well?

I stare at Evelyn's body and see Michael thrashing in the sunroom and Stanwin's baffled expression when Daniel shot him in the forest. Peter and Helena, Jonathan and Millicent, Dance, Davies, Rashton. The footman and Coleridge. The dead piled up.

How does somebody escape all this?

By saying a name…

"Anna," I mutter.

"I'm here," she says, clutching me fiercely. "We're going home, Aiden. You did it. You kept your promise."

She gazes at me, not a drop of doubt anywhere in her eyes. She's smiling, jubilant. One day and one life. I thought it wouldn't be enough to escape this place. Perhaps it's the *only* way to escape this place.

Keeping tight hold of me, she looks up at the Plague Doctor.

"What happens next?" she asks. "I still can't remember anything before this morning."

"You will," says the Plague Doctor. "You've served your sentence so all possessions will be returned to you, including your memories. If you wish. Most choose to leave them behind, and go on as they are. It may be something worth considering."

Anna digests this, and I realize she still doesn't know who she is, or what she did. That's going to be a difficult conversation, but it's not one I have the strength to face right now. I need to pack Blackheath away, deep in the dark, where my nightmares live, and I'm not going to be free of it for a very long time. If I can spare Anna similar suffering, even for a little while, I will.

"You should go," says the Plague Doctor. "I think you've lingered here long enough."

"Are you ready?" asks Anna.

"I am," I say, letting her help me to my feet.

"Thank you for everything," she says to the Plague Doctor, curtsying before leaving the house.

He watches her depart, then hands me Evelyn's lantern.

"They'll be looking for her, Aiden," he whispers. "Don't trust anybody, and don't let yourselves remember. At best the memories will cripple you. At worst..." He lets that hang. "Once you're released, start running and don't stop. That's your only chance."

"What's going to happen to you?" I ask. "I doubt your superiors will be happy when they find out what you've done."

"Oh, they'll be furious," he says cheerfully. "But today feels like a good day, and Blackheath hasn't seen one of those for a very long time.

I think I'll enjoy it for a while and worry about the cost tomorrow. It will come soon enough. It always does."

He holds out his hand. "Good luck, Aiden."

"You too," I say, shaking it and passing outside into the storm.

Anna's waiting on the road, her eyes fixed on Blackheath. She looks so young, so carefree, but it's a mask. There's another face beneath this one, a woman hated by half the world, and I've helped free her. Uncertainty flickers within me, but whatever she's done, whatever's waiting, we'll overcome it together. Here and now, that's all that matters to me.

"Where should we go?" asks Anna, as I sweep the dark forest with the lantern's warm light.

"I don't know," I say. "I don't think it matters."

She takes my hand, squeezing it gently.

"Then let's start walking and see where we end up."

And so we do, one foot in front of the other, pressing into the darkness with only the dimmest of lights for guidance.

I try to picture what's waiting for me.

The family I abandoned? Grandchildren raised on stories of what I did? Or just another forest, another house mired in secrets? I hope not. I hope my world is something else entirely. Something unknown and unfathomable, something I can't even imagine from inside the confines of Gold's mind. After all, it's not only Blackheath I'm escaping. It's them. It's Bell and the butler, Davies, Ravencourt, Dance, and Derby. It's Rashton and Gold. Blackheath was the prison, but they were the shackles.

And the keys.

I owe my freedom to every single one of them.

And what of Aiden Bishop? What do I owe him? The man who trapped me here so he could torture Annabelle Caulker. I won't give him his memories back. I'm certain of that. Tomorrow, I'll see his face in the mirror, and, somehow, I'll have to make it mine. To do that, I need to start again, free of the past, free of him and the mistakes he made.

Free of his voice.

"Thank you," I say under my breath, feeling him finally drift away.

It seems like a dream, too much to hope for. Tomorrow, there'll be no footman to overcome. No Evelyn Hardcastle to save, or Daniel Coleridge to outwit. No ticking clock hanging over a puzzle-box house. Instead of the impossible, I'll need only concern myself with the ordinary. The luxury of waking up in the same bed two days in a row or being able to reach the next village should I choose. The luxury of sunshine. The luxury of honesty. The luxury of living a life without a murder at the end of it.

Tomorrow can be whatever I want it to be, which means for the first time in decades, I can look forward to it. Instead of being something to fear, it can be a promise I make myself. A chance to be braver or kinder, to make what was wrong right. To be better than I am today.

Every day after this one is a gift.

I just have to keep walking until I get there.

READING GROUP GUIDE

1. What or who do you think are the deaths in *The 7½ Deaths of Evelyn Hardcastle?* Where does the half death enter the narrative?

2. *The 7½ Deaths of Evelyn Hardcastle* begins in a typically linear way, then shoots off in many different directions. How did the different narratives and perspectives enrich the story?

3. The mystery and escape in Blackheath is set up like a puzzle, and the reader plays along with Aiden as he puts the solution together. Were there any pieces you couldn't find a place for?

4. Aiden Bishop has a backstory that readers will never know in full; however, what we do know is there is plenty of revenge, cruelty, and questionable intentions wrapped up in who he was and why he entered Blackheath. With what you know about him, would you call him a hero? Why or why not?

5. Why do you think the Plague Doctor wears that particular costume, and how does it affect his relationship with Aiden? Is the Plague Doctor really the good man that the voice in Aiden's head claims he is?

6. Annabelle Caulker, or Anna, is unmasked as someone very different from whom Aiden believes her to be. What do you feel she did to deserve her time in Blackheath, and how do you think Aiden was able to forgive her?

7. Were there any tactics Aiden didn't think of that could have

solved the mystery of who killed Evelyn Hardcastle? If you were in his shoes, or hosts, what would you have done differently?

8. The construct of Blackheath as a prison feels like something from the future, but do you feel this sort of punishment (and possible redemption) could one day be considered a viable solution for criminals? What do you feel the advantages are, and in what ways could this be considered even more cruel than a standard incarceration sentence?

9. No character is ever what they first appear, something Aiden remarks on a few times throughout the novel. Who was your favorite character, and why did they resonate with you particularly? Which character undergoes the biggest transformation, and were there any characters you started off liking or loathing and changed your opinion about?

10. Was there one host who felt more important, or can you see how each character, despite their vices, provided something crucial to the story?

11. As Aiden switched from host to host, his protection against their memories and personalities waned until he was feeling their lust, their disgust, or their impatience. What characteristics do you feel are solely Aiden's? Outside of Blackheath, what sort of man do you think he is?

12. What recurring symbols or themes did you see throughout the book, and what role do you think they played in the story or Aiden's escape from Blackheath?

13. If you knew someone you loved had a devastating secret, would you choose to find out what it was or love them for who they've become? If you knew you did something terrible, would you want to remember or live with that shadow for the rest of your life?

A CONVERSATION
WITH THE AUTHOR

**What was your inspiration for *The 7½ Deaths of Evelyn
Hardcastle*?**

Inspiration is a flash-of-lightning kind of word. What happens
to me is more like sediment building. I love time travel, Agatha
Christie, and the eighties classic *Quantum Leap*, and over time a
book emerged from that beautiful quagmire. Truthfully, having the
idea was the easy part, keeping track of all the moving parts was
the difficulty.

**Which character was the most interesting to write, and in which
host do you feel Aiden truly flourishes?**

Lord Cecil Ravencourt, by miles. He occupies the section of
the book where the character has to grapple with the time travel
elements, the body swapping elements, and the murder itself. I
wanted my most intelligent character for that task, but I thought it
would be great to hamper him in some way, as well. Interestingly, I
wanted to make him really loathsome—which is why he's a banker.
And yet, for some reason, I ended up quite liking him, and feeding
a few laudable qualities into his personality. I think Derby ended
up getting a double dose of loathsome instead. Other than that,
it's just really nice seeing the evolution of his relationship with
Cunningham.

Is there a moral lesson to Aiden's story or any conclusion you hope the reader walks away with as they turn the final page?

Don't be a dick! Kind, funny, intelligent, and generous people are behind every good thing that's ever happened to me. Everybody else you just have to put up with. Like dandruff. Or sunburn. Don't be sunburn, people.

In one hundred years, do you believe there will be something similar to Blackheath, and would you support such a system?

Yes, and not exactly. Our prison system is barbaric, but some people deserve it. That's the tricky part of pinning your flag to the left or right of the moral spectrum. I think the current system is unsustainable, and I think personality adjustment and mental prisons are dangerous, achievable technology somebody will abuse. They could also solve a lot of problems. Would you trust your government with it? I suppose that's the question.

The book is so contained, and we don't get to see the place that Aiden is escaping to! Did you map that out, and is there anything you can share about the society beyond Blackheath's walls?

It's autocratic, technologically advanced, but they still haven't overcome our human weaknesses. You can get everywhere in an hour, but television's still overrun with reality shows, basically. Imagine the society that could create something as hateful as Annabelle Caulker.

There are so many puzzle pieces and characters and perspectives! How did you keep it all organized while writing the book?

A wall of Post-it Notes, an Excel spreadsheet, and a lot of muttering. My editor, Grace, will testify that I didn't nail it out of the gate. Every time I changed one small thing, it felt like the entire book fell apart because everything's so connected. One early draft was basically a David Lynch movie spread across four hundred pages. Each draft pushes you closer to the final book, though—which is worth remembering when fourteen impossible things are all happening at 1:42 p.m. and you're trying to fix it while hungover.

How long have you been writing?

This Q&A? About twenty minutes. I was a journalist for about eight years, and this book was happening for the last three of them.

What do you love most about writing?

Everything. Every single thing. I love that first blank page, finding that perfect first line, the moment your character says something unexpected and you realize they're a proper character. I love when it takes over a part of your brain and sits there, like a puzzle you're always working on, even while you're talking with friends or eating dinner with your wife. I love talking to people who've read my book and hearing their theories. I love beautiful writing, lines so good they bug you a week later. I love the collaborative spirit of editing and the joy of a good metaphor. Everything. Every moment. Wouldn't change a thing.

Do you have any writing rituals?

Is drinking a dozen cups of tea every day a ritual? Other than that, I like to write scenes for my characters that take place before the book starts. They're a way of getting into their head and finding their voice. Usually they have nothing to do with the story. They're little domestic scenes. A character planning a holiday, or shopping. Something unusual.

What do you do when you're not putting pen to paper?

I'm a travel journalist, so I'm always putting pen to paper. The poor paper must wonder what it's done to deserve my inky wrath.

ACKNOWLEDGMENTS

The 7½ Deaths of Evelyn Hardcastle doesn't exist without my agent, Harry Illingworth. He knew what this story could be before I did and helped me dig it out. You're a gent, Illington.

For her wisdom and word scalpel, I'd like to thank my editor, Alison Hennessy, a.k.a. the Queen of Ravens, a.k.a. glamorous (paragraph) murderer. I wrote a story; Alison made it into a book.

I'm also indebted to Grace Menary-Winefield, my U.S. editor, for asking the questions I never thought to ask and helping me prod at the edges of this world I've created.

And while I'm at it, I can't neglect the rest of the teams at Raven and Sourcebooks, who put me to shame with their talent, enthusiasm, and general loveliness. Of those, I'd particularly like to highlight Marigold Atkey, who weathered my panic—and last-minute edits— with good humor and wisdom. No doubt somebody, somewhere, heard her screaming, but it wasn't me. And for that, I'm very grateful.

Special mention must go to my early readers—David Bayon, Tim Danton, and Nicole Kobie—who read this story in its "David Lynch" phase and very kindly pointed out that clues, grammar, and reminders of plot points aren't a sign of weakness.

And finally, to my wife, Maresa. If you're going to do something stupid (like spend three years writing a time-travel, body-hopping, murder-mystery novel), you need your very best friend in your corner, all the way. She was, and is. I couldn't have done it without her.

ABOUT THE AUTHOR

Stuart Turton is a freelance travel journalist who has previously worked in Shanghai and Dubai. *The 7½ Deaths of Evelyn Hardcastle* is his debut novel. He is the winner of the Brighton and Hove Short Story Prize and was longlisted for the BBC Radio 4 Opening Lines competition. He lives in West London with his wife and daughter. Find him on Twitter @Stu_Turton.